ALEXANDER ZELENYJ

BEWARE US
FLOWERS OF THE ANNIHILATOR

The following stories were originally published in a variety of publications:

"The Deathwish of Valerie Vulture"—*Helion Science Fiction, Print Edition #3-4*, Romanian-English issue, 2024.

"Maleficia Falling"—*Helion Science Fiction, Print Edition #3-4*, all-English issue, 2023.

"Houses Within Houses Within Houses Within"—*Helion Science Fiction, Print Edition #3-4*, Romanian-English issue, 2024.

"Little Boys"—*Galaxia 42, Issue #58-59*

"Peace Machines"—*Animals of the Exodus*, Eibonvale Press, 2019.

"Oppenheimer's Door"—*Shallow Waters, Volume 4*, Crystal Lake Publications, 2019.

"Spiders in the Temple"—*Strange Days, Midnight Street Anthology 4*, Midnight Street Press, 2020.

"Sister-Biter"—*Night Light, Midnight Street Press*, 2018.

"We Are Alone"—*Solaris, Issue #236, Spring* 2025.

"The Punished World"—*Polar Starlight, Issue #9*, 2023.

Acknowledgments

Many thanks to the following for their support of my work over the years:

David Rix and Alice Howard of Eibonvale Press.

Brian A. Dixon and Adam Chamberlain of Fourth Horseman Press.

Steve Stred of Black Void Publishing.

Tim McWhorter of Manta Press for his generosity in taking on this project on such short notice.

Carl Lavoie; Greg Maxwell; Rachel Eagen; Andrew Murphy; Lindsay McNiff; Nick Cato; Tony Jones; Brittni and Peter Brinn; Des Lewis; Trevor Denyer of Midnight Street Press; Sami Airola; Nick Angelini; Roger Wurdemann and Louise Davis; and the Deathray Bradburys— the exodus awaits.

A special thank you to my family: Dan and Cindy Zelenyj; Tom and Lorrie Zelenyj; my mom and dad, R.I.P.; Elaine Walker and the rest of the Walker family; and of course, my wife Elizabeth, for everything; and our menagerie—Callie, Daisy, Dune, and Captain Janeway—for constantly reminding me of the good and simple things in life.

Contents

Break the skin of civilization and you find the ape,
roaring and red-handed.

- Robert E. Howard

Introduction

by Brian A. Dixon

They will tell you that you can't judge a book by its cover. But you can, of course. You must. Entering a bookshop or the library at day's end—be it brick-and-mortar or pixels-and-pages—is to step forth with a spirit of discovery and venture into a vast and varied landscape of literature. Each shelf represents another outcropping of stories, each section its own summit or valley. As readers, it isn't long before we're seeking some sense of direction, searching for something familiar, something that calls to us, some landmark amid the winding footpaths and crisscrossed roads.

That's the signpost, up ahead. The labels on those bookshelves promise us a sense of direction. Mystery to the north. The rolling hills of Humor to the east. Historical fiction behind us, to the south. And the smoldering sunset of Romance in the west. The enticing titles splayed out on the spines that pass promise excitement, stimulation, inspiration, contentment. Their brightly colored jackets and covers act as folded maps. They promise to show us the way.

Yes, the best designed of books signals to us what we'll find if we venture on, like the chaotic collage that adorns *Beware Us Flowers of the Annihilator*—but hold that thought.

We judge a book by its cover because, as readers, we long for a sense of genre. How are we to choose our stories? How are we to judge whether or not they bring us any entertainment, new insight, or satisfaction? How are we to face the insurmountable task of studying literature, a field so vast and diverse as to be all-consuming? How are we to choose an effective interpretive framework for that study? Genre promises to chart the terrain, to light the way, to ensure our safe passage in an inconstant land where it would be all too easy to lose our footing and lose our way.

The inclination to package ideas in this way is inherently human. We are possessed of a desperate desire to seek out discernible patterns in the world around us, an impulse imbued by our very biology, by the insurmountable logic of evolutionary adaptation. It is characteristic of the advanced intellect, of the raw, undeniable power of the human brain, the phylogenetic superpower that has enabled us not only to survive in a world of sudden death and unexpected dangers but to dominate. And here, at the absolute apex of the food chain, it has become our curse. As we venture out into the modern cultural landscape to hunt for that next great read, we hear whispers of more unsettling narratives, punctuated by the occasional shout of fear and cries of conspiracy theories. With a paralyzing paranoia, we come to feel that there are patterns absolutely everywhere—even where there aren't.

This reckless, hyperactive impetus for pattern recognition, this love of formulas and categories and Dewey decimals, is a trap. We begin to perceive the day-to-day experience of life in this strange and sometimes magical but often terrifying world as the result of a sinister blueprint, of a code, of a build-up of basic binaries, and in moments of weakness we begin to tell our stories using the words and symbols associated with the strict conceits of that masterplan. Witness the struggle of liberals versus conservatives. Blue versus red. Progress versus tradition. Freedom versus security. Art versus commerce. Alpha versus omega! Halloween versus Christmas!! Us versus them.

These labels will not help us to find our way and, though the power of storytelling is infinite and inexhaustible, our predefined genres are ultimately ill-suited to guiding us through the raw, wild wilderness of life in this incomprehensible world. As we venture through the shadowlands of narrative, we sense there is a problem with those crisply defined signposts to common genres that have been laid out for us along the path. Perhaps we should ignore them. Perhaps losing our sense of direction would help us to rediscover our sense of adventure. Perhaps we should find our own way. When you wander from that well-trodden path to a place that is far from the expected signposts, unmarked on any map, that is where you will find the flowers. That is where Alexander Zelenyj waits for you.

Alexander Zelenyj is among the most unique and accomplished authors of short form speculative fiction in the twenty-first century. He is the ideal guide to this wild continent of fiction that cannot be classified or categorized, the living embodiment of those problems that fester and rot deep inside of those whitewashed signposts. Such problems blossom into outright enigmas when we encounter this mysterious figure, the acclaimed author of this collection of truly remarkable fiction.

The problem lies in declaring that Alexander Zelenyj writes speculative fiction. There is no other genre label as flexible as it is concise, but it still bears the lingering tang of "science fiction," and even those with a passing familiarity with the author's works will recognize that it is woefully inadequate. In *Beware Us Flowers of the Annihilator*, you will find tales that shatter storytelling conventions, tales of everyday courage and timeless mysteries and creeping madness, tales that cultivate sprawling and inspired vistas in which the past and the future collide. It is the sheer invention of these stories, the author's willingness to remix familiar genres and symbols in new and unexpected ways, that renders them so unique.

There is a problem in the assertion that Alexander Zelenyj writes in the short form. Certainly, it is his preferred form, as exemplified by this collection. But *Black Sunshine*, Alex's first novel, lingers in the corners of my memory, with its spider's web of a narrative. And, after two decades of engaging with Alex's fiction in wide-eyed wonder, I have witnessed certain willful characters wander from story to story, anthology to anthology, as dismissive of narrative boundaries as the author who conjured them up. The punk band cum cosmic suicide cult Deathray Bradburys. The gritty detectives Clark and Kessel. The incredible being known as the Priests. The murderous and war-hungry McCall. In reading a new story, I feel that I have opened a door, and sometimes I am startled to find a familiar face staring back, there to warn me that there are no certainties here and I may be unprepared for the scale of this dark and sprawling literary cosmos.

I imagine each of Alex's books in this way, and this latest is no different; *Beware Us Flowers of the Annihilator* is a house of doors and mirrors that stands crookedly on the horizon of that atom-blasted wasteland far beyond the beaten path. It is a house through which a mob of driven and tormented characters rage, stumbling through the darkness of their reality, uncertain of where they are headed or where they have been and utterly unable to escape the inborn guilt of their humanity. Read on and you accept your place in their ranks.

In its earliest development, the book that you hold in your hands bore an entirely different title: *Oppenheimer's Doors* (derived from the titular short story, "Oppenheimer's Door"). It was a solid title, one that I felt beautifully captured this vision of the imaginative worlds and multitudinous genres that share space within. But Alex hadn't planned on the success of Christopher Nolan's latest cinematic masterpiece or the cultural phenomenon that it would ignite. Suddenly, there were preconceived associations, assumed intentions, expected destinations tied to that title. For a book like this, it simply wouldn't do.

With its new title—still more haunting and hypnotic and ominous—*Beware Us Flowers of the Annihilator* presents extraordinary narratives, captivating and compelling because of the ways in which they evolve and devolve the familiar literary genres that we have clung to in the past. There, on that chaotic cover, is the merest glimpse of the uncertainty that lies ahead. In this collage, curious figures desperately seek to portend the fate that awaits them beyond the wasteland, with doom burning on the horizon. This mix of classical works hints that this has all happened before and it will all happen again and, try though we might, we cannot paper over our guilt or mortal terror with the drawings and photographs that we collect along the way. It is the cover by which we judge *Beware Us Flowers of the Annihilator*, its arrangement disquieting. It promises everything and clarifies nothing, and for that, it is fitting. After all, the fiction of Alexander Zelenyj mocks your instinctive attempts at pattern recognition. It will not be pushed, filed, stamped, indexed, briefed, debriefed, or numbered. It cannot be programmed, categorized, or easily referenced. It is weird, it is wild, and it is wonderful.

Alex is a master storyteller and *Beware Us Flowers of the Annihilator* is the latest in a long line of *tours de force*. If you're brave enough to face Oppenheimer's door and venture within this labyrinthine house of doors and mirrors, you'll be rewarded with that giddy sensation that so often follows a sudden and terrifying lurch beyond the familiar and into the unknown. Wild hearts and thrill-seekers rejoice, you will find what you yearn for here but take care where you trod. There are abominable flowers blooming in these unfamiliar rooms and twisting, maze-like hallways, in these strange stories of fortune and excess and judgment and doom. Flowers that will feed on your fear and your uncertainty, on your delirium and decay. They have overgrown all signposts and obscured the path that has led you here. There is no turning back. Nevermind all that. Read on, and let Alexander Zelenyj be your guide.

Peacekeeper and the War-Mouth

"Your country took it from behind during the war—guess that means you take it from behind, too, Pete."

The confrontation, like so many before it, was taking place at the edge of the schoolyard, close to the fences of the neighbourhood houses that bordered the tarmac lot and that ran the length of the adjacent soccer field. Peter Eliáš took the same tack he usually did, feigning obliviousness to the bullying—though, as always, his tormentor didn't go away. In fact, as usually happened, Darren Dunlop's taunting words had drawn a crowd—mostly his equally moronic henchmen, but other kids, too. Even, most painfully of all, some girls. Most of these were smiling with a kind of eager anticipation, except for Jenny McGill, whose expression was a mixture of horror and fear. She'd sympathize with Peter's predicament, of course—he'd heard the popular girls call her names plenty of times, and wished he'd had the courage to say something to them about it.

"I said, 'Your country took it from behind during the war—guess that means you take it from behind, too.' Sound about right to you, Pete?"

Darren Dunlop's obsession was all things military. He got it from his older brother, a racist neo-Nazi skinhead trash-bag who'd been kicked out of most high schools in the city for various forms of violence and academic retardation. Rumour was that he was in jail at the moment, though nobody was brave enough to try and confirm the fact with Darren. The younger Dunlop had recently learned that Czechoslovakia had been occupied by the Germans during the Second World War. He had previously learned that Peter was Czech, and that his parents were first-generation immigrants who came to Canada back in the 1960s. Peter had shared all of this during his Social Studies oral presentation about his family's background. The result of this knowledge turned out to be fuel for primitive playground torture.

"That's a really smart equation you came up with." Peter was wise enough to bite off the remark there, though how he wished he was brave enough to finish, "...you mentally challenged ape."

"*What* was that, *Czech* boy?"

"Uh, just that Czechoslovakia was a peaceful country, and it had lots of, uh, resources that Germany wanted, and it's really a lot more complicated than that anyways," Peter managed by way of damage control. It was ironic—Peter actually loved similar things to the caveman who was terrorizing him. He liked military history, and obviously knew a hell of a lot more about it than Darren or his criminal brother. And he had the full run of the *G.I. Joe* comic book series and a lot of the toys too, because his mom spoiled him. He'd even made her take him to see *Predator* in the theatre the year before, and it was all he'd been able to talk about for months. He often played army in the woods behind his townhouse, though being friendless meant his were always solo missions infiltrating dangerous enemy lines to assassinate important generals or destroy weapons factories or, post-*Predator* viewing, a one-on-one test of cunning against an invisible alien hunter. He'd even given himself a codename, the thought of which made his cheeks burn red with embarrassment under the current circumstances: Kid Kombat. Jesus, what a joke.

Darren was sneering, and taking a moment to shake his head at Peter as if he were confronting the most pathetic creature he'd ever seen. "That's exactly what I said—*you guys took it from behind in WW Two*. What are you, *retarded?* You want me to smack some sense into you?"

Peter turned away, pretending to be examining the lawn with

interest, but the words escaped him, and he muttered, "Yeah, *you're* the one in remedial."

"*What* did you say to me, you little bitch?"

The playground tyrant's voice brimmed with theatrical incredulity. There was *no way* one of his lessers could conceivably *dare* to give back to him the insults he so readily dished out. He must have simply misheard this weak midget he regularly punished for being weak and midgetly, and therefore a guaranteed non-threat to his own greater physical stature and machismo.

"Nothing," muttered Peter, hating himself for living up to his abuser's expectations, wishing he had the courage to kick him square in the junk and then pummel the towering moron into unconsciousness.

"Thought so, peacekeeper. Since if you *did* say something then you might have had to eat some sand again."

Darren topped off the torment just as the bell rang signalling an end to recess, a heavy one-two-three clapping on Peter's shoulder in a brazen Alpha Male show of superiority, and with that reminder of the last shaming he'd made Peter endure one week before—dragging him from one side of the soccer field to the other in a headlock that had left his head ringing and his ears chafed, and then forcing his face into the sandpit while the kids practicing long-jump stood by watching. The ordeal went on for what had felt like forever, until Mr. Jefferies, the gym teacher, came rushing over and intervened.

"Hurry up, peacekeeper," called Darren loud enough for the whole schoolyard to hear, making Peter jump. "Unless you need me to drag you back to class."

The kids' laughter was sharp and malignant, sullying the autumn air. It was the sound of evil, Peter decided, especially the snickering he heard from a couple of the meaner girls.

But he felt it then—a tugging on his back, between his shoulder blade and spine on the left side; the familiar stretching of the skin, and this time with it came thoughts of violence and vengeance miles away from the usual thoughts Peter had in the aftermath of confrontations with Darren, when all he felt was relief and gratitude that the episode was finished with, and naïve hope that it might be the last time.

This sudden deluge of dark thoughts was strong enough that Peter dwelled on nothing else for the rest of the school day. It had been shockingly powerful. It felt wrong, but right, too. Because Darren deserved negative thoughts directed at him, didn't he? For all that he'd made Peter suffer over their years together at school, didn't he deserve the darkness of those thoughts, which were still so much kinder than the things he did to Peter? More than anything, these unexpected thoughts bothered Peter as much as they did because they felt like an awakening, of something dark inside himself that he hadn't known was there. And that thing, he now knew, had its own mouth—he knew the two were connected. He'd felt it in the pleasurable tautness of the skin stretching secretly across his back, in conjunction with the arrival of the bad-thoughts, of violent revenge.

Peter was just happy the blows from Darren had landed on his right side—his unblemished side. But the thought wormed its way into his jumbled thoughts: what would have happened if those hard claps *had* landed there? And as he hurried to the back of the crooked line of students filing inside the school, another thought began to form, one that lifted his defeated spirits considerably:

Maybe Kid Kombat had a secret weapon.

He'd been feeling the then-familiar movement all that summer, of course, but it had changed—grown stronger, the tugging of the skin more insistent. It stung sometimes, and afterward the skin around the deformity was sore for days.

He'd been feeling happy on the morning of his birthday and, just before his mom took him out to the comic book shop, he'd locked himself in the bathroom and pulled his shirt off. Turning his back to the mirror over the sink, he'd looked over his shoulder bravely, ready to confront it, and accept it for what he'd over the past few months grown to suspect it was. He saw the two rows of pristine white teeth, top and bottom, the distinct shape of the upper and bottom lips, a shade pinker than the rest of his pale complexion. He exerted himself and managed to slip his fingers into one corner of the mouth and gently pulled it back to peer into the dark recess.

The tongue had grown. Where before it had been a small nub, now it was fat and moist. He watched it with trepidation, almost willing the mouth to move like it so often did. He didn't have to wait long. A moment later, as he was about to put his shirt back on and pretend he was a normal kid like everyone else, the lips pulled to the sides, and the mouth smiled in the mirror.

He stared at it sullenly, telling himself this wasn't going to ruin his special day. What had he expected to see, after all? That the mouth had disappeared overnight, crawled back into his body and been made over with a clean patch of skin, like when his mom had the wart on her palm lasered away and a few weeks later she was happily showing him the smooth pad of healed skin. Peter's deformity had appeared as a small puckering lump the previous summer—by winter, it had formed distinct lips; by spring, teeth had grown in and the mouth had begun to move—opening and closing, grimacing, smiling, baring its teeth in silent snarls that gave him a shock when he discovered its expression reflected in the mirror.

Peter left the bathroom but, as he was walking to the front door where his mom was waiting for him, he felt it: a movement, *inside* his secret mouth, and then the distinct stretching of his t-shirt, the bulging of the fabric. He paused mid-step, the certainty of what it was sending a shudder through his body—the secret mouth's tongue was exploring outside of himself.

"One second, Mom," he called, not quite able to subdue the quiver from his voice. He turned and backtracked down the hall, ducking into his bedroom.

"Hurry up, birthday boy," came his mom's cheery reply from down the hall, though he heard her sigh afterwards. If she only knew the terrible secret of her birthday boy, she wouldn't sound so happy.

He came padding down the hall a moment later, the hooded sweatshirt he'd thrown on a little too thick for a warm spring day, but a safer way to be out in the world. It was his birthday, after all—he was allowed to do what he wanted. He could even try to pretend he was normal, even if he knew he'd never convince himself.

"Hey peacekeeper."

Peter looked up from his quiz paper, first to their math teacher Mr. Davidson; finding him seated at his desk flipping through the day's newspaper, he dared to turn to look across the aisle to the row of desks beside his own. Darren Dunlop was nodding toward Peter's quiz paper, mouthing 'show me'. Peter shook his head, aghast. The penalty for both cheaters and those who helped them was a fail, and possible suspension. He'd never cheated or been suspended, hadn't even been sent to detention, in all his years at Forest Grove Public School. The prospect of tarnishing his clean record in his last year because of the likes of Darren Dunlop was unthinkable, laughable.

He turned back to his quiz, began working out the equation on his scrap paper. A moment later, Darren's barely perceptible whisper came again: "Peacekeeper…"

Feeling the bully's eyes boring into him, Peter finally relented and shot a look at him. Darren was scowling at him, eyes glaring from Peter's face to his quiz and back to his face. Peter mouthed, 'no', gesturing to their teacher, and all that that implied for them both.

All he got was a muttered, "Man, I'm gonna beat on you so bad, Czech boy."

Darren's fury at being denied had caused his voice to rise a little too loudly. Mr. Davidson looked up from his newspaper. "Darren. If you have a question, you ask me, not Peter. Got that? One more word from you and you get an 'F'. Same goes for everyone in case anyone else needs reminding: Eyes. On. Your. Own. Paper. Back to work."

Peter felt a clammy sweat on his palms, and his heartbeat rise. He knew Darren would blame him for being yelled at in front of the class, though the idiot himself was totally to blame. What would the punishment be this time? A few hard slaps upside the back of his head? A loogie spit in his face in front of the whole playground at recess? Or the full-on beating he'd been promised, the same kind this racist Cro-Magnon had given Peter at least half a dozen times in their eight years locked together in a school that had long ago started to feel like a prison to Peter?

Peter willed himself to calm down and focus on his quiz, and got back to work. He was almost finished the next problem when it happened, and though it was the first time, Peter realized that he'd felt it coming for months.

The mouth whispered, a wordless sibilant noise one might make to soothe a cat or placate a crying baby; but it was distinctly a *voice* in the otherwise utterly silent classroom.

Coming after his recent reprimand and warning, all eyes turned to Darren, including those of Mr. Davidson.

"Okay, Mr. Dunlop. You want to goof off, you can do it in Principal Donnelley's office."

"Sir, it wasn't me…It was *Pete*…" Darren, bewildered, petulant, looked meaningfully to Peter in the row beside him, Peter who was watching the quiz paper on his desk in front of him, filling in his answers with his pencil.

"Really, Darren?" sighed Mr. Davidson with the air of a man at his wit's end. "How dumb do you think I am? Get out of here. Principal's office, *now*. And toss your quiz in the trash can on your way out. You've earned yourself a big fat zero today. Keep it up and you'll be in my class again next year."

"But sir, I swear, it was him—"

"*Now*, Dunlop!"

As Darren shuffled past his desk, Peter kept his eyes diligently on the quiz paper, making sure to keep his face emotionless, intent on his work. But underneath his shirt, he felt the movement, the tugging and stretching of skin: the war-mouth was smiling. And Peter felt it wash over him: the satisfaction of the vengeance enacted on Darren Dunlop, for asking him to cheat, and for threatening him with another beating and humiliation.

A scrap of paper, delivered through the rows of students at the opposite side of the classroom arrived on Peter's desk during homeroom the following morning. Of course, Peter knew the gist of the message waiting for him there, but he opened it anyway, staring for a second at the jagged angry scrawl of words before hiding the paper under his open binder. The four words there would prove to be the wall between him and the rest of Mr. Davidson's English lesson that morning:

Today you <u>DIE</u> peacekeeper

Peter fretted, thinking madly about how he might be able to escape the school and grounds. He could tell his teachers, but being a tattletale would only be digging his grave a few feet deeper because eventually Darren and his cronies *would* get to him. They always did.

He sat there, not hearing anything of the lesson being taught.

On his back, the war-mouth bared its teeth in a silent snarl.

Peter wasn't always able to undermine the war-mouth's plans and instructions. Sometimes he didn't want to. Often those plans were just right, after all. Peter would learn to meet it halfway. And so sometimes he'd have to relent and follow its wisdoms.

This is what he'd done that day, after spending an endless lunch hour locked in a bathroom stall on the second floor, off-limits during lunch break. He'd snuck up there during the bustle after the bell had sounded, sitting cross-legged on the seat so his feet couldn't be seen if Darren and his cronies came hunting for him. He clutched his books on his lap, and only realized after he'd shut himself in and the sounds of student conversation in the hall had long disappeared that he'd left his lunch inside his locker. Oh well—better hungry and alive than beaten-up and shamed on a full stomach. And the lunchroom would have proven the perfect arena for Darren to dish out some violence, with a huge audience and all his friends on hand.

But the lunch hour didn't prove without purpose for Peter. During those endless sixty minutes, he was tutored by the war-mouth, and by the time the bell rang and he slipped out of the washroom and rushed to his locker and from there to class, he was calmer than he had been before. And though he could feel Darren watching him from across the room, and heard him and his friends chortling from time to time, and knew that they were plotting his demise, he wasn't as frightened as he might have been otherwise.

The war-mouth was a fine teacher during such dire times.

~

As instructed, Peter made a show of loitering in class after final bell, pretending he had questions about the essay for History that was due the following week. He could hear Darren and his friend, Geoff, talking in the hall, their voices echoing in the increasingly emptier space as kids hustled off toward home. After five minutes with his teacher, Peter said goodnight and jogged down the hallway to his locker, pretending he hadn't seen Darren and Geoff loitering at the opposite end of the hall, peering around the corner. At his locker, Peter hurriedly grabbed his gym bag and ran outside. The lot and grounds were almost empty, with only a few straggling kids taking their time walking home at the edge of the soccer field. He crossed the tarmac at a jog and dove into the forest that abutted the school grounds on the east side.

Once he'd gained the middle of the forest, he slowed to a walk. He took his time, listening closely to the sounds of the woods around him: the birds singing and squirrels chittering in the trees, the buzz of flies around his ears, cicadas buzzing. It wasn't long before another sound intruded there, out of place, but just as he'd been expecting. Footsteps, brazenly loud as they snapped fallen branches, kicked up rocks and leafy litter from the ground.

"Peacekeeper."

Peter walked on a little, reaching into his gym bag.

"Czech boy. I'm talking to you, peacekeeper."

Peter stopped on the narrow path, feeling the two boys come up close behind him. The repeated meaty smacking sound he somehow knew was Darren imitating what they'd all seen in a hundred movies, and hitting the end of a baseball bat into his palm. The aggressors had come to destroy the pacifist, brandishing a weapon stolen from the gym's storage room.

What they found when their target turned around to face them, though, wasn't the frail kid they usually tormented, bending over for a beating he didn't deserve. It was a classmate wielding a canister of spider-killing spray in each hand. The spray had been an ideal example of environmentally unsafe and ethically unsound insecticides, and the perfect foil for the safer products Peter had discussed in his report for Science class, natural pest deterrents like basil and garlic and rosemary. But, just as the war-mouth had explained, the poison spray turned out to also be a good weapon against tyrants.

The change in the usual plot registered to the bullies only after Peter had opened fire into their faces. As the war-mouth had instructed, he aimed for their eyes and got them squarely. And, also as per the war-mouth's orders, he kept up the attack even as the boys stumbled backward, falling over each other in their pain and haste to escape, tripping over the tree roots emerging like fingers from the soil. And where Peter might have otherwise at that point turned and made his escape, the war-mouth urged him to complete his mission, and make certain that the aggressors were put in a place where they wouldn't pose a threat to his peace ever again.

"Go on, Peter! Keep at it! They'll just kill you next time!"

The war-mouth was right. And so Peter stood over them, leaning in close with the canisters and continuing to spray the poisonous streams into the boys' faces. They tried hiding their faces with their hands, turning toward the ground, but the relentless spraying into their ears and along their necks and backs of their heads caused a poisonous vapour to form around them, which they inevitably breathed in. They were choking on the noxious fumes and liquid, coughing, retching, screaming, clawing at their eyes, throats. And still Peter kept up his attack.

"Go on, Peter! *Go on!*"

They were deep enough in the woods that from the outside, their screams could easily have been misconstrued as the cries of kids at play. Playing at war, maybe, but still only playing.

Peter continued until both canisters were exhausted, at which point he threw the cans at the boys' heads, an anguished cry escaping him. They didn't appear to feel the blows; they were twitching and convulsing, streams of red vomit and saliva bubbling from their mouths and nostrils.

"We're almost finished here, Peter," said the war-mouth.

Understanding its meaning, Peter looked to the bat among the leaves.

It had been sweaty work, with the southwestern Ontario humidity making the air like quicksand, and Peter's t-shirt was clinging to him like a second skin. He became aware of the war-mouth visible under the sweat-soaked cotton and a flashback came to him, of all those past times of terror when gym class had called for team sports games of shirts vs. skins and the potential for his deformity being revealed.

And it was at that precise moment that he felt a physical touch on his back…directly on the war-mouth.

Like an electrical jolt, it sent him reeling around. Both he and the war-mouth cried out at the contact.

He found himself facing Jenny McGill. Her placid eyes calmed him a little, making him hope she hadn't seen the war-mouth, that she'd only coincidentally touched him there, oblivious, concerned maybe for the two stricken boys but unaware of Peter's secret shame.

But she said, her voice small like the rest of her, "I have one, too. Mine's down here, though." She was pointing to a place on her stomach, on the left side. "A little mouth. But it's getting bigger." She looked at the boys wheezing and spluttering on the ground. "I won't tell. I understand. I hate them both. They only make fun of people, and beat them up, and make them feel like nothing. Once, they said I looked like a dead fish washed up at the river." She looked away, adding, "Because I'm really pale. And they said I smell like a dead fish, but I don't. I smell nice."

Peter couldn't find his voice. It was all too much to process. A mix of horror and shame and elation and a sense of shared secrecy conspired to make him able to do nothing but stand gaping at Jenny, who turned to watch him with her docile expression, truly seeming to understand the situation just as she'd said she did.

He looked to his tormentors. They were still blubbering, twitching, gagging, crying, dying.

"There's no choice now," hissed the war-mouth, its voice clear in the hushed forest. "There's no going back after a death."

Peter understood that the war-mouth meant his death, the

gentle side of himself that had died after all the years of torment at the hands of people like Darren Dunlop and his thugs. It made sense. A line had certainly been crossed, though he was going to make sure he got back a little piece of his old self once this whole mess was over and done with. Because he never wanted to be a Darren Dunlop. He was going to try to be better than that.

"It's right," came a voice from Jenny, though by her solemn expression and by the way she was turning to look down at her herself, Peter understood it was her secret mouth that had spoken, its voice remarkably like Jenny's own: quiet, sad, but confident. "There's no going back."

Peter picked up the baseball bat Darren had brought with him into the woods, his chosen weapon for punishing Peter for the crime of the detention he'd been given, and the failed quiz. He walked over to Darren and Matt, a great calm seeping into him.

The birds sang in the tangled canopy. The late-day sunlight filtered through in long golden spears. Between these shafts of brilliant illumination the forest watched the confrontation from gloomy spaces.

"Do it," said Jenny McGill, her voice echoed perfectly by her war-mouth. "I don't want to watch, though," she added, in her voice alone. She turned and continued down the path toward home. "See you in class tomorrow, Pete."

He watched her go. He looked forward to seeing her at school. Maybe they could be friends. Maybe they could start a secret club. Or an army, just in case one was ever needed.

He turned back to his tormentors. Peter himself never had been Kid Kombat. He understood this now with a clarity he'd never really had before, about anything. He was Peacekeeper, and the thing on his back was the War-Mouth. They were opposites learning to live together, forever inseparable. They were the world.

He hefted the bat, and the War-Mouth smiled. The time had come to end a war and begin a peace long overdue.

The Deathwish
of Valerie Vulture

It was her. It was Valerie Vulture, in the flesh and feather—his predecessor's creation that this year was celebrating its one-hundredth birthday. The moment he saw it, Thomas understood its reality despite its inherent fantastical character: the bright purple feathers, long, hooked beak a brilliant orange, comically big cartoon eyes goggling at him. And blinking.

It was alive.

A real animal perched on the top of his easel, creaking the frame, its wings folded at its side, its eyes filled with all the melancholy his pen had ever imbued them with. And it was life-sized; that is, the same approximate size as a real-world vulture, though every aspect of the creature screamed that it had come from a different world.

And then the giant bird spoke, and it was the voice Thomas Kelly had always heard in his head when following its exploits in the funny pages as a boy, and while working on the strip himself as an adult; low and dopey-sounding, the perfect aural equivalent of the tragicomical face with its exaggeratedly large watery eyes and drooping beak and stooped neck, and the overarching hangdog aura that permeated the creature.

It—she—said:

"I need your help, Tom."

~

Thomas Kelly had taken over the *Valerie Vulture* comic strip in its eightieth year, just months after its long-lived creator, Jack McTavish, had died. Taking the job had proven the best career choice he'd ever made. His style meshed perfectly with that of the character's creator's style (being Jack's assistant and inker for five years assured that, plus the fact that he was one of the few remaining cartoonists who insisted on drawing straight to paper rather than on a computer screen and did no digital touch-ups), yet offered a bolder flourish that appealed to modern audience's tastes. Tom's Valerie was updated for a new generation yearning for the same character in a more streamlined guise, without the original version's scratchy linework, as remarkable as it was considered to be.

Valerie had been with him during his best years. She was there at his first marriage, through the births of his two daughters, and all through the difficult years of his divorce. She'd been a source of income during these tough times, when he'd churned out the strip with a diligent workmanlike efficiency for months on end. Val had been there when he met the woman who would become his second wife. Valerie had even brought him fame, something he'd never in his wildest dreams believed his work in the industry would get him, which in turn ensured that he'd never worry financially again. Thomas Kelly, chosen by the great Jack McTavish to continue the miserable story of the famed Valerie Vulture character, could get work anywhere he wanted.

Thomas had started his run the safe way—relying on long-established continuity while using his best gag-a-day ideas to pad out his first year on the strip. This was more than okay with Valerie's many readers—they yearned to see her suffer through the long list of tortures she'd been enduring since Jack McTavish had first drawn her into popular culture a century before. The most beloved, and hence most recurring, of these storylines was the introduction of some new character—and there had literally been hundreds of these over the years—with whom Valerie felt an instant connection and rapport; Valerie would become overwhelmed with joy and make proclamations that her long life of loneliness was finally over, that she'd found her one true partner; only to have the character in question meet an untimely (and always grisly) death right before Valerie's eyes. This was the classic tried-and-true formula for *Valerie Vulture*.

Readers ate it up. Enthusiastic fan mail inundated newspaper offices' inboxes everywhere. Fan groups abounded. Valerie was a popular costume at cosplay events and on Halloween. There were books and a cartoon series, even a documentary about her. People loved tuning in to Valerie's never-ending misery.

The first recurring storyline of Tom's own invention was introduced at the start of his second year on the strip, when he'd felt much more comfortable with the character and the various secondary characters and classic narrative threads. This original contribution sent Valerie on a full-on quest to find others like herself (where before she'd been entirely passive in waiting for any good fortunes to materialize). During the McTavish years, she'd met many characters she felt a connection with, but never one of her own species: a purple-feathered vulture.

The year-long storyline was the most relentlessly dismal of the famed bird's career, and one of the most popular among readers. They devoured Valerie's fruitless quest and what they foresaw as its inevitable doomed resolution. This was how countless strips had ended, of course, in Valerie trying to come to terms with her singular aloneness. Readers loved that the poor bird had gotten her hopes up so high this time, while simultaneously questioning over and over again whether she would always be alone in the world; unlike any other bird or animal, and infinitely less equipped than other birds at eking out a life among the solitary aeries and peopled towns she frequented.

Indeed, her solitude among the nameless cliffs that had always been her home led to long philosophical ruminations on her seeming immortality, set against the mortality she saw all around her, and that she yearned for. Valerie Vulture was contemplating the merits of her own death, and end to her misery. And of course her interactions with the humans in the towns she passed through led only to her being shunned over and over again, as was customary in the strip.

People didn't take kindly to a carrion bird, even one as gaily clad in ironically bright feathers as Valerie was.

Then, the *Valerie Vulture* strip was given a jolt that got readers sending in mountains of concerned messages, and had them more than a little worried. It amused Tom to no end because he knew all the fear was unfounded (though he was more than a little shocked at how angry some of the mail was—it bordered on hate-mail, and included several hundred messages that contained outright threats on his life).

Readers needed never to have feared. The controversial story arc, which depicted Valerie seemingly finding true love, would turn out to be Tom's cruellest joke on her.

In the second-to-last strip of the year-long quest story, Tom introduced Valentine Vulture, a handsome purple-feathered(!) carrion bird with a big heart and a bad-luck streak on par with Valerie's own. Like Valerie, he'd lived his long life in solitude among a different series of mountain crags, lamenting his lonely existence and the revulsion he was met with whenever he tried to befriend another animal or human.

The two were perfect together, and in the final strip of the quest story Val and Val enjoyed two panels of wedded bliss, a third panel of joyful flight toward an undisclosed honeymoon destination…before the fourth and final panel, in which Valentine was shot from the air by a hunter (off-panel, the hunter was never identified, which was in keeping with countless other such murderers of Valerie's friends and fellow lonesome travellers she felt some kinship with).

To rub salt in the wound, the whole storyline was shown to be a dream in the following day's strip, one of the regular nightmares of death and violence and loneliness that had plagued Valerie from the beginning of her life, which simultaneously proved a horrible experience of its own right but also cemented the certainty that Val was *truly* alone and never had been able to find true love, not even for a few panels. She remained the loneliest outsider in the world. Even the hopefulness of her dream existed solely to be torn down.

Tom's name was made after the conclusion of the strip with its big reveals, so cathartic for his readers in meeting—and then exceeding—their expectations. He was beloved all over again.

~

Tom's and Valerie's long shared history had crashed over him in a span of seconds, a tidal wave of remembrance that left him nearly as shaken as this latest and most surreal moment in that relationship.

"But…how?" was all he could manage.

Above him, from her perch along his easel, Valerie Vulture said sedately, "I needed to see you, Tom. I flew in the direction opposite from any compass directions, toward where I could sense you. I knew you were there. I flew as hard as my wings could take me. And here I am."

"You flew from my…You flew from the comic strip." Tom's voice sounded very far away to his ears. He felt as if he were floating, watching the scene from a bird's-eye view—a scene in a weird movie, an episode of a science fiction TV series. He looked to the sheet spread across his easel, the latest Valerie strip which he'd completed only minutes before Valerie's arrival. As if to remind him of the reality of the moment, he saw the single bright purple feather resting among his brush pens, the same feather that had appeared there at the same time as he'd felt her presence, and turned his eyes up to see the manifestation of the legendary cartoon character watching him hopefully.

Jesus, he was lucky it was Easter and his fellow artists were at home with their families—only he came into the bullpen on holidays, where he could concentrate on his work without the distraction of kids, allowing him to crank out work quickly but without sacrificing quality.

He felt his hands trembling where they rested in his lap and knew that he'd never be able to draw a steady line no matter how hard he tried.

"Yes, I did. I was as surprised as you that it worked. I didn't know…that it would. I just had to try something. I needed to. I tried so many times over the years I've lost count, but this time it felt like…it was like everything I'd been through, all the bad experiences, filled me with this sort of energy, a desperate energy, that shot me like a cannonball from there to here. I *had* to see you, Tom, and talk to you."

"But you can't be real."

"But I am."

"But it's crazy."

"Feel my feathers—maybe that will convince you."

Valerie stretched out a long wing, its lush purple feathers spread like a decorative fan before him. He reached out gingerly, stroked the feathers. They were soft, silky, like he'd imagined they would be.

"Okay," he said, still feeling stunned, numb, but yielding to the inevitable. Valerie was there with him. They were having a conversation. He'd touched her and she felt real. Life was strange. There was so much more to the universe than science had ever taught him in the Space Channel documentaries he liked to watch.

With acceptance of the situation's reality, Tom felt an unexpected wave of guilt wash over him. What he'd put this creature through, oblivious though he'd been…it was horrible. To be made to endure such suffering, and for so long…It was unfathomable. He would do anything to make things right.

"I hope you know, Val, that I had no idea about any of this. It's so fantastic. I'm still half wondering if I'm having some intense delusion and that I'll wake up in a hospital bed or padded room. But I'm feeling fine, relatively speaking, given the circumstances, and I want to do what I can to…to make things right. I'm sure Jack McTavish would have wanted it, too."

"I doubt that, Tom. I could sense him through his lines, too. The link between him and what he created for me—my world, that he made for me to live in and for him to benefit from—the link told me a little of the kind of human he was. He wasn't good. Maybe not evil or anything close to that, but he wasn't all that good. You, I sense you're a good human."

"I'm going to fix this, then," Tom said, eagerly standing up and snatching a pencil from his easel. He was prepared to unleash ideas onto paper of a new story for Val, that would change her secret life for the better.

"You can't, Tom, though I really appreciate you wanting to try. But you can't."

"Why can't I fix it? Why can't I draw a new story, with new characters, and make you happy? Why can't I? Tell me. Because I will. I'll do whatever I can. My editor and readers be damned." He was already thinking of the backlash, knew it would be tremendous. At least he'd had a great run. At least he was financially secure enough that career suicide wouldn't leave him penniless.

She told him.

"Because when I was created, by that tyrant of a man back in 2024, he put nothing but sadness in my heart. That's what he made me from: pure misery. I've been everyone's sad little scavenger bird for over a century. I've known nothing but. My heart is broken. If you tried to put happiness in it, it wouldn't—it couldn't—work. It couldn't accept it. It would be like poison. That's how it feels to me now when every week you introduce some new false joy—it burns in my heart. Like fire. Like acid. I'm ruined. My soul is tarnished. I only know how to be miserable, because it's what I was written to know, and nothing else. And I always felt it, somehow it was communicated back to me though the pages—the sick glee so many humans got from watching my suffering."

Tom spoke past the lump in his throat, feeling sick. "I always thought it's because people could relate to you. Because a lot of people—most people—aren't happy."

"Maybe it should give me comfort, knowing there are others who might understand what I've gone through, just a little. But it doesn't. Maybe it's because it's always seemed to me that a lot of people—not all, but a lot—are cruel at heart. That they enjoy the misery they see all around them, because that misery is bigger than their own misery. I've been that measuring stick for too long to bear."

She shook her head, closing her lids over her big ludicrous eyes. "And the thing is, that now when I meet new friends—*characters* to you—who are kind and good-hearted and who love me and accept me for who and what I am…I don't feel anything. Before, for decades and decades and decades, I did. I was happy sometimes, filled with so much joy whenever you or Jack would give me new friends, even though that joy was always cut short when those friends were taken away from me. But I was always hopeful, optimistic about the next day…the next comic strip, for you. But now there's nothing. I'm broken. After all the years, my heart can't feel good things. There's been too much disappointment, and sadness. You can write my lines and make me say how happy I am to have found a new companion, but that's not the real me. I'm dead inside." Her beak tapped softly at her fluffy chest in a gesture that pained Tom to see.

He waited, thoughts a jumble as he tried to decide what action he could take to help Valerie, and shake off the weight of his guilt.

"There's a place between the comic strip panels," Valerie went on. "You can get there by pushing through them to what lies behind. It's way out past where it's hazy to the eyes of the people reading the comics. Most people don't even sense it, though."

She paused and looked out the window, following the path of a gull wheeling against the blue sky.

Tom had known about the place between the panels, had always suspected it existed. He'd had the inkling when he was a little boy reading his first comic books, and while poring over the funnies in the weekend newspaper. When he was sad, or upset by something, the comfort of the comics he adored called to him, and within them something else called to him—beyond their inherent escapism, an escape to something much more tangible but just beyond his grasp. By the time he was a teenager and fancied himself a serious comic collector, he was certain about the existence of the place, though he never spoke a word about it to anyone, because who would have taken the idea seriously?

He said, feeling as if he were unburdening himself of a heavy weight, "I knew it existed. I've always known." He wondered if other cartoonists and readers knew it, too.

A subtle light seemed to seep into Valerie's watery eyes. "I knew you did, Tom. I could sense it, even more than with Jack. Your renderings, the way you moved me, gave my words life, joy, and the way you drew the world around me—the forests and mountains and valleys, and the towns and roads and highways—I could sense that the artist that drew it understood the curtain that existed between what the reader saw, and what was behind the picture." Then she added, "I've caught glimpses, a peek now and then over the years. It's beautiful. It's Paradise. Or Heaven, or whatever you want to call it. It's peace, and that's what I want, Tom, more than anything. I need peace.

"And I think you owe me, Tom, after all the years of…It's been so hard all these years. One hundred years of torture—of people laughing at my expense, all the cruel characters, all the readers. There's never been a break from it. It's all I've ever known. Through all your personal history, and the history of your world during your lifetime and before—the good and the bad—I was suffering. The bad of New Vietnam, the good of the first Mars colony. It didn't matter for *me*. *My* existence was the same misery. I couldn't celebrate along with you all. I couldn't mourn with you, even though those events were always woven into the background of my ugly little stories. There was no light for me. There is no light for me. All I have is the darkness that's been in my heart since I was created. And I think that, after all of that pain, you owe me, Tom. You took over from that monster who made me, but you haven't done any better. I've been nothing but a vehicle for your success. You've gained a lot at my expense, haven't you? I know you didn't know about me, Tom, about the real me, but you have to admit the truth in it—that I've helped you, when all you ever did for me was cause me pain."

"Jesus, I…I'm sorry, Val." He was shocked to realize how sincere the apology was, though he knew it couldn't mean much to Valerie. 'Val'—he felt embarrassed at using the abbreviated form of her name, too intimate-sounding considering how little good he'd ever done for her. But it was how he'd always thought of her, and referred to her to his friends, family—'Sorry, can't watch the news with you right now, honey: I've got a Val strip to draw before deadline tomorrow morning.'

Valerie Vulture shook him from his uncomfortable reverie.

"And I don't have much time here, Tom—it takes a lot to visit this place, your world, and I don't know if I can ever manage it again. Maybe it will take me another hundred years. By then you'll be gone and there'll be a new human writing my day-to-day torments. And now, I feel the pull of the paper, like it's going to suck me back in." Her beak tapped at the art paper clipped to Tom's easel.

He said, "Of course, I'll do whatever I can to help you…But what are you saying? What *can* I do?"

"I'm asking you to kill me."

Tom only stared at Valerie.

"Only you can do this for me, Tom, or at least I think this is how it works. Because you're the one who draws me, and my world. There's only ever been you, and the monster that made me so many years ago."

"Val," Tom said, "Even if this were true, I don't want to…*kill* you. I'm not sure I could."

"Please, Tom. For me, and my broken heart. End the pain for me."

He watched the big cartoon bird for a moment. Then, "How?"

"Draw it. Draw my death. It's that simple. I can feel that this is the only way I can be freed. But please make it quick and painless. I deserve that after everything else."

He shook his head, giving a weak, rueful laugh. "It's…it sounds made up."

Valerie's voice was soft. "I sound made up, too, Tom."

"So, what—I draw this strip, showing your death, and…that's it? You'll really die? How can that be?"

"I was born, wasn't I?"

"But even if I do this…someone else will just take over the strip. They'll bring you back." Of course they would—*Valerie Vulture* was big bucks.

"But it won't be *me*, Tom. That will be another poor creature, with my name."

There was logic in the illogical lunacy of it all, he admitted to himself. Then, "I can do it right now. Do a quick sketch, and…"

Valerie Vulture said, "I'm not sure it works that way. This is all new to me, too, Tom, I hope you understand. I don't have all the answers. Maybe I don't have any of the answers. I'm just going by instinct. I'm a wild animal, after all, even if I'm a cartoon one, so maybe my instincts are good. And they tell me that it isn't just you drawing my death that will free me, but that the people need to see it, too. The readers need to know that I've been freed from their everyday routine, their everyday world where in one tiny corner there's a cartoon animal suffering the way she's suffered for their whole lives."

Tom thought of the decades of Valerie's life, and the countless historical happenings great and small that comprised those years: Russia invading Ukraine and pushing for a third global conflict; the election in the United States of its first female president, a moment of reckoning and progress; and, as Val herself had mentioned, that moment overshadowed by New Vietnam a few years later, the old war-nightmare all over again; the glory of the Mars colonies changing over time into a reflection of any Earth city, divided sharply into regions of affluence and economical despair; the ruining of the oceans and the extinction of the whales but for the two dozen surviving specimens in captivity, freakishly stunted and physiologically sullied by pollutants; Robert Wilson's ingenious invention of the lightweb chamber and light-shard interstellar travel, a high-point in astrophysics and space exploration…and his first journey revealing a truth nobody had expected nor wanted to hear: that we are alone in the infinite, ever-expanding universe, our notions of life elsewhere a myth, the wishful thinking of a race of dreamers; births and deaths; conflicts and tentative periods of peace; scientific advancements and societal regressions; countless steps forward and back.

And through all of it, the joys and disappointments, Valerie had endured; suffering, giving her readers what they expected, what they needed, all while existing—truly *living*—in the unsuspected and incomprehensible world behind the panels.

Valerie Vulture and Tom sat in silence.

She said, "It all sounds crazy, doesn't it?"

Tom laughed. "Sheer lunacy. Straitjacket-level, yeah."

The sun dipping behind the buildings in the west bloodied

the bullpen.

"Please—will you help me, Tom?"

Tom looked through the window and into the parking lot six floors below, and the city beyond, where things carried on as they always did, without pause for the contemplation of daily miracles. He found that he was okay with going through with it, and likely losing his job because of it. After all, a cartoonist working on a long-established character—one created by another artist, no less—doesn't just kill off that character without getting permission from his editors. But as fate would have had it, the already complicated situation became much thornier.

"My *god.*"

Cartoonist and cartoon vulture jumped at the voice invading the quiet bullpen. They found Edwin Palmer, editor-in-chief of the Daily Tribune and Tom's boss, peering with wide eyes from where he stood among the rows of desks and easels.

Tom found his voice, managed, "Sir, I'd like you to meet an old friend of mine. This is Valerie."

"It's…it's inconceivable."

"You see her."

"I know, Tom. I know. It's only that…it defies logic. It defies science. How could it be?"

"I don't know, sir."

"It said that it feels pain. It feels *emotion*? But how can this *be*? How is it *here*? Is this *real*?"

"Yes, it's real, sir. But I don't know how it can be, not really."

As if to prove her existence, the sudden sound of wings flapping sounded loudly in the room. Tom and Palmer both jerked. It had the distinct note of a thumping heartbeat.

"Sir, maybe you heard our conversation, but…she wants me—needs me—to kill her. She says that only I can do it. I have to draw her death. And then she'll be free."

Palmer watched him with an expression of sheer incredulity. "Not a *chance*, Tom. Not a chance in the world. We're keeping this thing alive *forever*." He looked at the clock on the wall. "Speaking of, Tom, it's getting late and I'm guessing you haven't had time to finish up tomorrow's strip. Chop-chop. You get to work while I contact the people at the science institute."

The only thing more insane than Valerie Vulture materializing from his latest comic strip was the pragmatism and demented logic of his boss, Mr. Palmer. "Sir, could you just take a moment to think about what I—"

"Lock that thing in the storage room, Tom. And then get to work on tomorrow's strip. And it *better* be one of the garden variety kind. It's going to end with a run-of-the-mill death, right, Tom? A new friend or lover killed—got it? The bird stays alive."

Tom stared at Palmer in disbelief, speechless. Then he nodded, but vowing to draw his most original strip yet, personal consequences be damned.

~

"I've got just two panels left and it'll be done."

Valerie, perched on Tom's easel, stared down with wide eyes. "It's beautiful, Tom. Thank you."

He'd stayed late, too scared to leave Valerie alone at the office in case Palmer's call to the science people meant an evening visit by some people in lab-coats. He'd been drawing and inking quickly, while trying to preserve his usual style, keeping the integrity of his work alive. It was going to be his most famous piece, after all, and his pride made him work hard to ensure it was of the highest quality he could manage under the circumstances.

The story was simple: Valerie decided in the first panel that she was going to go to Heaven; panel two she flew high among the clouds; panel three showed her among stars and comets; in the final panel she would be floating lifeless in the darkness, with a very final-looking 'END' in the bottom right corner, a first in the Valerie Vulture strip, and for good measure a memorial stating 'R.I.P. Valerie Vulture 2024–2124'.

He was putting brush to paper, the tip touching inside the final panel where he would add his initials as per his usual signature, after which he would scan the strip and submit it to the distributor directly, bypassing his editor completely. By the time he learned of what Tom had done, it would be too late—the strip would be out in the world.

"Step away from your easel, Tom."

Tom and Valerie turned, found Palmer filling the doorway. Behind him was a huge dome-topped cage, its narrow bars the gaudy gold that so many birdcages were made from. He'd evidently purchased the thing from a pet store and lugged it up in the service elevator.

Tom, stomach knotting with dread at the implications of that cage, tried for levity, talking past the lump forming in his throat. "You need to stop surprising us like this, sir."

But Palmer only repeated, "Step away from the easel, Tom."

"No. No way, Palmer, sir. I spent so long on this strip. It's the best work I've ever done." He knew as soon as he'd said it that it was true. A deep pride filled him, like nothing he'd ever felt before about his art. He'd done good work. He'd done good in drawing it.

"Step away, Tom. That strip has to be destroyed. If what you say is true we can't let it exist." He looked to the desks and easels around him, snagged a large bottle of India ink and uncapped it. "Step aside so I can fix this mess you've drawn up before it goes to print. We'll miss our deadline so we'll have to run our first-ever reprint. But better that than an end to the strip." When he saw that Tom was standing his ground, Palmer shook his head, added, "And I'll be forced to call the police on you, Tom. I don't want to, but I will."

"What, are you going to charge me as a criminal for this? On what grounds? Assisted suicide for a cartoon that I draw?"

"It's a new world, Thomas. I'll do what I have to."

Insanely, Palmer had snatched an Exacto knife from somebody's desk and was edging toward him, brandishing it menacingly in one hand, the ink bottle in the other.

"No, sir, it's the same world it's always been," Tom said. Nothing had ever been clearer to him, and with the knowledge came a pang in the heart he felt was his penance to endure. "Sir, we can talk about this."

But Palmer wasn't to be dissuaded by logic. "This creature is either a miracle of science, or just a plain miracle. I'm banking on the former. I've contacted the science institute. They'll know what to do with this situation. Be happy, Tom—your bird will be more famous than ever."

"I'm famous enough already," said Valerie.

Palmer jerked at Valerie's voice. Staring at her as if for the first time, a wide smile spread itself across his face. Tom thought his boss looked utterly unhinged.

He said, "She's been in syndication in every major newspaper for one hundred years, Palmer. She has how many books, cartoons, documentaries, comics, toys. Think of all the suffering she's been through."

"Who hasn't seen me cry myself to sleep on my branch every night?" Valerie said.

Palmer scowled. "Don't try to make me feel guilty, Tom. This thing is—I don't even know what the hell it is. But it sure isn't like you or me. I'm not sure what Jack created when he made it, or how he did it, but it most certainly isn't normal. It isn't *natural*. And science would learn a lot from studying it, and if some of us benefit from that, well, what's the harm?" Palmer lowered his voice, leaned toward Tom. "And Tommy, I'm thinking of you as much as me. You're in on this with me. You...called the bird. Or drew it out of wherever it existed. I know that. I *appreciate* that. I may be your boss and I may be in charge here, and I may seem like a hard-ass about all this, but I want you to benefit from this thing, too."

"Palmer," said Tom. "I can't in good conscience do that."

Palmer's expression darkened. Shaking his head in disappointment, he said, "Tom, step away from the bird. And *you*," he pointed to Valerie and then to the golden cage, "get in there, now."

Valerie gingerly stretched out her wings, began beating them languidly in preparation for the short flight across the room and into the cage. Tom stepped between her and the open cage door, "Wait, Val. No. This is wrong. I—"

"It's okay, Tom," Valerie said, her mopey voice painfully suited to her acquiescence to being caged. "I'm used to this sort of thing."

"But—"

"You heard the thing, Tom—now step aside."

Tom did. He saw in Palmer's hard eyes that there was no appealing to him—any decency he'd had was dead. He was the audience of *Valerie Vulture* all rolled up into a single miserable man looking to help himself at the expense of an innocent.

Before Tom could utter a warning—and he would have, he really would have, he would try to convince himself in the days following—the vulture lifted into the musty air of the bullpen and, beating her wings, flapped erratically across the room. It was as she was nearing the cage that she altered her course, and descended on Palmer.

He had no time to dodge her, or try to bat her away with his hands. Valerie was draped over him, long talons biting into his shoulders and immense purple wings enfolding the man completely. From within her feathery embrace the man's muffled protests rose in hysteria and pain until a muted shrieking was the only sound in the office, like a man screaming into thick velvet curtains.

Palmer's knees buckled, and he collapsed. The Exacto knife fell harmlessly from his limp fingers. Valerie unfolded herself, her wings lifted ceilingward, long feathers splayed wide and predatorily as she surveyed the ruin of the man with her goofy cartoon eyes.

Her long beak had torn out Larry's jugular in an explosion of red.

Thomas stared, unable to speak, taking in the sight of his dead boss: a ragged hole where his throat had been, the wound so large that he looked nearly decapitated, his head askew at a crazy (the word came to Tom: *cartoonish*) angle.

A minute later he found his voice. "Aw jeez, Val, why the hell did you do that? Maybe we could have convinced him. Ohmygod, ohmygod…"

Valerie Vulture turned a mortified gaze on him. "I'm sorry, Thomas. I guess I'm not so good at handling things in *this* world either. But I think that you and I both know that he couldn't have been convinced of anything. But believe me, Tom, it breaks my heart that I had to do it."

Tom watched in disbelief as Valerie wept over the body of the man who'd been planning to exploit her misery for himself—the same gigantic blue-white cartoon teardrops Tom had been drawing falling from her eyes for twenty years.

He'd scanned the strip and sent it to their distributors. He spent the night and early morning hours in conversation with Valerie Vulture.

They ignored the dead man lying in his own blood between the easels. Vaguely, Tom wondered what conclusions the police would come to when their investigation showed the unmistakable wounds from a wild animal, a large bird's talons and beak, or whether they'd simply overlook the evidence in favour of more rational explanations—a disgruntled employee lashing out with some commonplace weapon. He wondered if he would be implicated, though he'd had a good enough working relationship with Palmer, and nobody besides his wife and kids knew where he'd been all day. He put these thoughts aside—he was tired, and other things needed to be attended to now.

Around sunrise, at about the time the day's newspaper had been delivered into the inboxes of subscribers and the first breakfasting readers were scrolling to the comics pages to start their day the way they'd been starting it for years and years; at around this time Valerie Vulture grew quiet, and tired-looking, her eyelids drooping lower than Tom ever drew them. She sagged on her perch until he offered to take her into his arms. She accepted, perhaps feeling close to the man who'd drawn her for so many years, and comforted by his presence despite the pain he'd given her. Maybe her gratitude for the one gift he'd been able to give her was enough for her to grace him with her feathery touch in her final moments.

He held her through it. Like an infant, he coddled the vulture across his lap, gently stroking her wing feathers. By the end, those feathers, which had been a bright purple for over one hundred years, had paled to magenta, and soon after faded to a sickly pink; a cartoon death if he'd ever seen one. Her eyelids slid closed over her big sad eyes. She became lighter, nearly weightless, then insubstantial altogether. Soon after, all colour was gone, leaving a deflated and indistinct black shape in his arms that even as he watched turned the soft grey of a pencil-rendered, smudged drawing, quivering subtly in his hands.

He felt honoured to hear it, the single word flying from the collapsing outline of her beak before she disappeared completely:

"*Look…*"

The word brimmed with awe—joyousness—the first good emotions Valerie Vulture had ever felt in her long life that weren't to be sullied by tragedy. He was happy he'd been able to help her feel them.

Then she was gone and the only evidence of her that remained were the ink stains and pencil smudges covering his hands and arms. Tom thought that a lot of his readers were going to be feeling sadder than usual that day, for all the wrong reasons.

Maleficia Falling

"The sculptor said the pieces are meant to be representations of gifts from Heaven."

The two men—Emperor Hadrian and his quaestor, Casteleo—were standing side by side, appraising the three sculptures in the sunlit atrium of the emperor's villa. Daylight from the *compluvium* and windows shimmered in the placid water of the pool in the room's centre. A shrine occupied one corner, while the funeral masks of dead ancestors stared blindly from their cabinets lining one wall.

The piece that held their attention stood on a squat ivory pedestal that accentuated its size, which was ten feet long, and its shape, which was cylindrical. Its topmost half had about it the look of a great urn, sleek and unornamented; or perhaps a giant's club. Decorative, streamlined ridges like the fins of a great fish rose at evenly spaced intervals from its square base. The sculpture, and its two companion sculptures, seemed to fill the capacious space, exuding a powerful aura. Truly, the artworks had a presence. They had, indeed, supplanted the two men's discussion concerning recent political happenings, the building of the wall in Britannia, the rebuilding of the Pantheon, the ongoing trouble with the Parthians.

"This one is rather phallic," Casteleo observed, and glancing toward the other pair of sculptures, added, "Those two remind me of a strange fat fish, and a giant egg." Indeed, the pieces' bulbous shapes conjured the quaestor's descriptions succinctly.

"Astute in your artistic critique as ever," quipped the emperor, adding, more warmly, "It's wonderful to have you back from your trip abroad, my friend, and to host you here at Tibur. I've missed your wisdoms greatly these past days. The older I grow, the more I rely on your counsel." And then, turning back to the sculptures, "They're sculpted from marble, by that vagabond-cum-prophet, Gallius, though how he came into possession of so much marble remains a mystery. Each of them life-size to real-world counterparts, he was to have said."

"Gifts from Heaven, you say? But of what are they sculptures?" Casteleo said, frowning at the piece before them, seeking meaning from its sleek, dangerous shape, its economy of detail. "I'd thought this one an urn."

"Different incarnations…of God."

Casteleo turned an outraged and delighted eye on his companion. "Incarnations of a single, *Christian* God? Gifting Himself to
the people?"

"It seems that way. In fact, the name Gallius gave to this piece before us was 'God in the Child'".

Casteleo's eyes grew wider.

The emperor chuckled. "Turn your gaze to the inscription."

"Inscription?"

"There," the emperor pointed at a place near the object's middle.

Casteleo leaned close, squinting at the characters etched there. "This language—I can't read it."

"Nor I. Being curious, I sent for an interpreter."

"And what did he say the inscription says?"

"He couldn't read it either, and wasn't able to identify the language. However…"

"Yes?"

"Gallius made a series of notes and sketches while working on the sculptures, which I also have in my possession. In those notes, among other things, is this same message," he gestured to the words in the marble, "and its translation into Latin. Apparently, he had no idea what this foreign language was either, but was convinced he understood it, hence the translation he appended."

"This whole affair grows more curious every moment," said

Casteleo. "But what does it say, supposedly?"

Turning back to the alien characters, Hadrian quoted aloud: "'Greetings to the Emperor.'"

Casteleo looked shocked. "I…This is…The *audacity*. Does the sculptor believe himself the vessel through which God speaks to you, his emperor? He should rather speak of *you* as his Lord. And to say that this travesty," he waved a hand at the sculpture, "should be the embodiment of any deity, Roman or otherwise—sacrilege."

Hadrian nodded gravely. "It would seem so, yes. Gallius, I am told, had a series of visions that resulted in the creation of these sculptures—he entered what his acquaintances attest was a fugue state, sculpting for days on end without respite, without food or water, completing this trinity of sculptures in a mere week's time. He was, of course, brought to a physician in the end. One can imagine the bloodletting and leeching administered to the man." He gestured to the other two sculptures. "This one—your fat fish—he called 'A Second Kiss', while this one—your giant's egg—he called 'The Test'". The meaning of these names I do not know."

"I find the pieces somehow…obscene. All of them." When Hadrian made no reply, Casteleo added, "There is enough cause to have Gallius executed for his sacrilege."

"There's no need to think of it now—he hung himself while receiving treatment for his eccentric behaviour." Then, more reflectively, Hadrian added, "You know, though, some might interpret his inscription as being a generous one, showing love for his emperor. I guess we will never know."

"I've missed much these past days," said Casteleo, stunned-sounding.

"Indeed, and you're much the luckier for it," said Hadrian. "Imprisonments, tortures, executions, artists hanging themselves…I don't relish such happenings, though they do have a place, I fear. A part of the natural order and so forth." He sighed, in that moment missing the former empress, now passed away: Pompeia Plotina, who'd so often lent him her sage advices—he sometimes felt that she'd been his conscience and that without her, he was a colder ruler.

Coming out of his reverie, he said, "Interestingly enough, Gallius maintained that the inscription does *not* refer to me."

"Then who?"

The emperor shrugged. "He claimed he didn't know. His vision, he said, contained only as much as he captured in the sculptures. In his heart, he swore, he knew it didn't speak of me."

Casteleo shook his head, bewildered. It was his turn to chuckle. "Blasphemous art indeed. And yet here his work rests, in your home, my lord—quite bold of you, I must say, to embrace a purportedly divine message, interpreted through a commoner and seemingly dedicated to you…even if Gallius himself defined it otherwise." He indicated Hadrian's beard, adding, "But then you are, after all, bolder than most, my lord—how many men imitate you, and wear beards now, as well? Many, many." And Casteleo ran a hand over his own neatly-cropped beard, smiling.

"Art is art," Hadrian said, ignoring his adviser's compliments. "I am a connoisseur, as you well know. Be it the lowliest beggar whittling a birch branch into the Roman eagle of his daydreams, I show bias to no master artisan. And these pieces have about them…an inevitability I found myself wholly unable to resign to the *midden*. They simply had to exist in the world. I only wish I could decipher their mystery—Gallius said that in his vision he saw them as gifts, as I've said, falling from Heaven to earth, in a distant land and time. God returning to the people, or something like this." He waved a hand dismissively in the air, adding, "Much of this comes to me second-hand from the men I sent to fetch the pieces. Gallius himself was nowhere to be found when I first set eyes on the works, at the urging of a fellow collector. By the time I'd located him, he'd taken his own life."

"Some did call him a prophet," murmured Casteleo, voice hushed as if he was frightened of being overheard by someone outside the room, or perhaps apprehensive of the visions described by his emperor. He leaned a little closer to the sculpture in reappraisal of its artistry, its vision. He murmured, "But then some always believed him a lunatic."

"Indeed," said Hadrian. "Indeed." And then in a subdued voice of secrecy, "Most interestingly of all, Gallius claimed that the pieces contain something inside of them."

Casteleo raised an eyebrow. "They're *hollow?*" He moved his fist toward the sculpture as if to rap against its marble surface, though he only held it there uncertainly, as if he were wary of touching the object.

"They certainly weigh a great deal," said the emperor thoughtfully, "suggesting they're solid blocks, or that whatever they contain is very heavy, and certainly encased closely within their marble shells."

He remembered how the dozen men had toiled to move the sculptures into the atrium—first using the complicated contraption of wooden rollers and ropes to hoist the pieces from the three separate wagons in which they had arrived from the city; and then, because the rollers would not fit through the door and the things weighed far too much for the men to carry, they'd had to send for a crane. Hadrian had watched the workers walking in a steady rhythm inside of the great wooden wheel, spooling in the ropes that were secured around the sculpture to lift it slowly into the air. The pieces were successfully lowered, one by one, through the atrium's wide *compluvium*, guided to one side of the room's central pool and onto the empty pedestals awaiting their arrival. Altogether it had proven to be a far more formidable task than it had been to move any of the many other artworks displayed throughout the villa.

"Did the prophet-artist reveal what lies within his trinity of final works?"

The emperor noted that there was no longer the hint of casual mockery in his friend's voice when speaking of the sculptor, an astonishing fact given that Casteleo was known to show contempt when speaking of most people, commoners especially. And this coming shortly after he'd referred to the sculptures as *travesties*.

"He did," the emperor said. "Fire. He said that a great *fire* was inside the sculptures."

Casteleo watched him quietly a moment before saying, "A metaphor? An allusion to the creative fire—the passion—which the artist poured into these works?"

The emperor ruminated on this for a moment. "Perhaps. Though…"

"Yes, my lord?" Casteleo spoke quickly, a quiver of excitement in his voice.

"Well, there's more to this Gallius character than most had thought."

"Oh?"

Hadrian nodded, frowning. "Yes. All evidence suggests he was…a sorcerer."

Casteleo watched the emperor silently, waiting.

"We sometimes tell ourselves we have left behind notions like these," said Hadrian. "That such ideas belong to the past and that we understand our world differently than we once did. That the amulets and books of spells some still keep hidden in their homes are no more than harmless adherence to superstition." He paused, raising a hand to the sculpture but, like Casteleo, not letting himself touch its smooth surface. He finished, "But we are deceived: sorcery remains in the world."

The emperor crossed to one of the cupboards and unlocked its doors. When he returned, he was holding an object cupped in his hands. It was a large, smooth globe, and appeared hewn from the same ivory as the sculptures.

"This piece Gallius called *Pluto*."

Casteleo frowned at the globe. "Why? Has it some meaning that relates to the underworld? Or to Pluto himself?" The pantheon of Roman gods was great and much-celebrated, and attributing a deity's name to an artwork could be no accident.

"Gallius claimed ignorance about this, as well, said it was merely another component of his vision. But most interestingly of all, he also claimed that striking this smaller sculpture with great force will somehow act as a catalyst and, through means I cannot fathom, cause one of the sculptures to…open, revealing this supposed fire that it contains. I do not know which sculpture—that knowledge was lost with the artist's life. Perhaps he would have sculpted similar companion pieces for the remaining two sculptures had death not halted his work."

Casteleo looked from the globe in Hadrian's hands to the urn-like sculpture, and then to the others. When he spoke, his tone was subdued. "Fantasy, surely…though if it *were* true, then…"

Hadrian watched him earnestly, and his whisper was like the sharing of a dark secret:

"*Maleficia.*"

The word seemed to hang in the air like smoke.

"I can't understand how…" began Casteleo, shaking his head, his expression disconcerted. Then, a feigned jocularity in his voice, "Well, it may just be a lot of trickery, as I say. A large-scale farce. Gallius *was* an eccentric, after all, by all accounts. Let us not forget that."

Hadrian said, voice distant, "Perhaps." It was enough to silence Casteleo, submerging him beneath the fear that had steadily mounted in him.

Hadrian set the companion piece down on the floor before the urn sculpture, and the two friends, as if helpless to do anything else, continued to study the sculptures without comment; and the longer they looked, Hadrian felt the things' presence—their power—grow. A sorrow seemed to pulse from them, too, and into his heart; and into the room itself, and the world beyond the room where, seen through the villa's wide and tall windows, the sunset's final fire was quickly giving way to night's darkness, shrouding the distant Sabine hills in morose shadow.

"My lord," said Casteleo breathlessly. "I hadn't noticed it before—look!" He was pointing a finger at the red flower nestled at the base of the sculpture. "An oleander."

"And another," said Hadrian, staring. "And there, another!"

The men made a circuit of the sculpture in opposite directions until they met on the other side. The entire piece was wreathed with the flowers.

"A servant didn't place them there?" said Casteleo.

"No, certainly not without my permission. But how did we not notice the flowers before now?"

"A mystery, my lord. It's as if they sprang up while we admired the pieces."

"It seems we are surrounded by mysteries. And…sorceries." He gave his friend a lingering look of gravity before returning to the cabinet from which he'd retrieved the marble globe. When he came back he was holding a papyrus scroll, and said, "These are the sketches and notes Gallius kept. The entirety of the notes appear in both Latin *and* the same mysterious language etched into the sculpture." Unrolling the papyrus, he came to the place he sought and showed it to Casteleo, who read the words scrawled there in a barely legible cursive:

"The red oleander was the first flower to bloom from the irradiated rubble of Hiroshima. Since then, the flower has symbolized both the dangers of nuclear war and the hope of a more peaceful future."

When he looked up from the papyrus, he was pale and frightened. Voice small, he said "What is this 'Hiroshima'"?

"I do not know."

"And this…" Casteleo looked to the papyrus again. "This 'nuclear war'—what does it mean?"

"All I am certain of, my friend," said Hadrian, "is that the red oleander has appeared upon this sculpture, and it was not there earlier. The connection between this happening and Gallius's text is beyond question."

Casteleo dared to utter the words aloud: "It is a spell!"

They stood staring at one another, unspeaking, lost in thought. Then, into the deep hush, the emperor ventured, "My friend…may I confide something?"

Casteleo's eyes were riveted on him. "Of course." His whisper was loud in the darkening atrium.

Hadrian reached beneath his robes and unsheathed the gladius from the scabbard on his belt. The dusking light glimmered in its steel blade. "All day—in fact, ever since the sculptures arrived here two days ago—I've felt the strangest, nearly unquenchable desire…to strike this sister sculpture"—here he motioned with the sword to the marble globe resting on the floor—"with the pommel of my gladius. To set in motion the supposed magic that links it to the larger sculpture. Sacrifice the artwork that I might see the fire the prophet-artist promised lies at its heart. And…unleash it. The fire."

The men watched one another expectantly. Casteleo found himself nodding, slowly and hesitantly at first, and then with great eagerness.

The emperor, having received sanction from his trusted adviser and old friend, turned back to the sculptures. He avidly appraised each of the trinity in turn, and then eyed the marble globe with an intense calculation. And he raised the sword over the globe. And in his heart, he felt the rightness of it, even if his mind could not comprehend.

Houses Within Houses Within Houses Within

The castle was round and about them, widespread and as unchartable as a dark day.

— Mervyn Peake, *Gormenghast*

Across the chemical-ruined river, Detroit brooded behind the sheeting snowfall. The outlines of its buildings wavered uncertainly in the frenetic precipitation, imbuing them with the unsettling semblance of life, like restless leviathans biding their time before crashing into the water; and making their way inevitably to Windsor, Detroit's crippled little Canadian cousin, a herd of crepuscular predators on the hunt.

This view held Peter's attention where he stood at the attic window after midnight, the long pane flecked with a crystalline powdering of snow. A gust of wind found its way through the insulation. He shuddered, despite his thick wool sweater. This invasion of the elements distressed him—his designs were flawless, and he'd of course overseen the installation of the window himself, as he'd overseen the building of the rest of the lavish riverside house. Maybe he'd grown careless since he crested the hill of middle age. Or maybe it was only another indication of the world coming apart, the way he'd been watching it do for years, here in his city especially. Maybe come this time the following night when he resumed his ritual vigil the window glass would be gone completely, with no barrier at all between him and the hungry wind and hungry cityscape across the river.

Another surge of wind lashed at the glass, stirring him from his thoughts. The high-pitched keening it caused in the space between his house and his neighbours' home made him anxious.

The snowfall had intensified, obscuring the saurian architectures across the river completely. For all he knew, they were halfway across already, an army about to lay siege to this house he'd built. Another test, of whether it was fortress enough against the things in the world he'd long known were there, hungering to undo the things made by ambitious men like him.

He heaved a sigh, laden with the heaviness of the heart that, until recently, had been utterly foreign to him, but which now vied constantly with his periods of manic industriousness. If he succeeded in his work, then all might be well again, for himself, for Audrey. And he would have created something truly without precedent.

There was no use putting it off any longer, he thought, and slumped his way to the door in the floor, and descended the pull-down ladder into the expansive house below. The time had come for him to return to his work, while his wife Audrey fed the Knowledge-Eater.

Peter and Audrey Beaumont no longer spoke of what the thing might actually be. Words like *demon* and *monster* and *thing*, though superficially appropriate, were never used by them. It in every way surpassed the paltry definitions connoted by terms like these. It was by definition alien, and yet its presence—its omnipresence throughout recorded history, and long before—suggested the label fit more comfortably on themselves rather than it. And since it never admitted to having a name, they would simply come to refer to it as the Knowledge-Eater, after its particular appetite.

They'd been in their home for a little over one month when it first appeared to them. It had been the day before Christmas Eve; an early snowfall provided the wintry outdoors vista framed in the picture window before which they sat. The record snowfall and subzero temperatures added to the splendour of their indoors comfort. Peter had been telling Audrey about the old prohibition days of rumrunning across this very river, when bootleggers would drive cars laden with liquor over the ice from Canada to the United States. She'd been feigning interest; her hands playing with his shirt collar, and then tracing lines along his neck, showed her real intent—they'd been determined to start a family, and their failed attempts to get her pregnant had been a disappointment they were trying to rectify as frequently as possible.

He was just giving in to her advances when the voice said:

"How very often you crawl on each other, and for naught."

They leapt from the iron-framed accent sofa, clutching at one another in their fright; when they saw the thing, resting at the back of the room where warm orange light from the floor lamp illuminated it in all its horror, they screamed like children, and scrambled toward the entrance to the kitchen in an instinctual bid for escape. But the thing rolled across the floor with a sound like thunder among distant clouds, trapping them hopelessly.

They goggled at it, too frightened to say or do anything.

It was like a nightmare somehow siphoned from the mind and poured into the waking world: a huge lumpen orb that, standing at a little less than twelve feet and nearly brushing the high ceiling, dwarfed Peter, who was six feet tall. It would come to remind Peter of a grotesque, grey-skinned beach ball a giant's child might have played with; though unlike the uniform patterns that often decorated such balls, the thing's entire body was webbed with a haphazard maze of deep, scar-like lines, and appeared to have a coarse texture. It had limbs of a sort, though they were tiny and nub-like and contributed to its locomotion merely by pushing off from the ground and walls, propelling its immense body to roll through the house. Its impressive girth, the Beaumonts would come to know, made passage through doorways difficult, even in a house such as theirs, whose reliance on a foundation of classical Brutalist design meant wide and tall entrances; in such spaces, it would take a moment to squeeze itself through, its rough, pliable skin making a rasping, scratching noise that set Peter's and Audrey's flesh crawling, its little nubs frantically scrabbling at the walls, seeking traction so that the thing could continue on its way.

A scattering of eyes lay in a rough band across the entire circumference of its body near its centre—these were pupil-less, yellowish and round as coins, and seemed impervious to the violence of the orb-thing's movements, which saw them constantly being mashed along the ground. It had other, weird red bulbous appendages, a little longer than its nub-limbs, sprouting at random from its body, that Peter and Audrey would never learn the function of (who the Hell would ask?), though everything about them (their lush, blood-like colour, their perpetual moistness) exuded a grotesque sexual energy. These too were trampled beneath the orb's movements without any apparent effect on them.

If it had a mouth—presumably it did, because they had heard it speak—it was nowhere to be seen.

After a moment had passed, Peter managed to master his terror enough to ask the creature what it was. Its answer, loaded with enigmatic suggestion, made him wish he'd remained ignorant.

"I am old. I am always. I am creation. I am annihilation. I am master here."

Its baroque English was tinged with an accent hinting vaguely at Eastern European influences, but overlaid with something else unclassifiable. They would learn in the coming days that it spoke many languages, and come to recognize the same alien quality in every dialect it spoke.

Peter had ventured, as bravely and reasonably as was possible under the circumstances, "But...*we* live here."

The voice that boomed from the thing shook the house, sending pictures falling from their nails on the walls:

"*I* live here. This is *my* home more so than it is yours. This has been my home for many years. Many more years than you have been alive, little animals. I will not go away simply because you do not want me here."

"But...I *built* this home."

Indeed, Peter had every right to be defiant in this: it was his profession, after all, that had made it possible; his calling, which he'd put to painstaking use with the building of this house. Known throughout the province for his bold and innovative designs, he was certainly one of the most successful freelance architects in the region, certainly the most successful Windsor had ever seen. He'd come a long way, his mother had told him only last week while he was giving her a tour of the city's new Medical Lab building he'd designed, from the boy building castles out of bright plastic blocks on his bedroom floor.

He'd searched for over two years for the ideal site to build this, the home he hoped to live the remainder of his life in, and raise a family in with his wife. And on that bare plot of land—a scarce commodity in this section of the otherwise built-up riverside community, and an expensive one—he'd found everything on his long list of must-haves, most notably an unimpeded view of the river with their American neighbour on its opposite shore. He'd poured a great deal of time, resources, work and passion into the home, creating something truly idiosyncratic, and unapologetically opulent (his tastes always had veered toward the grand).

Yes, this was *his* house.

"Little animal does not understand," retorted the thing, its stentorian voice dripping with scorn. "You fling up these frail walls around me and think to claim this space as your own? You. Think. To. *Displace. Me?* But I was always here."

Peter, recoiling from the fury in the thing's voice and sensibly fearing where that could lead, ventured in a much gentler voice, "I'm sorry, but why haven't we seen you until now?"

It was certainly a valid question: the thing was, after all, impossible to miss, and there simply could be no place for something as massive as it to hide in the open-concept rooms. More practically, Peter had reasoned desperately that keeping the abomination talking was the only way he could think of to ensure it didn't do him and Audrey harm. For her part, though she'd always been the most fearless person he'd known, Audrey remained peering out at the thing from behind the meagre shelter of Peter's shoulder, silent.

"You see me now because I allow you to see me."

"But how?" His voice shook. He couldn't help it. The thing

was hideous, and horrifying, and, worst of all, intelligent—he was having a conversation with it, after all! It was all nearly too much to take. Had Audrey not been there with him, shuddering at his back, he'd have thought himself experiencing a wild hallucination.

"You could never understand."

"I-I don't believe that. If you—"

Suddenly it was gone. Where the incomprehensible horror had sat was empty space, the only evidence of its having been there the puddle of black mung soiling the large hand-knotted *Rilievo* rug.

But it wasn't gone. Peter could feel it; indeed, he now recognized the fact that, from the very beginning of their living in the house, and even while he was supervising its building, he'd felt the same sensation that now enveloped him: an awareness of observation; of being un-alone; of a *heavy* presence, one that had the ability to alter a person's mood, sully their good cheer, cause lovemaking and the conceiving of a child to be so very difficult.

"But…for how long?" He winced at the plaintive note in his voice, weak and young, at the fact that he'd now openly accepted the impossible, unfathomable truth they'd been told; and the reality of the thing itself.

"*Always*," intoned the empty room where the thing had sat.

And then it was before them again, though its reappearance likewise carried no visual or auditory fanfare; it simply was there, as if it had never left. As if echoing this thought, it said, "I have always been here. I *am* always."

"Before…Before we chose this site to build on? But…"

"Before the site for your Byzantine box was chosen, yes. And before this land was first formed. And before this world was formed. When no world was here at all, nor other nearby worlds or suns, I was here."

"But what…What do—" Peter faltered. "What was here when…" He drifted into silence, uncomprehending, or simply unwilling to take his belief that far into the realm of the fantastic.

"There was no world as you know it. But I was here. In this same place. Occupying the same precise place in the vastness between celestial bodies, and long before this in the vastness of the void during the great Before-Time. I would provide you with specific details of spatial and temporal coordinates but, being that these are not your fields of expertise, the knowledge would provide no enlightenment. Any further elaboration beyond this relating to details of time and space and other dimensional analogs would pose potential danger to your limited mental and emotional faculties."

"…Space." Peter heard his voice as if it were being transmitted from very far away.

It was referring to *outer space*, in the billions of years before the planet was formed from the elements of the cosmos. He had his mouth open to protest the preposterousness of the claim and instantly shut it as the present scene came home to him once more: he and Audrey having a conversation in their living room…with this incomprehensible entity. If someone had described this scene to him only the day before, he would have laughed at the absurdity, relegated it to the sphere of pulp fiction spooks; had they sworn to its reality he would have referred them to a psychiatrist.

A sound that might have been chortling came from the thing, humourless, icy. "You understand, if only in the most rudimentary terms. Good. Perhaps you are the first spark of something intellectually hopeful in this savage land, though it *is* unlikely. And so, *perhaps*…" It heaved a sigh, laden with resignation, before concluding, "You might be able to help me."

"H-help you? But…how can I help you?"

"This house. Its design…intrigues me. Perhaps your building it here, upon the site of my lifelong home, is the profoundest of synchronicities. This most remote of possibilities is one I am compelled to explore."

"Thank you. I—"

Audrey, finding her voice, cut into the conversation. "Here, in this neighbourhood, the houses are all very large and different—"

"They are beneath my notice," it intoned. "So much flotsam."

Peter, understanding that Audrey was seizing an opportunity, trying to lure it away from their home to haunt one of the others in the affluent suburb, only managed, "Oh, er…Well then, if I may ask, what exactly do you find intriguing about *this* house?" Peter was aware even as he spoke that he was relenting to a desire to have his ego massaged, even in this most lunatic of scenarios.

Indeed, this won him a look of exaggerated, nearly comical disbelief from Audrey that was extraordinary to see. He could feel her resentment like a tangible force pushing against him, a sensation he'd experienced often enough, though now as before he reasoned that whether he deserved it or not, it came from him expressing his individuality, an inalienable right he would never shed for another person, not even her.

Before the thing could reply, Audrey said, "Why should we help you? If you're so all-powerful, why do you need our help?" Her tone was scornful, though her fingers digging painfully into her husband's shoulder betrayed her fear. Still, the bold woman he'd always known was resuming control. It was oddly thrilling. He felt remotely aroused.

Most importantly, hearing her confront their visitor brought Peter back to a semblance of rationality. Rallying his courage, he said in as challenging a tone as he could muster, "Yes, if you can remain undetected by us, and were watching us for the past month, why show yourself now and ask for our help?"

"As a prison of frail walls, I barely notice this box, and initially simply regretted having to share my space with creatures born of this world. But as I was saying, I must confess that though I initially thought little of it, I now find myself inexplicably drawn to what you have created. It possesses disparate qualities I have seen elsewhere, though never in quite the same combination. A cultivated sprawl. The mess of humanity at the edges of overwhelming austerity. It is unique. I have studied it closely. I now give you an ultimatum."

"You…like my work?" Peter's voice was aghast, though he relished the slow swelling of pride that came flooding through him. He sensed Audrey shake her head with theatrical deliberation, disgusted at the insane egocentricity she was witnessing.

She said, as much to Peter as to the being, "*Ultimatum?*"

It was then the thing revealed a new depth to its powers. "You, female animal: you think you can dupe me, to play at acquiescence and then refuse me, and escape from this box. You cannot. Your time would be better spent listening to what I have to tell you."

Peter glanced at Audrey. He saw panic seep into her face, proving the thing's accusation was spot-on. Sensing Peter's eyes on her, she turned a look of fury on him. He had his mouth open to try to explain but she wouldn't let him.

"How can your *ego* even *exist* in this situation? What's *wrong* with you?"

Nothing, he thought, wisely keeping his mouth shut. Maybe I'm just a superior animal.

"Perhaps you are, little builder-animal," said the being. Again, the weird chortling came from it, more like a droning this time, heavy and like another wedge laid down between Peter and Audrey. Understanding that some secret communication had passed between Peter and the thing, she only shook her head, looking disgusted, afraid, defeated.

Into the heavy silence the thing said, "I now confide in you, little animals: I am unwell."

"Un…well?" Peter ventured.

"Perhaps it is the three hundred thousand years I have spent among you—the disease of you spreading and encroaching until it may have infected me as it has affected the many creatures of the world. The fault is partially my own: I am a curious mind. I wished to study this species risen from slime and simian, to follow its trajectory through all its peaks and valleys. But now the toll lays upon me: the disease of you is in me. It eats away more every day. To be surrounded by so much stupidity, and cruelty, and savagery…and for so long. Wherever I have travelled—though I always return to this site, which is *my home*—I *feel* you always. Humanity, that is. It is loud and bores into me. It is a psychical pain, reaching depths unplumbed by any pain I have experienced besides. Perhaps this weakness of mine—this need to always return to my home-place, and remain here—will be my undoing, after all this time."

"What can we…How can we help you?" Peter found he felt a desperate desire to make the thing feel better, to cure it of its pain, that went beyond any need to safeguard his own and Audrey's well-being.

The deep droning came from the thing as it seemed to ponder his question. Momentarily, "You are a builder. This is providence, or the finest example of synchronicity. It can be nothing less. Build me a home. A refuge that dwarfs this structure we are now in. A sanctuary, that I might dwell there without bother. Without contact with the human contagion. Enshrined therein, I hold hope that I will recover from what ails me."

"Why don't you go to some remote place, uninhabited by people?" said Audrey hopefully. "There are so many places like this around the world. Like, for instance, the middle of the Arabian Desert."

"There are those who dwell there, in the deep desert, though very few know of them. Remote and sparsely populated, yes. But so much sand—it gets in the fissures of me."

Here, the thing performed a startling manoeuvre, first flexing its body, bulging itself outward so that the design of lines zigzagging across its surface grew distended, wider; and then using its nub-limbs to spin itself around. Peter found himself thinking of the time he'd watched a Harlem Globetrotters game when he was a child, marvelling at the seeming magic of the team's players performing tricks like spinning a basketball like a top on the tips of their index fingers. He was smiling stupidly, entranced with the combination of the coddling childhood memory and the alien display in his living room.

He was shaken from his reverie by Audrey's valiant effort to save them from whatever fate the thing had in store for them.

"Okay, noted—deserts and beaches are out. But there's an unlimited number of places out there—how about, uh, the Tibetan Plateau, in China? It's vast, high up between two mountain chains. The only people there are scattered nomads, and these days not many of them. Or what about Alien Island, in Yemen? The few locals speak an unwritten language, which is fascinating, right? And the rare Dragon's Blood trees that are only local to this region are totally unreal, it's like you're on another planet. Or if the population numbers are still too high for your liking, you could pick any of the countless *deserted* islands in the world."

With barely a pause for breath she finished, "Here, though, in *Windsor?* Pollution through the roof, crime on the rise, summers so humid it's like you have to swim through the air. Basically the worst place you could be, really, and it's not getting better anytime soon from the looks of it."

Audrey was a sales rep for a travel agency specializing in adventure packages to remote, off-the-grid locales—she was in her element now, and Peter knew her impassioned attempt to sell the entity on plans of relocation was much more animated than the rote way she said she sometimes ran through her spiel with clients—their lives may have depended on it, after all. He found her brazen efforts to rid them of the thing commendable, though by then he sensed the futility in it; or perhaps a growing desire to give in to the thing's wishes, to help it, to see where all of this would lead.

The entity echoed his thoughts about Audrey's motivations. "It is an admirable effort you make to lure me away from this box you believe to be your rightful home, but know that the pollutant and climatological and criminal elements you cite have no impact upon me whatsoever. I am above such things. And though I have of course visited each of the locations you name—as I have visited every inch of the planet, from distant atmospheric reaches to ocean bottoms the human race will never see—and though certain of these sites possess remarkable natural beauty, still the human stink reaches them."

"But nobody *lives* in some of these places," Audrey exclaimed, her voice pleading, looking from the entity to Peter for support.

"Oh, yes," he said, catching up with what she'd said. "That's true. All of these places are so remote, they're mostly uninhabited. Some of them are virtually unreachable except through extreme efforts. And think about the wonders that just aren't available here—Easter Island's moai, for instance. The mystery of those statues, why the Rapa Nui built them, and the sheer beauty of them staring out to sea—it's all so breathtaking…"

He drifted off, thinking he must have scored an incontestable point with this last—the raw architectural grandeur of those monolithic statues had always enthralled him. For this reason, Easter Island had been the first place he and Audrey had vacationed together, the year before they were married. She'd likewise always been fascinated with the place (and all remote locales, hence her chosen profession), and had gotten them a steal of a deal on a travel package.

But there was no appeasing the thing. It said, "The Rapa Nui did not build the eight-hundred-and-eighty-seven statues of Easter Island."

Peter and Audrey waited breathlessly, unprepared for this sidetrack into a possible revelation relating to one of the world's enduring wonders and mysteries. But the thing went on before they could say anything.

"Oh, but the *psychical* disease of you has infiltrated even such rare sites. Where no humans physically live, still the air is sullied, the waters and air ruined and the better animals affected. The hand of humanity reaches its fingers into the remaining clean places, dirtying them along with the rest. And even the remotest places, inaccessible to animals like yourselves—the tops of mountain peaks, the bottom of the deepest oceans, the heart of the darkest jungles where no human has ever trod—even there I can *sense* you. I know this, for I have tried. Oh, how I have tried over the years! But always the human presence grows, takes more, encroaches there and there and everywhere—where before this world was wild and beautiful and pure, now it is property to be fought over by sentients somehow so puerile as to believe in written laws of boundaries, with governments dividing the bountiful spoils as they might a table of food. It is a pain I feel, every day, all of the time."

It paused, and a heavy silence hung in the spacious room.

Then, "Let me be clear, as perhaps you do not fully fathom my abilities. I could leave this world completely if I so desired—I could leave this place and be across the galaxy in the proverbial blink of an eye. I could be in any number of different galaxies, farther away than your minds could grasp. I could journey to the heart of your world's sun, or into any sun, anywhere. I could exist inside the wake of a comet and be pulled along on its journey. I have, in fact, existed in each of these places, and countless others. But, as I have said and must repeat, I always feel the homeward pull, and wish to reside here, in *this* space in the universe, my lifelong *home*. And so, therefore, still I need you to build me a refuge, to keep out the physical and the psychical presence of humanity. A castle, if you will, the likes of which no invader might ever gain ingress to."

Peter tried to let it all sink in. "But…*how* can I do that? Where would I build it? You don't understand the legal hurdles to a project of this sort. The financial obstacles. It's imposs—"

"You will build it in your mind. I will inhabit it."

"What do you…I don't understand."

"You cannot, not truly. But you have nothing to worry for: *I* understand."

"But…what do you mean?" Audrey said, aghast. "You have to explain it to us."

"I *need* explain nothing to you, little animals."

Silence, laden with unease.

"But I will try," the thing relented. "This is the simplest rendering of the formula. You need not understand—nor are you able to—its nuances. You may trust that I do understand them. Attend to my teaching, little animals:

"The end of this world is imminent.

"I will survive this doom, though my sickness due to human contamination means my own life will come to an end between one hundred to three hundred years from today.

"Peter-animal contains the knowledge, skill, and genius to build the fortress I require to survive—one that is impregnable to the psychical presence of humanity.

"Audrey-animal is linked with Peter-animal through human socio-sexual relations, and is therefore an inextricable component of Peter-animal.

"If Peter-animal (with his creation of my fortress extant in his mind) were to exist inside of me, my mind would have access to his knowledge—amalgamating it into my personal experience, making of it a shared experience. In doing so, the fortress as an intellectual, metaphysical, and corporeal construct would exist inside me, and I would be able to inhabit it as well, both theoretically and in actuality. I will vacate this space, here and now, and enter the sanctuary, our shared stronghold.

"Peter-animal and Audrey-animal represent an inconsequential percentage of humanity—sharing the world of the fortress with these two human beings would pose little to no threat to my ongoing health and recuperation.

"Therefore: Peter-animal plus Audrey-animal will physically live inside of me. There, they will be safe from the cataclysmic dangers looming in the world outside of myself, while I reap the benefits of existing within the boundaries of a home where I may regain and sustain my health. That house—that fortress against humanity—will be able to exist here, in this space, indefinitely, and I—we—within it. Peter-animal will imagine the fortress, and design it detail by detail, imbuing it with the capability to withstand all such human and catastrophic elements. I will make it a reality.

"*We will all live happily ever after*—this, I believe, is the appropriate conclusion to a formula that will no doubt seem far-fetched and fantastical to your ears."

Peter and Audrey were silent a moment, taking it all in. Then Audrey blurted, "Wait—did you start off your equation with 'the end of the world is nigh'? You don't mean that literally? You mean the planet isn't doing so good, so thousands of years down the road—"

"I believe you understood my meaning," the entity cut in.

"But how could you possibly know that?" said Peter. "There's no way..." He drifted off, considering what they'd seen so far of this hyper-intelligent, physics-defying alien creature, and found that in his heart he indeed believed it—why wouldn't prophecy be among its powers?

Audrey, Peter sensed, believed it, too. He saw it in her resigned posture, arms wrapped around herself, tapping her fingers against her arm as if ruminating on a problem. Her eyes, distant, seemed concentrated on trying to solve it.

"I see you believe the truth of what I have said."

"When?" Audrey's voice was quiet but resolute.

"Within your lifetimes," said the entity.

"How?" said Peter.

"You."

"Me? You mean, I—"

"Your *species*, which exists to obliterate what it builds; a fact well known. This ending has been underway for a long time, though foundationally it began when you arrived on this planet. The steady degradation would have continued until the threshold of planetary tolerance was broken, even if no dramatic event were to occur, though this cataclysm is, in fact, coming."

After a lengthy silence, Audrey, pragmatic as always, said, "You said Peter and me would…live inside you? So, um…how, exactly?" A frown of worry marked her forehead.

"I will eat you."

A pregnant moment passed during which Peter and Audrey's jaws dropped and they stared at the entity, speechless.

"Eat us?" Peter managed, voice a squeak.

The weird droning that they'd learned to be the thing's laughter came from it now. "I jest. I will not so much *eat* you as *swallow* you. This detail is not as fatal as the description suggests. In fact, it is the key component to your potential survival."

"But you don't have a mouth." The way Audrey said it was like a dare she was frightened of proposing to the thing.

"I have a mouth," said the entity.

"I…I don't see it," she said, defiantly, voice quivering.

"Audrey," Peter hissed warningly, searching the giant orb-body, anxiously turning away from its many emotionless yellow eyes.

The creature said, "Best wait until the time has arrived when necessity dictates what we must do."

All at once the gruesomeness, the insanity, of the scenario came home to Peter. "I refuse. It's lunacy. No. I won't subject myself to this…this *torture*."

"Why torture? Perhaps it will be ecstasy. In any case, refuse and you will die in the apocalypse which lies on your horizon. Acquiescing to my plan will save your lives. I should point out that, should I wish, I could easily persuade you, Peter-animal, by taking away the sole thing you cannot bear to lose."

"Take me and let Audrey go—you don't need her anyways." Even as the seemingly noble and protective words left him, he understood their hollow character.

The being heard it, too, or else understood his nature innately. "She means less to you than you pretend. The thing you will lose and that would forever haunt you for having let it slip away…is the opportunity to design and build the masterwork of your life, the summation of all that you have worked and lived for, that which would once and for all set you far above the accomplishments of your contemporaries, and all those great builders who came before. And though I find potential in your creations, without your obeisance I could be compelled to seek another talent comparable to your own elsewhere."

Peter felt shame. He couldn't bear to look at Audrey, though he could imagine her watching him, angry, confused, hurt. But on the heels of this, he felt the encroaching urge to please the creature, and prove himself—he deserved to have this ultimate project see fruition, more than his contemporaries.

Perhaps sensing Peter's being swayed, the entity said, "As I have said, I am compelled by your work, Peter-animal, this structure you have designed and built to house yourself. Logic dictates that the mind behind this creation could theoretically create what I desire and need, and perhaps prove itself…intellectually and artistically superior to the minds of its contemporaries. Thus far, I confess you make me less sick than the rest of your species, though I admit to being at a loss as to exactly why that is." A pause, and it added, "Audrey-animal. While your mate deliberates the situation, I cannot help but inquire— from you I feel waves of resentment and loathing. Your mind is above average in intellect—surely you understand the logic in the proposal I have outlined."

Audrey stared at it. "What else could I possibly feel? It's a lose-lose."

The entity droned to itself a moment. Then, "I would think you might feel…awe. Fascination. Curiosity. Admiration. Love, perhaps only of the sort a canine of this world feels for its human master. These are only a few of the many, more positive emotions you might theoretically feel for me."

Audrey's face twisted into a mask of disgust.

The entity droned on, mirthless-sounding now, only a steady ponderous groaning before falling into a meditative silence.

Peter, in that moment, after having processed the tale spoken by the thing, accepted it; all of it, including the certainty that the thing really could see the future. He did what he had to. "I'll start right now."

Again, he sensed Audrey turn an aghast look at him, though she didn't say anything to try and dissuade him. And then the thought struck him. "Wait…Then you must know whether I'll succeed or not. If you can see the future…"

"Indeed I can, and indeed I know. Peter-animal, you *will* succeed."

This time Audrey muttered something unintelligible under her breath, though her voice brimmed with resentment, outrage.

I can do this, Peter thought. *I'm a builder. This incredible creature* believes *in me!*

"Indeed you are. Though perhaps a more fitting title would be *re*builder. For all that you build, you build upon the ruins of what came before, the carcass of that which you destroyed. It is a cycle uniquely yours—no other species, here or elsewhere, is gifted with such folly and brutality, banes to your sometime ingenuity. But we will do better—we will place your castle in a new geography, away from the rotting touch of your fellow human. It will reside inside me, and I will remain unscathed, even eons from today when this site is celestial space again."

I can live with this, he thought. His confidence had returned, and it felt good, following his terror and confusion. A glimpse of his old self, outside of responsibility for anyone but himself. He was an island—Audrey, his wife, an outlying neighbouring island. Already ideas were percolating.

"There is one final matter I must discuss," said the entity. "And it pertains to you, Audrey-animal."

She glanced up, looking surprised. Peter hoped whatever it was might give her the same sense of purpose he now had in their inexplicably new day-to-day world.

"I am hungry. You will read to me. Today I want a fat book, of history. I want to chew on the fat of irony. I wish to gorge myself on the succulence of tragedy. With this new role, you have a stake in this project, as well, it would seem."

Peter felt relieved: the entity did have something in mind for Audrey to busy herself with.

"Read to you?" Audrey said. Peter saw that she'd left his side at some point and returned to the couch, no longer as afraid of the being, or perhaps only resigned to the inescapability of it. Indeed, her voice was calm, her words measured though stiff.

"Yes, your readings will be my feeding. While I wait for the construction to conclude, and to alleviate my suffering a small degree, I need succour. This is the sole thing that brings me relief, though it is a transient one, or sometimes simply a distraction from the sickness that spreads within me more every day. You will feed me *knowledge*, from books, from your machines with their finite virtual-realm access—knowledge, from wherever you may obtain it. Stories. Dictionaries. Histories. Philosophies. Sciences. Poems. The daily news, here, in this stinking city of automotive factories and smog and cancers. You will read these to me because my physical form presents a barrier to my doing so easily myself. Before my sickness, my body was capable of manipulation—many appendages were at my disposal, with which I was able to engage in routine activities, such as holding a book. Those abilities, at least until I am healed within my new sanctuary, are no more."

She surprised Peter, and quite likely the entity as well, when she said, "Are you alone? Do you have relatives, or other members of your species?"

For a moment Peter wondered if they were in the presence of God.

"I am alone, yes. My species lost its ability to procreate long ago. Little by little, we died. As far as I am aware, and I have searched widely, I am the last of my kind."

In a small voice, Audrey said, "Okay."

Peter was trying to think of something polite or sympathetic to say, but the entity turned the conversation elsewhere.

"The only further stipulation I must make is that neither of you is permitted to leave this house until the endeavour is concluded. And neither of you is permitted to answer the door, or the telephone. Audrey-animal, you will call in to your place of employment and explain that you are extremely ill and require an extended leave of absence. Peter-animal, you will release all clients for whom you have projects ongoing. Put simply, I cannot trust either of you to not betray this project. After all, it is, I understand, an entirely alien and disconcerting experience and, though I know you understand the greater implications of the situation, yet I also can envision you acting on emotion, from out of fear or rebellion, and thereby destroying our joint project. The sooner we begin, the sooner success will be achieved, and all negative associations related to it will be a thing of the past. We will start this process now. Time is truly of the essence, for all of us."

"What will *we* eat?" Audrey's voice was calm even in asking this most pressing of questions, a fact that chilled Peter. It was as if she'd actually accepted the strange turn their shared life had taken. Miraculously, she appeared to be back to her old pragmatic, reliable self. He felt his old affection for her in that moment, remembered the way she calmed him down when his creative pursuits over the years reached the mania that had left him friendless, but for her.

"You need not be concerned," said the thing. "I will create sustenance for you, once the current cache of your food supply is exhausted."

"What, you're a chef, too?" Audrey said, deadpan.

A moment of awkward and tense silence. And then Peter couldn't contain himself and erupted in a fit of unexpected laughter borne of terror and a new and lunatic world-view suddenly thrust on him. Because, really, the scenario was comical to begin with, in a mad, dark, down-the-rabbit-hole sort of way. Truly, he loved Audrey then, with all his heart. He gave her a tender look but she only watched him with cold eyes before levelling the same gaze on the entity desecrating their home.

As if mocking the venom in her stare, the entity rolled away toward the hall, emitting a horrid flatulence in its wake that sounded like the growling of a grizzly bear and stunk like a jungle of rotting vegetation. As the stench permeated the room, the entity called after itself, "Audrey-animal, come along to the meagre library you keep here, and gather my first meal of knowledge. Peter-animal, gather your thoughts and begin your Herculean labour. Our great endeavour begins now. Chop-chop."

The leviathans of Detroit had moved closer.

Peter stared out the attic window, willing himself to believe that it was a trick of the uncertain nocturnal light, the wispy strands of fog curling in the breeze, though his heart remained unconvinced. The buildings indeed appeared closer tonight than they'd been last, hugging the distant shoreline at the river's edge as if prepared to slip into the icy water. Then, illuminated by the moon penetrating the overcast, they became clearer, and he saw they were merely the handful of high-rise buildings rising from the city's downtown core—impressive perhaps when one stands among them but, when you conceive architectural designs of groundbreaking quality, fade into the lacklustre aspect of yesterday's accomplishments.

When he was a young boy, in the 1980s, Detroit had seemed bent on orchestrating its own apocalypse: soaring crime rates setting shocking new records each year passing; Devil's Night an annual epidemic of arson, seeing the streets burn bright enough to tinge the smog clouds red like some citywide annual rite of sacrifice; all of which was presided over by the shadow of the Fermi atomic plant disaster, when a reactor suffered a partial fuel meltdown; although no radioactive material was released, the incident was a reminder that worse fates were always waiting. All of this he'd watched as a child from afar, experiencing vicariously the thrill of his neighbouring city's dangerous character through television news and the stories told by his father at the dinner table; his dad who worked as a teller at a bank located inside the Renaissance Centre in downtown Detroit itself, a building that to young Peter had epitomized an architecture of the fantastic future rising from the ghetto his parents' conversations and the nightly newscasts had helped to mythologize in his impressionable mind.

Audrey's words came back to him. She was right: now things had gotten somewhat better across the river—homelessness, while still a problem, was a much less significant one than it had been; the statistics for violent deaths and crime were likewise lower than in past years; whereas in Windsor the collapse was in the ascendant: the numbers of homeless risen so staggeringly that in the crumbling downtown core alone their makeshift homes of tents and cardboard boxes gave the impression of an army encampment, the base of operations from which its soldiers would prepare to lay siege to the city. And just this year alone there had been more murders than in the previous decade combined, and the year had just gotten underway; and the pollution: the smog was so thick you could cut it with a knife.

The little brother city—Little Detroit, as some still called it; *his* city—was in trouble.

"But then who isn't in trouble?" he said, breath frosting the window glass, an unfamiliar heaviness in his heart it took him a moment to understand was a sense of failure. Close on its heels though, returned his old determination, and a desire to succeed, to create a sanctuary to withstand whatever the world hurled at him. He looked to the thing in his hand: a globe of grey; it looked like clay or putty, but it had come *from* the Knowledge-Eater. It was the sustenance it had promised, once their food had run out a month before. The process of how it created the food was never broached by either of them. It was tasteless and, once musings of its origins were pushed from the mind, edible enough.

Audrey had looked as if the mere thought of eating the stuff was going to make her retch. All the more remarkable that, two days later, she ate the globes diligently and without protest. Peter was learning just how strong his wife was.

Suddenly, he felt compelled and pulled the food-globe into two pieces, held together by gluey stalactites of tissue; then these he pulled apart into smaller pieces, on and on, until a dozen lumps of the stuff lay scattered along the windowsill. He stared at them, willing them to become something else, something more.

Somewhere, in the depths of his mind, some mostly-formless

idea that had been quietly percolating began to gather its strength, to gain the embryonic touch of clarity.

With this idea fuelling his courage, he hurried to the library. He began pulling the largest tomes they owned. The Knowledge-Eater was voracious and had had Audrey read everything they'd had in the way of history and science books. He was scanning the remaining books when he caught sight of the familiar section of volumes, displayed prominently in the centre shelf.

He ran a hand along the spines of the journals, randomly pulled one from among its counterparts. *New Sights*; its title had spoken to him, encouraged him to get a subscription five years before and to submit his own news to its editors not long after. He'd made the cover, his second title appearance for *NS*. The photo was of one of his, an imperial tech company headquarters located on the city's south side, in one of the wealthiest suburbs. The caption was as bold as the structure itself, a thick-charactered, bronze-coloured font emblazoned along the length of the cover bottom: *Experimental Brutalism: Peter Beaumont and the Future Wave.*

And in that moment, it happened, as it had happened for him countless times in his career: Peter was struck with a lightning bolt of inspiration; and this idea, he was sure, would stand as his ultimate genius, and the most challenging project he'd ever dared to undertake. The reason for this genius, he knew, was his inspiration, a thing he'd never experienced before in relation to his architectural design work, and certainly never so profoundly.

Fear, of living in a world teetering near the brink. It was certainly no place to try to raise a family.

And with that fear filling his heart, he said, "I won't build you a *house* in my mind—I'll build you a *city*."

Months passed. The thing stunk more all the time, a sign of its progressing sickness.

The foundational odour was of metal, coppery and stinging to the senses, but as the days turned to weeks to months, a fouler stench grew from the thing. It conjured decomposition of a scope vaster than would allow one to specify any single source: flesh, foliage, foods. It reeked so strongly it was almost suffocating for Peter and Audrey if they stayed too close to it for too long.

Once, Peter cupped a hand over his mouth as the Knowledge-Eater—this name that Peter and Audrey had given it only grew more apt as the months wore on, as its voracious appetite for knowledge became its most defining quality—passed him by in the living room; seeing this, Audrey whispered from where she sat on the sofa, surrounded by crooked stacks of books she'd had delivered from the library and online booksellers, "Peter—maybe it'll die soon!"

Before Peter could reply, the Knowledge-Eater's voice echoed forth from the hallway where it had rolled: "If your game is to outlive me, foolish animals, remember that, without respite from my illness, my projected lifespan is between two to three hundred of your years. I have never been wrong in prognostications. And so, to use death as your weapon, your only means of escaping me is to await, or expediate, your own deaths."

The silence in the house was monstrous, anxious. Without any further conversation, Peter rushed back to his office and Audrey continued opening the boxes of new book arrivals.

Another time, as the Knowledge-Eater was passing the dining room where the couple were sharing a conversation-less supper, it sensed their discomfort. "Don't turn your noses up at me. Yes, I see how you avert yourself, grimacing at the sight and smell of me. My sickness rots me from within, the fault for which lies in you. Do you not know how badly *you* smell, on the *inside* most especially? What scent do you imagine exists bottled up inside of your body, in the dark cramped spaces between your organs and the skeletal architecture that moves you through your brief, inconsequential life? I've seen that landscape—I have gone inside many of your species out of a scientific curiosity and oh, what a pong of putrescence lies inside you! A putrescence of *ages*! Oh, my regret at having investigated such foul territories!"

Peter was just beginning to wrap his mind around this idea— and it was one he felt he'd almost but not quite pondered before at some point—when the Knowledge-Eater added, "And dark. It's *dark* inside you."

He opened his mouth as if to refute the accusation, defend himself in some way, but already the Knowledge-Eater was squeezing itself through the doorway with its portly imperial columns, and rolling down the hall, its bulk making a scratching racket, leaving a trail of black in its wake.

Peter frowned after it, wondering suddenly whether he had a soul, or if such a thing truly existed at all. He found himself troubled in a new way, in a way he'd never been disturbed before. The Knowledge-Eater was right. He was dark inside. He may have had a bright disposition, at least compared to some malcontents he knew, but *physically*…he was filled with darkness. Literally and physically. It was in his nature. His *human* nature.

Ten minutes later he was brushing his teeth before turning in for the night, when he set the toothbrush aside, spit the frothy toothpaste into the sink, and hurriedly rooted about in the beneath-sink drawer. From among the clutter of hand cream tubes, tweezers, grooming scissors, Audrey's hair-bands, and assorted bathroom paraphernalia, he pulled the tiny flashlight he used for searching his neck for thin stray hairs that the electric shaver always seemed to miss and that the overhead light never seemed able to illuminate. He opened his mouth wide enough that his jaws ached, and played the flashlight's beam into the back reaches of his throat.

Suddenly, he understood the simple mechanics of himself in a way he never had considered it before: he was looking down a hole that led into himself, into his *darkness*, a darkness that indeed undoubtedly stunk and that his feeble handheld light could never hope to reach. He was staring into that hole, past his epiglottis like a weird stalactite and marker of the drop into his bodily abyss, when he realized his teeth were biting down into his knuckles where they helped prop his jaws apart; and with this came the epiphany that these were *bones*, pieces of his skeleton peering forth from the flesh of his gums, as if the mortal frame that held him together was seeking to escape his darkness the same way his mind in that moment wanted to escape, too.

The smile he made was less a smile than a simple baring of his teeth. He stared at this silently snarling animal reflected in the mirror and wondered how he might find the true path into it, to light up its darkness, and what he might find there if he could.

Peter could tell Audrey was focusing hard on his rhythm, willing herself to reach a climax her heart likely knew was beyond reach.

When she stopped abruptly, he only lay there on top of her, hopeful that she'd climaxed. But she was looking toward the bedroom doorway, which he'd stupidly forgotten to close on his way back from the bathroom.

"Get out! Leave us alone!"

Her outburst startled him. Her voice was broken, the words wavering with despair. Peter, startled into flaccidness, clambered off of his wife, swung around to glare at the intruder squeezed into the creaking doorframe. It was dark in the dim glow thrown from the nightlight, but he sensed its many eyes watching them, could see the moist glimmer of its appendages stirring on the air.

Laying curled in a fetal position beside him, Audrey's words came muffled as she wailed into the tight embrace of her hands covering her face: "It's hard enough without it watching us."

He found his voice, shaky as it was. "You have to go. *Now.*"

The Knowledge-Eater said, "I gift you, with family."

At this, even Audrey turned to look. Peter fell back beside his wife, clicking on the bedside lamp. Together they stared from the bed, swaddled in sheets like a pair of cartoon ghosts. Indeed, the Knowledge-Eater had truly gifted them.

A pair of creatures—unmistakably, they were diminutive versions of the Knowledge-Eater—sat on the floor between their parent and the bed. They were the same spheroid shape, though milky-pale and coming up to only about a quarter the height of the Knowledge-Eater. Like their creator, these progenies pulsed and hummed, and their many, tiny yellow eyes watched the humans impassively. They exuded a sickly stench that reached Peter and

Audrey: meat gone bad, though nowhere near as potent as their parent.

Peter ventured, "You're asexual? I thought your species had died out. How…"

"My species has the ability to reproduce through both syngenesis *and* parthenogenesis—sexually, asexually."

"But you said that you'd lost the ability to…" Peter began.

"The procreation act comes with more difficulty than it once did but, unlike my extinct brethren, I retain that ability. A mystery beyond even my solving, it would seem. This set of twin infants is a product of parthenogenesis."

Peter could have sworn he detected pride in the Knowledge-Eater's voice.

When they continued to stare in silence, the Knowledge-Eater moaned dismally. "I had thought giving you that which you have tried for so long to create would be a source of happiness—the growth of your family unit. You are…displeased. You would prefer to continue your ineffectual attempts to conceive together. These two children would need your ongoing assistance and supervision, and I have burdened you both. I will destroy them."

Before Peter or Audrey could utter another word, a pair of thin sharp-tipped spines thrust from the Knowledge-Eater's rotund body and skewered the children. They made no sound, only spasmed violently where they sat, spurting blood and pus. They visibly deflated, crumpling in on themselves like blowup lawn ornaments whose air seal has been popped. Soon they lay in heaps, like moulted skin, and the Knowledge-Eater dragged them away without further word.

Nobody ever spoke about the incident again.

Six months passed that felt to Peter like eternity. He toiled, slaved. Audrey endured.

He found the Knowledge-Eater feeding: Audrey reading to it in the living room: the book opened in her lap was the Brittanica Encyclopedia, Volume 7, Letters G-H. Published in the early 1990s, the books were hopelessly out of date, and he wondered what sustenance it could possibly give to one like the Knowledge-Eater. Was it mere junk? Fast food it took into itself the way a man might gobble a quick cheeseburger and fries at a rest stop diner before continuing his travels? It must be so, he reasoned. But, looking to the landscape of books towering all over the large room, and the laptop with its infinite online access, he reasoned that at some point, the novelty itself of outdated books like the encyclopedias would satisfy a certain hunger. At any rate, he had news to share that would change the strained, difficult atmosphere—the atmosphere of sickness—that had come to saturate the mansion.

"It's done."

His words cut Audrey's reading voice short like a knife slicing silk.

The Knowledge-Eater filled the silence after a heartbeat.

"An extraordinary moment is upon us."

Peter found he couldn't speak. The excitement, the emotion— the pride in his achievement realized—stifled any words he might have said. For her part, Audrey watched the Knowledge-Eater solemnly and silently, though Peter wished she'd offered him congratulations. But it didn't matter, he thought. Time enough for everything later.

A strange, sonorous sound began, filling the room. It was at once deep and thrumming like the sliding of a heavy door on its rollers along a track; and yet fleshy and moist, like pushing through curtains of blubber. Peter and Audrey watched, spellbound:

A seam was forming in the Knowledge-Eater.

"Our bodies are temples," Peter breathed, the import of what was happening coming home to him. "Audrey, I think this is what it meant. I think we have to climb in—"

"I know," Audrey said. "The Knowledge-Eater told me already."

Peter frowned, then smiled incredulously. He'd been so immersed in his labours that much had passed him by. But no matter. All was going to be well in this most incredible end and beginning.

The dark fissure, located a little beneath its eye-band, grew wider and wider as the bottom third of the Knowledge-Eater drew upward and backward. In that darkness, glimmerings could now be seen, growing brighter with each second. Peter couldn't imagine what they might be, though his first thought was that they reminded him of stars seen in a night sky. An appropriate visual parallel, of course, given the incredible nature of the entity. As the hole became large enough to allow light from the room's lamps to penetrate, they saw that these shimmering objects were embedded in the flesh of the cavernous mouth, its back-most reaches, its roof, though what the things were they couldn't be sure.

When the groaning thunder had stopped and its mouth stood fully open, Peter and Audrey stepped inside its star-mottled darkness with neither discussion nor hesitation. They'd long known this moment was coming, and there was no reason to delay it. The floor beneath their socked feet was warm, pliant—was it the Knowledge-Eater's tongue the couple stood on? Peter was too overcome with emotions to ask, or to say anything at all.

The thunder started again—louder now because they heard it from within—and the mouth of the Knowledge-Eater closed over them.

Peter thought of the bizarre gestalt animal they made together, comprised of one animal swallowing the others. He admired the architecture they made together, another masterwork, in flux. Like a weird living model of Russian nesting dolls. Tears blurred his vision, this time tears of joy. There was nothing left for him in the world anymore. What more could he have given a world that was plowing straight toward the annihilation of all the dreams of its greatest builders, its creators of lasting beauty?

And he thought, *It'll be a new beginning for us.*

He reached for Audrey's hand, found it, clutched it. She felt cold, and lifeless, and he squeezed her tighter, as if to communicate it without words: that everything was going to be okay. They were in this new adventure together. His greatest accomplishment lay waiting, and it was going to save them.

The mouth closed with a final meaty thump and the light from outside, in their old house, was extinguished and replaced with the warm red universe of the Knowledge-Eater.

A thunder as wide as the sky, and from it, words:

> *I feel you, little animals. Welcome home, now, and always.*
>
> *Peter-animal: thank you. Your dream-design is the pinnacle of architectural genius. You have outdone yourself, truly.*
>
> *Audrey-animal: my eternal thanks for your readings, for the library that lives inside of you.*

Time passed—a nanosecond; a million years—

Peter opened his eyes and drank in the scene before him.

There was *so much*—a cornucopia of imperial architectures and labyrinthine layouts unseen in the Old World; visions unknown; impossible vistas to threaten the mind; and yet here they were, unspooled from the fever-dream of his toil and manifested in this incredible reality. A sprawling marriage of styles running the gamut from Classical Antiquity to Modern, with his beloved Brutalism as the foundational school underlying it all. His heart felt a fulfillment he'd never known. His great hunger was sated—his masterpiece had been wrought.

The sky overhead was twilit, dark and dotted with a familiar scape of glimmering red stars. In the distance, the vast aerodynamic contours of an Arcology-inspired community glimmered with moonlight.

He took Audrey's hand, and they ventured into the streets, burning to know it all.

After a time, he wondered why Audrey hadn't commented on the splendour around them or at least congratulated him on his creation. He'd done it for her, as well as for himself, after all. But he let it pass, marvelling at what he'd dreamed up, poring for months over his growing catalogue of inspired blueprints. He was leading them toward the Grand Kitchens—he'd designed the sumptuous series of buildings with her in mind, remembering her loathing of the sustenance provided by the Knowledge-Eater in the days before they'd realized the creature had the ability to replicate recipes that tasted astonishingly good. Here, inside the universe of the Knowledge-Eater, the vast kitchens contained all the delicacies he'd been able to find in old cookbooks and online sources, transfigured from detailed concept to tangible reality through the mysterious conduit that was the Knowledge-Eater. Exactly like every other square inch of the city Peter had designed, and their benefactor had breathed into life.

They were walking down a wide colonnade, its emerald columns as fat around as oak trunks, when Audrey told him:

"I'm pregnant."

Peter stopped in his tracks, spun to look at her. He smiled stupidly, awed that things could have gotten even better than the realization of his professional and artistic dreams. His dream of family would be realized now, too, and here, no less, in this heavenly metropolis he'd created. He'd built a new home for their family, even better than their old riverside mansion, which now took on a shabby quality, a house made of matchsticks. He'd built them a city. A city like no other that had ever been built before.

"Audrey, that's wonderful. But...*how*? We were having such problems conceiving. And when was the last time we...I've been so busy, we both have—I can't even remember when we were together last."

Maybe some of the Knowledge-Eater's powers were rubbing off on him, because even as Audrey opened her mouth to tell him, Peter felt the words coming, as if he'd foreseen it, if only vaguely.

"It isn't yours, Peter. I decided I needed to be with someone less narcissistic than you. Someone who loves me for who I am. I'm...I'm the first human that hasn't made him sick."

There were tears in her eyes. Joyous tears.

"But it...it despises us," he said, throat tight. "Both of us. All people."

"He always loved me, first from afar, and then..." She paused, and finished, "He did it all for love."

Then, averting her eyes to watch the skyline of regal structures across the way, she said, "He doesn't like you, though, Peter. He's going to…come after you. But he said he'll give you a chance to run and hide. He's not as familiar with the city as you are, even though he made it real. You designed it all, Peter. You might be able to find someplace to hide away…" She drifted off and then after a moment added, "He doesn't look the way he did before. He was sick then. He's healthy now. Now he…I don't have the words. You can't even imagine. But maybe you can find a place to hide."

Peter's mind reeled. He imagined himself, a harried Theseus pursued through the labyrinth of the city by his alien Minotaur—ironically, and oh so tragically, in this rewriting of the myth Peter was also Daedalus himself, the architect of the maze. And in this case, his hunter seemed omniscient, or certainly like the fastest learner in the universe. Not all retellings ended the same, he thought bitterly.

She left Peter there, slipping between the columns and onto the expansive lawn beyond. The city, which was his supreme masterwork, was his to revel in alone. He imagined Audrey, reading to the Knowledge-Eater all those months while he dreamed up this place for them all, and for himself and his ego especially.

Stunned, he wondered vaguely which parent the baby would take after more.

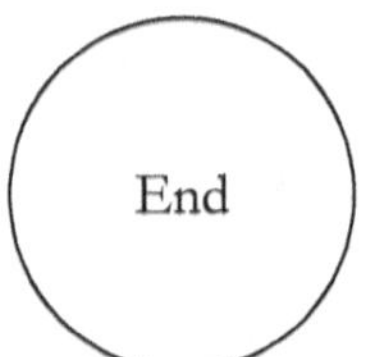

Silver the Starfallen

I

Even in death the beast was majestic.

Stags this size were rare. The animal was huge, its grey-furred chest pierced in two places with deep spear-wounds. Its black lips were drawn back in a death-rictus to reveal pristine white teeth; its black eyes glowered as if it were imparting a challenge from beyond the mortal plane.

"You were mighty, like Dvalinn and Duneyrr and your other brothers," said the Dane chieftain, Heimdall, examining the animal with admiration. He ran a finger along the impressive architecture of its massive curving antlers, adding sombrely, "'The rivers of the world form from the dew gathered on your crown each morning.'"

A few of his men murmured their agreement, though most weren't prone to reciting poetry recalling the great stories. More practically, the animal was sustenance for the party of half-starved warriors. They'd become separated from the main body of Guthorm's army after its defeat at the hands of Saxon forces at Eþandun, during the mad retreat to Chippenham. In the days since, they'd remained hidden in the woods and bogs, trying to escape west to their longships moored in the Bristol Channel while avoiding the parties of Saxons combing the area for them.

They'd tracked the hart since the previous day and finally found it feeding in a small dell early that morning. They had no bowmen among them and had to use their spears to fell the animal. Doing so had been a battle: even with all ten Danes surrounding it, the hart had been deadly and had landed a savage blow on one of the men with a thrust of its antlers.

Ulf, seated on a rock, nursed his arm, the tunic wrapped around it soaked through with his blood. He grimaced at the pain, and the memory of his bone thrusting through his gored flesh haunted the others. Days away from their ships, they knew his chances of surviving the journey with such a grave wound were slim.

"Heimdall."

The chieftain and his men turned toward the speaker, hearing clearly the warning in his voice. It was Haakon, who'd been keeping sentry to the rear of their party. Beyond him they could already see the approaching men weaving among the trees.

"Saxons."

The word fell like a curse from Heimdall's mouth. He stepped to the vanguard of his men, his hand resting on the pommel of the sword hanging at his hip. A quick scan of the woods showed him that they were surrounded.

The Saxons drew closer, fanning out into a ragged line, the clatter of their arms the only sound besides the keening of the wind through the oak trunks. Most were on foot, though a handful rode sturdy little horses. Heimdall saw that the force nearly doubled the number of his men. There would be no escaping this time.

The Saxon chieftain urged his mount forward, preceding his warriors into the perimeter of the glade. He was a giant, blonde-haired and hard-eyed beneath his battered helmet. His voice cut through the stillness, clear and uncompromising.

"It's over. Chippenham has fallen, and Guthorm surrendered and sworn to be baptized. There's no reason for you to fight us. Come with us in peace and we'll let you keep your lives."

"What say you, brothers?" said Heimdall, following the Saxons' movement with wary eyes. "Who thinks we should bow to these men, and undergo this rite of baptism?"

Shouted taunts were hurled at the Saxons. Swords were unsheathed and ready in Dane fists.

But the Saxons were too distracted to pay heed to any of it; their eyes were now drawn to one of the Danes: a diminutive warrior at the centre of their group, over whom the other men towered. The

Saxons exchanged whispered words, vying for a clearer look at the curious figure.

"What is this?" barked the Saxon chief, leaning forward theatrically in his saddle and squinting at the little Dane. "Do you bring your children to fight for you? Or is that a dwarf you're hiding? I'd heard whispers of a strange stunted creature in the ranks of the Heathen Army but didn't believe it."

His comrades laughed derisively, though with a nervous quiver in their voices. Rumours of this inexplicable Dane had been circulating for months, and held a touch of the supernatural—tales of his outlandish appearance, his prowess in battle, stoking further rumours that the Heathen Army had recruited some new mysterious barbarian race in their bid to expand the territory of the Danelaw.

At a silent sign from Heimdall, the Dane men stepped aside, offering a clear view of their comrade. He was indeed small, child-like in stature, but wiry. And he was clad in the strangest armour any of the Saxons had ever seen. Every inch of the little figure's body was covered with immense spikes—six inches long and sculpted to a deadly-looking point, and of a pure silver that reflected the bright daylight into a weird kaleidoscopic aura that hung all around him, confusing the eye.

The Saxons likewise had trouble getting a clear glimpse of his face, because his skin, like his armour, was like burnished steel, a brilliant argent that the daylight flashed from, though from what they could make out his features were unfamiliar, alien, unsettling. His helmet obscured his face further, though his shockingly silver eyes peered out brightly from that nest of spikes thrusting outward in all directions. A beard of these spikes sprouted from beneath his jaw, seemingly growing from the very bone.

"What the *hell* is that?" barked the Saxon chieftain.

As the figure stepped forward to stand alongside Heimdall, the Saxons saw that the same bizarre armour covered the entirety of his arms and legs, front and back. Astonishingly, there seemed no place on his body where the deadly armour didn't reach—even the tops of his little hands and feet bristled with it.

The small warrior said, his tone measured and clear in the

wind-whipped air:

"I am Silver. And though I'd rather shed no blood today and simply be on our way, I warn you, Saxon: walk away from this encounter, or your bones and those of your men will forever remain here."

"Ho-*ho!*" laughed the Saxon chieftain, looking to his men on all sides. "It speaks, it does! And what does our little dwarf think will happen when he crosses swords with the real men who've come to capture him?"

Some of his men chortled, though others kept silent, watching Silver with guarded eyes.

"You'll find I'm no creature from fable."

"Then you play a dangerous game…whatever you are."

The little silver warrior shook his head. "You sadden me, friend."

The Saxon's eyes darkened, all mirth gone. He snarled, in a low voice, "You're no friend of mine, Godless *dog*. You'll die slowly for that insult to Edgar, son of Siegfried, stripling or not." He looked to Heimdall. "What say you, heathen? I challenge your dwarf cub to meet me in trial by combat, here and now. Should he win, your freedom remains yours, at least until King Alfred finds you running to the sea. Should I win, as I certainly will…you come with us, and follow the example of your defeated king, Guthorm."

Heimdall turned to Silver. The little warrior nodded sedately and without hesitation, light glinting and shimmering from his spikes.

"Man to man, it is," said Heimdall.

Edgar smiled cruelly. "Man to *man*, you say? We will see."

The challenge accepted, Edgar dismounted and strode toward Silver, sword swinging in his fist. His men followed.

Once the Saxons arrived in the dell, the men of both sides wordlessly formed a loose circle around the combatants.

A moment later, and just as wordlessly, it began.

Silver pulled the blade from the scabbard at his hip: a sax, the long dagger favoured by the Danes, but in the grip of his small fist it was like a sword. He moved toward his challenger swiftly, which seemed to startle the Saxon. He padded across the grass, crouching low to the ground, sax pointed before him, his piercing silver eyes watching intently over the rim of the circular shield he wore on his other arm.

A vicious opening thrust from the Saxon chief was parried with ease by Silver, who moved with a fleetness difficult to follow. His movement left a phantasmagoric imprint shimmering lingeringly in the air. Edgar's face registered shock at his opponent's uncanny nimbleness and this strange mirage of light, but he immediately lunged at the little warrior again, delivering a powerful downward slash of his sword. But Silver battered aside the blow without trouble, staggering the Saxon back a step.

What followed happened so fast that Edgar didn't even react, his reflexes unable to keep pace with his opponent's mind-numbing speed. Silver smashed his shield across Edgar's face, following the blow through fully with his sax ready—as the Saxon stumbled, a shimmering sweep of Silver's blade sliced the chieftain's leg through at the knee, sending Edgar toppling to the ground, a scream tearing from his throat. Blood gushed like a fountain to stain the wildflowers.

Silver spun all the way round, landing in a crouch and delivering an effortlessly powerful backhand slash of his blade that bit through the Saxon's outstretched sword-arm, cleaving it clean at the elbow. Sword and arm clattered against a thick oak root protruding from the grass. The prolonged shriek from the Saxon held the spectators enthralled.

The entire contest had taken mere seconds.

Edgar goggled at his diminutive attacker, shuddering violently from the shock of pain. Bloody foam ran from his mouth as he spluttered, "Wha-wha-what—*are* you?"

At this, a look of sorrow crossed Silver's features. "I don't know, Saxon. Though I know I have more honour in my heart than you in yours."

Edgar's eyes grew wider, and he barked, "Magic! *Scucca!* You are an…abomination! Give me my sword and…I'll sh-sheathe it in your—"

Silver's sword-arm flashed, and the Saxon's head toppled from his neck to roll splashing in the grass beside his devastated body.

Heimdall stepped forward.

"Ho-*ho*! It kills, it does! Do any of you others challenge our friend, Silver? Would you stay a while to dispute ownership of the hart with us? Or to try to convince us to be…baptized?" He curled his fingers conspicuously around the grip of the sword on his belt.

The Saxons eyed Silver waiting calmly before them, surrounded by the bloody pieces of their chieftain. Silver's sax edge gleamed redly. The shifting silvery aura hung over him, strange and unfathomable.

One of the Saxons, finding his voice, said, "We mourn our fallen chief today. But another day will see you dead by our blades, when a scucca is not on your side."

"What's this idiot saying?" asked Heimdall of his men. "What's this 'scucca'?"

Silver obliged. "He says I'm a *draugr*. Or something like this."

Heimdall laughed. He gestured theatrically to Silver beside him. "A draugr, man? This little one, an undead monster? This cub who's proven more warrior than your mighty chieftain? Bah! Be gone, weaklings, or we'll keep your bones here for the crows."

The Saxon shook his sword at the Danes, even as his men were turning in retreat. "Watch yourself, dog! You'd do well to heed—"

He didn't finish his threat.

It was in that instant that Silver became aware of a great shadow that enveloped them all, as when a storm cloud passes before the sun. As one, the Danes turned to follow the wide-eyed stares of the Saxons, looking behind them, and skyward.

"Odin the Almighty!"

"Swords at the ready!"

"Valhalla, prepare thyself for us!"

Death, as ancient as the beginning of the world, had come for them all.

II

The wyrm was colossal.

It reminded Silver of the great skeletons he'd seen scattered across the lands everywhere when he'd first arrived on this world long, long ago. Perhaps this dreki was some distant relative of those mighty creatures? His heart ached at the thought of ridding the world of its savage beauty. But, as ever, he would do what he had to in order to survive.

The beast had appeared without warning, slipping stealthily through the trees and into the glade, to tower over the bickering Danes and Saxons. It held an assortment of wicked weapons in its half dozen fists: swords and hammers claimed from Northmen and Saxons it had felled in days past looked like children's toys in its long-fingered grasp; and slivers of rock and oak branch honed to ragged and deadly points by fang and claw, and great boulders to crush its enemies scrambling in its shadow. Its serpent's body was wide around as an oak trunk, and a long tapering neck supported its massive head, which was made all the more impressive by its staggering array of horns. The beast's amber eyes glared down at them ravenously.

Heimdall's voice strove to be heard over its ear-shattering shrieking: "Circle it! Circle it!"

Without discussion, the men of both parties moved to obey—but they had no time to close their circle.

The wyrm struck, fast as lightning.

In an instant, three men were dead, two Saxons and a Dane hacked apart by a flurry from the beast's weapons; a fourth man from Edgar's raiders was struck by the thing's stout tail and sent hurtling through the air to crunch heavily among the trees along the edge of the dell, his spine crushed. The wyrm snatched Ulf from where he stood, bravely baring an axe in his good hand—snapping its iron jaws closed over his head and shoulders and rearing away from the men to chew its meal while taking in the havoc it had wreaked so far. Amid the crunching of bone, Ulf's muffled screams could be heard from within the beast's maw.

His friend's dying cries tore Silver from his daze—he threw himself into action. He approached the creature at a swift run. Sensing his approach, the dreki lashed out its tail in an attempt to swat him away. Silver leaped agilely over the undulating appendage and, when it swept back along the grass, managed to drop down on it and scampered like a flea along its length. He lunged up onto its back, thankful for the distraction of the men harassing the beast below.

Even so, the wyrm's violent movements nearly sent Silver flying off. He narrowly darted out of reach of the beast's snapping jaws, and scrambled his way to straddle the wyrm's thick neck. He plunged his heels into the creature, locking his spikes between its armoured scales. He began a methodical assault with his sax: stabbing and stabbing and stabbing with all his strength. It took several blows for the weapon to break through the dreki's thick armoured plating but eventually Silver felt the blade penetrate and sink to the hilt into the meat and bone beneath.

The wyrm roared in pain and fury, and lashed violently from side to side in an effort to shake loose its assailant. Silver continued his relentless attack, stabbing and stabbing, a cloud of scales and blood and flesh flying about him. Below, the Danes and Saxons were landing blows with sword and axe and spear, though several more men were crushed by the wild whipping of the animal's muscular tail.

In the madness of its agony, the wyrm succeeded in tearing Silver from its neck with one of its hands. He was thrown high and far, clear over the tops of the trees. He crashed heavily among them, causing a small avalanche of branches and leaves. When he hit the grass far below, he didn't come to a rest, but found himself rolling headlong down a steep slope he and his comrades hadn't known was there.

He came to rest at the bottom of a small vale, battered and dizzy. As his vision cleared, he was dismayed to find that his sword had been claimed by the skull of the wyrm, left behind to feed its pain and rage. A puddle of silver blood bubbled between the spikes on his right forearm, where the dreki's long curved claw had gauged him deeply when it wrenched him from itself. Slowly, in pulsating waves of sensation, he grew aware of the pain enveloping his arm.

As his vertigo dissipated, he looked around himself, and a chill crept over him. He stared for a moment, forgetting his wound and his pain, awed, sickened. Then quickly he rose to his feet and scrambled back up the precarious slope. He could hear the shouts of the men in the glade above, the hissing and roaring of the wyrm, the clash of steel on armoured saurian body.

He gained the summit and hurried through the trees. When he burst into the glade, he raised his voice over the tumult of the battle raging before him.

"Stop!"

Silver held his hands outstretched. Catching the eye of the wyrm he called, "Let this battle cease, all of you, and come see what I've found."

The men of both sides eyed each other and the wyrm warily. Following the violence of battle, the silence in the glade was profound. Slowly they made their way to where Silver stood panting from his climb, keeping their distance from one another. The dreki, bleeding now from many wounds, rumbled warningly in its throat while swaying where it stood, its tail listing menacingly from side to side. It had the opportunity to flee but chose to remain, seemingly torn between the sating of its curiosity and its bloodlust.

They followed Silver through the trees until together they looked down from the edge of the precipice and into the vale. Across its floor stretched a graveyard for as far as the eye could see.

"Odin's all-seeing eye," breathed Heimdall in astonishment.

The valley was heaped with wyrm dead.

Near to the base of the cliff, a long spear was driven through a young wyrm's skull. Attached to its end was a banner that whipped in the wind, its coat of arms clearly visible: the heraldic shield belonged to the Northmen's great English nemesis.

"Alfred," muttered Heimdall.

"*King* Alfred," amended one of the Saxon men, though he sounded sullen, uncertain.

The Danes exchanged meaningful looks. Several looked around them among the trees, to the opposite slope, as if anticipating the appearance of a great horde of Englishmen.

Silver scanned the vale, and after a moment picked out the signs of ambush. Tellingly, mounds of scorched timber lay directly before each of the wide cave mouths at the base of the slope opposite to the one on which the men stood: the English had smoked out the wyrms from their nest and, judging from the number of creatures, likely while they'd been engaged in their annual mating orgy. Silver imagined the men hacking the creatures to pieces as they escaped the smoke-choked tunnels, confused, half-blind from the smoke and daylight. Dozens of arrows lay in the grass, those that had missed their targets. Silver imagined the Saxon archers raining down volleys of arrows into the tunnel mouths before the main ground force had commenced the massacre.

The thought of such slaughter, the Englishmen butchering the helpless, smoke-befuddled drekis, sent a shudder of fury through Silver. Too often over the years he had met such men, and only rarely honourable people like Heimdall, though even among his warriors there were those who killed just as freely, with just as much inexplicable glee.

He spat in the leaves, disgusted, as the wind gusted and blew the pungent stench of death over them all.

Silver gestured to the wyrm eyeing them warily from the edge of the trees. "Please, great wyrm, come see for yourself."

Its voice split the air, brimming with fury, anguish. "I *know* what lies there! My tribe—my *family!*—For this, you deserve my bite!" It bared its mouthful of knife-length fangs at him, clenching and unclenching its long fingers.

Now, following the relentless action of battle, Silver found himself overcome with awe—not only that a wyrm so gigantic existed here in the Danelaw, but that the stories were true: the creatures *spoke*. This one, incredibly, even spoke rudimentary Old Norse.

"No, friend," he said. "I don't believe you do know. Please, I beg of you. This is no deception. We need to show you this so that you might understand."

It watched him with baleful eyes, but it came, cautiously, slithering to a place a short way from where the men were gathered. It peered down into the vale—the look it turned on the men a moment later showed its lack of surprise, its hatred of them all. It indeed knew this scene well. It had survived the slaughter, after all.

Silver called out, "Look, o mighty wyrm! *That* is not *us!*"

He was pointing at the banner fluttering blasphemously among the corpses. Heimdall was watching Silver, admiration gleaming in his eyes.

Again, Silver shouted, *"That* is not *us*. That is the mark of another tribe."

Heimdall echoed this. "Aye, we owe no allegiance to that banner. Alfred seeks to displace our gods, our ways. To build his churches on top of us. How can a warrior ascend to Valhalla if he must first climb up through the roof of a Christian house?"

Angry murmurs of agreement from his men greeted the words.

A Saxon warrior, prideful but voice hushed with worry as he eyed the wyrm, stammered, "I serve the banner, but I'm no butcher of children. My men and I had nothing to do with this, dreki. I give you my word."

"So you claim, soldiers of Alfred," the wyrm said, this time in West Saxon, causing Edgar's men to whisper among themselves in disbelief. Silver noted, though, that the venom of earlier was gone from its voice.

Indeed, the men of both parties had lowered their weapons, and watched the wyrm with eyes of sympathy, and awe. The Saxons had even forgotten about Silver, his alien appearance at least temporarily accepted.

"You speak our languages," said Heimdall in wonder.

"And the language of my kin, and other much older languages."

The creature turned to once again look out across its many dead brethren. It held the scene in its volcanic gaze for some time.

Finally, it pointed to a corpse that lay directly below it on the slope. The frail creature coiled there was a slitherling, a child, no more than twenty winters old, its head nearly severed from its neck, its beak-like snout buried in the grass. Black blood streaked from its mouth and nostrils; one of its amber eyes stared sightlessly at the ground, while the other socket stared black and empty; blood lay in a congealed black pool all around its coils, wound tightly in a final death-convulsion, its wounds spilling tangles of veins and muscle. A hand was outstretched among the leaves, where the slitherling had been reaching for the lip of the slope, and the hope of escaping the slaughter in the vale below.

"All men are the same", the dreki spat and hissed. "Our great wyrm brood shunned mankind. We made no war against you. And you brought fire and smoke and slaughter to us, here as elsewhere. *Why?*"

Silver spread his arms in a show of peace. "I am no man, and yet I'm part of this tribe of men. Does this not show the truth in what I tell you? *These* men are *honourable* men. They're no butchers of children." Turning his eyes to the Saxons, hovering together nervously, he added, "And from what these others say, I believe they had no part in this, either. Some men do such things—others could never."

The wyrm said, "I know nothing of this cruel religion you speak of, only that its disciples have left wyrm-blood in their wake." Its eyes were troubled as it watched the English banner billowing in the wind.

Silver said nothing. He had seen this same thing before, many times, and was weary of the sight. There were more men in the world who wreaked senseless havoc than men who preached for peace. A great weariness came over him, and he wished he could find a lonely place where he might lay down his head and rest.

The wyrm turned to Silver. "What are you, little silver one? I am very old and have been to many lands, but have never seen one like you."

The old sorrow came into Silver's heart. "I don't know. I only know that I've never met another quite like me, either."

"Lies!" hissed the wyrm, its body rippling, as if it were preparing to strike. "Evasions! What deceit is this? Where is your tribe? Where is your kingdom? What is this strange armour you wear?"

Silver remained standing as he was, calm and loose-limbed, the fading afternoon light glimmering from his body. "It's no deception, I promise you, great wyrm. And this is no armour—this is me."

He ran his fingers along one of the many spikes thrusting from his body, this one from just beneath his neck. He made a show of grabbing the spike in his fingers and attempting to tug on it, to pull it away from himself as one would a jerkin or chainmail. The spike, and those surrounding it, remained firmly in place. Silver said, "If I had a tribe before these men took me in, then I don't recall it. And if I have a kingdom of origin, then…"

He drifted off, uncertain how to go on.

"Yes?" The wyrm was leaning toward him, its aggressive stance gone now, only curiosity remaining. "Tell me."

Silver turned his gaze up, eyes searching the sky. "My earliest memory is falling like a star from the sky."

Silver's words were like a spell, bewitching the wyrm.

"The *sky?* Have you wings? It is said that my ancestors had wings, long ago, and that we too flew down from the heavens."

The Northmen and Saxons, sensing an end to hostilities and weary from the fight behind them, relaxed, and squatted or sat down on the large boulders that dotted the edge of the slope. The latter were as spellbound by Silver's tale as the wyrm.

"No, I can't fly, though sometimes I wish that I could. I simply fell from the sky long ago, and that is my earliest memory—falling toward the world far, far below. I suppose this strange shell kept me alive." He lifted his arms, the silvery aura that surrounded him shifting at the movement. "It isn't impervious to a well-aimed sword-strike, but it's quite strong."

"Quite," chuckled Heimdall. "I've seen Saxon swords shatter on it. Silver wears a shield like the rest of us, but his naked arm can do the job damn well. If all that silver wasn't attached to him, we'd have stripped those spikes for our coffers when we first found him in Danemark."

"Wait—you said you fell from the sky…*long ago?*" said the wyrm. "But you are so young—a child."

"Oh, but I'm not," said Silver. "Though I have grown since my falling, that time is dim and misted with the years. I am much, *much* older than you can imagine."

"Forgive me, I meant no disrespect. You are…different to the creatures of this world that I have met."

"I'm not of this world at all, it would seem," said Silver, a melancholy smile on his face.

The dreki cocked its head. "Your teeth—they are silver, too. And your blood, there on your arm." There was wonder in its voice as it stared at his wounded arm, dripping silver droplets that flashed like jewels in the sun.

"Indeed, for these reasons I'm called Silver by those who are my friends," he said. "Again, I have no answer to these things, besides that I'm me, and I've always been like this, and unlike others."

The wyrm nodded, a thoughtful murmuring coming from deep in its throat.

"I am Ultek, of what was once known as the Farhover Warren, though that place is no more. I have no tribe now either, Silver. All that I have is the fire of fury and sorrow that burns in my heart. And though I have no hatred for you, all I know to do now is to wage war on all that are not wyrmkind."

Silver watched Ultek pensively. Then, "Perhaps we wage the same war."

When he turned to Heimdall, the chieftain was already nodding, a knowing glimmer in his eyes. "I believe Silver speaks of something that's crossed my own mind, as well, great Ultek. Go on, Silver."

To the wyrm, Silver said, "Perhaps together we might both avenge your family...and strike a blow against Alfred, enemy of the Danes."

III

The Saxons manning the stone walls of Daw's Castle stirred uneasily at their posts. Before them, the waters of the bay shimmered crimson with dawn—there were no Danish longships in sight. But behind them, where the small burh known as Wæced was just waking, a disturbance came that set the men's skin crawling with fear.

A great roaring boomed from the east, and though the wind was cold and strong on that sun-bright dawn, that voice was no wind. It bounced from the walls of the hillfort, its echoes eerie and endless. Most of the men had been present a few weeks earlier at the slaughter in the valley of the wyrm, and knew that roar well, only this time the advantage of surprise was not on their side. And the burh, until the soldiers could come to its aid, was undefended.

They signalled the alarum, awakening the rest of the garrison.

A moment later, their chieftain, Æthel, strode from the barracks, tying his sword-belt around his waist.

"Report," he called to the nearest man as he ascended the ladder to the wooden rampart that ran the length of the wall.

One of the sentries, ashen-faced, said, "Wyrm-voice, my lord, from Wæced. Maybe the beasts come for vengeance."

"What beasts?" he said. "I thought we'd rid this area of them with the last hunts." The chief looked wide-eyed to the east, then, "Come. A full company of bowmen should do it. We'll rid ourselves of the vermin once and for all."

The Saxon war party was nearing the outskirts of the burh when the entourage came fully into view. It occupied the entire breadth of the dirt road that ran through the town.

Æthel stared a moment, confused, aghast…and then a smile creased his weather-beaten features. His men saw, too, and smiled like their chieftain, a great relief settling over them.

A half dozen horses were struggling to pull a vast cargo: a great wyrm, subdued with coils upon coils of rope lashed tightly around its body from head to tail. It lay on a makeshift litter made from felled oak and left a deep furrow in the dirt over which it was dragged. A small band of Danish warriors surrounded the beast, keeping it cowed with occasional jabs from their spears.

"Will those ropes hold?" muttered a man beside the chieftain.

"The thing's likely wounded in a hundred places beneath those bonds." Indeed, the wyrm bled from gashes in its skull, where chunks of its armour-like scales were missing. "See there, its brains are fit to spill from its head," Æthel added. "No, no, we're safe enough."

Heimdall and his convoy drew close to the Saxons. He and his men were doing their best to calm the horses, which whinnied nervously so close to the wyrm. The animals had been a parting gift from Edgar's men. The remaining warriors of his band—a mere handful had survived the battle with Ultek—refused to take an active role in the deception of their fellow Saxons, though they'd sworn to give no warning to the stronghold either. To a man, they were ashamed of what they'd found, the aftermath of the slaughter of the drekis, and the last that Heimdall's raiders had seen of them they were marching westward through the forest.

"What's the meaning of this?"

The Danes found the speaker among the men lining the road in front of them: the Saxon chieftain, with hard eyes set in a proud face, the hint of a mocking smile pulling at the corners of his mouth.

"A gift from our war chief to you," declared Heimdall, spreading his arms in a show of peace. "We're deserters from Guthorm's forces, bound for the sea where others who no longer wish to serve him will meet us. We found this wounded beast in a vale less than a half day's march to the north., crawling among the corpses of its blasphemous brethren. Seeing your banner flying in that field of carnage and knowing that those responsible for this brave feat likely dwelled here, we maimed the loathsome creature more and subdued it. And we dragged it here…"

He paused, and when the Saxon chief continued to watch him incredulously, added, "If you want the thing, but don't think us worthy of your Christian hospitality, we'll leave it here, and be on our way. Or we can do the killing of it, if you like—it matters little to us."

Ultek screeched, the breath from its nostrils gusting like a savage wind. The ropes lashed about its snout strained as the wyrm struggled to open its jaws. Several Danes delivered blows to the beast with the aft end of their spears, settling it down.

"And how do we know that your story is true, and that you are indeed deserters? After all, the news is everywhere, that Guthorm was defeated. Maybe you're simply running, and hoping to escape to the sea?"

Heimdall nodded grimly. "Guthorm defeated. We thought as much. The tides of war had been moving in this direction for some time." He gestured to the wyrm, said, "If we're simply running from defeat, why should we drag a monster with us? Were we going to squeeze it onto a longboat with us?"

Laughter trickled from the ranks of the Danes.

The Saxons shifted nervously, looking to their chieftain. After a moment, Æthel chuckled, too. "You make a good point, Dane." And then he said magnanimously, "This is indeed a rare gift, and a boon for your kind, Northman. King Alfred will be pleased to hear of it. Maybe this is the beginning of a new era between our peoples. We accept the monster you've gone to such trouble to gift to us, and will rejoice in the slaughtering of it as we rejoiced in the destruction of its kin. God's world must be rid of demons like these. And indeed, we insist that we repay this good and brave act. Come, sup with us, and drink with us. Let the light of Christ Himself shine upon this gathering."

Heimdall and his men made a show of exchanging uncertain looks, before Heimdall offered the Saxon leader a smile. "This is kind of you. And trapping godless beasts *is* thirsty work. We thank you for your hospitality."

"I am Æthel, and we man Daw's Castle."

"I am Heimdall. We thank you for opening your keep to us."

"Come."

The two parties commenced down the road leading into the hillfort.

As the Danes followed their hosts toward the looming walls of the fortress's eastern side, a pair of heavy metal portcullises were opened to them.

Dragging their heavy burden was difficult, and as they inched their way forward into the narrow expanse of the barbican between the first and second of these gates, they eyed the shadowed forms flitting on the other side of the apertures lining the walls and ceiling—the Danes had heard the tales of these new fortresses Alfred was building, and how the Saxons would use these structures to trap enemy forces, and slaughter them with arrows fired from the holes in the walls, and burn the trapped men with boiling water poured down from above. A cowardly tactic, but brutally effective. And with Æthel and his men preceding them into the keep itself, it would give the Saxons just enough time to close the gates and shutter the Danes within.

But it was not to be: the brief trip through the neck of the barbican seemed to last an eternity but finally the Danes emerged into the daylight of the open courtyard beyond. Heimdall and his men breathed easier, though lines of Saxons three men deep hemmed them in on every side, and archers watched them from the walls above, arrows nocked.

Once the entire group was within the walls, Æthel instructed the Danes to drag the wyrm into the centre of the courtyard. Here, he walked boldly among the ranks of the Danes and squatted beside the bound wyrm to gain a closer look. He smiled a cruel smile. "Ah, so we missed one, did we? And what a specimen! I never imagined a dreki this size could exist except in song. Perhaps this beast was cowardly, and hid itself deep in some hole where brave Christian warriors wouldn't have thought to look?"

In answer, the wyrm growled, a sound deep and loud that the men felt trembling the ground beneath their feet.

The chieftain laughed. "Maybe the things do understand the language of men, after all. We seem to have angered the ugly brute. No matter—after we've dined, we'll make sport of it."

"Sport, aye," said Heimdall, running a hand along one of the long horns that curved upward from the wyrm's skull. And then, more quietly, he murmured, "'The seas of the world form from the dew gathered on your crown each morning.'"

"What was that?" said Æthel, a frown of suspicion on his face. "Was that verse?"

"Aye, just a snatch of it, from an old tale."

Æthel watched him a moment before smiling. "Well, poet Heimdall, I hope you and your men drink well. Our cellars here run deep and when we play host, well, our guests are near drowned with wine."

Heimdall barked a laugh. "Oh, great Saxon chieftain, I fear you haven't enough wine in all your barrels for the one among us whose thirst runs deepest."

A voice like thunder filled the courtyard:

"Only when all Saxon blood has been drained shall I turn to your wine."

The wyrm rose upward smoothly, its bonds severed by the swords of the Danes on either side of it. It towered higher than the walls of the castle. It spread its arms wide, revealing the swords and hammers in its fists, and freeing the secret cargo it had held hidden from sight against its armoured bosom—Silver, sword in hand and shield upon arm, sunlight flashing blindingly from his spike-sheathed body. The Saxons, bewitched by the spectacle of the freed dreki and this bizarre glimmering enemy landing in their midst, stood rapt for a moment…a moment too long.

With a speed too fast to follow, Ultek smashed its way through the assembled ranks of Saxons, sending men flying through the air, crushing others beneath its immense weight. It snatched Æthel in its jaws, biting through leather tunic into the bone beneath; and stabbing and clubbing Saxons all around until the courtyard lay strewn with the dead and dying. The wyrm surged forward into the greater compound, all the power of its plated grey coils and its hatred of the Saxons at its command.

And among the chaos wove the blinding silvery blur: Silver, his blade licking out to sever heads from shoulders and spill guts on the flagstones. The Saxons' swords clanged harmlessly from his cocoon of spikes, and when the occasional blade found its way between them and drew his argent blood, the strange warrior felt nothing—he fought on, maddened by visions of the slaughter he'd witnessed in the vale: dreki families blinded by smoke and fire, and cut to pieces for no reason he could understand. Recognizing in this heinous act the same crime perpetrated against him by so many men over the years: a hatred of him, simply because he was different from other men.

Into the bedlam roared Heimdall and his warriors, axes rising and falling, hammers pummelling, swords slashing. Despite the vaster numbers of the Saxons, the tide of the battle swept them into disarray—those that weren't cut down where they stood were run to ground as they sought to flee.

Over the roar of the fighting, the voice of Ultek boomed, a judgement of the Saxon butchers and an elegy to the slaughtered wyrmkind that put a grim smile on Silver's face:

"This vengeance is for the Farhover Warren—from Ultek, and his new brothers!"

The screams of the Saxons rose into the bright, frostbitten air.

IV

The unmistakable hush of death hung over the garrison.

The Danes had left the dead where they'd fallen. They belonged to the Saxons alone—Heimdall's men hadn't suffered a single fatality. It had been a slaughter, though certainly a less wanton one than the extermination that had taken place at Farhover Warren. Where that had been all vindictiveness, this had been vengeance.

They were taking shelter in the garrison through the night, and would be off by morning, leaving the Saxon dead to rot and be found by their kinsmen from Wæced in the days ahead. The Danes were scattered throughout the compound, some sleeping, some drinking from the much-celebrated ale barrels, and others sharpening their weapons. The sentries posted along the eastern perimeter of the hillfort watched for signs of approaching Saxon, though the night drew on and the general feeling was that they would remain unvisited. The news of Guthorm's final surrender at Eþandun had been spreading far and wide, but though the Northmen were in dire straits, with more and more becoming baptized into the cult of Christ, for that night at least Heimdall's band was safe.

Ultek lay coiled in the centre of the courtyard, the only space large enough to accommodate it. Silver sat cross-legged beside it, close to the fire the men had built in the yard. Light from the flames danced and glimmered from Silver's spiked body, enchanting the eye of the wyrm. They had eaten, and were resting following the long day behind them.

"You fought well, Silver." Ultek's voice was drowsy, content-sounding.

"As did you, Ultek—perhaps once this world is finished with us, we'll fight alongside each other again, among the stars."

"I hope that day comes to pass, though I sense we have more fighting waiting for us here on this world before that day comes."

Heimdall, seated across from Silver and nursing a flagon of wine, saw the distance in his companion's gaze.

"What thoughts trouble you, Silver?"

"I'm thinking of tomorrow," said Silver, his argent gaze looking deep and far. Beyond this death-field, what other fields of battle waited for him? He'd arrived in the world before man existed, and often found himself looking back to those early years with longing—the peace of that time was something he missed.

Silver wondered how many years he would live to wander the world. Having no others of his kind to judge by, he didn't know how long his lifespan might be. He wondered what things he would see, what new and unguessed darknesses? He wondered whether he would ever feel un-alone, and if he could ever truly fit in among the greater tribe of man? He wondered if he would ever know peace again. He wondered these things but, in his heart, felt that he knew the answers, and these answers troubled him.

He said, "I have to go, Heimdall."

"I know it, Silver. I've seen this coming for some time. Your eyes tell it even when your tongue is silent. There's something you need to find that isn't here in the Danelaw. I fear it may not be in the Northland either." He paused, then, "We're much stronger—and much better men—with you in our ranks. I hate to lose you."

Silver looked to his chief wonderingly. He smiled, silver teeth shining in the firelight. "You are wise, Heimdall, old friend, and have read my thoughts well."

"'Old,' yes," Heimdall said, chuckling. "'Wise', well, *that* is uncertain."

The old friends shared a reflective silence.

Then Heimdall said abruptly, "I dislike maudlin farewells. Take as many provisions and arms as you can carry. Then be gone."

Silver said, "You're generous as well as wise…and old."

Heimdall laughed, stood, stretching his muscles. "Farewell, brothers. May your travels yield the treasures you seek."

"Thank you," said Silver. "Fare thee well, and let us meet again someday."

Silver and Ultek watched Heimdall cross the courtyard and disappear into the garrison in search of a bed. The wind whistled weirdly through the compound, reminding Silver of wailing gulls.

"I will go in the morning, too," said Ultek. "Though I do not know where I might go. There is nothing for me here, but then there is nothing for me anywhere else, either. Farhover Warren was the last of the great wyrm strongholds—I have never seen another of my kind elsewhere here, or heard tell of others. Perhaps I too will go back to the North."

Silver took in the import of what he'd heard, and he didn't know what to say. After a moment of staring into the fire, he said, "Two always fare better than those who walk alone." He was surprised to find himself hoping earnestly for the wyrm to agree with the statement, and its implication.

"We are alike in our loneliness," Ultek said. "We would make for a curious pair of travellers."

"Indeed," agreed Silver. "We'd certainly draw attention to ourselves."

"And likely it would be attention of the evil kind."

"Ah," said Silver, "but maybe the world needs to see us. Maybe it needs to see us, and if it doesn't like what it sees…Well, maybe the seeing is what matters." And then suddenly the thought occurred to him. "But Ultek—our longboats are big and mighty vessels, but never could you fit on one of them!"

Ultek rumbled with laughter. "How do you think I arrived here all those years ago, friend Silver? Wyrmkind do not build ships. We do not need them. We swim."

"Swim?" Silver looked on in wonder. Truly, Ultek was a creature stepped from out of myth and into the natural world.

Ultek said, thoughtfully, "I think that a warrior who survives the sky throwing him down to the world below would surely survive a ride across the sea. How fast are your longships?"

Silver said, "Under favourable conditions, the journey from here to Danemark could be made in three to ten days."

"Ride with Ultek and you will touch your shores in three days."

Silver knew the wyrm wasn't exaggerating. An excitement he hadn't known in some time awoke in his heart, but still something troubled him. He thought for a moment, and then it came to him.

"What if I don't feel compelled to return to those cold northern shores? What if warmer climes call? What if the rest of the world calls?"

Ultek extended his long neck to peer above the fort's wall, and toward the bay beyond.

"That journey will take somewhat longer."

It wasn't yet dawn when they took their leave.

They followed a circuitous path down the slope to the rock-strewn beach below the fort. From there, Ultek slipped into the foaming shallows of the bay, and Silver clambered up to a point behind the wyrm's head, where its shield-like skull ornamentation provided sanctuary from the wind, as well as a convenient nook to nestle himself when he needed to rest.

The wind rose. The waves lapped. The world called.

Little Silver and the old wyrm set off together, the moonlight casting ghostly designs from spike and scale.

Young, But Tomorrow

Chuck was sitting in darkness, the lights of his apartment turned off and the black, light-killing drapes drawn tightly against the July afternoon burning brightly outside. He felt vacant, as if whatever had made up his inner self had been emptied over the years, leaving only the shell of him behind. He had no more faith left: neither in himself or in the world he'd always felt so weirdly misplaced in.

If there was a God then He must have made a mistake with me—this thought had haunted Chuck since he was a child. Chuck had always seen himself as some sort of failed experiment, whether biological—as young boy, he used to ask his parents whether he'd been born in a test-tube, in a laboratory—or divine (his recent experiences had awoken a spiritual belief he'd never known lay dormant in him). The sound of his voice was always alien to his ears, and made him uneasy. He hadn't spoken out loud in several days, not even to himself, and vaguely wondered whether the human voice was something that, without use, might fall into disrepair.

He examined the coffee table in front of him. It was a haphazard landscape of the junk of the week past: several potato chip bags in varying stages of completion; empty glasses and paper cups; the remains of several T.V. dinners and fast food meals, the surfaces of the Styrofoam cartons and the compartments of the plastic trays encrusted with congealed condiments and inedible chunks of gristle that passed for Salisbury steak and fried chicken; an assortment of prescription and over-the-counter pill bottles; the television's remote control, sticky with food grime.

This was a good approximation of his mind, Chuck thought,

cluttered and filthy and destined only to get dirty and cluttered all over again if he could find it in himself to actually sweep away the detritus that had accumulated. He said it out loud, hoping to gain some shred of courage from the boldness of his voice piercing the heavy silence of the apartment after so long: "What a dump. I should maybe clean up around here." But he heard the smallness of his voice, the defeated character of what had come out of his mouth and shook his head at this latest small failure. Why was it that cleaning up—and cleaning up his act and making something of himself, like his dad used to say—seemed so far beyond his reach?

He closed his eyes, felt the old lethargy stealing over him and threatening to pull him down into sleep. Sleep was always the easiest way. And the oblivion of the pills to get him to that familiar and blessed sanctuary of unconsciousness.

Like an atom bomb dropping from the heavens and landing squarely on his head, the telephone on the end-table beside him jangled into terrifying life. He leapt half out of his sofa seat, knocking his knees against the low coffee table, causing pop to spill from the glass that had been sitting there since that morning's breakfast of pills. The phone's clamour echoed in the sparsely furnished living room, bouncing from the walls, hammering at his eardrums; chilling him.

Who was calling? Whose voice—what mind with what motivations—existed on the opposite end of the copper wire? What did it *want* from him? Was it a bill collector? The relentless student loan collections agent with his calculatedly demonic voice whose purpose was to instill fear in those he harassed, and who always succeeded? Some other faceless being waiting to seed its dark message in his ear, where it would fester in his thoughts, a virus of worry and fear?

The telephone cut off mid-ring, leaving the ghost of its voice hanging in the air. Chuck exhaled the breath he hadn't even realized he'd been holding in. He felt his heart stuttering, and slowly, slowly resume its normal rhythm. Who could have been calling him? What had they wanted from him? Why did he fear the phone—and the world outside—so much? These questions clung in his thoughts, pulled in from the periphery of his awareness where they always floated like airborne virus spores.

But of course Chuck had much worse problems to contend with than bill collectors and collections agents and dirty dishes and stale apartment air and prescriptions on the cusp of needing to be refilled. Poverty; joblessness in a city with unemployment at a crisis-level high; the scant promise offered by a welfare cheque a week away in the mail while the refrigerator haunted the kitchen like an empty casket, waiting: these troubles paled beside certain other problems a man could have.

The words fell from Chuck's lips without his consent, as if his unconscious mind were pushing him to confront the reality he'd been trying to avoid:

"There's a giant skull floating outside of my apartment window."

Chuck's heart immediately returned to its jackhammering rhythm of a moment earlier. Voicing it out loud brought the terrifying reality of his predicament home to him all over again.

He actually had seen the skull. No joke. It was there, a presence, a spirit, or a tangible entity floating there for him and him alone, just outside of the single window of his tiny bachelor apartment. He felt that it was waiting for him to do something, though he couldn't imagine what? He knew it could see him despite the drapes, but still he kept them closed, an instinctual defence against observation. No one else saw it, of course, or else someone would have dealt with it; the authorities, the people, the army, God.

Sadly, Chuck had grown to understand over the last several days that he had no one else in the world he could depend on, for good or bad, except for—in its own perverse way—the skull. He was a recluse, a single child whose parents were both long dead and buried. Having always shunned social contact had left him utterly friendless. The years since he'd graduated from university had been an unending epoch of fruitless job searches while coasting by as he could on the scraps afforded him through his welfare allowance, a solitary existence enabling his hermit-like tendencies and social inhibitions to grow like a rampant cancer. People terrified him, more so even than phantasmagorical visions floating outside of his window—at least the skull had mystery about it, a potential for something supernatural beyond the dreary everyday, even if its dark gaze seemed to signal its intent on consuming him, body and soul.

This is why he combated the predicament the way he did.

Even now, he pulled the old Halloween mask from where it had been nestled between the couch cushions and slipped it with practiced ease over his head. Immediately a wave of relief washed over him. It was the rubber type of mask that's pulled all the way over the head, far superior in appearance to its cheap plastic-moulded counterparts that were attached with an elastic fastened around the back of the head. This particular mask was a chalk-pale, skull-faced ghoul with deep black orbital sockets, a leering grin, and a splash of red paint circling its mouth, spattering its teeth.

Chuck believed that the skull knew about his ritual wearing of the mask, though he'd never dared to actually open his curtains and show himself in his supplication. But of course the skull knew—it was a deity, or something so far beyond the inconsequential lifeform he was that it may as well have been a god. And a god could see through flimsy veils of curtains the way it could see through lies and deceptions and into the soul of a person. Chuck knew innately that the skull recognized his obeisance when he wore the mask, as if he were an acolyte paying respectful tribute to the skull's might and horror, and so he sensed that wearing the mask helped ward off its full-fledged advances. Maybe his perceptiveness pleased the spectre, his ritualistic costume showing his efforts to rise to its level of perfection, while accepting the truth of what he was: a phantom drifting through the harsh world of humankind.

Whatever the root cause of his actions, Chuck had felt an immediate compulsion to rifle through his cluttered storage closet and find the mask when, one week before, he'd crawled out of bed and opened the curtains to greet another day and been greeted with the death-mask of the colossal skull floating outside his window; its gigantic black eyes watching him like all the judgment of the world.

He'd worn the mask and kept the curtains tightly drawn ever since, only removing it so that he could eat and drink, and only cracking the curtains to peer outside when his hope got the better of him. But always the skull was hovering there, with only the flimsy barrier of window glass separating it from him shuddering in the gloomy room.

Again, the nerve-wracking racket of the telephone assaulted the uneasy quiet.

This time it actually elicited a cry from Chuck. A girlish, high-note yelp that made him instantly ashamed, and furious with himself. What a weakling he was. What a complete goddamned wimp of a man-boy he was, jumping at a ringing telephone. Worst case scenario, it was collections, or the phone company with threats to cut him off from the possibility of communicating by telephone with the greater world, which needn't have bothered him because who in the greater world did he have to communicate with anyways? There was no one. He was alone in the world. *He. Was. Alone.*

The thought—and it was one that haunted him always—was just settling into its usual small, tight ball of burning depression in the pit of his stomach, when its manifestation was obliterated by another thought:

Was it the floating skull outside the window that was waiting at the other end of the line, finally managing to hack into his phone line and calling him up the way nobody had ever called him out of friendship, or companionship? Would it never stop calling because it knew he was there hiding futilely from the day, from his future waiting like a hungry evil thing on the other side of the glass and brick of the building?

With shaking fingers Chuck grabbed the bottle of anxiety meds from the coffee table and, pulling the skull-mask up above his mouth, popped a half dozen of the bright red capsules. He swallowed them dry, quickly pulling the mask back down as he did.

The telephone's voice stopped as abruptly as it had begun its raping of the apartment's tomb-like silence. He shivered in its aftermath.

It had been real. The real thing: *attempted contact* from outside his small, tentatively safe world. The second such attempted contact in one day and the day was young. Much, much too young at only two in the terrible afternoon. He felt his heart quicken. He fought down the tears he felt coming. He turned his eyes in their sockets, remaining otherwise frozen on the couch, at the soft, nearly undetectable sound: a tapping on the window glass; a reminder, a warning, a promise of dark mysteries to come.

He had to piss but he willed himself to stay where he was, unmoving. It could wait until after his lunch of another pill or two or three, and through the endless late afternoon stretch when time would seem stilled as it always did at that time, like it would be all through the endless night waiting for him.

He drifted to sleep before he'd even felt sleep coming for him, assassin that it was, getting him like it did every day just when he might have finally been ready to be brave; to seize the day by its horns and find himself some of the happiness that had always been in such short supply.

He dreamed a dream of worms.

A huge congress of worms deep in the earth, worms pink as newborn mice and fat as his arm, coiling and sliming in the darkness, indifferent to the ticking of human clocks in the world far above; thriving in the cold moist soil and operating according to their own infallible and primordial time-keeping system.

Waiting for him.

He was shocked into panicked wakefulness by a rapid machine-gunning clamour echoing throughout the apartment.

It took maybe two seconds for his befuddled brain to process the sound and give it its dark meaning: knocking…

There was someone at the door of his apartment!

He instinctively reached for the mask covering his head, making sure it was securely in place. It was probably the landlord with another warning that he pay his rent before week's end, or else. If he were to actually answer the door, he couldn't do so wearing the skull-mask—Mr. Clemens already thought he was a weirdo, and

Chuck was certainly one of his most unreliable tenants. Seeing him like this—dressed for his secret devotions to the entity haunting his window—might get him evicted, and fast.

Again, the loud and fast knocking came, jangling his nerves. Resigned to dealing with this new situation, he steeled himself and pulled the mask from his head. His heartrate shop up—he felt naked, exposed, weaker than he'd been with his head swaddled inside the comforting rubber warmth. He placed the mask gently onto the cushion beside him, then eased himself from the sofa, wincing at the wheezing sound of its faux-leather reforming itself following his hours-long sprawl. He tiptoed across the threadbare carpet and into the small hallway, wincing at the groaning of the loose floorboard he'd forgotten to avoid stepping on as he neared the door; and then, a moment after, the noise of his foot kicking over a plastic pop bottle from the stash of empties waiting for the recycle bin. Its clattering din as it skidded across the floor caused an icy sweat to break out down his back. He mouthed curses at himself in the gloom, willing the noise of the rolling bottle to stop. An eternity later, it did.

A moment passed. He crept close and, holding his breath, moved his eye to the peephole. But a nebulous smear of grey-white greeted him, as if whoever waited on the opposite side of the thin wooden door was covering the hole. This possibility awakened a new, deeper fear in him—why would they *do* that? What possible reason could they have for not wanting him to know who they were?

Ratatatatatat!

The machine gun-knocking directly in front of his face made him jump, startled out of his wits. He shook his head at himself, ashamed and annoyed at his fearfulness. What were they going to do anyways? Keep knocking like those relentless door-to-door salespeople? Kick down his door?

But what if they did? What if they did just that, and found him right there, cowering like a mouse before their wrath? And what would compel them to go to such drastic measures and force their way into the apartment?

He reasoned with himself: he was being paranoid. Of course he was. Relax, Chuck. Calm down. Give it another minute and they'd be gone, and he could back to his couch and his pills and his sleep and the comfort of his mask and—

"Chuck."

The voice had come from the other side of the door.

It had been loud, as if the speaker was standing very close to the door…very close to where Chuck cowered in the shadows. He waited, breathless and tense.

Again: "Chuck. Chuck-Chuck. Open up. We know you're in there, man."

We? There was more than *one* person out there calling on him? Why? Who were they? What did they want from him? *They knew his name!*

Chuck, frantic, panicking, gathered what wits he could manage and, acting on impulse, did what he had to, to regain a shred of the dignity he'd been steadily losing since the awkward years of his childhood. He exhaled sharply, steeled himself, and, leaving the chain-lock securely in place, cracked the door.

He looked out at the sea of skeleton-men.

They looked as big as an army squeezed into the musty claustrophobic hallway, its intermittently flickering light fixtures illuminating their ranks in spectral rows. He saw that the identical masks they wore were much like his own. It was an unsettling sight to say the least, and it took Chuck a moment to take in the fact that, beyond this single uniform detail, the skeleton-men were all dressed differently: some wore dress shirts and suit jackets, others denim jackets or hooded sweatshirts; some sported baseball caps and some were in jeans. Instinctively, he strained to see the masks' telltale puckered trim beneath the chin where the rubber fit was tightest. He couldn't find it, and swallowed in a dry throat.

"Hi Chuck," said the skeleton-man directly in front of him. His voice, Chuck thought, was the voice that had first addressed him through the door. It was a perfectly normal voice. Perfectly human, high and a little nasally. But why would he even question the humanity of the people calling on him?

The skeleton-man interrupted his thoughts: "No need to introduce yourself, Chuck. We've known you forever."

"That's right," said another skeleton-man standing beside the first, voice husky, a life-time smoker's voice. "Just come along with us now."

Chuck hesitated, his stomach tightening at the edge of threat he detected in the words, his fingers instinctively finding the doorknob and tightening around its round brass curvature. "What? What do you want?" he said, voice small.

"Come on, don't be such an asshole," said another skeleton-man, his tone both whiny and exasperated, as if he'd been trying to coerce Chuck for some time. The vulgar words startled Chuck. He didn't like language like that, and avoided speaking it himself. There was something a little too barbaric about that kind of talk. Maybe he just didn't like being reminded that he lived in a world of barbarians, crude, savage, stronger than he was.

"You can't hide in that shit-hole you call an apartment anymore. It's been way too long." The voice, female, came from a skeleton-woman somewhere behind the first row of skeleton-men. Again, he recoiled from the crude words.

"Yeah, this is long overdue, dumbass," said another skeleton-man from somewhere to the rear of the skeleton-mob.

"Yeah, hurry up, fuck-up," affirmed another skeleton-man before Chuck could compose himself to respond. "You always take so long to do even the smallest thing."

There was such derision in the voice, in all their voices. Such *disgust*. Such *loathing*. Chuck heard it as clearly as he felt it within himself. Jesus, he *was* such a fucking *fuck-up*. He felt shame and resignation at thinking so vulgarly, but then sometimes truth was a tough pill to swallow.

He could only agree with the skeleton-men, about everything.

"Okay," he said. "Let me get my mask." This felt right to him, all things considered. He'd always wanted to feel welcome somewhere, to be a part of a larger group, and if he were to join the ranks of the skeleton-men he wanted to look right, fit in like he'd never really fit in anywhere else before. The reason for their collective get-up he could learn afterward: he felt naked at the moment and had to clothe himself properly. Besides, he should be overjoyed that they were dressed like they were—maybe he'd at long last found kindred spirits.

"You don't need to do that," said a skeleton-man, gloved skeleton-hand raised peremptorily on the air, halting Chuck as he was turning back into his apartment.

"Nope," agreed a skeleton-woman. "You don't need to do that at all, Chuckster."

Another skeleton-man peered over the shoulders of those in the front row and explained: "You're *wearing* your real face, Chuck. *Finally*. After all the long years."

The figures before him parted so that a pair of skeleton-men standing behind lay revealed. These were holding a long rectangular mirror between them, its reflective surface aimed at Chuck. He saw his reflection watching him: pale-faced, black-eyed, teeth completely revealed and leering in his naked skull as if he had something to laugh at; which maybe he did, he thought. Maybe the joke had always been on him, and this was the punch-line. Pow.

But hadn't he removed his mask, and left it on the couch? He reached a shaking hand to his neck, feeling for the puckered rubber trim but, as he'd known he would, he found none. His heart fluttered. Something heavy thudded inside him. He realized it was his acceptance of his situation. Acceptance of some things was a heavy weight to bear. Maybe he was finally growing up.

"Come on, fucktard," urged a skeleton-woman.

Another skeleton-man's voice came from somewhere in the throng: "Yeah, hurry up, loser. The clock is ticking."

Before he could move, another voice said: "Come *on* already, Chuck, you dumb fuck. Tick-tock, tick-tock. Time's a-wasting."

And another: "Come along now, Dumb-Fuck Chuck. You're late for your important appointment."

He heard muted laughter among some of the skeleton-men, and whispered snippets of their mocking exchanges:

"Look at this idiot."

"Ha! Taking his time now like always—pathetic."

"Truly. A shit-stain on this toilet-bowl Earth."

"When is he going to get it through his thick skull?"

Into the chaos of voices, Chuck stammered, "O-okay. Sure, I'll go. It makes sense. It'll be like a…a new beginning?"

Several skeleton-men sneered at this.

"What a moron," one said.

Another said, "If you say so, dummy."

Another: "Chuck the shmuck."

Laughter continued to trickle from the skeleton-mob.

Chuck felt tears brimming in his eyes but fought them back. This was no reason to cry. This was going to be the only reasonably good thing he'd ever done. He nodded and stepped into the midst of the skeleton-men. He didn't bother to shut his apartment door behind him. Something told him that he didn't need to do that.

"There we go, dummy," said a skeleton-man at his ear. He felt a cold hard hand clap him on the back.

"Let's go, chump," said another skeleton-man off to his right.

Another skeleton-man confirmed Chuck's afternoon dream, and his destiny as he'd always secretly known it: "Come on, Charles—the worms have been waiting in your hole for years. They're itching to meet you. Let's go. We're late for the big supper."

As Chuck moved along in the claustrophobic swell of the throng he grew conscious of a sound, which at first he mistook for his own frightened heartbeat in his ears, and then for the mechanical movements of some enormous clock's hands; but then he understood that it was a chant, the collective voice of the skeleton-men speaking as one and surrounding him:

"Tick. Tock. Tick. Tock. Tick. Tock."

He cleared his throat, and joined them, feeling the rightness in it: "Tick. Tock. Tick. Tock."

Behind him someone snorted and said, "What a fucking chump."

Chuck maintained his marching step with the skeleton-men as they led him down the narrow corridors and stairwell, and then finally toward the bright light of the outdoors waiting at the end of the first-floor hall. He squinted as they neared the glass door. He hadn't seen the sunlight in a very long time. His mole-like existence had kept him in the dark for weeks, or had it been years, or had it been his whole life so far? He kept up his mantra-like recital as he passed through the door into the world waiting outside, his voice never wavering, one with the greater voice pulsing in at him from all around.

Tick.
Tock.
Tick.
Tock.
Tick.
Tock.
Tomorrow.
Was.
Finally.
Here.

Little Boys

I

The Pacific Ocean was spread out before them, divided up inside the cockpit's array of armoured glass window panels. The water glittered brilliantly in the pre-dawn light. No matter how many times he witnessed it, the sight never lost any of its rapturous beauty.

Colonel Paul Tibbets was settled in for the six-hour flight to Japan, admiring this view, trying to keep calm, when he saw the flower. He frowned, reaching up to retrieve it from where it clung to the bulkhead. He had to exert a surprising amount of force to pull it free, and as it peeled from the metal, he saw the gluey black film that held it fixed in place.

He examined the flower, turning it over in his fingers. He'd never seen one quite like it, though he certainly wasn't an expert in botany. Its size was startling—it dwarfed his hand, and brought to mind the drawings of prehistoric megaflora he'd seen in books on dinosaurs when he was a boy. Its long teardrop-shaped petals were a lustrous black, speckled with tiny circles of an even darker black that only became visible when he turned them toward the light.

Looking to his co-pilot, Lewis, he smiled and said, "A memento from some young lady seeing you off this morning?"

Lewis cocked an eye at him, and then to the flower resting across Tibbets' palm. He shook his head. "No, sir."

"Any idea where it came from? I can't believe I didn't see the thing until now. It's hard to miss." They'd been in the air for almost three hours already, and flowers weren't the type of thing that easily blended in with the surroundings of the cockpit, let alone a weird and exotic specimen like this.

Lewis only shook his head, frowning at the flower lingeringly before turning back to his instruments. Tibbets considered pursuing the conversation, then dropped it. Lewis either didn't care, or just didn't want to talk to him. Likely both. Tibbets placed the flower on his instrument console. A good luck charm, he told himself, then thought better of it and swept it to the side—there was something about this flower that he found vaguely unsettling.

He rubbed his eyes, and let his thoughts drift.

Tibbets knew that what they were doing that morning was important. History would remember it as the right thing to have done, the turning point that would end the war for good. Whenever he'd had any doubts about the moral implications of Little Boy, it was always his mother's words that came to him and offered wisdom and comfort:

I know the goodness that's in you, son. And I know you will be all right.

These words, and other snippets from their conversations, he would often repeat like mantras while on test flights and missions, though now, when he needed to summon her most, he was distracted by a sudden bickering among his men. Their voices came through the radio in a tinny static and echoed up through the pressurized tunnel that connected the front and rear cabins. They'd been experiencing severe interference with the radio, and even their in-ship coms had been unreliable and he couldn't make out much from the general clamour.

Annoyed, and getting the anxious feeling that something might be seriously amiss among his crew, he called behind him to Private Nelson, the radio operator, and Captain Dutch, the navigator, "Any idea what the hell's going on back there?"

A moment's pause, and Nelson's uncertain voice came to him, "Don't know, sir."

Dutch said nothing, remaining focused on his instruments.

Tibbets listened as the shouting continued. It was impossible to tell what they were arguing about, though he thought the volume of the exchange had risen, taken on a violent note.

"*Boys!*" he shouted into his com. "What is going *on* back

there?" When the arguing only continued, Tibbets said, "Dutch. Crawl through to the rear cabin and tell them to cool off."

"Yes, sir," Dutch said, just as uncertain-sounding as Nelson. He climbed up into the pressurized tunnel and scurried toward the rear cabin. He might have been halfway there when Tibbets heard him call to the men, though what he said was drowned out by the engines.

The voices quieted, and a moment later Dutch returned.

"What was all that about?" Tibbets said.

"Well, I'm not exactly sure, sir. It might just be the jitters coming out."

Tibbets frowned. "The *jitters?* Since when is my crew made up of children?"

He exchanged a look of incredulity with his co-pilot, but Lewis quickly turned his attention back to his instruments as if he hadn't looked at him at all. Lewis had been like this since they'd departed from Tinian three hours before—withdrawn, uncommunicative, going about his duties mechanically. On one hand, Tibbets couldn't really fault the man, considering that the Enola Gay was his regularly assigned aircraft and he'd been ousted in favour of Tibbets at the eleventh hour.

Still, while the Superfortress was his to command, he expected—and needed—his men to act like men, like soldiers. He'd been given the command because he'd logged more test flight hours than anyone else, and was already an experienced B-29 pilot. It was only fair. It was for the greater good of the mission. And the mission itself was for the greater good, of all.

He was opening his mouth to bring the thorny subject into the open when a renewed commotion from the rear cabin reached them through the com. This time, the static interference in the radio had quieted and he could make out several individual voices:

"Maybe Little Boy *isn't* the best answer we can give to the Axis—all we've been hearing about for months is their dabbling in things nobody should touch—"

"Listen to this kid—scared of fairy tales. Go back to the nursery and your momma's tit, the army's no place for—"

"He's right, Morris—the Nazis have been using *something* in the war and it ain't just Panzers. Explain Stalingrad, then? That should have belonged to the Russians! But the whole city *wiped out.* How do you *explain* that? And the few that made it out alive, and pilots flying over the city, all reporting—"

"*Shellshock* is all those poor bastards were reporting, you dummy. But if you believe in monsters and other enemy propaganda, be my guest—I got your answer to the Axis locked up in the bomb bay right here."

"So we escalate the war like *this?* An *atomic bomb* is the answer? What's the ratio of Jap military to *civilians* down there? Use what little brains you—"

A burst of static noise buried the voices.

Hearing the exchange had caused a clammy sweat to break out on Tibbets' palms—his men had given voice to the conflicted voices inside himself. It was a shock to his system to hear the argument put forth at all, let alone with such passion, such *anger.* It was the worst thing he could have heard at that time, because it fed all of the self-doubt that had been gnawing at him ever since he'd been assigned the mission, and that he'd succeeded so well in hiding; even before, in fact, during each of his test flights, during conversations he'd had over the months with friends and fellow soldiers, some patriotic, some pacifist, others arguing from a more universal, humanitarian perspective. He'd told himself that morality didn't exist in warfare, and he'd mostly convinced himself. The façade he'd been wearing so well felt, for the first time, as though it had a chink forming in it.

Even worse, his crew's argument awoke the embarrassing superstitious dread he felt whenever the subject came up of the enemy's rumoured use of experimental sciences—some went so far as to claim they used arcane magic—and the supposed things it summoned to help their cause. He'd seen the grainy images, though, photographed on battlefields in Russia, France, showing things he couldn't deny. Gargantuan and hulking and utterly alien, and certainly not images of machines or men. He tried to convince himself that they were hoaxed, part of the Axis propaganda machine, but logic only went so far when his heart believed; the Axis represented true evil, after all—didn't it make sense that they should have forged an alliance with unspeakable things like these?

A prolonged shudder of turbulence roused Tibbets from his reverie. He shook his head, clearing his thoughts. He eyed the com, which continued to crackle with the heated argument between his crew. Fury boiled up in him. Of all times to be betrayed by his men, this was by far the most treasonous. Over halfway to their objective, and the greatest gambit in the Allies' bid for victory, and his crew was fighting like drunks on shore-leave.

He unbuckled his safety harness, stood from his seat, and said curtly to Lewis, "Take over. This bullshit ends now. We have a job to do."

It was at that precise moment that the daylight was put out.

And with the sudden pall of darkness, there came a great roaring that swallowed the sound of the Superfortress' engines completely.

II

"Sweet Jesus, what in the hell are we seeing?"

Tibbets distantly registered the sound of assistant weaponeer Jeppson's voice coming through the com amid the static noise. He was the only one of them to say anything in the moment of shock that followed the great voice booming in the darkness, shaking the bomber—a god-voice.

In the cockpit and front cabin, Tibbets gawked along with his crewmen, disbelief vying with horror, and a kind of fear that was new to them all. Unlike the fear they'd all experienced during combat, which was rooted in something they'd been trained to deal with, this new fear came from the overwhelming sense of the unknown that confronted them. This catalyst of fear came from outside of them all—from outside the experience of men.

It took a moment for their eyes to adjust to the sudden gloom, but little by little they understood that a light was in fact present, filtering from somewhere above them to illuminate the landscape through which they flew: one transformed utterly. Gone was the wide-open panorama of the ocean glittering in the early morning sunrise, replaced with a vista so absolute in its singularity—so alien to anything the men had ever seen—that it truly felt like they were in another world; the plausibility of which sent a quiver of dread snaking along Tibbets' spine. He goggled at the vision, taking in the details one by one.

A series of colossal structures rose from the darkness below to tower overhead. These stretched seemingly without limit into the nebulous distance before them and, indeed, were so densely concentrated that Tibbets found it necessary to make constant small adjustments in their flight path to navigate among them. Like immense pillars, their twisted contours were nearly as breathtaking as their monumental size. The maze of channels that covered some of these were deep enough for the Superfortress to have entered; while other columns were furred in what appeared to be a lush carpet of green and red mosses.

Slowly, Tibbets recognized the inherently geological quality of the structures and imagined that they must have been created through some cataclysmic tectonic event. Behind him, Nelson's and Dutch's whispered conversation came to him.

"They look like what do ya call it—dryads. All those twisty sections, there and there." This was Ferebee, the bombardier, from his place at the front of the cockpit.

"What the hell's a dryad, Ferebee?"

"These things from old myths."

"It looks like bark to me, but super-sized."

With a start Tibbets understood what it was he was looking at: trees, though on a scale that defied belief. It was their sheer size that made them completely alien to the men. Beside these trunks, the Superfortress was like a mosquito buzzing through a forest of redwoods.

"You got it Nelson—they're trees," Tibbets said, awe in his voice.

There were gasps from the men around him.

"But…how?" said Dutch.

"I don't know," Tibbets said. "But look up there."

He'd been slowly steering them to a higher elevation, after catching a glimpse of something overhead that disturbed him—a shape, a structure, where clouds and empty sky might have been, especially given the light source that came from above.

They were flying close enough to it now that the bombers' outboard lights shone a faint illumination among the complex latticework of shapes, which also seemed lighted faintly from above, presumably by the sun. Like before, it took a moment for his brain to accept that he was looking at foliage; colossal vegetation-laden branches, dense with green and amber leaves and shoots, hung with roots and creepers, but all on a scale relative to the trees that spawned them. Scattered among this verdure were titanic night-black flowers that dwarfed the Superfortress. Tibbetts realized with a sinking feeling in his gut that these were counterparts to the much smaller flower he'd discovered in the cabin earlier.

Like a roof over the world, this dark, shimmering flora stretched overhead as far as the eye could see.

The radio crackled and Jeppson's voice came through:

"Jesus, are you guys seeing this, sir?"

"We're seeing it," murmured Tibbets.

Though the density of the canopy still stifled the sunlight, they were entering a stretch where it pierced through in places in long golden spears that cut the gloom. This only accentuated the nearly palpable darkness, creating a staggering sense of isolation. It was almost as if they were no longer outside, but moving within some vast subterranean space, with the added claustrophobic feeling of being surrounded on all sides by the monolithic trees. Curtains of vines hung down in places now, each tendril as thick around as an oak tree, adding a further obstacle for the bomber to navigate in the gloom.

"Let's see what we've got downstairs," Tibbets said, announcing his intention as he slowly descended. Soon, they came to a zone of low-lying mist—lit by the outboard lights, it shifted and swirled uneasily. After a minute, it thinned out considerably and Tibbets saw a landscape of great grass stalks swaying in the wind. The blades were relative in size to the trees, and so likewise were larger than the bomber.

After a few minutes, the grass thinned in places and Tibbets saw with a rush of relief that the ocean was still there, the waves reflecting the dim light in iridescent flashes. He watched the flashes, mesmerized, the only anchor in this otherwise unrecognizable vision they now found themselves in. The grass continued to poke up through the water at irregular intervals, making for an odd juxtaposition of elements, the ocean seemingly belonging to the world they knew and yet looking like the gentle lapping of water at the shoreline of a creek when set against the colossal grasses and trees towering from the depths. Logically—scientifically—Tibbets knew this made no sense. But there it was.

The Enola Gay was, inconceivably and yet undeniably, flying through what appeared to be a great and alien wilderness, megaflora for a world of giants.

They flew on, all conversation ceased among them. He wove the plane among the trees and curtains of vines, while each of the men considered in stunned silence the incomprehensible puzzle of their situation.

And then the great voice boomed once more throughout that landscape, shuddering the Superfortress' frame. They listened to it thunder on and on, robust and menacing, lasting almost half a minute before rapidly dwindling in volume and finally disappearing.

In the wake of it, several of the men burst out with oaths. Tibbets realized he'd been trying to convince himself that the voice had been something directly related to the blackout, the catalyst for the transformation of the landscape around them—and so a one-time occurrence. A massive warhead detonated, something similar to Little Boy, maybe. Another type of new, experimental weapon. Something rational, even if on a scale beyond what they'd seen before. Something explainable.

But no. The voice had returned, whatever its source, and it was an undeniable element of this new world.

And that's exactly what it was, Tibbets knew, having heard it again: a *voice* thundering from the void.

The crew was peering from every available window and porthole, trying to find its source. There was nothing out there but the endless labyrinth of trees, though Tibbets had a sense the sound had come from below them somewhere. Wherever and whatever its source, he'd noted that the second time it had been distinctly louder than the first.

They were getting closer to it.

In the wake of the voice, another sound soon came to haunt the night-darkness: an incessant buzzing that grew louder and louder as they flew on, until it was nearly unbearable. It was punctuated by loud cracking sounds, like firecrackers going off in a bed of autumn leaves.

"I feel like my head's inside a shorted telephone wire," whispered Dutch.

Nobody replied.

A shadow threw the cockpit into full darkness, and was gone an instant later. Before the men could so much as exchange startled looks it came and went away again. And again, the third time with an accompanying heavy thud from somewhere along the top of the bomber's armoured hull. The impact was strong enough that it knocked the plane off-course slightly.

Tibbets said, "I'm taking us down lower."

Lewis nodded, face expressionless, eyes focused and searching the darkness outside the window.

Another shadow blanketed the cockpit, and this time Tibbets got a clearer impression of its speed and size. Something was racing past the Superfortress—something huge.

"What the Hell is it?" shouted Ferebee, rigid in his seat, up close to the armoured glass in the plane's nose.

"I don't know, but it wasn't a plane," Lewis said.

Tibbets knew it hadn't been a plane, either—he'd caught a fleeting, blurred glimpse of a long cigar-shaped body, and clusters of segmented appendages beneath…

They were navigating a particularly dense area of the wilderness and, passing close between a pair of trees, the plane's outboard lights caught the trunks at close range. And so their lights caught full-on the host of creatures clinging to the bark everywhere.

"Oh my God," said Ferebee, throwing his hands in front of his face. "What are they?"

As with the details of the trees, it took the men a moment to grasp what it was they were seeing, to extrapolate its normal Earthly counterpart from the supernormal scale of the creatures. They were insects, grasshoppers, Tibbets thought, though they might as well have been armoured spacecraft from Mars.

"Grasshoppers," he answered Ferebee. "But ones to match this place."

"Locusts."

Tibbets turned to Lewis. "What was that, Lewis?"

The co-pilot was staring at the insects with wide eyes.

"They're locusts. The locust swarm—my great army that I sent among you."

Tibbets eyed Lewis a moment, unnerved by this odd behaviour from such a steady man. But of course their situation was enough to rattle the best of men, so he let it pass, and turned back to his instruments.

They dwarfed the bomber. And even as he said it, one of the insects scudded past them again, its shadow drenching the cockpit in darkness, its relentless buzz-sawing voice filling the cabin. This one had flown from behind the bomber and alighted on a tree directly ahead of them. Having had the opportunity of watching its flight clearly, Tibbets marvelled at the creature's vast wings, and the unexpectedly slow beating of those wings—on one hand, it seemed remarkable that they carried the gargantuan insect, but on the other hand, the sheer power in their movement was undeniable.

Tibbets didn't hear what his men were shouting, though he of course knew the gist—he was seeing the creatures with his own eyes, in all of their ultra-magnified horror. Luckily, though, the insects didn't seem interested in the bomber. They were left more or less alone as they continued on their way and, soon enough, they'd left the swarm behind them. But something troubled Tibbets about the encounter, something beyond the obvious otherworldly terror of it. After a moment it came to him.

"Grasshoppers don't live on the ocean," he said.

Lewis turned to him questioningly. The silence from the crew told Tibbets he had their collective attention.

"It's a fact that there's no insects on the open oceans, except for those water jumper things, but even those are rare."

"So, what's it mean?" asked Stiborik in the com.

"I don't know for sure, Joe," admitted Tibbets. "But if that is the Pacific down there—which we're going to find out for sure soon enough if we hit Japan like we're supposed to—then it's almost like…it's like our world is here, but there's all of this—what looks like a new world—mixed together with it. Superimposed on it."

It sounded insane. It *was* insane. But it was an insanity Tibbets shared with the entirety of his crew, which gave it its reality. His men understood this too, he knew, because rather than deny the wildness of the idea, he listened as they began an earnest discussion of it. The part of him still lucid enough to note such things found himself pleased that they were working together again like the efficient unit they'd been before the insanity had commandeered their mission.

During a lull in the debate, Dutch said, voice hushed, "Let's hope we don't see any of the birds in this place."

His words hung like poison gas in the claustrophobic space, deadly and unavoidable. Nobody wanted to consider the logical train of thinking that led from the monstrous insect that had nearly collided with the Superfortress to the next step up in the chain of predators. But the longer they thought about it, the truth of it became unarguable.

"Better birds than what I'm seeing coming up," said Ferebee.

They followed where he looked.

It was most noticeable where the mammoth vegetation grew thinnest; where what appeared to be a different stratum lay entwined among the branches. This surface was a mottled grey-black and appeared rocky, though the longer the men examined it, the more they recognized the sinuous quality of the whole structure. As with the insects, their minds needed time to process and accept the scope of this detail, its vastness stretching out of sight ahead of them, in order to see it for what it was: scaled, ridged…and moving. Shifting subtly among the mottled greenery, and belonging to something decidedly alive.

It was Tibbets, telling himself to act the part of commanding officer, who dared to first utter the incredible truth. "The texture of it, and the way it moves…And if you look at it in the distance, the way it sways in different places, I'd swear that it looks like…It's moving. It's *living*. It's a *living thing*."

The next logical questions remained unspoken among the crew—how large exactly *was* the thing? And did it pose a danger to them? Tibbets was tempted to edge a little closer to get a clearer look at it but knew he wouldn't—both fear and his responsibility to his men and the mission urged him to stick to caution. But he was brave enough to say it out loud:

"It's a snake."

No crew member of the Enola Gay said anything.

They flew on, a prayer in the darkness of this strange place.

III

Theirs was a predicament to overwhelm the mind and the heart, and so the men turned their attention to the familiarity of manning their stations, or bent to the pull of staring out into the new landscape in mute awe.

Seargent Caron's voice crackled from the com, startling Tibbets. "Let me have a shot at that ceiling, sir. I'll try to take out a chunk of it—make a way through." He was their tail gunner, the man responsible for the sole gun the refitted bomber had. Like Dutch, he'd tried to sound courageous, but nobody was buying it.

"Not a chance, Bob," Tibbets was quick to say, grateful for the distraction of countermanding Caron, the seeming normalcy of acting out his role of commanding officer. He was much more grateful that they'd passed beyond the unthinkable monstrosity among the trees— and that it hadn't pursued them, though being as small next to it as the Enola Gay was likely meant that they were beneath the thing's notice. The idea led Tibbets to wonder whether the opposite scenario had come to pass—that they had, through some incredible process, been shrunken down in size and were experiencing their own world on this new scale? But really, it amounted to the same thing, he knew: they were completely insignificant here. Whatever the case, caution was best at times like this. "It looks way too dense to get the job done right with the gun we've got. We'll keep going and wait for a break in the trees."

Because logically speaking there had to be a break at some point, right? Though a second thought harried this first one: why would logic work here in a world that looked as alien as this, and that had taken over the former world in the literal blink of an eye?

Tibbets shook his head in wonder at the lunacy of the conversation, then accepted that the madness of their situation did nothing to alter their mission: the horror outside the plane might be alive, but until his superiors told him otherwise, they were still going to drop Little Boy on Hiroshima.

It was ten minutes later when the trees thinned out somewhat and naked sky could be glimpsed. He scanned the stars and immediately saw something amiss. Not wanting to alarm his men without reason, he called to Dutch in the cabin behind him.

"Dutch, what are you reading?"

"Not much, sir." He tapped his instruments. "Still dead back here."

"We've come up on some holes in the ceiling," Tibbets said. "I need confirmation on where we are. Take a look from the astrodome."

The navigator looked rooted to his chair as he digested Tibbets' order, then came to. "Yes sir." He moved rigidly, fear making every step he took come grudgingly. In his absence, the men only continued to stare out the windows in silence, into the nearly impenetrable darkness ahead.

When Dutch returned from the observation station a few minutes later he lingered in the pressured tunnel, avoiding Tibbets' questioning eyes.

"Nobody said we live in a sane world," he dared to quip, though his voice was low, scared, merely the mechanical response to crisis he'd long ago become accustomed to giving, though now devoid of bravado. He added, "It's definitely…this place…"

"Dutch?" Tibbets had never known the man to be uncertain in expressing himself.

"I don't recognize things upstairs, sir. It's like some of the stars are in the right place, but then all the others aren't. It doesn't make sense. I got just a quick look because the canopy was back not long after I got up there, but from what I saw, I don't know where we could be."

Tibbets nodded. He considered turning around so that Dutch might get a better look at the stars, and possibly make an educated guess as to their position. But logic dictated that, with diminishing fuel and no clear sense of whether Japan still lay ahead of them—or Tinian waited behind—they needed to stay their course, and hope the mishmash of the stars was the same when it came to the geography of this place so that, among the new and alien, they'd find the old, too.

"Thanks, Dutch. That's a big help. Everything you saw confirms what we've been seeing down here—there's the old mixed with the unfamiliar. We'll…We'll figure this out." Tibbets was turning away when the navigator cleared his throat.

"Sir. I don't understand it, sir, but…I found this in the dome."

Dread awakened in Tibbets as he stared at the massive black flower the navigator held in his hand, and with it the overwhelming knowledge that the unknown had now truly infiltrated the meagre illusion of safety that was the Superfortress. This specimen was larger even than the first one Tibbets had found in the cockpit, its petals as long as the arm of the man that held it.

"The dome's full of them," Dutch said in a tremulous voice. "I had to fight my way through them to get a good view. Flowers and vines. Sticking to the walls and the dome glass. They…they weren't there when we took off."

Tibbets saw that the vision had summoned Lewis' attention, too—his co-pilot stared in silent horror at the flower Dutch held.

When he met Tibbets' eyes, it was to guide him with a wordless nod, to look to the floor. There, between the two men's chairs, were clusters of the flowers. These grew on thick black vines that clung to the sides of their chairs and instrument consoles. The skin of the vines was pocked with deadly-looking black thorns.

Tibbets swore under his breath. "Jesus, what the hell is going on?"

Lewis stared at the flowers a moment longer, then returned his attention to his instruments.

"Sir. Guys."

Tibbets, as if in a dream, felt himself turn slowly, mechanically toward the voice.

Private Nelson, the radio operator, was ashen-faced where he sat at his station, listening intently to something inside his headset. Tibbets would have been relieved that Dutch had made contact with someone if it wasn't for the expression on the navigator's face.

When Dutch looked up, his words came so quietly that the men in the front cabin leaned toward him as one, innately understanding that whatever it was he was going to tell them was important. The quiet in the com told Tibbets that those in the rear cabin were likewise riveted to Nelson, hanging on his mouse-like voice.

"I managed to get HQ on the horn for a minute. I told them our situation. And they…I asked them to repeat, because it's so…I asked them to clarify, but I heard it right the first time. It's for *real*, just like all this." He waved a hand upward, encompassing their incomprehensible surroundings. He went on, "Berlin got…Berlin's been wiped off the map. Civilians, military... Happened in the night."

"*What?*" Tibbets said. The dread now felt like icy fingers closing over his heart.

"How?" said Duzenbury, the flight engineer. The single word came muffled through his fingers where they were clamped across his mouth in a gesture of mounting panic.

Nelson was pale as a cadaver. "Sounds like some sort of situation like the one we got here." Here he turned quickly to one side and vomited beside his station. Tibbets saw the black flower clinging to the right side of his headset, as if placed there in hideous decoration. He didn't mention it to Nelson.

"I thought those bastards were using magic to fight *us…*" Stiborik's voice erupted in the com, sounding stunned.

Jeppson's voice came through, "Maybe they lost control of whatever it was they were doing? Maybe they, uh, *called* something that they didn't really understand, or…"

"Sergeant, what else did they say?" said Tibbets, as much to drown out Jeppson's and Stiborik's paranoid talk as anything else. The sergeant finished dry heaving, shoulders hunched and trembling. "Nelson," Tibbets prodded. "Look at me. Okay, now listen to me. What did HQ say *exactly?*"

Nelson wiped his hand across his mouth, brow wrinkled in studied concentration. Slowly, he said, "They called it a…*colossus*. They said a *colossus* destroyed the city. And that there's nothing left. Thousands dead. And that's all I got because then the radio died again. I wasn't able to raise them again. What…what does it mean, sir?"

Tibbets continued staring at Nelson until the man began to cry silently. Then he turned away, letting him have some privacy with his emotions, though Tibbets doubted it offered much comfort. He tried to dispel the images that returned to him then, the unexplainable things he'd seen in photographs, the gargantuan hulking shapes looming in the mist and smoke of battlefields and razed cities, but he wasn't able. Only a few days ago, he'd been flipping through a newspaper when he came to a black-and-white photo that chilled him, and seized his imagination though he'd wanted nothing more than to be able to close the pages and un-see it.

As with other such images Tibbets had seen, this one was grainy and indistinct, and blurry, as if the hand that had snapped it was shaking violently, though some details were clear enough. For one thing, its size was titanic, relative to the overturned personnel carrier that lay in its shadow—like a child's treasure chest at the foot of a giant.

The most horrifying quality of the thing portrayed in that photograph, doctored or not, was its distant yet undeniable approximation to the human. Humanoid in its basic structure as a bipedal being, and yet utterly inhuman with its shocking size, its bursting musculature that pushed it far beyond humanity into grotesquerie…into *otherness*. It was a human being, but so much more. A human, but not. A humanoid, and yet the term did nothing to remotely define its supernormal characteristics. The only fact that seemed certain was that it stood at a scale that was inconceivable.

And what Tibbets had initially thought might have been an array of long curved horns erupting from the figure's head, he wasn't so sure about the second and third time he scanned the picture, while his friends were at the bar getting drinks or hitting the bathroom. From a certain angle, with a certain skewing of the imagination, they could have been ornamental, a headdress; or maybe a primitive crown or helmet. The photographed figure held some indistinct object—a piece of machinery maybe, or a soldier like a doll, plucked from some battlefield or trench in Russia? A veil of smoke obscured part of the image here so it was hard to be sure, but it had unnerved him.

The thought had come to Tibbets that maybe the thing *was* human, but the next evolutionary step; or many steps down the evolutionary chain. And the thought of that abomination existing in even a latent genetic coding inside of himself made him sick with revulsion. He'd been with friends in a bar when he'd come across the article and had laughed it off as more overblown Nazi scare tactics, tossing the newspaper aside, but the image had haunted his thoughts the rest of that night.

"Heads up, everyone," said Ferebee.

The skyscape above the tree canopy changed suddenly, and shockingly.

The tangled latticework of the forest canopy fell away, and a star-stitched sky stretched out above them. The brightness was almost blinding following their passage through the gloom-soaked forest, due in a large part to the moon—beyond being full, it loomed much closer than Tibbets had ever seen before. He was grateful for its light, though the sight of it—once again, the familiar tainted with the strange—made him uneasy.

But even as relief at having broken free from the oppressive clutches of the forest came over the men, it was crushed by the alien nature of the vista they'd entered: the same confusing array of familiar and unfamiliar stars.

Adding to this alien environment was a colony of the giant flowers, these somewhat taller than those they'd seen in the forest. The chief difference in these, though, was their colour: they were white. The Superfortress was flying close among them, and the men were startled by the glaring white petals. Tibbets wondered about the jagged red structures embedded in their centres, like skeletal trees or sea anemones preserved in amber. He stood from his chair, straining to get a clear glimpse through the overhead window, dismayed to have to pull a flower-covered vine from where it clung to the glass. The whispery noise it made as he pried it loose sounded far too much like an exhalation of breath and Tibbets flung it to the floor in revulsion.

He was just easing back into his pilot's seat when Nelson's voice, hushed with terror, came from the front cabin.

"*Oh my God.* Eyes. Those are *eyes*. Like the flowers in here."

Meaning flooded into Tibbets' apprehension, and he took in the sight of the gargantuan orbs watching them in their tiny Superfortress bomber. The men jumped when a long fleshy mass in the eye closest to them—its lid—came sliding across the surface from top to bottom; a moment later, it slid back in the opposite direction, revealing the eye again with its snarled networks of vessels, its black iris watching them coldly.

On the heels of this latest of horrors came Ferebee's exclamation from the nose of the plane: "Look!"

The crew members found him staring out of the window with his fingers clutching at his hair and exchanged spooked looks. Tibbets, frustrated that he wasn't able to see what his radio operator apparently did, shouted at the man.

"Ferebee! What is it? Tell me what you see."

"Stairs."

They looked together. Nelson hadn't imagined it: it was indeed a staircase rising from the centre of the ocean ahead of them, and climbing up as far as the naked eye could see; dwindling with distance but rising and rising to disappear—as impossible as it was to accept—among the stars.

As they drew closer to the structure, they saw that each step was like an airfield that the Enola Gay could easily have landed on had they chosen. But they flew on past the staircase, desperate to understand, but afraid to do anything other than stick to their course.

IV

They flew onward.

The giant eye-flowers lay scattered everywhere. Fearing their proximity, Tibbets guided the bomber to a slightly higher altitude. He found, though, that the change in altitude did anything but offer him comfort, as the increased distance from the things only confirmed their reality by granting him a greater perspective of their size.

He could sense the growing anxiety of his crewmates, except for Lewis, who continued going about his work methodically, and just as removed emotionally from his interaction with Tibbets as he had been since they'd embarked.

"Lewis," Tibbets said, the need to break through his co-pilot's distant veneer overcoming him. "Your thoughts?"

From beside him, eyes watching his instruments, Lewis replied, "Sir?"

Tibbets watched Lewis, his hope for finding comfort or clarity in conversation with him flagging. "Your thoughts, Lewis. What do you make of all this?"

Lewis frowned pensively. When he spoke, it was with quiet precision. "It's out of the ordinary, sir. We're dealing with it in as satisfactory a way as we can. I'm sure General Spaatz would commend you."

Tibbets sighed, shaking his head in frustration, disbelief. *Out of the ordinary, Lewis? Well, that was putting it a touch fucking mildly, wasn't it?* He resisted getting into that with Lewis, though he knew he should; should have right from the outset of the mission, in fact. He reminded himself that each of the men, himself included, was dealing with their extraordinary circumstances in whatever way they could in order to preserve their calm—maybe Lewis was handling the situation by barricading himself behind this aloof and efficient front. Tibbets had heard it, though, the unveiled antagonism of Lewis' mentioning General Spaatz commending him, another jab at him for being given command of the mission.

Beyond the anger he felt, Tibbets couldn't quite believe that his co-pilot could still be acting this way given their current plight. He considered the nature of human frailties, the self-absorbed ambitions of men, and how trivial—how utterly *unimportant*—such pursuits were when seen against the magnitude of the world, the unknowable mysteries of the universe. He remembered a time—

The commotion startled Tibbets from his thoughts—a combination of Dutch's sudden screaming and the flurry of movement as the navigator stomped frantically on something in the floorspace between his chair and Nelson's station. Beside him, Nelson cowered, feet pulled up onto his chair as if he were afraid to touch the floor.

Tibbets hurried over, trying to calm Dutch with a hand on his arm. "Dutch! Hey! What is it?"

Dutch gave one final stomp of his heavy boots and uttered a lingering guttural cry, then sagged against Tibbets. The captain stared, and shuddered: there, crushed to a pulpy ruin by Dutch's boots, was one of the flowers, though this specimen differed markedly from the others: in place of an iris was a perfectly round amber eye which, even in its crushed state, oozing pus-like ichor, still turned about in its bed of black petals to behold the men with a venomous glare.

Does it think, Tibbets found himself wondering, even as he felt the thing's alien sentience scrutinize him. *What is it thinking when it sees us?*

Dutch's sobs stirred Tibbets, and he hurriedly threw a towel over the thing before delivering it one final, obliterating stomp that made his stomach heave. The men continued to stare at the towel as the pool of soupy yellow liquid widened around it, ignoring the questions of the crewmen from the rear cabin who had heard the disturbance through the com.

"Sir?"

Tibbets looked up to find his weaponeers watching him from the pressurized tunnel, Parsons up front and Jeppson visible just behind. Parsons' eyes were unsettlingly calm, but his voice was hushed with awe.

"See, sir? Do you see what Little Boy is? A *key*. To the same door Germany already opened. This is *it*. The end-times. Things have been heading toward this moment for years now. If they knew the weapon we had, they'd probably have *asked* us to use it on one of their cities."

The circumference of the tunnel, Tibbets saw, was lined with flowers, huge and black-petaled, impossible but real, a new element in this new world. Even as he watched his men, one of the flowers opened an eye, swivelling in its bed of petals to appraise the men.

Jeppson noticed the eye, too, started, but then relaxed. He said, "They started waking up in the rear cabin a few minutes ago, sir. We killed a couple but there's too many now. They haven't done any harm, just watch us and creep us out."

Parsons went on like before. "I'm telling you, sir. Little Boy is a key, and the end-times are—"

"No!" There was a desperate anger in Tibbets' voice. "Cut this bullshit doom-talk! It's been giving me a headache since Tinian with you monkeys arguing in the rear cabin. We have a job to do, and we're going to carry it out to the letter. And that's *all* it is: another mission. A damn important one, yes, but a mission we're going to finish. Stop attaching such importance to yourselves and your damn theories."

But there were tears threatening to well in Tibbets' eyes as he said it, all of this military rhetoric he'd been taught to believe in, *had* believed in—so when had that changed? *Had* it changed? The world, and his place in it, had never been confusing like this before.

She was conjured in his muddled thoughts the way she often appeared to him. He wanted to make her proud: his mother had always believed in him and supported his pursuits. He didn't want to let her down so profoundly. The key he held—if Little Boy was indeed that—was supposed to open a different door altogether from the one Jeppson and Parsons were prophesying; one that opened onto a new era of peace following the past years of global conflict.

As the incomprehensible Berlin situation became a reality in the men's minds, compounding the madness of their own predicament, they each dealt with it in their own way. Several simply looked out the windows and began an ongoing muttering, more monkeys than men, only another regression during the endlessness of the war. Others took what small refuge they could in silence, a ghostly glaze in their eyes as they looked inward, to the people they were, or had believed themselves to be. And here was Tibbets, acting the part of commanding officer in this remade world, barking orders as though he meant it, a man who knew his place and what needed to be done so that—

The great roaring erupted again.

Like being inside a thunderhead, it cracked the sky. It was so loud it felt like a tangible force, shuddering the Superfortress, shaking the men's skeletons inside their skins. It lasted longer than the previous times, going on and on and on: a sound of unbridled power. And Tibbets would have sworn he heard it—a distinct, primal note of triumph inside the bedlam of it; the voice of a hunter overwhelming its prey; a voice far greater than they were in their flimsy flying machine; a god-voice mocking them for their efforts, their futile purpose.

As the voice tapered off, the crew looked around themselves mutely, as if confirming that their companions had shared the experience. After a moment, the men simply stared off through the windows again, watching the strange stars above, the roiling surface of the ocean glimpsed below, their reflections in the window glass, the flowers clinging to their chairs or uniforms; or peering inward and moving down personal paths of remembrance, looking back into simpler times.

Tibbets wondered if men could—or even should—be brave in a world with terrors like these: stairs leading from the stars to the ocean, and bombs harnessing the power of the sun to kill like no man-made weapon that came before. These different judgment days. Could he equate bravery with the mass death-dealing locked up in the plane's bomb bay? Did he have the right to wield this power? Was he playing God or Devil by unleashing Little Boy on a sleeping Japanese city? What was Little Boy when set against these other horrors being unleashed in the world? Were Parsons and Jeppson right? Was their atomic weapon only another enabling force pushing the conflict toward some unfathomable, irrevocable end for all? What waited at the summit of this colossal staircase?

Even as he thought this, Dutch, remarkably calm-sounding, said, "Sir. My guess is that we're approximately thirty minutes from target."

Thirty minutes from Hiroshima—the designated time had arrived to arm Little Boy.

Tibbets turned meaningfully to Jeppson and Parsons, who were still squeezed inside the crew tunnel, watching him like a pair of Neanderthals peering from a frond-veiled cave entrance. It was their job to arm Little Boy—theirs would be the last human contact with this new and ultimate weapon before it was released from the plane's bomb bay and into the world for the first time. They held Tibbets' gaze a moment before wordlessly returning down the tunnel to complete their duty. A couple of the black flowers on the edge of the tunnel were disturbed by the men's movement, and trembled. As Tibbets was about to look away, one of the flowers' faces swiveled to reveal a horrid yellow eye—the orb darted around in its bed of black petals, as if getting its bearings before it fixed on him.

A shiver crept along the nape of his neck as he held that inhuman gaze. He managed to say without a tremor in his voice, "Nelson, Dutch. One of you—take care of that thing. And the others."

Tibbets quickly turned away, while his crewmen swore at the sight of the hideous thing. They were getting set to destroy it, when Tibbets called back to them, "Actually, cancel that. Leave them be. More of them will just take their place in no time."

Indeed, as he'd turned back into the cockpit, he was greeted with dozens of the flowers that hadn't been there minutes earlier.

When he looked at Lewis, the man only shrugged before checking on his instruments, as if to say he didn't have an answer but was getting on with his job. Good man, good soldier, thought Tibbets.

He looked out into the dense darkness, and realized after a moment that he was able to make out a darker mass in the distance: the Japanese mainland coming within range. He recognized the land, even though the colossal trees now encircled the coastline; several dozen of them had even taken root on the land mass itself.

It took a moment longer for his mind to fathom the nature of a new light source coming up below them, one that allowed him to see the mainland so clearly: a series of dark masses spread out in a wide line, encased in a vivid golden effulgence, which were surging inexorably toward Japan, casting the tossing waves of the Pacific into weird, otherworldly relief.

Ferebee's voice drifted from the nose of the cockpit: "Sir? What *are* they?"

Tibbets watched a moment longer, unable to find his voice.

My God, there you are, he thought, awed, humbled by what he saw.

V

Giants.

The ones who ruled in this incomprehensible mega-Eden. It was only appropriate that they rode in vessels as magnificent as these.

Their design was reminiscent of ancient galleons, though, as all things in this new world, on a scale that boggled the mind—each ship taking up so much room in the water that the fleet of them stretched out of sight on either side of the bomber. Each ship was made of a brilliant gold, the group of them together creating a shimmering light that pushed back the night.

The longer they watched, the men realized their monolithic size—an aircraft carrier could fit tidily in the bow of any one of them. The V-shaped waves that billowed out in their wake were high enough to drown ships of the old world.

Several members of the host flanked each vessel, sitting astride some sort of leviathan whose topmost portion alone emerged from the water. Judging from what little he could make out, Tibbets estimated that the creatures made the blue whale look like goldfish. Indeed, he reasoned that beside these gargantuan ships, the Superfortress bomber was like a whalesucker skimming unnoticed among a school of whales.

The giants didn't seem to notice the Enola Gay as it passed over their ranks. Even when Tibbets guided the Superfortress down a little closer to them—though still far out of arm's reach. The plane was like an insect buzzing around them, unworthy of their attention.

Tibbets used the binoculars to scan the ranks of the giants massed on the deck of the nearest vessel. They wore no clothing, no armour or ornamentation. They needed none. They were warrior enough to go into battle with their bodies alone, their hands the weapons to vanquish weaker kingdoms and their armies of boys playing at being men.

The longer Tibbets watched them, the more he saw that the giants radiated a god-like quality that couldn't be denied. He'd never felt so insignificant in his life. He panned from one giant to another to another, and confirmed what the view from a higher elevation had only suggested: the giants were human, but also…more.

Their faces were each different but each singularly beautiful. And yet, there was something in this beauty that Tibbets found repellent. He stared entranced, until it came to him, just as they passed the flagship and were clear of the fleet. Here he saw one of the figures leaning forward from the prow of the vessel and over the chaos of waves, raising a great silver trumpet to his lips and, puffing out his cheeks and blowing, sending out a great booming voice—the same voice that had followed the Superfortress since its entrance into this transformed world. A call into the night, declaring war.

The trumpeter—one knee raised on the golden prow of the vessel, chin thrust forward regally, was the picture of perfection, but perfection pushed into its furthest reaches, into a place where it became something else—something hideous. His clearly defined muscles rippled with strength, looking swollen with power; too large, as if his anatomy had outgrown the genetic code he had been born with and continued on at some super-accelerated pace, pushing his evolution into a new phase that was alien to the minds of men like Tibbets.

He actually had to turn away, from revulsion; and from fear. He and his crew shouldn't exist in the same world as beings like these.

The sheer size of the beings continued to astonish, no matter how long the crewmen stared. And the fact that they were unquestionably more fearsome than any man-made machines of war they had seen. Finally seeing them in the flesh put Tibbets in mind of those unexplainable photographs they'd all seen in the newspapers, showing things apprehended less in their concrete details than in their more general, overarching form; the idea of the things conveyed to the mind and the heart, and shuddering both.

"Looks like Little Boy got beat to his mission," Tibbets murmured. And besides, he thought, what was Little Boy next to the monstrosities moving toward Japan from the ocean? What power—what message—could their puny atomic warhead carry now that it shared its world with things like these? What did it all mean?

"What does it all mean?"

He was startled to find that he'd spoken the question out loud. He was even more surprised when Lewis answered.

"Maybe we're not supposed to know. Maybe…we're not able to know."

Tibbets watched his co-pilot, unsure how to respond. Lewis' words hung heavily in his thoughts, and he found himself wondering what new horror beyond their understanding would come next?

And, as if in answer to this thought, Tibbets followed where Lewis was staring, ashen-faced: Tibbets' own hand resting on the instrument console.

He told himself that, just like the others, the flower had simply materialized from the air and clung to him as it had to members of his crew, to the interior walls and outside hull of the bomber. He told himself this even as he reached out with his other hand, clasping the thick stem and, pulling, felt a resistance that went beyond the resistance he'd encountered when peeling the flower from the bulkhead. He felt the pull of the flower *inside* himself, and with a sudden calm accepted the fact that the black flower was growing from his hand. With this detached lucidity, he imagined he could feel its intricate system of root filaments merged with his own nervous system, his veins and muscles. It was part of him; or, maybe more accurately—who could say for certain—he was part of it. The world was a changing place, and they would change with it, ceasing to be what they'd been and becoming…what?

He felt Lewis still staring at him, and spoke to his co-pilot without looking at him. He kept his voice low, unheard by the others over the engines. "Lewis. Please. Let's put aside issues of rank. None of that matters anymore. That…It won't ever matter again. I need you here with me now. I need you to be honest with me. What…What would you do?"

Tibbets felt it like a weight slipped from his shoulders and presented to his companion as a burden they might share: the responsibility for their lives, an honour and a curse under most wartime situations, but here, incalculably heavier.

Lewis watched him a moment. The stoic mask he'd worn since the Enola Gay had taken off hours earlier fell away. The transformation was startling, and in its aftermath Tibbets was relieved to see the man he recognized, his friend of old.

Lewis' expression, though, was grave as he said, "You know there's only one thing to do, Paul." He paused, then added, "Sorry, Paul. I've just been…I'm scared."

Tibbets watched as Lewis undid his flight suit and turned to face him. Lewis' entire torso was thick with a garden of white flowers. Released from the confines of his clothing they burst forth, to sag downward uniformly as if bowing in humility.

"They're Lily of the Valley. In the Bible, they mean starting over."

Tibbets had never known Lewis to speak of spiritual matters. Maybe he was changing to better fit into this new world they found themselves in. Or maybe it was only the fear he'd admitted to, doing its work. Fear, the great motivator, was often a catalyst for drastic change.

Lewis looked down at himself, frowning. "But these are so big. Like everything here."

Indeed, the flowers were as large as the black flowers filling the bomber. Tibbets gestured to the flower growing from his own hand. "What do these black ones mean?"

Lewis said, "I think they're black roses. At least, they look like black roses. I think it says that they have to do with being able to overcome anything."

"If only."

"Amen."

Tibbets smiled wanly at his co-pilot, then turned to look out the cockpit.

He thought of his mother, alive in this world that men like him had helped to make; his mother, who along with his wife, had seen him off that morning, showering him with kisses and embraces, believing in his actions, believing in his goodness.

And he made his decision.

Into the com, he said, "Boys. Everybody listen up. The world's different right now than it was when we took off this morning. I need to know you're with me."

VI

They sighted it in the late afternoon: Tinian. They'd found their way back.

It remained dark as midnight. The unknown atmospheric disturbance had continued to plague them, the bomber's radio communications remaining inoperable for the rest of the homebound flight.

The unfathomable starscape had continued throughout the whole journey, though the constellations were different now than on their outbound flight. The eye-flowers had sprung up in greater profusion as well, standing vigil over the new, strange Pacific. Tibbets had kept their distance from them, and with this distance came a more comprehensive view of the things; they were all the more horrifying simply because they were instantly recognizable for what they were: slowly blinking, the orbs swinging to and fro within the flesh of their vegetal sockets, keeping ceaseless watch over the waves rolling beneath them.

The Enola Gay had also passed two more of the astonishing staircases rising from the waves and climbing, seemingly, among the stars. The first of these disappeared over one of the Aleutian Islands the bomber flew over. Pillars of smoke, small with distance, rose from the landmasses. Fires burned down there, shockingly bright in the night.

The second staircase, a few miles beyond, simply disappeared beneath the waves like the first that they'd passed, within sight of a nameless island not on any map in the old world. The ghostly opalescence in its stones made it impossible to miss in the starlight.

This ever-shifting state of the heavens and geography confirmed it in Tibbets' mind: things were in flux, a world not fully formed. And so maybe he and his crew still had a part to play in this inexplicable drama. He'd never felt so small—so insignificant—as he did in this between-place, flying in his bomber like a paper airplane tossed among giants. Would the giants rule this world? Or was something greater coming? Would it be a force of good, or the adversary to goodness?

Tibbets didn't know. How could he? He was just one man, a speck of stardust.

They spotted a second host of giants surging toward Tinian, as massive as the fleet they'd seen approaching the Japanese mainland. It was perhaps less than fifteen minutes from landfall. Seeing them helped lift a weight from Tibbets' heart. He'd made the right choice, turning back and returning here, to their base, to his family, to the start of this most important mission of his career. The great war-voice of the host preceded its arrival—Tibbets could see the trumpet-blower in his position in the ship's prow, resplendent as he leaned far out over the tumult of the waves.

Tibbets hadn't expected to see another host moving parallel to the one en route to Tinian—this other fleet, though, was sailing in the opposite direction, passing Tinian on its eastern side. Where might they be going, he wondered? Japan, maybe. The thought made sense to him—the giants would claim all lands everywhere. They were the enemy of men everywhere. Or, more likely, man was beneath their notice but they would take what land they wanted. The old rules were no more. Old allies and foes had ceased to exist. It was a new world.

The strange, alien flora that had afflicted the bomber from the beginning of its journey continued to spread. Though how it was growing, let alone at such an accelerated rate, remained a mystery: the flowers and tendrils and leaves filled the plane, crawled across every surface. The crew members were forced to constantly clear the growth from their instrument consoles, the windows. The crew tunnel was so overgrown the men had to cut through it with their knives in order to pass through; then, on heading back the same way only minutes later, the passage was filled again.

There was a brief scare when Stiborik found a scattering of the flowers clinging to the bomber's wings but, though the flora did continue to appear on the external surfaces of the plane in greater and greater abundance, it had so far stayed away from the engines and propellers. A few flowers continued to cling to the exterior of the windows—terrifyingly, the majority of these held eyes that watched the men avidly.

Like Tibbets, each of the men had reacted with the same unexpected calm when they discovered the first signs of the flora invading their bodies: flowers sprouting from scalps, vines bulging forth from throats, cactus spines stippling arms, legs, faces. As the hours wore on, they grew more and more cloaked within the weird flora, and more and more at peace with the transformation.

They'd begun to encounter others mired in the same plight as they were—several planes had passed them, three friendlies and two enemies, though the planes' markings had been nearly impossible to make out. Each was, to varying degrees, forested in the queer vegetation, wings and hull fluttering with leaves and branches, trailing clusters of vines that gave them the look of strange deep-sea anemones taken to the air; the pilots of these terraformed flyers with their faces pressed to the cockpit glass, haunted eyes peering from among the gigantic flowers. One plane, the last they'd passed, had what appeared to be a juniper tree growing from the top of its cockpit, its roots strangling the entire circumference of its hull.

The crew didn't land at Tinian, while the many military personnel, journalists and photographers who came to greet them stood about on the runway looking confused, uncertain as they watched the bomber cross the alien sky. Floodlights illuminated the area, revealing the hopeless look of the gathered people, tiny with distance, tiny set against the horrors rampant in the world. How could they look otherwise, considering the things surrounding them in the water, and with the news from Berlin fresh in the minds of the Superfortress' crew? Who knew—there might have been worse news still that the bomber crew hadn't yet learned, telling of further horrors stalking the land? In all likelihood, the thing had spread far and wide already. And if it hadn't yet, it would: what could possibly stop it?

Tibbets leaned forward in his pilot's chair, brushing the garland of flowers that now encircled his head away from his eyes, searching the people below. His face looking down on the crowd, he knew, was not the same face of the jubilant pilot who'd left half a day ago, posing for the cameras, a time that seemed a lifetime ago to everyone onboard; this man stared among those gathered below with grim, determined eyes. Of course, he couldn't pick out his mother and wife standing in the throng, but he knew they were there. He felt them. It was a comfort. He was going to save them from what was coming for them at Tinian, surging toward the island like a tidal wave, like a tempest of Biblical fury.

When his roving gaze found the large box-shape that was General Spaatz's HQ building on the far eastern perimeter of the site, he straightened in his seat in a gesture of ingrained formality. Tibbets could envision the hard, questioning look on General Spaatz's face as he followed the weirdly transformed Superfortress in the sky. It was a look he knew well. He wondered what fate had reached Japan that morning, what madness its people had faced when they looked toward the ocean bearing the darkest dreams of men.

Tibbets offered a tired, rote salute and called into the radio in a weary voice, "General Spaatz, sir. I hope you can read me. I wanted to tell you. Mission accomplished, sir."

He was going to do the only good that he possibly could.

The weaponeers, Captain Parsons and Second Lieutenant Jeppson, had removed the safety devices from Little Boy thirty minutes before reaching the island. They'd cut away the mysterious flower-festooned vines that cradled the bomb in their tight, black embrace. Hearing their commander's words now—their signal—they released Little Boy.

Tibbets turned the Enola Gay in a steep plunge that followed in the wake of the bomb. He closed his eyes, the black roses growing from his body trembling in anticipation.

Thank you, mother.

VII

And a sun burned brightly over Tinian, helping to usher in the final darkness the world of old would know.

Peace Machines

It had been another long day of toil beneath the perennially rust-coloured sky. The ridding pit gave its final convulsions of his shift, swallowing down its mouthful of eliminated. Their dying screams echoed in the tired shell of his skull, as they always did.

Bin wiped a filthy hand across his face, breathing heavily from his exertions on the deposit station platform. The air he gulped was flinty and sooty, and he longed for his clean quarters ten miles beneath the crust of the earth. His strong blue pulse of earlier in the shift had waned considerably: he was tired. He felt his work in his bones. He'd been a feeder for too many years and wasn't sure how much longer he could hack the labour. And that was only the physical weight of the years—never mind what it had done to his mind, though this he kept to himself; and, of course, Lolisr. He was fortunate, to have a partner with whom to share his deep-private thoughts.

He dismissed his small team and began gathering his tools. The other feeders trundled off in silence, too tired for conversation. Like Bin, they pulsed a wan blue of weariness. It had been a busy day. Bin was turning to follow them into the subterranean corridor, past the next feeder team milling there prior to the commencement of their shift when a small thudding sounded in the tubing leading down to the collecting box. He followed the long curve of the tube trailing into the sky and disappearing, far above, into the belly of the immense collection ship docked at the ridding station. It cast a great shadow over the platform, and though working beneath that shadow all day long had gone as usual the sight of the ship now sent a shudder of despondence through Bin. This was a peculiar reaction, he considered, a little stunned. Then he reasoned that he was very tired, so perhaps it wasn't that strange a response after all.

The noise in the tubing concluded with a metallic crash inside the large box and, professional that he was, Bin paused and set his gear down. He motioned to the next team to hold off, several of whom saw and were making their way forward to offer assistance, pulsing the deep icy blue of work-diligence and emotional detachment. He quickly swung the steel door open, reached in and efficiently grabbed the first of the pair of creatures with one hand while batting its appendages away from his arm with the lasher in his left. He kicked the gate-control switch at the base of the box, sending its gridded steel door sliding from top to bottom, trapping the second of the pair in the box.

He hefted the baby Trillip, holding it steady with practiced ease despite its flailing appendages, and quickly swung about to drop it shrieking over the steel lip of the deposit station platform. Its cry echoed back up to him, its acidic expulsions spattering on the air, across the protective skin of his gloves and suit.

He winced at the chittering clamour, young and terrified, and at the frantic cries of its still-living counterpart locked in the box and witnessing the death of its fellow through the bars of the gate. Maybe it had simply come at the worst possible time, after his shift had already concluded following a very long and arduous work day. Death-dealing on a slow day could be difficult, after all, let alone at the conclusion of a particularly busy one. The endless shifts of multiple-species deliveries took their toll on any devoted servant of the Ganshars.

"Shut up!" he screamed, his voice ragged.

He looked up, startled at his outburst, to find the silhouettes of the security detail standing alertly behind the window glass overhead, and the next feeder team still idling in the doorway of the corridor watching him with stoic expressions; and then Bin realized it was only the echoes of the Trillip's cries he'd heard—his own seemingly shouted words had remained in his mind only. Sometimes his inner voice tricked him into believing he'd spoken out loud, so vociferous was it. Sometimes this was more frightening to him than the idea of his having actually made such an emotional outburst.

Quickly, he kicked the gate open and reached into the holding box, grasping a thick cylindrical limb of the remaining Trillip. This one, in its terror, had succeeded in crawling up a ways into the tubing toward the futile promise of escape back the way it had come, but he pulled it down through the greased tube to flail and screech in his arms. This one—an adult, and female, he believed, though it was difficult to distinguish her female plume-colouring amid the blood leaking from her gashed skull—he was forced to stun with the lasher. She was too strong otherwise for his weary limbs. Even as the bolt coursed through the creature's body he pulled it from the box and, in a single fluid motion—veteran feeders like himself were masters of this—he tossed the creature hard over the lip of the platform. Its cries were muted somewhat from the electrical charge numbing it, but for its final terror-filled scream as it neared the teeth of the pit below—this scream bellowed up at him briefly before being cut abruptly short as the ridding pit commenced its hungry duty.

The gnashing of steel through flesh and bone sounded loudly, followed by a prolonged sizzling—the ever-present burning-voice of the ridding pits—deep within the cavity's belly.

This was good, he reminded himself, in a practised rebuking of his queasy stomach, the barely-acknowledged needling of guilt in his heart: this was one more morsel of energy to fuel the ever-expanding might of the Ganshars spreading peace among the stars.

Onwards! Onwards, for the greater good!

The deep silence of the elevator whisking him down and down and down was huge following the ceaseless noise of the ridding pit. His ears and thoughts rang with it, would continue to ring with it long into the night. He was long accustomed to it. Possibly its voice would find entry into his dreams as it often did, changing them, giving them the dark flavour that had characterized his dream-life for so many years.

He was going to quit someday, and that day was coming fast. He was eligible for retirement soon—only one more cycle of his five hundred cycles left. He was going to retire from his job at the ridding pits and use his stature to buy himself a one-way trip to a colony in the Old World's Living Vex where he would live out his days in the way of species of old. In a green and fertile place, with only the amenities offered by that place, of which there were many because riches, as his father had told him so often, came in different forms than payment for hard labour at ridding pits and war machine factories and prison holding facilities and serving dutifully with the army spreading the name and honour and wisdom and violence of the Ganshars far and wide. He would, in his later years, devote himself to scientific studies, or work, perhaps, for one of the horticultural or agricultural companies, like his beloved Lolisr.

Yes, he would be finished with his years of ridding work, and soon. His day of retirement loomed on the horizon: it was the beacon that he focused on during every final death-scream screamed in his presence, though his pride in his work never flagged.

The elevator made a satisfied-sounding exhalation and the doors whisked open. The long dim corridor of his warren-hall stretched before him. The silence of the hall made him feel as wealthy as a Ganshar high leader as he drifted toward his compartment at the far end.

The door-hummer sounded. He knew who it was before he saw her face centred on the greeting screen. She seemed always to arrive when his mind needed calming most. It was as if she *knew*.

"Lolisr," he said into the voice-channel. "Welcome." He let her in.

She hovered in the entryway, pulsing a gentle emerald. He averted his eyes. Sometimes her face—so genuinely gentle—held too much beauty for his weary eyes to bear. Too much innocence, and innocence following a workday was simultaneously amazing and difficult to bask in.

She came bearing the gift of food as she often did. She was

thoughtful and affectionate, and a skilled cooker. Her life had changed after she'd met Bin, and they'd made the decision to couple. Relocating from the central core of a small city in the Living Vex to the border region between it and the Labour Vex. The border wasn't too bad of a place, though it certainly wasn't a place of splendour like the interior of the eastern hemisphere. But then it wasn't nearly so disheartening as the Labour Vex proper. Lolisr was able to continue her scientific and philosophical studies, though here she needed a tutor, which was both expensive to her family as well as less intensive than a traditional program of study at the university. But she was happy to set aside the rigorous former curriculum of her schooling for her life-partner-to-be. As she'd told him several times over the past year, she believed that they were meant to remain together and explore and solve the great secrets as partners.

Bin, weary as he was, forced a smile of contentment and a pulse as close to an approximation of warm-green as he was able. "My Lolisr-one. What delicacy have you created and brought for us today?"

She pulsed radiantly at his greeting and, placing the hard plastic box on the foyer shelf, opened its sliding lid. A thousand aromas leapt out at him as he looked at the meal within. It was an omnivore's feast: maldow vegetables and Loo-loom meat. He found his salivary glands reacting strongly, a tingle of excitement rippling through his limbs.

"My master-master cooker," he said, and the green pulse he pulsed this time was genuinely warm, and nearly as radiant as his lover's.

After they'd dined, they copulated and after this they lay dozing together in their bodily excretions. Her voice was so soft it seemed to come from a very far place. It sounded like it came to his ears from a dream, both for its sound and what it said.

"Bin…Let's decide on our peace-place soon, and go there soon after that, and live there until our time in the world has gone…"

He closed his eyes to the beauty of her glistening body, pulsing softly red beside him, and after a time sleep came to rescue him from his turmoil of thoughts.

~

This day's batch of tossed were delivered to the holding box of ridding pit 177, Bin's placement pit for going on ten years. He heaved a sigh when he'd scanned the invoice scrolling up the tabulator sent down to him by the driver. Last-wave survivors of a major metropolis on Elam-4, all adults.

Elamians were, by and large, difficult to handle for their sheer size alone, which said nothing of their volatile nature, especially the war-seasoned military type imprisoned in the box. He could hear their collective voice of fury muffled but clear behind the impregnable titanium walls. The muted thundering was their stone-like fists pounding on the walls.

"Maffar," he called to his first assistant down the way.

"Master Ridder."

"You and Tannish distribute the heavy lashers to everyone. Key them on full. This is a tough batch."

This was the one drawback of the work done at the ridding pits—only the lowest-energy tools and weapons were allowed them to help in their duties; anything more powerful—a simple projectile gun for instance—risked setting off an explosion in the pit itself, and a consequent chain reaction among neighbouring pits. The cataclysmic energies of the pits were contained only by the sheer natural might of the planet's shell itself—letting them loose would prove apocalyptic.

This of course made the ridders a crucial piece in the military regime: it was essential that the vast energies required for the Ganshars' machines be stoked, but the volatility of those energies meant that each pit needed to be regulated to perfection, overseen by experienced ridders with both the highest level of technological expertise, as well as an inherent feel for the work. Like Bin, who could feel in his bones when one more batch of Mafreeti fed to his pit would prove too much, despite what the energy counters told, and would cause a quick-flare to rupture a pit wall. Some likened the work to handfeeding a Bokr beast: extremely dangerous no matter one's experience with deadly creatures. But sometimes this was necessary, if only to gain the beast's trust so that it could then be trained to kill your enemies in close-quarters combat.

"Yes, Master Ridder."

Bin heard the poorly concealed dismay in Maffar's voice. He felt it too. But nothing could be done about it. The work had to get done. There were many worlds and many darknesses and the work of the peacemakers never ended. For the greater good of the Ganshars. All, for the greater good.

She came to see him in the hospital ward. Of course she did. He felt her pulsing from the doorway of his room before he opened his melancholy eyes to behold her, beautiful and concerned.

"My Lolisr-one."

"Oh, my Bin-Bin." She came to him, quickly, and clung to him, careful to avoid placing pressure on his bandaged arm. Her amber pulses enveloped him like an additional medicine to alleviate his pain.

"I'm fine. You don't have anything to worry about."

She looked at him. Touched a gentle hand to the sticky white compress pasted against his temple. Despite its thickness a tiny spot darkened its centre: his blood, staunched but barely.

"What did this?"

"Elamians. Two of them broke loose before we could toss them."

She recoiled a little at the words. His casualness, as if he were engaged in work-speak with fellow feeders. He winced. She often was shocked by direct discussion of his work, though she of course knew what he did. For this reason he avoided talking to her of it, or at least tempered it with gentler language.

"I'm sorry you were worried, Lolisr. But I *am* fine. A day more of bed-rest here and a day of rest at home, and I'll be back to work."

She blinked at him, nodded in understanding, though her amber pulsing continued: the colour of despair.

~

Right back into the thick of things, his supervisor had commented to him on his way onto the platform his first day back.

Indeed, thought Bin as he looked from the invoice screen to the shuddering containment box. This batch was one of the worst species regularly encountered by the ridders. They were currently embroiled in their second worldwide war, and a continuous stream of smaller but no less violent wars ran the course of their entire recorded history, misguided by complicated political agendas and religious fanaticism: all of this in their genetic memory. Of course they were vicious. It was unfathomable but true. If ever a species epitomized pure and primal savagery, this was it. It was one of a handful of types loathed by all ridders, the only good thing about them being that eliminating them always felt especially rewarding.

"Third-planet batch, G-52," Bin confirmed when Tannish sidled up beside him to study the invoice over his shoulder. "Always difficult, one of my least favourite jobs. And frightening, to consider some of them have found the means of far-wide inter-dimensional travel."

"Among the worst and most cruel." The feeder's tone was matter-of-fact, analytic, his gaze as it scanned the electronic invoice full of disdain. "I dislike thirders."

Beside him, Bin opened the shield so that they could view the interplay behind the observation glass, evidently a scene of great drama among the creatures within. Bin keyed the com so that they could eavesdrop, the frantic furious clamour of the creatures' unintelligible voices sputtering from the speaker.

As they watched violence erupted among the creatures. Fists pummelled; feet kicked; teeth tore; fingers raked skin; and one animal voice, feral and unsettling, rose over the general hubbub, filling the containment space and spilling from the speaker to chill the spectators, for they realized that the creature was watching them through the glass, and was addressing its words to them:

"Greetings! My name is Heinrich Hassel. My rank is Captain,

Eleventh Division, Waffen SS. I implore you as one intelligent being to another, stop this, let us stop this and work together and be stronger through our collaboration. If you could see the might we wield: military, scientific, *magic*. …We found *you*, after all, didn't we? This was our mission, and I have achieved it. We *found* you! Our vision is one of peace and order, and the machine with which we disseminate it is undefeatable. I can see that you have the same vision. We are the same. *We* are the *same!*"

The being stopped talking, a manic desperation in its eyes, as it waited expectantly.

Bin, of course, could understand nothing of the language it spoke, though he was fluent in ten off-world languages (as well as a dozen local) and was able to muddle his way through at least a handful of other alien tongues. But the universe was large and here in the Labour Vex they, of course, got all kinds. And fearing the wild-eyed being and what they'd learned of its primitive legacy of bloodshed, he did what he had to in order to help clean the universe.

He opened the box's door, raised his lasher, and electrified the being into immobility. He then dragged it to the edge of the platform while Tannish slammed the gate shut. Seeing the implication of this gesture its companions raised their voices in protest, and made to struggle against their captors. Bin ignored the voices as he'd long ago taught himself to do, relegating them to the silent room in his mind where all such voices were (usually) squashed efficiently. And he hefted the being up and threw it from the platform into the peace-making mouth of the ridding pit churning far, far below.

Coincidence or luck or fate had sent Bin back toward his work station to pick up the lasher he'd forgotten there.

This in and of itself was a strange occurrence, as he wasn't forgetful at all, least of all when it came to his work, which he treated with a methodical diligence and pride. He blamed the fact that it had been a remarkably slow shift, and he and his team had only needed to use the smaller lashers, and these only for two group of beings (the Thirders; and Mitisi, a slave-race that had grown war-like following numerous rebellions against their Thirder conquerors). And so the heavy lasher, which he hadn't lifted even once, had remained neglected where he'd left it propped alongside the wall overlooking the platform at his shift's commencement. Also: it was his first day back to his job after a two-day absence, and he hadn't missed a shift in nearly ten years as a Ridder. He could be forgiven for being a little discombobulated.

The sight of her, there, in the gloomy subterranean corridor leading to the ridding pit, was surreal. He blinked hard, as if testing the reality of what his eyes told him must be a phantom-vision. But no, there she remained, pulsing an anxious pink, exposed with her shocking cargo in tow.

"Do not move, Lolisr," Bin said slowly, surprised at the level command and outrage in his voice as it boomed out across the corridor, despite the roar of the ridding pit thrumming in the walls. "What are you doing with those Skandri?"

He turned his eyes—reluctantly, as if he wished to ignore their presence but of course knew that he could not—to the small forms huddled around his beloved. Their insect's carapaces glinted in the dull overheads, their little mandibles vibrated frantically, and an electric chittering came from them. He sensed their fear, and the fear from Lolisr.

She tried to reason with him. "Bin," her voice soft-sweet and wheedling, her eyes leaking tears. "I learned what this batch was to be. I opened the tubing, between shifts." She held up a hand—a slender blade glimmered there, her tool for freeing the Skandri. He knew her background, of course, and that she'd taken a field placement in a facility devoted to studies of insectoid races considered a threat to Ganshar supremacy, of which the Skandri were regarded as one of the fiercest. Highly intelligent and technologically gifted, they'd posed an obstacle to expansion beyond the rim worlds of the solar system. They still did, even in this age of their defeat: rebel insurgents had migrated everywhere. They were bugs, after all, and everyone knew how difficult it was to exterminate quickly-reproducing vermin like these.

She went on in the same imploring voice. "Bin. Please. These are *children*. They have so much life left to live, if only we let them have it. Not all those fed into the pits deserve it, and these children least of all."

Bin frowned at the sight of her, surrounded by the diminutive creatures, their many leafy legs wrapped about her ankles and arms. He frowned at her naming of the unnamable thing, the thing of which they never spoke because the thing caused great conflict to awake in him, and this mixed-up feeling only ever threatened his livelihood, and their future peace-years together.

Always his reason triumphed over his heart. And always duty conquered the frailty of emotion, and the good work continued. But then there were times of weakness, apparently even in those most reliable servants to the Ganshars.

"Go," he heard himself saying, knowing in the moment he'd spoken that he'd made a mistake.

"Thank you, Bin-Bin," she said, instantly pulsing a green of deepest gratitude and warmth. "Your mercy will be rewarded, love-love."

He watched her as she shuffled forward, ushering the younglings before her. Her smell of simi leaf and lullur oil washed over him as she passed him in the narrow space. The pulsing came from her to fill the corridor like the glow of a forest beneath bright sunlight. And he heard his voice, again, as if from a great distance. It sounded hard, full of importance. It was not the voice of his brittle breaking heart. If his voice had been a colour it was the coldest blue, a blue to blister away the warmth of the green tunnel, a blue to match the icy pulsing coming from him in steady, resolute waves.

"No. Wait. My heart *does* mourn, Lolisr. But I do what I must."

His hand with the small lasher was raised. It flashed and flashed in the darkness and one by one the would-be escapees fell. He moved about them a moment later and they watched, goggle-eyed and numbed and helpless, as he dragged each through the doorway and onto the platform. The hungry roar of the ridding pit came up from below.

Lolisr shrank from her partner, cried and pulsed anguished amber while watching the methodical and efficient process she'd heard tell about but never witnessed until that moment, though she never once looked away. Bin felt her watching him, and it seemed to him as though she were trying to understand it, seeking to glean some meaning from the work he did in that moment.

He hoped she did. For her sake, he hoped she did. Or maybe she only stood by him then as she always had because of her love and duty to him. He loved her too, he realized all over again as he euthanized the final-final batch of the day.

One more full cycle completed—the day had finally arrived.

The morning air felt different than it usually did. A vibrant quality suffused it, and placid sunshine penetrated the perpetual foundry-clouds that polluted the skies in the western hemisphere and fell through the glass ceiling of the waiting vestibule. Bin, looking at the confirmation-communication in his talk-screen for what might have been the millionth time, felt a mixture of numbness and elation. After a few minutes of re-reading the message over and over, he punched the line to his chief.

"Master Ridder Bin," came Chief Gemlor's sonorous voice through the speaker, his immense face materializing slowly in the centre of the vis-screen overhead. "Congratulations are in order. You are, of course, here to have your final cycle completion processed."

Bin's voice quavered with emotion. "High Ganshar, thank you. But I would like to put in a request for an extension of my service in your division."

The Chief's expression changed from amiable to a neutral quality that betrayed nothing, though the wry, hard humour in his next words sounded forced to Bin. "Not ready to quit just yet, are we? Can't say goodbye to my handsome face yet, is that it?" There was something else in the chief's voice, though Bin couldn't quite place what it was.

Visions of green land, abounding with leaf and tree and grass and vine and hill, swam like a dream before Bin's eyes. His heart pounded loudly. He fought the amber pulse that threatened to flood his pores, succeeded in maintaining his cool, controlled blue pulsing.

He said, "The universe needs me, High Ganshar. There's so much work still left to do."

"Once we put in your re-app, you're back in for good until the next cycle. You, more than most, know how long a cycle is." The Chief's voice had lowered, sounding as close to concerned as Bin had ever heard it.

The sound of Bin's own voice came to him as if from some very, very great distance. "I understand, High Ganshar."

"A Ridder until the very end," the Chief said with a combination of admiration, pride, and astonishment. Then, as his eyes looked off-screen, seemingly immersed in the inputting of information in some machine, "What about your God-place of peace, Bin? You and your life-partner were planning for this, no? You've earned it. It's waiting. It's yours now, if you want it. Last chance-last chance." He spoke casually, though Bin understood that the gesture, so far outside of formality in such a scenario, was one of friendship.

The thunder-voice of the ridding pit awakening for another day of feasting reverberated in the floor, walls, rumbled inside his bones. Its familiarity soothed Bin, reminded him of who he was and what he did and why he did it. He and his Lolisr-one would have forever to share together, but he still had a few more good cycles of work to give to the goodness of the Ganshars.

He said, "But maybe I'm standing on it now, High Ganshar."

It was the first time he recognized true admiration in his superior's face as he looked at him. Chief Gemlor winked in a chummy manner—another first—and disappeared from the screen, presumably gone into the maze of interior cubicles of his work station to retrieve a re-app package.

Bin became aware of her presence as he stood quivering with excitement and nervousness in the corridor moments before his shift was set to begin—it was like a cold wind refreshing him from the hot breath of the nearby pit-mouth.

"Lolisr," he said, startled by her presence in this place where she'd only ever dared intrude once before, a time he worked hard to force beneath other, pleasanter memories, though he never succeeded. His job, and his place of work, were sacred to him, as they were to every Ridder. Any anger he might have felt at the intrusion was overwhelmed with confusion and concern. "What are you doing here? Is everything okay?"

His mind didn't know what was going on, though his heart felt a great imminent *something*. Mixed into this was a nascent feeling of gratitude: she always knew whenever he needed something and, whatever that thing was now, here she was to give it to him. Maybe he was being rescued, though from what he wasn't able to comprehend in that moment.

Her eyes held him fixed with a melancholy intensity. Her blue pulsing cast a cold colour over the platform. This was a rare colour for her: she always relented to her emotions, never quelled them, and warm colours were her only colours, he'd learned over their years together.

"I was told of your decision, Bin-Bin. Word has spread among the laboratories. I foresaw it, too, in spite of our plan to retire now to a green colony, in our God-place. And so I planned for this day. And so now I have brought your peace-place to you. And to me. And to many others."

Her voice was sweet as water, as ever. Her eyes were full of gentleness and sadness. He felt himself warmed by her voice, beneath her gaze, though her cold blue pulsing made him anxious.

"What? Lolisr, I don't understand—"

"The God-place—*God*—is here," she said in her sweet, crying voice.

She opened the tessellated folds of her robe and he saw the quaker in her long fingers. The device was only ever used in the eastern hemisphere, as an excavation tool. She was familiar with them from many fossil digs. They were, of course, banned from entering the west.

"Lolisr," he said, voice so quiet it was nearly drowned beneath the grumbling of the ridding pit. "An explosion here, inside a pit..."

He thought of the chain reaction, the inevitable series of explosions running from one pit to another and through the adjacent foundry district and war machine and armament factories and among the storage prisons and out across the remainder of the country and the hemisphere, and the atomic power that would be let loose within each of them; and the combined annihilation this would bring. The green zones in the east would be completely corrupted, if they survived at all. Over time, the ruined atmosphere would ensure that they couldn't.

"Billions will perish. This is not like you. It is not in you to *do* this, Lolisr-one."

She smiled. Her blue pulsing remained. Her free hand rested lovingly on her swollen belly. Her voice was full of reason and sweetness: "But so many more will be born to live."

Bin stared aghast at her bulging belly, and their creation living inside her pulsing a deep and innocent emerald that coloured her skin warmly from within, amid her blue colour. In that moment of unprecedented emotional turmoil something in Bin died, and something else became freed. He nodded, eyes and heart filled with gratitude. He pulsed the deepest green. She always knew what he needed most.

"The God-place is here, my good Bin-Bin. We'll all be together." And she held the device aloft, and she cried.

She depressed the small silver button on top of the quaker.

In the darkness a star was born.

Its light was beautiful, and bountiful pulsing into the blackness all around.

Oppenheimer's Door

"What did you fools *do?*"

Leo Green said this before he'd fully woken from his shaking dark dream. He opened his eyes, lids crusty with brine, to the sky raging overhead.

He lay on the scrap of land, the Atlantic surging all around. He hated the sky: its sickly yellow-green-tinged poison clouds, back-lit with glowing red, its constant thunder-voice like an insane god murmuring to itself. If he'd indeed been addressing a potential deity it could only be a lunatic one who would have allowed whatever had happened. Although the details of the event remained unknown to him their catastrophic evidence lay all around, in the pulsing, ruined sky; the incomprehensible infinity of black water where once there'd been land; the utter absence of any human life but his own.

He had Maria, of course, though she was only a skeleton sleeping in the narrow pinewood coffin that formed the centre of his little shuddering world. Some things remained constant, even in the midst of cataclysmic change. He leaned his head against the wood, and felt comforted.

He turned accusatory eyes upward. "Answer me."

The only answer was the rumbling conversation among the loathsome clouds, a language beyond his comprehension.

~

He'd been at her gravesite when the Great Emptiness began. He visited her every Saturday without fail. A ritual of comfort, of need, without which he would have felt (been) lost and adrift in the world.

Then, chaos: thunder; fire; seismic quaking.

He'd frantically dug her out of the earth with a shovel pilfered from the cemetery caretaker's shed during the first tremors that sent Florida sliding piecemeal into the Atlantic. He'd scavenged the half-submerged carcass of a boat from the nearby pier, returning to rig a pair of pontoons to the ragged edge of the ever-shrinking peninsula that wound outward from the cemetery. Days passed, and segments of the land continued to erode into the water. Newly-formed islands in the distance sank, too. His makeshift safeguard couldn't help them stay afloat if the islet severed at its base yet, beyond reason, he maintained the pontoons.

Pain in his stomach interrupted his reveries, sent him crawling to the islet's edge. Squatting, he let loose a violent stream of diarrhea into the waves. He'd been sick all week, a consequence of his diet. The meagre fish he'd caught (like a Neanderthal fisherman he trawled the depths with a fraying rope-net) had been diseased-looking, scales flaking from weirdly blackened bodies, as if they'd suffered severe burning. Indeed, he was troubled by the temperature of the water: unnaturally *hot* to the touch. He was parched, but dared not drink the black, salty water.

He jumped as a blackened fin cut the water inches from his feet dangling over a pontoon. It splashed furiously, spraying him with hot water, and disappeared. He imagined the shark swimming down into darkness, too sick to eat, waiting to die.

Leo's thoughts drifted.

He remembered a professor he'd once known, in a time that seemed incredibly long ago. This man—middle-aged, an enthusiastic instructor of physics at the University of Florida—had had an equally avid interest in other poles along the spectrum of wonders: the mythologies and religions of cultures around the world.

The professor had once made a striking analogy to a graduate class, comparing man's inherently self-hurting nature (Oppenheimer and his most infamous creation had been the subject under discussion) to a substance from Norse mythology: *Eitr*, a miraculous liquid representing the origin of all living things and, conversely, the same annihilating poison produced by the dreaded Midgard serpent. And of course one needed look no further than that book of paradoxes, the Bible, for scenes rife with goodness and carnage, rebirth and apocalypse, Alpha…Omega.

A wave capped over the islet, slamming Leo's head onto the casket. With the concussive impact returned knowledge of the professor's identity:

Dr. Leonard Green, before man's poison had taken root in the world and rotted away transient flesh and the importance of giving names to things.

Laying there, senseless and shaking, he coughed up salty water and cursed the way of things. He was a student of history, after all, and saw the patterns woven through its epochs. He thought, we were always coming to this. This was always the end of our saga.

As before, so now: a great fire-plume descended from the sky to burn into the ocean close to the shoreline. Leo cowered and, acting instinctively, pried open the coffin lid with a screaming of splinters. The stench of death swept outward, staggering him. He looked at her nestled in the claustrophobic space, this physical framework on which so much else had been built to house ever so much more: Maria, his beloved, taken too soon by illness, spared the immutable hand of extinction waiting for them all.

Awkwardly, he climbed in and lay among her bones and skin-dust and stink.

"My dust and yours, darling. Forever."

The islet rocked. Fire hissed like serpents. He drew the lid closed over them. Water poured in.

They sank, the islet of Florida submerging beneath the waves, falling to a better place than what remained behind.

But then:

Their descent slowed, stopped, until Leo felt inexorable movement upward on a great swell of water, or something more substantial.

They tossed violently on the waves.

He peered through the narrow crack between casket and lifted lid, and found himself looking up at two titanic figures towering from the Atlantic like children might stand in a play-pool: true colossi on a scale that his mind rebelled from. One of these behemoths was bathed in the supernal fires of the sky, brilliant red and green and violet—its adversary draped in a shroud of blackness, as if the figure were moulded from the void itself. Their heads and faces were lost in the churning clouds far overhead. The blows they rained on each other carried a concussive thunder. And their voices—a primal roaring, a collective rumble felt in the marrow—were the sound of mountains shifting, landslides burying the fragile architectures of man.

He closed his eyes, shutting out the incomprehensible vision. And in that moment, relinquishing all he'd ever taught or been taught, some part of Dr. Leo Green began to fathom the nature of how the Great Emptiness had been let loose in the world.

An atomic flash brighter than a million suns, opening a door to the final conflict the world would ever know.

But this was too much for Leo and his skeleton-wife to think about any more. Too much for any man or woman. He was tired, and Maria, oh, how very tired she was. And so he pulled the lid back into place, and in the warm death-stinking darkness of their tomb man and woman finally drifted on into the most comforting dream of all.

The Threat from Earth

"Damn it—missed him."

The two boys, Brent Riley and Patrick Ellis, watched the hoary gull glide past to disappear over the tops of the sun-glazed trees. As the echo of the gun's report faded, the heavy August quiet came back in full: drowsy, humid, broken only by the distant electric chatter of cicadas in the depths of the woods.

"Yeah, you sure did," laughed Brent. "Watch me get the next one."

"Yeah, your first one ever."

They were nestled cozily in the foxhole they'd dug at the start of the summer, nearly flush against the tree-line. They'd been using the rifles all summer, because their friend Billy was Native, and his dad was allowed to carry a licence for shooting birds. Billy owed them a favour for all the pot they scored him. Boom. They'd have preferred something much less archaic (and much quieter) but nobody they knew could afford a laser rifle. Beggars couldn't be choosers. At least they were a step or two above slingshots, or bows and arrows.

"Pass it here," said Patrick. "My turn."

"Here you go, sharpshooter Ellis."

Patrick gave his friend a look. Brent chuckled.

They watched the field, the air.

"You like her?"

"What? Who's that?" said Patrick, playing dumb, knowing he wasn't fooling his friend.

"Who the hell you think? You've only rode your air-scooter by her place like a thousand times this month, hoping she goes out on her porch."

Patrick laughed. It was true. He'd been obsessed with Julie Bantin since the beginning of last school year. She'd only gotten better looking as time went on. He was proud of himself for having gotten up the nerve to actually talk to her a couple of times during that time. Just small-talk, but it had given him the hope that something more might blossom from it. He'd hoped that summer would have given him the ideal opportunity—without her cool friends hanging around, and the jock guys who no doubt wanted her just as much—Patrick would have been able to talk to her without the distraction of other people and had the chance to show her that he was just as cool and interesting as those other kids. He said, "I don't know if I *like* her. I like how she looks."

"You want to get with her?" Brent turned to watch him with eyebrows raised mischievously.

"Who doesn't? Don't you?"

"Sure. Sure, I do. Who doesn't? She's easy on the eyes." Brent turned back to the rifle in his hands, and searching the sky for birds.

After a few seconds of silence, Patrick added, "Brad Dunlee said she's easy, period."

"Brad Dunlee wouldn't know anything about the subject *at all.*"

They laughed. They felt safe in their foxhole, invisible to anyone who might be looking from the distant backyards of the townhouses that bordered the field they were facing. They could see a couple of people milling around in their respective yards—there was Mr. and Mrs. Mackelroy, retirees who seemed to enjoy nothing more than spending the afternoons drinking lemonade (or was it alcohol?) in their backyard by day and drinking coffee (was it spiked with something stronger like the neighbourhood kids claimed?) after supper on their front porch; there was old Ms. Gabowski reading a paperback novel (probably a Romance story) in her lawn chair in the middle of her little yard, the big brim of the straw sunhat she wore hiding her wrinkles in shadow; and there was Mr. Halchek kneeling in his garden along the edge of the chain-link fence, flush with the wild grass of the field that, unbeknownst to him, separated him from the two boys trying to shoot birds from the air.

Every once in a while, he, or one of the other backyarders, would turn in their direction after a shot from the rifle, or look elsewhere, distracted from their book or lemonade or garden vegetables, and search the hazy distance for the source of the noise. At that distance it probably sounded more like a loud firecracker than a rifle, and so after a second of scanning the field and forest and sky, they would turn back to their respective activity. It had been that way all summer, no one suspecting that a couple of neighbourhood kids were using a real rifle. Fireworks had been for sale all summer long at the convenience store, long after Canada Day had come and gone, and kids were setting them off all the time, as well as the smaller firecrackers and whizz-bangs.

Feeling brave, or at least enabled by the great hush and their secret shared hideout, which reminded him of being in the confession booth at church, Patrick said, "Yeah, I guess I do like her. Like, she's nice, I mean, and not just easy on the eyes. Seems nice, at least."

After seeming to think about what Patrick had said, Brent said, "Yeah, seems." His was voice neutral and therefore confusing to his friend. They left the subject there, which had somehow turned out to be a tricky one to discuss after all.

"There's one."

Patrick followed where Brent was looking. "I see him. He's gonna be tough, though."

"Cry-baby."

They watched the sparrow speed toward them from the grounds of the water treatment plant that bordered the field to their left—he came skimming over the field of wild grass that bowed in the humidity, a blur against the sun-bled green stalks. He was gone in the bushes that fringed the woods behind them before the boys could blink.

"Nice shot, sniper."

"You hit a sparrow at high speed that close to the ground I'll give you my whole comic book collection." Instantly following his outburst, Patrick felt a faint twinge of fear—his friend was a pretty good shot. But no; even if he did achieve the miraculous feat, he wasn't going to give him his comics. Too bad.

"You'd never give me your comics," laughed Brent.

"Nope."

They scanned the sky, but it was bird-less, and the field, too, where sometimes small sparrows and gulls cold be found daintily hopping among the tall grass stalks, pecking at bugs. A wiry grey cat was slinking through the field closer to the townhouses, but there were rules that prohibited trying to shoot it. Back at the start of July, they'd taken out a couple of ground hogs but had stopped after that—the animals were too cute to be shot, the boys thought, and ground hogs and other flightless animals, like the squirrels and rabbits and raccoons that were so abundant in the woods, didn't make for tough targets. They decided that only birds would be true tests of their marksmanship, being fast, and being moving targets (they weren't allowed to shoot them while they were foraging in the grass or trees) and because most of the species around those parts were small, except for the heron they'd killed last month; but then that had bordered on being too beautiful an animal to have been shot down at all—so big and majestic, its wingspan startling as it flopped back down into the trees it had risen from like some great creature from prehistory.

This was an important factor the boys took into account: size. The rule was that if it was a heron or around that size then it couldn't be shot at. So geese were out, and owls, too. Hawks, on the other hand, were allowed, on the basis that getting a hawk, which was a rare bird to see let alone shoot down, would be a great achievement. Same went for the eagles, which were even rarer than hawks, but they had seen a couple, flying higher in the sky than they'd had any hope of hitting with their lousy aim.

They waited for more birds but they were scarce. Maybe the humidity was too fierce for them and they were opting to stay at home in their nests among the trees. Maybe they'd grown wise to the danger that had plagued them all that summer, and that had claimed twenty-four of their number since the end of June. Patrick knew those stats didn't say much for their marksmanship, though he figured it probably was news in the bird community. 'Another bird—a gull, the eighth this summer—felled by mysterious force over field near home forest.' When he thought of it in such terms the whole scenario struck him as kind of cruel, and sad. But he drove it from his mind, turning to those things he got from this weird sport he and his friend had devised for themselves: the companionship of it; the way that they could share things about themselves and speak their thoughts while in the foxhole that weren't as easy to talk about elsewhere, like when riding their bikes down the streets, or hitting up the convenience store for comic books and penny candies, or while waiting in the cool, dark theatre for the matinee movie to start, with the summer breathing its furious hot breath all over the building outside.

Brent said, "I read that they're calling this the Season of the UFO. They're watching us. They're coming, man."

"Yeah? To do what?"

"Kill us. Obviously. Why else would they come here?"

"Why else?" Patrick echoed, trying to feel the truth in it, the logic. Thinking he'd found it, he said, "Where'd you read that?"

"One of the magazines I got at the 7-11. It was *True UFO Stories*, I think."

"I wonder if they're watching us."

"I bet they are," Brent was quick to answer. "Don't you sometimes feel like we're being watched?"

Come to think of it, Patrick had felt that way. "Yeah, sometimes."

They scanned the blue sky and the scant white clouds.

"I wish we'd seen something this summer," Patrick said. "A UFO, I mean."

The two of them, and a couple of other friends from school, along with John Delson's dad (an admitted conspiracy theorist and UFO nut), had braved the mosquitoes on many a night, setting up Mr. Dalson's telescope on top of Suicide Hill and taking turns looking at Jupiter or the constellations, though Patrick had always been hoping for a sighting of something a little more remarkable.

Maybe he should have put back the last couple comics he'd bought with his allowance money and grabbed one of the UFO magazines. They were pricier, but they sure had some fascinating and scary stuff.

"Careful what you wish for," Brent said. "What are we gonna do against their deathrays and flying saucers and probes worming through our bodies? We gonna fight the invasion with these puny things?"

Patrick saw that his friend was running a hand caressingly along the undercarriage of the rifle Patrick held. Lovingly, the way Patrick often imagined touching Julie Bantin's cheek, arm, thigh. The way he sometimes touched himself while dreaming of touching her in these ways.

"Huh," was all he could think to say, his drifting thoughts catching up to the moment again and his friend eyeing him curiously.

"Your mind on the hunt, Ellis?"

Patrick smiled bashfully. "Yeah, Riley. For sure. It's getting dark. Maybe I'll get a bat."

"Bats are bad luck to get."

"Where did you hear that?"

"Same magazine I told you about, but different issue. It talked about urban legends and weird true stories. That was one of them: don't ever kill a bat. Bad things will happen to you."

"Alright," he said. "Forget that. Give me a nightbird, then." Being superstitious, he was completely convinced, and scratched bats off his list of potential targets, though he knew he was unlikely to get one anyways—their erratic and frantic flying style made them nearly impossible targets.

"We'll get us some nightbirds, bro, for sure."

"For sure," agreed Patrick.

They kept up their vigil. The afternoon wore on, and soon the air darkened perceptibly, and the air cooled a little, and dusk was nearing. They waited through it, knowing they'd both get yelled at by their moms for being late for dinner. But they were in it deep, in the depths of the hunt, of the wait for the prime bird. There was always one like it at the end of every day, at least so far it had always been that way. The gloaming deepened, throwing the shadows into sharper relief in the trees rearing up behind them. The first mosquitoes came out, stinging their bare arms, legs.

They still felt safe in their foxhole, despite the descending dark. Boys pretending to be soldiers with a single ancient weapon between them, though they didn't kid themselves about being brave. They were just having some fun, letting off some steam before school called them back into its clutches in only a few days' time. It had been a good summer, but not long enough. They were going to miss the late nights of movie-watching and the afternoons idling at the convenience store; the bike rides down the streets and along the trails that wound through the woods they were camped out in front of right now; the bird-hunts that stretched the afternoon hours, and made a safe space for them to talk about anything in the world.

But the friends didn't bother voicing these things now, or lament the unfairness of summer's looming end. Today, as the dusk settled over the woods and fields, they left all those thoughts behind. They revelled in the moment, exhilarating and special. Patrick felt these emotions stir him, and could tell it was the same for his friend.

Brent said, "You want to get that bird there?"

"Which one?"

"The big one. That big bird puttering around over there."

Patrick followed where his friend was sighting through the rifle's scope. The only movement was in the backyards of the townhouses abutting the field. Miss Gabowski had retreated into her townhouse, and the Mackelroys had disappeared from their yard, too, likely eating supper or maybe already relocated to their front porch. But in the backyard second from the end of the row of houses, Mr. Halchek was still puttering. He hobbled to and fro in his sad excuse for a garden, the one Patrick's mom sometimes made fun of because their garden had one row more of veggies than his. As the boys watched him, Mr Halchek paused a moment to remove his old John Deere baseball cap and wipe his face with it while contemplating his meagre vegetables.

"Yeah." Patrick heard the word fall from his mouth like something special, something unique from all of the other things he'd said that day, maybe that whole summer.

"Yeah?"

"Yeah. He's big, and the rule is only smaller birds, *but*…we did get the heron last month."

"Yeah, we did. And this won't be like that anyways. This will be better."

"Yeah."

Patrick felt a nudge from Brent. He was hefting the rifle an inch or two off the lip of earth in their hole, gesturing toward the prey.

"Together. So it's both of us doing it, and both of us getting the bird if it's a good shot."

"Yeah. I like that."

"And nobody'll know it was us. We'll cut back through the bush and double back, hop the fence back into the neighbourhood from the far end."

"Yeah. I like that."

"On the count of three and. Okay?"

"Three and…shoot?"

"Yeah. Exactly. Three and both our fingers press the trigger. Here, slide yours in, on top of mine."

Patrick saw his friend move his finger down the length of the steel trigger a centimetre. He slipped his finger through the loop of the guard without hesitation. Both boys' fingers fit snugly in the guard, it wouldn't take much strength at all to pull the trigger toward them, and send the bullet shooting from the gun and at their bird.

"Okay," said Patrick.

"You cool doing it?"

"Yeah. I am."

He was, he realized. He wanted this. For whatever reason, Patrick wanted this. He felt the Mystery of it seep into him, through the pores of his sweating skin, through his nostrils smelling the damp grass and earth, through his eyes watering in the humidity, through his heart smashing behind his chest in the strange energy of the moment. The summer had been good and bad and this was the way to call it done. This was a proper end to it.

"Okay then," Brent said. "Here we go."

Patrick was dizzy in the grip of the Mystery as, distantly, his heart and his senses and his finger on his friend's finger on the trigger all kept time with the voice of Brent counting down to three and.

The Mystery filled him, and he knew it in all its power.

The skies remained clear that night, empty of cloud and bat and death-raining alien machine. But a cold wind blew. Summer had fallen to Fall.

In local news, before one other happening buried all other newsworthy items, there was one curious report. A number of people described witnessing a strange phenomenon in the early evening sky—what appeared to be a falling star or meteor but, inexplicably, travelling *upward* at a high velocity and leaving a bright fiery red wake that was clear in the night. Several of the witnesses had a different take in their account, and swore that what they'd seen was a large, disc-shaped machine—a flying saucer.

The Electric Voice of Summer

The dusty yellow school buses were disgorging their bellyfuls of children. They spilled out into the gravel lot in long lines like ants exiting an anthill. It took the entire dozen camp counsellors to corral the more rambunctious boys and girls as they tried to reach the adjacent trails leading into the greater camp grounds and the forest beyond.

"Welcome to Camp Chipmunk, all you Chipmunks!"

This megaphone-boosted greeting came from a portly man of about forty years old, balding and moustached. If his face hadn't been so kind more kids might have wanted to poke fun at his belly showing above his khaki shorts and his brown wool socks pulled up nearly to his knees. As it was, only a couple of older boys sniggered to one another, while most of the kids calmed down enough to stand and listen to what he had to say.

Jane surveyed the surging mass of kids from the rear of the lot, feeling an overwhelming sense of anxiety coming over her. She wondered how so many of these kids knew each other, or seemed to know each other. Had they come to the camp in summers past? Was this a big reunion for them, with friends made one or two summers before? The thought made her nervous—she'd had the idea that coming here was sort of like wiping the slate clean. She'd envisioned everybody being newbies here, and having to start from scratch when making friends. She turned to look after her parents' car, just now disappearing around the corner of the long winding drive. Then it was gone amid the emerald branches and she felt her aloneness settle over her like a blanket.

The megaphone-man continued his introduction, but Jane tuned out completely. She was looking around herself: tall walls of trees surrounded the lot on three sides, their lush green leaves shimmering in the sunlight. She saw the narrow footpaths disappearing into the green gulfs and imagined them crisscrossing into secret glades, past waterfalls, passing beaches whose sands were burning hot and whose lake waters were busy with fish.

She cast her eyes up and saw the great wooden arches that led into the central part of the campgrounds. Etched into the wood were the words:

Camp Chipmunk, Port Elgin, Ontario, Est. 1935

She realized the other kids had formed into two lines—boys and girls—and were filing beneath those wooden arches. She scurried to a place last in her line. She took a deep breath. She silently repeated the words like a mantra to calm her nerves and bolster her courage: *You can do it. You can do it. You can do it…*

Quietly, so no one might hear her, she said, "Okay. Go get 'em, Jane Montgomery."

And she scurried under the wooden arches, excited and scared, her runners kicking up dust as she went.

She looked up at the dainty girl standing in the doorway of the bunkie, suitcase in hand. Despite the heat, she was wearing a button-pocked denim jacket, and Jane could make out the logo of the Deathray Bradburys t-shirt she wore underneath—she was vaguely aware that this was a band of some sort, possibly a punk rock band, and, having very little knowledge of loud music, she immediately felt intimidated by the newcomer.

When the girl spoke, her voice was as small as the rest of her.

"Hi. I'm Lila. I'm your bunk-mate. I got here late. I missed my bus so my mom drove me."

Jane stood. "Hey. I'm Jane." She gestured to her suitcase and bags spread across the lower bunk bed. "I just got here, too. I was just unpacking. But you can have the bottom bunk if you want."

The new girl eyed the bunks, then turned a furtive look over the rest of the room. It was tiny and panelled in rich dark wood. The wooden floorboards creaked as she stepped fully into the room.

"That's okay. You can have it if you want."

Jane smiled. "Well, we can always switch later on. We're actually pretty lucky that we even got a bunkie. Usually only counsellors get them, and sometimes senior campers." She was thinking of how anxious she would have felt having to sleep in the main cabin with a dozen other girls, even though that would have increased her chances of getting to know more people, and making friends.

"Yeah," Lila said. "I'm cool with a bunkie instead of rooming with—" She stopped, and turned to look through the large open window in the centre of the wall. Jane thought Lila looked as scared staring out the window as she'd felt walking under the wooden arches into the camp a few minutes earlier.

"What *is* that? It's so loud."

Jane listened, then realized what Lila meant. "That's the soundtrack of summer," Jane said, a big smile materializing on her face.

When Lila gave her a questioning look, she laughed and explained. "Those are cicadas. They make that sound by contracting and relaxing muscles inside their bodies. It sounds like a constant noise but it's actually a bunch of clicking noises really close together. And only the males make the sound." As she finished she realized just how teacherly she must have sounded, and hoped she hadn't annoyed her new roommate—first impressions weren't her strong suit.

"It sounds like electricity."

Jane had been trying to decide whether to continue listing off other weird and fascinating facts about cicadas but found herself too stunned to say anything. When she found her voice, it was brimming with excitement. "Yeah. That's what *I* always said about their singing, except nobody else ever got what I was talking about."

Lila tossed her suitcase up onto the top bunk. "How come you're such an expert on insects?"

Jane was disappointed that Lila didn't seem to think this common thinking was a sign of some deeper connection they might have. That maybe it represented the first indication that they'd both just met their best friend. But she only laughed. "I'm definitely no expert. But I love science stuff. Full disclosure: I am a nerd." The thought arrived immediately as these last words left her mouth: *what kind of a first impression am I making here?*

Lila smiled. "That's cool. Nerdy is cool." Then, cocking an ear toward the window, "Oh my God, please tell me *that* is *not* a cicada!" Lila was staring out the window.

Jane concentrated for only a moment before her ears picked out the new sound from the rest of the outdoors noise. She said, "Oh, that's probably only a short circuit in the power lines." She didn't know exactly what a short circuit was, but had heard her dad talk about them more than once when discussing his work day with her mom. His job with the telephone company kept him busy, and the work itself—climbing up on rooftops and swinging out on the crane-arm inside the company truck's little steel nest to fix damaged and dangerous power lines among the trees—always worried her mom. It worried her a little sometimes, too, but mostly she just thought her dad was superhumanly impervious to everyday dangers.

"How can you be sure about that?" Lila asked.

Jane made herself sound as confident and teacherly as she could. "Well, did you notice all the power lines connecting to camp? They go all through the trees and disappear way off somewhere..." She waved a hand vaguely. "Plus, once you get used to it enough you realize they do sound different—the cicadas and this kind of man-made noise. Cicada-singing is prettier."

Lila's eyes grew less worried. "Well, okay then. Because if that was a monster-cicada I think I might be hitchhiking right back home this afternoon."

She smiled a little smile as she said it.

Jane thought: *don't go home,* and was surprised at how forcefully the thought had come to her.

The electric voice of the cicadas didn't go to sleep. It buzzed on and on and on all through the rest of the afternoon, and long into the wee hours after lights-out.

They were woken up the following morning by the amplified voice of a camp counsellor booming through the campground with morning announcements:

"Good morning! Rise and shine, all you Chipmunks! The calendar says it's July third, nineteen-eighty-three, and the forecast is calling for a real scorcher. Breakfast is served in thirty minutes and then it's down to the lake to beat the heat on this first day of the summer's first heatwave…"

But Jane didn't hear any more of what the camp counsellor said. She'd turned away from the wall and found Lila, hands draped easily on the wooden rungs of the ladder leading to the upper bunk. She was upside down, her long hair fanned out in a curtain silhouetted by the sunlight streaming in through the window. She was watching her, and though Jane usually didn't like being stared at, this time it felt okay. This time it felt good. There was nothing cruel or judging in the placid green eyes watching her. There was nothing but curiosity and goodness in that stare. And some other thing that Jane couldn't quite put into words, but it was a thing that endeared Lila to her even more.

"I got woken up bright and early," upside-down-Lila said.

"By what?"

"The cicadas. Your summer soundtrack."

Jane tuned in. There it was:

The song of the insects buzzing out among the trees like all the electricity in the world.

The girls listened to the music in silence, smiling sleepily at each other in the morning stillness.

~

"So what is it like in Windsor?"

Jane had never been there, and was curious. From what Lila had said of it—which wasn't much—it sounded like the big city compared to her quaint little hometown of Goderich.

They were playing outfield, though calling it "playing" suggested that they were actually participating in the game. They loved the daily baseball games, but only because being as inept as they were in all sports meant the coach always relegated them to the very back of the playing field where the ball was only rarely hit. So baseball for them became talking-time (unless they weren't selected for the same team, which made the game excruciating for both of them). Sometimes, like now, the coach and other players seemed to not even notice them at all, so they sat cross-legged on the warm grass, plucking dandelions and blowing their seeds onto the burning air while talking in drowsy voices. The trees fringing the closely-cropped lawn shimmered in the heat-haze.

"Boring, kind of. But okay, I guess. Not as nice as Goderich, that's for sure." Lila was wearing a pair of large purple-framed sunglasses. Their lenses were scratched, and Jane thought wearing them made Lila look somehow older, more mature.

Jane felt a little self-conscious hearing her talk about Goderich. She'd never really thought about her parents being well-off until she'd met someone whose family might not be so well-off. This was something she could tell about Lila's family. Not that it mattered to her in the least—it was just something she could tell. Maybe it was the one battered suitcase Lila had brought with her to camp compared to Jane's two new suitcases and heavy-duty backpack. Maybe it was the something she glimpsed in her eyes every once in a while, behind the green gentleness: something murkier, as if she'd seen things or lived through things Jane had never, having lived the relatively privileged life she had. And maybe living where Lila did was partially responsible for that. Maybe where Lila lived there was a greater population of jerks than where she lived.

"But that's good for you," Lila said quickly, as if realizing she might have committed a faux-pas. "I'm glad you live in a nice town. And it looked *really* nice from what I saw on the drive up here."

Jane reached behind her and pulled her t-shirt from where it clung to her sweaty back. "Holy, it's hot." Then, turning to Lila, she said, "Aren't you dying in those layers?"

Lila had pulled her green team shirt overtop the button-down flannel shirt she'd been wearing. She seemed always to wear one long-sleeve shirt or other, even on the hottest days. She even swam with long sleeves. It was one of her Lila-quirks. "Yeah, I'm snug as a bug in a rug," she said. "But I don't like showing my skinny arms to the world. So."

Jane, afraid she'd offended her, said, "That's cool."

They became aware that there was shouting going on, from off in the hazy distance, and that it was being directed at them. They looked to the other players, who were waving their arms excitedly and looking at them expectantly. A single player wearing the opposite shirt colour—blue—was running furiously from second to third base. They saw the baseball land and bounce off to the left of where they sat.

"Oh crap," said Jane, getting to her feet.

"The game found us," said Lila.

Jane liked the sound of that. It sounded just right. They ran awkwardly to where the ball had rolled to a stop and Jane snatched it up and threw it in the general direction of their gesticulating impatient teammates. The friends watched the ball's wobbly path as it, of course, fell far short of where it needed to reach. The little blue-shirted runner was rounding third and heading for home plate, a dust cloud rising behind his pounding feet.

Their teammates were shouting things at them, condemning their play and lack of baseball skills. It was a little like the school year they'd each left behind them in their respective schools in their respective cities on different sides of the province. But it was okay now, here, in this warm, sunny place in the heart of the forest. Here they had each other, and it made all the difference.

"Wake up, zombies!"

"Nice catch, ladies!"

"Zzzzzzzz…"

"Oh, shut up," Lila muttered under her breath.

Jane turned to her. She could see Lila's eyes glimmering mischievously behind the scratched plastic lenses of her sunglasses, and laughed. She couldn't help herself. And when Lila smiled, and then laughed too, the complicated world of a baseball game being lost in the middle of a blistering-hot afternoon in the middle of a summer in the middle of a forest on a lake became the best place to be in the entire world.

Their team, it turned out, lost the game: Blues 10, Greens 4. But it didn't matter in the least.

Because Jane and Lila had won. It might have been a secret victory known only to them, but then that was what mattered most. As far as Jane was concerned, they'd hit a homerun straight into the burning heart of the day and made it home safe and sound.

Two weeks into camp letters began to arrive from home.

The mail truck was the centre of a chaos of kids, jumping in their places, eager to hear their name called as the mail carrier read them off one by one from the envelopes and packages he retrieved from the vehicle.

"Lila…Pollard!" called the mail carrier, squinting at the envelope in his hand as if he were reading hieroglyphics.

Lila said to Jane, "That's my mom—her writing is *so* bad."

Jane watched her move into the crowd, one hand raised high on the air for the carrier to see. When she returned a moment later Jane wondered at the way she clutched the letter protectively to her chest but made no move to open it the way everyone else was eagerly tearing their envelopes open. She appeared to be waiting for something to happen, eyes fixed on the man reading out names.

Jane's name was called and she came back a moment later with a large package in a bubble-wrapped envelope. Her mother's tidy cursive—surrounded by several sappy cartoon hearts—was surprisingly nice to see.

Before Jane could say anything Lila said, "Can we go back to our room now?"

The way she said it—quickly, quietly, like she was sharing a secret—made Jane anxious. "Yeah. Of course. Let's go."

And together they left the crowd of kids and hurried down the footpath to their tiny bunkie.

Jane had the contents of the bubble envelope spread open on the floor between them:

One letter, two pages long and covered—*covered*—in her mom's meticulous cursive, but signed by both her mom and dad at the bottom in radically different handwriting; and two rectangular shapes wrapped snugly in aluminum foil.

"This," and Jane pointed to the larger of the two aluminum foil-wrapped mounds, "is a loaf of chocolate chip banana bread— delish. And this," she pointed to the smaller of the silver-shrouded lumps, "is apple crumble—not quite as delish, but not bad either."

"Did it keep okay in the mail, do you think?" wondered Lila.

"Yeah, it should be okay. Goderich is close by. Mom probably mailed it, like, yesterday."

Jane looked to Lila sitting across from her. She'd received a letter, but no package of goodies from home.

"Lucky you," Lila said, indicating the pastries.

"Half of this loot is yours if you want it," Jane said quickly, feeling somehow embarrassed by her parents' devotion to her. "It's way too much food anyways. My mom is nuts. And if it sits around too long, it *will* go bad, so…"

But Lila shrugged. "That's okay. I don't mind the food here. I don't eat too much anyway."

Jane wasn't surprised about that. Lila was tiny, and though she devoured all three meals and all the snacks they were given at camp she could tell she was the kind of girl that just wouldn't gain any substantial amount of weight. Unlike herself.

Jane nodded to the unopened envelope on the floor. "How come you don't open yours? You don't want to hear from your parents?"

Lila shrugged again. "The letter's from my mom only. I don't know. Maybe later I'll open it."

"Oh," Jane said. "Why just your mom?"

She watched Lila look down at her grass-stained running shoes, eyes obscured by her auburn bangs, then wordlessly begin picking lint from the sleeve of her flannel shirt. And that's how she knew she'd trespassed into some kind of taboo territory, said something fatally wrong. The likely transgression, the most adult scenario Jane's mind could produce, came to her then: divorce. Her new friend was dealing with her parents' separation, and here she was making things awkward by dragging the touchy subject into the open.

"I'm sorry." Jane lowered her voice conspiratorially, which somehow seemed to make it all worse. And she placed a hand clumsily on Lila's arm. When Lila shrugged it away the gesture felt cataclysmic.

Jane thought frantically. She wanted desperately to make things right, to make this fragile girl feel better. The words she blurted out sounded inadequate but it was all she could come up with: "I'm sorry, Lila. Look, I'm an idiot. I didn't mean to upset you. And we don't have to talk about it anymore, obviously."

But Lila kept coming with the surprises, though her revelation went beyond being merely surprising, and right on into shocking.

"I came here to get away from home. Because it doesn't feel like home anymore. Suicide definitely does that. I was the one who found him. My dad."

She'd said it matter-of-factly, which somehow gave the words an even darker cast, a weight that seemed to stifle any hope for the conversation to climb from the abyss it had so quickly slipped into. She then said, more thoughtfully, "He was a crisis counsellor. He talked to people on the phone, people who were having problems and wanted to hurt themselves. So it's kind of, like, super-ironic, I guess."

Giving the unspoken thing a name had bestowed it a reality so harsh that Jane was literally rendered speechless hearing it. This was all so far beyond her realm of experience, she simply had no way to process it, let alone offer comfort or advice. That Lila's dad had been a crisis counsellor made it somehow so much worse a truth, as if it were proof of a weight to the problems the world hoisted onto people's shoulders everywhere. It made her feel small, and unequal to the task of living life.

Lila's words continued to hang heavily in the air.

Before Jane even realized what she was saying, she found herself having asked the question. "How did he do it?" She immediately stammered, "Ohmygod, Lila, I'm so sorry. So dumb, Jane, so dumb. Please can we pretend I didn't just say that, please?"

An expression somewhere between startled and angry and amused crossed Lila's features. Then she said, in a brazen voice, as if she were acting on a dare, "It's fine. I'll tell you. The counsellor at my school says it's good for me to talk about it. It was last fall. My dad used to work from home sometimes. He had a private line in his office for work. He'd been working up there all morning, I guess. He got a call from someone in distress. They talked all morning. There were city workers there that day, working in the neighbours' backyard. They were cutting down tree branches, so it was really loud, and I could hear my dad talking louder than usual over the noise. After the call, I heard him hang up, but he didn't leave his office. I was in my room, right beside the office, drawing in my sketchbook. I guess what happened then is he just climbed out of his office window, and walked along the flat roof of the back porch to where the wood chipper was set up in the neighbours' yard, on their side of the fence that we share with them. He jumped in."

Jane stared at her friend, mouth open, a kind of dread settling over her that she'd never until that moment known. It was the feeling of knowing that things like this could and did happen in the world she lived in; all while the inevitable questions came to her, and those questions she made sure to keep locked deep inside herself where they could only cause her pain: questions like what would a woodchipper do to a human being's body? She'd seen the city workers back home tossing branches taller than her into the machines, marvelled at the savagery with which they devoured them, sucking them relentlessly through their immense steel teeth to spew them out as fluffy wood pulp. It was that remarkable transformation, Jane found, that carried the greatest horror of the whole scenario.

She stirred from the prison of her horrific imaginings when she felt Lila's hand on hers. She stared, and Lila's face coalesced from the brutal vision, concerned, tragic.

"Earth to Jane," she said. Then, more soberly, "Sorry. That got real pretty fast, I guess. I shouldn't have told what really happened. I'm not sure if my counsellor was right about me talking about it, at least not at summer camp."

Jane gathered herself. Not knowing where to begin to offer anything resembling adequate condolence, she just said, "I'm sorry, Lila."

"Thanks," Lila said, turning to the low coffee table beside them and snatching the issue of *National Geographic* from the top of the magazine pile. Eyes scanning the pages with disinterest, she frowned and added, "Actually, I think my mom wanted to send me away, so she could deal with stuff on her own. Without any distractions. As in, me. A distraction."

"Is that why you chose this camp?" Jane said. "I realized a while back how far Windsor is from here." Her own town was relatively close by, and a lot of the other kids were from nearby places too—Sauble Beach, Owen Sound, Collingwood. Windsor, judging by its place on the provincial map tacked to their bunkie's corkboard, was at least six or seven hours' drive away.

"You hit the nail on the head," Lila said, then added, "I found it on a map sort of like that one." She nodded toward the map on their corkboard. "It looked so far away, and the area was coloured all green, with little cartoony trees and tee-pees all over it. And it had a lake. I needed that. I needed 'so far away and green.' I'm actually pretty lucky that my mom let me come here. It's pretty expensive."

Jane, in that moment, wished more than anything that she could comfort Lila. Make her feel better somehow, if not specifically about her home situation which was beyond her control, then generally.

"I'm here because I don't have any friends."

Jane had never confided this to anybody: not to her parents, who just believed their daughter wanting to come here involved her indulging her passion for all things nature-related, nor even to the diary she kept so diligently. It was almost as if committing it to paper would make it truer, and seeing it written there would make it more real. She was surprised to feel unburdened by the confession, and added, "I was hoping to make friends here since I don't have any back home. Or at least one good friend. I'm what you'd call *socially super-awkward.*"

Lila brightened a little. The wan smile she smiled looked brilliant to Jane. "Nah, you're okay. You're a really good talker and listener. And you know interesting facts about insects that nobody except maybe insect-scientists know, and maybe this kid Colin in my class—huge science nerd, but a nice guy. So, it's their loss, whoever your stupid classmates are."

"Thanks." Jane, emboldened by Lila's kind words, put a gentle hand on her friend's sneakered foot. "I'm sorry about being stupid about your letter. And about...you know, all that stuff you told me about. But...We'll have a good rest of the summer here. Okay?"

She heard the pleading sound in her words and cringed. How could she encourage her new friend when she sounded so needy herself, so totally *lame?*

"Yeah. But while we're telling each other our deepest darkest secrets, I should say that the situation with my dad...it's not even the worst thing, though." Lila's voice was so small it was nearly drowned out by the insistent buzzing of the plump bumblebee kissing flowers outside the open window.

Jane felt like a cold hand was squeezing her heart. She leaned closer. "What? What else, Lila?"

"I'm haunted."

The girls made the best of the days.

They hiked the trails, pocketing blueberries they couldn't resist picking and then popping them into their mouths when no one was watching. They played baseball and badminton and tennis, never to win but for the simple fun of swinging the rackets and bats as hard as they could. They dutifully wrote letters home, though they never shared what they wrote to their respective parents. They swam in Lake Arran and pointed out imaginary sightings of the lake's legendary cryptid, the giant plesiosaur known in local lore by its old indigenous name, *Aashk-ozhi* (the camp manual they'd each received explained this Ojibwe word translated to "Wave-Maker").

They dutifully finished their assigned projects for the daily arts and crafts class that took place underneath the long gazebo overlooking the lake, and they were surprised to find that they actually enjoyed making origami birds and painting watercolours of landscapes inspired by the park and its plants and animals, even if neither one of them was very good at drawing anything but very cartoony-looking animals. They sang along to the songs sung over night-time campfires and chugged their hot chocolates and shivered and shrieked and laughed along with everyone else during the recounting of creepy local urban legends.

Best of all though was that whenever the two of them found themselves inside the greater group of their camp-mates they occupied their own little world inside of it—their "bubble-world", they called it. And they were lucky enough to find plenty of opportunities to sneak off on their own, to escape the greater tribe and explore the expansive parkland together. They were never missed by their counsellors—either they were too busy and had their hands full with the trouble-making kids, or maybe they didn't care all that much, or maybe some of them even recognized that two kids off on their own didn't pose a problem for anyone, and was maybe even necessary for the two of them to deal with whatever things they were dealing with. Whatever the case, there were days and nights with secret stolen moments that belonged to Jane and Lila and no one else.

It was summer. It was *their* summer. It was good. It was good enough.

But always at the edge of things—and all through the nights especially—lurked a shadowy presence, nearly tangible, and growing more so as the days moved closer to summer's end and the first breath of September could be felt in the nip of the evening wind off the lake. This presence was Lila's ghost, and it grew to haunt Jane, too, though not in the same way. She worried about her new friend. She worried about Lila a lot. And so sometimes their adventures, which began with the two of them feeling free, and excited, and comforted by the other's presence, would end in a mood of sadness.

One afternoon during the first weekend in August, all of Camp Chipmunk hit the lake. The plan was to make a circuit of the entire lake in canoes, and be back for supper. Jane and Lila, sharing a canoe, had quickly fallen behind their fellow campers, though they'd started somewhere near the middle of the pack. Their progress had been lazier, and soon enough they'd let themselves drift off into one of the several inlets that dotted the shoreline. No one had noticed them meander from the main group—neither counsellors or kids. It was like they were selectively invisible, and had the power to sneak away in secret when they needed relief from the noise and commotion and to share a quiet moment with just each other.

They were basking on the muddy banks of the lake like a pair of beached fishes, the front end of their canoe dragged up onto the bank close by, its rear end bobbing in the shallows among the cattails. They felt luxuriously sleepy in the warmth and sunlight, and their conversation meandered. They talked a little about their respective schools, and their hometowns, but mostly they stayed away from any subject that existed outside of the green sanctuary of Camp Chipmunk.

Instead, they made up stories relating to the parkland, something they'd been doing for a few weeks and that had grown into a rich lore filled with benevolent spirits and mischievous pixies who lived in the wildflower colonies in the deepest part of the park, far off any trail. Kid's stuff, but that was okay: kid stuff was good to dive deep down into sometimes, even when you'd gotten just a little too old for it in the eyes of the world. What did the world know anyway? The world, after all, was what they were hiding from.

Jane was embellishing their latest addition to their folklore with one final detail.

"And the chipmunk tribe helped the pixies put out the Great Brushfire of 1950 by each of them carrying a tiny bucket of lake water deep into the heart of the forest and dousing the fire. It took a whole day, and the help of all the hundreds and hundreds of chipmunks, but they did it. And the pixies declared the chipmunks honorary members of their tribe, and the parkland was named after them because of their bravery and heroism."

Lila, her head close to Jane's on the muddy bank, smiled lazily. "Long live Camp Chipmunk. I love it."

Sometimes the camp schemed to help the friends when they needed magic most—a sudden and very small chittering startled them. Sitting up on the bank they followed the direction of the clamour and found him: a tiny chipmunk watched them from the lowest branch of the black oak that rose up near the lake's edge, its branches hanging over the water. His chestnut fur was bright and shiny and his little eyes were excited.

"A chipmunk!" exclaimed Jane.

"He came right out of your story!"

The girls laughed, delighted, astonished. It was incredible, but also made some kind of perfect sense.

"What's your name, little fella?" called Jane. "Oh my God, you're so adorable."

The tiny creature cocked its head at Jane's voice, then renewed his chittering.

The girls sat in silence a while, watching the animal watch them, before scampering out of sight into the leafy canopy over their heads.

Jane said, "Funny. He's the first chipmunk we've seen, and we've been at Camp Chipmunk for like a whole month. It's like he answered the call of our story. He's magic."

Lila smiled. "You're totally right. He is." But then her smile faded, and her eyes grew distant, as if she'd just remembered something that ruined her good cheer.

Seeing, Jane said, "What? What is it?"

Lila spoke reluctantly, as if she didn't want to ruin the goodness of their moment lounging in the sunshine. "But there's bad magic out there, too. Not that anyone believes me."

She was talking about her ghost, of course. The one that she'd told Jane about in bits and pieces, a detail one day and another a few days later. The strangeness of its visitations, and the mystery of what Lila swore was its even creepier appearance, though these details she hadn't felt brave enough to share with her just yet (and Jane, out of courtesy, didn't ask, though her curiosity about it bordered on fanatical).

And without warning, Lila covered her face with her hands. The sound of her crying was muffled through her fingers but to Jane it was the loudest sound in the world on that still, humid afternoon. It hurt Jane to hear her broken voice in the green stillness:

"I *feel* it, Jane. It's looking for me, Jane. It's looking for me *here.*"

The tenacious way of Lila's ghost—the way Lila made it sound as if it was hunting her—was what frightened Jane most about it. But she was as brave as she could be for her friend. She said, "Don't worry, Lila. We're safe here. You and me, in the Kingdom of the Chipmunks."

They lay without talking on the muddy banks, watching dragonflies glide elegantly across the sky, their emerald bodies flashing in the bright sun like mysterious coded messages. They could hear the sounds of the other campers drift to them from out on the lake, the canoes and their occupants tiny with distance.

A moment passed with each lost in their own thoughts. Then, Jane ventured, "Did you ever ask it…why it haunts you?"

Lila turned to her briefly, eyes wide with shock, before looking back to the water and saying vehemently, "*No.* Would *you?*"

Jane didn't answer, and by doing so showed her friend she understood her predicament.

"I mean, if you *saw* this thing…" Lila trailed off, small and helpless and afraid. "Not that anyone would believe me. They'd say I'm nuts. Maybe I am."

Into the huge quiet Jane said, "I believe you. And you're not."

Lila didn't say anything. In answer she only reached over and put her warm, clammy hand over Jane's.

The deep shadow of the woods was cooler on their skin after the open sun in the main campground. The perfume of flowers grew more potent the further they went, a heady mix of violets and lilies. A few minutes later and the outline of a man-made structure could be glimpsed among the trees.

Campers weren't allowed to use the observation tower without an accompanying counsellor or scout leader, but by mid-August Lila and Jane had mastered the art of being invisible. And so they'd been able to sneak off unnoticed from the open-air pavilion during lunch and hustle through the woods to the observation area. The tower reared from the forest floor close to the lake's edge like some great and ancient medieval machine of war, though everything about it and the land spread out in front of them filled the girls with peace.

"You first, my lady," Jane said, stepping to one side for Lila. She was a little afraid of heights, and watching her friend climb up before her might give her the confidence to follow. Lila gave a clumsy imitation of a curtsey and they climbed up through the creaking skeleton of the tower, out of breath by the time they reached the top. The view from the high-railed observation platform was breathtaking, taking in the entirety of the lake and the forested opposite shore. The canoes moored at the jetty were bobbing in the current, waiting for the campers to finish lunch and take them out again. The sun flashed from the waves in a million places.

Jane summed it up perfectly for them both: "I love this place."

Beside her, Lila was nodding agreement, quiet, just looking, looking.

Then Jane realized. "Oh, yeah. Me first." And she crossed to the ancient-looking observation binoculars, whose circular steel base was bolted into the wooden floor. She put her eyes to its eye-piece and slowly swivelled the sturdy steel body to take in the view below. It took a minute of playing with the focus knobs along the side of the machine but soon the picture became clear and crisp, and Jane was methodically scanning the landscape on their side of the lakeshore.

"I can just make out everyone eating lunch at the pavilion," Jane said.

"Do you see Marcy Stansfield bossing everyone around?"

Jane watched a moment, then laughed. "Yes! I do see her, and yes, she's pointing to someone and it looks like she's yelling."

Lila laughed. "Of course she is."

Marcy Stansfield, it was understood between the friends, was the girl to avoid whenever possible: mean-spirited and bossy, she seemed to genuinely relish pointing out people's flaws. It was almost like Marcy was trying to bring along all the baggage of grade school that some of the campers—Jane and Lila, for example—were all too happy to leave behind. And this place, Camp Chipmunk—should never be a place where things like that happened. This wasn't the schoolyard, or classroom, or the walk home from school with the bully giving you shoves in the back as you hurried on your way, suns of shame burning in your cheeks and tears threatening to leak from your eyes and reveal your weakness. Camp Chipmunk, Jane and Lila had decided, was different from the rest of the world, its cute, innocent name like an extra layer of camouflage that hid its secret power from anyone in the world trying to look in.

She swivelled the binoculars up and scanned the opposite shoreline shimmering in the afternoon haze. Gulls were making a commotion on the water, feasting amid a school of fish or a camper's lunch remains tossed from a canoe.

"You want a turn?" Jane had stepped away from the binoculars and made a sweeping gesture taking in the lake.

"Um…Okay," Lila said, and stepped forward to place her eyes to the eye-piece.

Jane wondered about the way she'd hesitated, and the careful, almost reluctant way that her friend panned the instrument across the water. It was almost as if she was scared of seeing something out there, something worse than a Marcy Stansfield being bossy and loud. But what? Well, Jane knew what her friend was afraid of seeing, and she wished so very much for no dark vision to lie waiting for Lila's eyes to find floating over the water or among the trees on the far shore.

"Jane." Lila had stepped back from the binoculars, indicating Jane should put her eyes to it. She was pointing in a vaguely north-easterly direction, and Jane felt her stomach tighten anxiously. "On the lake. Not too far out from the little pier closest to us."

Jane searched a moment, making minute adjustments to the binoculars, fearing what she might see. Then she stopped, gasping, and understood the sighting for what it was: only another of the many magical ingredients of Camp Chipmunk's endless folklore.

There it was: a shadow. Very large and moving beneath the placid water.

The girls would never be able to say for sure whether they'd seen some physical evidence of the creature that cast that great shadow break the surface of the lake, though they believed they had: a dark curvature slowly rising from the green-blue water, a humped back or a fin or the sleek curve of a long neck. They were so excited that they couldn't be certain, but their hearts told them that they'd seen. And that was truth enough.

"It was Wave-Maker," said Jane in an exhilarated whisper.

Lila didn't say anything. But she was smiling, lost inside the magic of the miraculous sighting, and that was answer enough.

Jane would never know what woke her in the deep A.M. She lay there in her bunk and sensed something amiss.

Quietly, she stepped from her bed and confirmed what she already knew: Lila was gone. Her bed was dishevelled and, glancing to the doormat she saw that her running shoes were missing, too.

Without thinking she slipped her bare feet into her own shoes, grabbed the electric lantern from its peg beside the door, and crept into the moon-lit night.

She knew to go to the lake, and she went quickly, the lantern in her hand casting a warm orange glow across the trees and path before her. As she whispered through the grass, grasshoppers jumped at her progress—she felt them pelting her bare legs, heard them rustling like autumn leaves in the tall grass fringing the path.

She followed the trail until the quiet lapping of the lake came to her, and soon after she was following the sound of crying and a moment after that she found Lila at the shoreline. She was silhouetted against the moon-shimmering water. Overhead, the Milky Way frosted as far as the eye could see.

"Lila."

She needn't have worried about startling her friend. Lila

sounded as if she'd known Jane was there all along. Her words clamped an icy hand over Jane's heart.

"I can't, Jane. I can't anymore. I'm sorry, but it won't leave me alone. It's always there."

That's when Jane edged closer and saw the moonlight glimmering from the knife blade her friend held pressed to one wrist. She saw the tears on her cheeks. She saw the thin dark trickle from Lila's wrist that was blood from her first cut. Standing there she saw her friend's moonlight-washed arms criss-crossed with scars, some dark and new-looking, others old, pink and faded. It was the first time she'd seen her in just a t-shirt—another puzzle piece falling into place, helping Jane see the greater picture of her friend a little more clearly.

"Lila," Jane said, coming down to kneel beside her, and placing an arm around her small shoulders. Desperation made words fall helter-skelter from her mouth. "Don't. Please? We'll hang out now. We'll have an adventure, in the forest. On the trails. Off the trails. On the water, in a canoe. We'll steal a canoe, and take it out. We'll find the lake monster, and the treasure he keeps in the secret cave, like the Camp Chipmunk guidebook tells about."

"No," Lila said. "It found me. It's…It's here with us now. The *real* monster. My ghost."

Jane felt it then. A distinct presence. Goosebumps pimpled her skin as she heard the whispering of leaves touching in the forest darkness behind them. It was followed a moment later by the rustling of branches, and then the snapping of a branch like a thunder-crack in the nocturnal stillness: a footfall in the dewy loam behind them.

Together, the friends turned to look into the shadowed forest.

The thing drifted out of the trees.

The girls gasped.

Jane saw it, too. *She saw it, too.* It was real. Despite its terrifying appearance—maybe because of it—the girls couldn't help but stare at it, bewitched, though of course Lila had seen it plenty of times before:

The first thought that struck Jane about the thing, though she couldn't tell what it was she was seeing, was its weird and remarkable beauty. The cumulative effect was of a vast red-white cloud, like a detail from a painting by one of the impressionists they'd studied in art class last year, but somehow materialized in these woods after midnight, painted on the very air itself. It hung among the trees, shifting and swaying like a colossal jellyfish, entrancing the eye with its countless points of crimson; its ethereal white vapours comprised of particles ranging in size from motes to small stones; and the long red filaments like streamers curling and drifting on the night breeze—these individually moving elements that formed its essential structure stretching out across the moon-shimmering lake to the west and deep into the shadowed forest to the east, wrapping around the trunks of the black oaks, whispering among the leaves on their branches.

But then indefinable details and suggestions of details emerged from the greater canvas, and all at once Jane understood the horror of what she was looking at: the streamer-like appendages coalesced into millions of shredded strips of flesh, pulped muscles and organs—red and glistening; the cloud of whitish dust particles that she instinctively knew was ground bone; and the floating red cumulus of uncountable blood drops like a universe of stars.

Lila's father, Jane suddenly knew, had returned to visit his daughter in the final form his mortal body had known, after it had been devoured and regurgitated by a wood chipper just waiting for a man in distress to climb into its churning mouth. A shudder crawled the length of her spine, and she reached to her side to clench her friend's hand, and felt Lila shaking, too.

The phantasm floated over them like a spell, its presence somehow exuding an imploring quality, holding the girls captive with its fathomless horror. There was no portion of sky unoccupied by the thing—it now stretched as far as the eye could see in all compass directions. It felt to Jane as if they'd been transported into another universe completely.

A nauseating gurgling spluttered from somewhere within the red ruin as pulverized vocal cords struggled hopelessly to reform. The girls instinctively clamped their hands to their ears but it did nothing to shut out the cacophony of wet noises that made up that horrible voice. They stumbled backward, splashing ankle-deep into the cold water. Jane snatched a fallen branch that lay among the cattails. Lila just stood staring with eyes like moons.

Jane brandished the gnarled branch like a sword.

The thing drifted forward, bending grass blades and cattails in its wake, shaking acorns from the trees to plunk in the water around them. Its watery clamour grew louder.

The words flew from Jane before she even knew she'd been conscious of the insight.

"She *forgives* you, Mr. Pollard. Lila *forgives* you."

She turned to Lila for confirmation, and Lila was nodding her head vigorously, looking confused, trembling now less with fear than sorrow. Jane clenched Lila's hand tighter, imploring her, "Tell him, Lila."

Lila stared at her friend a moment, still confused, before a startled understanding seeped into her eyes. She managed, amid her convulsive sobs, five words:

"*Yes*, dad—I forgive you."

The deafening wet whisper-voice stopped instantly.

The girls watched mesmerized as the gigantic red-white cloud drifted up and up, silently through the entwined arms of the trees, up over the forest and the lake and high into the night sky. They stared skyward long after the apparition had disappeared, merged with the stars shuddering in the darkness.

The silence of the woods was huge.

The girls looked into the forest, hearts smashing.

Where the phantom had hovered menacingly a moment before only the white lilies and cattails stirred in the gentle breeze.

One by one, nightbirds took up their songs. A moment later and the crickets and cicadas resumed their electric symphony in the tall grass and trees.

The girls looked to one another. There were tears in their eyes. But these were the good kind of tears. Something overwhelming and dark had been defeated.

"I miss him," Lila said. "I miss him so much."

"I know you do," said Jane, thinking that whatever his troubles had been, Jane's dad must have been a really good person to have helped raise someone as special as her new friend.

They collapsed into each other's arms while all around them the electric voice of the night pulsed and pulsed like the most comforting music in the world.

They stood facing one another in the thick air of the bunkie cabin they'd shared for the past seven weeks. Their suitcases sat between them on the wooden floorboards. A megaphone-voice making announcements drifted in through the open window.

"I guess we better mosey," Lila said.

"Yeah."

They retrieved their bags from the floor and shuffled into the bright air. A moment later they were standing at the periphery of the dusty gravel lot, with the school buses and several cars lined up on the far side, with parents standing around waiting for their children. The sound of excited conversation was everywhere. Lila waved a hand at the thin blonde-haired woman standing beside one of the cars at the lot's edge. When she waved in return and made as if to come over to her she held her back with a finger raised on the air: wait. She stopped mid-stride, smiled, and returned to stand beside the door of the car.

Words came with difficulty, but Jane managed to begin the conversation she'd dreaded for days leading up to that inevitable moment.

"Will you come back next summer?"

"You know I will. Once a Chipmunk, always a Chipmunk."

"And you'll write me?"

"You know I will."

They stood there in the dust and sunshine. Their eyes were hidden behind sunglasses (Lila had bought Jane a pair—purple, like hers—from the little general store at the edge of the park as a farewell gift the day before) but they both knew there were tears in the other's eyes.

"Thanks," said Lila.

"For what?" It was Jane's turn to be bashful, looking at her hands.

"For believing me. And seeing my ghost, too. And…for making me feel like a whole person." She laughed, shook her head. "Oh my god—listen to sappy me. Can Lila get some pancakes with all this syrup?"

Jane looked up and met her eyes.

They smiled through their tears.

They held each other in a farewell that was as good as it was heart-wrenching.

Lila turned and crunched through the gravel toward her mom waiting amid the idling buses and cars. Jane watched her go. The day was bright. The day was so *bright*. No more ghosts lived inside its warmth and light. Not anymore. She imagined Lila opening the package she'd given her earlier that morning while making the long drive home with her mom. She imagined her smiling as she lifted the lid of the small wooden box to see the shell of the cicada, perfectly preserved with a thin coat of resin, mounted on the little square of green construction paper. Jane had found the hollow husk of the insect's shell clinging to their window sill one morning, as if waiting for her to discover it and gift it to her friend. She imagined Lila reading her attached note:

Listen Lila, and you'll hear.

And she imagined Lila listening, and hearing the song of their summer, wherever and whenever she needed to hear it.

You did it, Jane Montgomery, she thought, and began murmuring the words like a new mantra, one that would help her face all the days that were waiting: "Lila Pollard. Lila Pollard. Lila Pollard. My friend Lila Pollard…"

The summer was over, but that was okay: next summer was waiting, and it couldn't come fast enough.

Jane adjusted her new sunglasses on her nose and turned to look for her parents in the bustling parking lot.

Bright Sons
of the Morning

I: The Mission

He'd spotted a darker movement among the heat waves shimmering on the horizon, confirmed its reality with the binoculars. He watched it closely, marking its hulking shape, its loping and purposeful progress: a wolf, travelling in their direction.

"Company, Cerby," he said, but the mutt was already standing at his side, its ears raised alertly, eyes fixed on the approaching animal. Nine times out of ten, Mackey knew from long experience, Cerberus sensed imminent danger before he did, and his senses had been attuned to picking up threats even before his Change. The military helped instill that in a man, along with other, much less desirable traits—or maybe it only sanctioned the expression of those traits, gave them the vessel through which they could flourish. Maybe—

He shook his head, irritated with himself. *Focus, old man.* The older he got—and he'd certainly hit elderly status long ago—the more he worried that senility would come for him, and to be in its grip while living out his interminable existence, well...

Again, he willed himself to focus like the hardened pro that he was.

"Stay, girl," he said, voice firm. Cerberus had taken a step forward, her right paw dangerously close to the protective line Mackey had drawn in the sand, encircling them, as soon as they'd stopped for a water break. "Stay inside the castle." Because of course castles like these were sometimes necessary to repel the kind of invader they were dealing with.

Cerberus was one tough dog, but the monster coming toward them dwarfed her. The wolves of the Iraqi desert were fierce in and of themselves, but this specimen had the telltale signs of *otherness* that elevated it to an entirely different category of deadly. As it neared them, Mackey saw that, indeed, everything about the animal was unnatural: its size was staggering, less a wolf than a lion; the off-kilter way it moved, by turns graceful and then suddenly displaying a queer herky-jerky gait, like an automaton whose limbs were being manipulated by an unseen puppeteer, which was of course an accurate metaphor in describing it; and its eyes: the keenness of intelligence watching him from those two amber slashes was the real giveaway that he was confronted by an otherling, in the guise of a terrestrial creature.

He wondered if the wolf had been chosen for its size, or whether through some horrific transmutation the thing inside the wolf had caused the animal's physical form to grow, engorging it with its malignance, stretching its bones, ballooning its muscles, as well as augmenting its prowess, its hunger. And then also the fact that it came alone, when most wolves travelled in packs. Maybe, Mackey thought, the thing had eaten the rest of its pack.

That their position had been compromised came as little surprise, though it was disheartening. They'd only been dropped off at their designated debarkation point by his Reclamation Society contact that morning at dawn. They'd wiled away the hours in the tiny oasis, alone except for the trio of Domari, members of a travelling family of musicians. He had shared a simple meal of bread and figs with them, allowing the songs they played to calm him, help him adjust to his new surroundings after having spent the past six months in the comforts of college life back home, teaching, preparing for the rigours of this mission. They hadn't questioned him about his purpose in the inhospitable Al-Dibdibah region, a Canadian with his military gear and dog, and he'd appreciated their courtesy.

He and Cerberus had helped themselves from the fresh-water

spring and relaxed in the shade of the date palms, conserving their strength for the work ahead. Mackey had stared with awe at the vista of the Arabian Desert surrounding them, stretching out into the shimmering miles. He'd felt humbled by this rugged geography, this reminder that he was in the heart of an ancient land, untouched by modern society with its technologies that hid the natural wonder still abundant in the world.

Around midday, while the men took a siesta, Mackey and Cerberus had set out on foot. They'd crossed a monotonous dune sea dotted with scrub brush, the eastern horizon marked by a series of gas flare stacks, the colossal plumes of flame billowing from their summits giving them the appearance of Hellish candles. They hadn't seen a single living creature since, until now.

Of course, agents of otherness had plenty of safeguards against attack, and steeped in ritual cloakings though he was, Mackey had been too long at this game to believe his skills and knowledge went as deep as those of the secret deities and their earthly disciples. He kicked himself for not having made better use of the techware he'd brought along, which might have warned him of the wolf earlier, though out in the open desert he wasn't sure what he could have done to avoid the encounter. He hadn't thought such precautions were necessary until they made camp for the night. Well, live and learn—even after this long, there was still more to learn.

The wolf was dangerously close now, baring its fangs at them, leering and ugly. Cerberus growled challengingly, eyes avid. Mackey tracked the wolf's progress in the scope of his C7 rifle, sighting its chest as it sidled sideways, its snout low to the sand, watching them.

The animal opened its jaws obscenely wide, until an audible cracking sounded in the stillness as the bones became dislocated; and a voice spat at them, a grating falsetto that came out not as if garbled through vocal cords that weren't meant for human speech; but seeming to churn up whole and undiluted from deep within the beast, as if another creature resided there—which was, in fact, essentially the case.

"Go back go back go back. Fool infidel almost-human, we *see* you."

A messenger, then.

Mackey granted that he might be a fool, though he was no infidel—he was a believer through and through. But the thing likely meant it as a warning to a foolish wanderer, that those who weren't disciples of the deity it served weren't welcome in its territory. But why had it called him *almost-human*? He knew agents of otherness relished talking in riddles and nonsense, confusing their prey; likely this thing's remarks were exactly that. He'd had to bite down the desire to reply to it, reminding himself that communicating with such abominations was potentially deadly. His curiosity had nearly compelled him past his reason, however—otherlings, after all, represented a tenuous connection to the shadowside he was inextricably linked to himself.

But Mackey's face betrayed no emotion—it had taken decades of encounters like this for him to master his stoic façade, and even now, on the inside, he felt the same devouring terror he'd felt that first time, back in the trenches of the Somme, when he'd been made to understand that the engines of war operated on a profoundly deeper level than he'd ever guessed, so much deeper than the surface-level machinations of powerful men moving armies like pieces on a chess board. With this memory, a sudden cognizance of time swept over him—*that had been so long ago*. Over ninety years gone by in a flash—he'd been so young then, and naïve about the nature of the world, and other worlds and other worlds.

But he only raised his gun meaningfully, his finger itching the trigger. The otherling, understanding glinting in its eyes beyond the fire of its mania, and with the message for which it had been sent delivered, turned to be on its way into the sandy wastes it had come from.

But then, it stopped to peer over its shoulder and called, fangs bared mockingly, "Oh, the orgy of suffering beneath the bottom of the world goes on and on and on—*Jenny sends her regards*."

And it loped off, cackling like a hyena as it went.

Mackey stared after it. Then, biting down on the desperate fury that threatened to throw off his aim, he raised the rifle to his shoulder, sighted the creature in its scope, and let off a shot like he'd done too many times to remember: he watched, briefly satisfied when the bullet found its mark, blowing the wolf's head clean off. His heart sank though, when the thing only continued galloping across the sands, headless, silent, evil.

At his side, Cerberus snarled at the vision, a comfort to Mackey as always.

"Good girl," he murmured, following the retreating thing's progress. "Good Cerby." And then, "Don't worry—we're going to find her." Words he'd said to the dog countless times over the years, a promise he'd yet to make good on.

But, as ever, beyond the hardening of his heart, he felt it: the stabbing deep inside him, at the thought of his wife, Jenny, who he'd last seen over ninety years before; Jenny, who was lost in darkness, all because of him.

He shouldered his pack and, with his dearest friend in the world beside him, stepped from the protective circle and followed in the wake of the apparition.

"First watch is yours, Cerby."

The dog immediately stood from where it sat at his feet and climbed the small dune beside them to scan the dusking desert in the west.

Nothing beat a living, breathing sentry, though Mackey made what use he could of the state-of-the-art experimental tech the military provided him with, and sent up a pair of Invisibles. He liked the miniature drones—besides scanning the surroundings for signs of danger, they emitted a constant electrical pulse that disrupted all known forms of surveillance equipment in a radius of ten kilometres; this, plus their size—roughly the diameter of a golf ball—essentially cloaked them completely. He shook his head, still annoyed with himself for having overlooked the use of tech earlier, then told himself to let it go.

But it wouldn't go so easily. As always when he got down on himself for some shortcoming or another, Mackey thought of his father. Military through and through, he'd brought the army straight into their home. Growing up, Mackey had quickly begun to think of their house less as 'home and much more as 'HQ'. By the time Mackey was in high school, his hard-ass dad had gotten even worse by way of drinking like it was a mission every night—this led to full-on war between him and his mom. His dad won all the battles, bully piece of shit that he was, even if he'd lost his family in the process.

Mackey cut off the memory. He wouldn't let the son-of-a-bitch rent space in his brain while he was on a job, let alone this job. He didn't deserve to be in Mackey's thoughts at all. So he turned back to rummaging in his pack, and a moment later removed the half dozen Scuttles. These he scattered in a circle around himself, satisfied when the tiny globes silently sprouted their needle-thin legs and stood poised in the sand. Devised by the nanotech team of the Experimental Sciences Division, though much larger than their usual work, Scuttles were about the size of jumping spiders and, like arachnids, had eight legs that allowed them to effectively navigate sandy terrain. Most importantly, their superior computer systems allowed them to link electronic signals across vast distances in the formation of a tripwire web—calibrated to a frequency compatible with the Invisibles' signal-nullifying pulse, they created an efficient ground-level alarm system, at least when dealing with corporeal threats.

Mackey watched the things scamper off to take up surveillance positions in the distance. The trouble with tech when it came to missions like this was that the enemy didn't use new-fangled technology; much older sciences were always the chosen medium for spying on foolhardy men and their brave dogs when they tried to infiltrate places they never should have dared.

"Caution never hurts, right?"

Cerberus snuffled.

"Don't worry. I got us covered with all the usual wardings, and then some."

Luckily for Mackey, he knew a thing or two about the old sciences, too. Some considered him one of the rare experts, though he hadn't let it go to his head. It was a sobering reality, after all, dealing with the things he did on his covert missions. Those things made him realize just how amateur-hour his store of knowledge was. So if using Invisibles and other techware, even if only as a precautionary measure, offered an illusory sense of protection, he figured why the hell not go with it.

He unrolled his blanket and was settling down when he saw a camel spider scamper toward him. It stopped suddenly at the barrier of the protective circle, unmoving. His first thought was that it might be an otherling, but when he sensed no supernormal quality emanating from it, he knew it was just seeking the relief his shadow provided from the relentless sun. Mackey simply held up his hand in a gentle warding sign, and watched the immense spider scurry off to bury itself in the sand somewhere.

Sleep well, he thought, knowing he would not, despite his tiredness. The weariness he felt was a different, deeper kind—on days like this, he felt his age. This in spite of, or maybe because of, the gift-cum-curse wrought by his Change. The truth of it was that he constantly felt the inner tug of war—it defined his existence, caught as he was within the chronological passage of the years and what he'd come to think of as his inexplicable suspension outside of time; like an armour against the visible rigours of the normal aging process, his condition (he often thought of it as an "affliction") took its toll in different aways: mental, emotional, spiritual. It had nearly broken him in the early years, and it had taken a vast amount of mental training for him to be able to function as time wore on.

Sometimes he thought his greatest achievement had been managing to stay out of the psych ward—that and, on a more pragmatic level, continually faking his death and reinventing himself while remaining within the confines of the military. No easy feat, and he knew there were some that harboured suspicions about him, though the inherently cloak-and-dagger nature of his role as a police investigator at the military college provided good cover. Besides, what could anyone do or say, and who would believe their loonie notions about a preternaturally long-lived cop and instructor anyways?

He glanced at Cerberus, looking majestic on the dune summit, her snout etched against the red gloaming sky. He called to her,

"Quick shifts, okay? Quick shifts. I know you're tired, too, sweetheart." Of course, she was—she endured the same tug of war as Mackey did; she'd been Changed, too, at the same time as him. They were by far the world's oldest living soldiers.

The electric chirp from his wrist drew him from his reverie. The implant's digital screen had awakened, the information it held glowing through his skin: the Invisibles had given the all-clear. He felt safer knowing they hovered overhead, however misplaced that sense of comfort might be. He thought of the Scuttles and felt the same hopeful sense of assurance knowing they were out there, securing a wider perimeter beyond that of the protective circle he'd drawn around the dune. Naturally, Mackey took the most comfort from this boundary, made by his own hand and imbued with the incantatory strength he'd learned from the one teacher he'd had that he felt confident had been a true master. How he missed Antoni Dury on mission-days like this, when he was on the cusp of entering the country of the otherness.

Mackey stretched out on his sleeping bag, pillowing his head on his pack roll. Laying down allowed some trigger in his body to relax and physical weariness immediately washed over him, though his mind remained acutely alert. They'd spent most of the afternoon on the march, after all, skirting their target and then doubling back in an attempt to approach from an unexpected direction.

Mackey knew they needed to get what rest they could before making their strike in the hours before dawn. His sources put their objective within a mile of their present location, though any hope of their presence remaining undetected had evaporated after the encounter with the wolf. Somewhere south of them, very near, lay the tiny village of Dai-Rappur, and past this, out in the wastes, the nameless colony that was their dark destination. This was where Lieutenant Delson was.

But beyond the Lieutenant—beyond the thing it was that he'd become—a greater danger was waiting. A much more important otherling that the Lietenant was a slave to. And being as powerful as it undoubtedly was meant that it knew Mackey was coming. And so of course it knew *why* he was coming. It knew he'd been waiting for this mission—preparing for it with all the countless other missions—for over ninety years.

He closed his eyes, pushing away the vision of Jenny that, as it always did while he struggled for sleep, appeared to him; she was the phantom that dwelled in the cavernous cathedral of his mind, in the pain-riven causeways of his heart. But he managed to hold her at bay—and, as always, it was a struggle—and began the practised breathing techniques designed to bring on sleep, at least in theory. But though his body eventually grew comfortably limp, his thoughts continued to race, and he found himself contemplating the recording that had come into his hands four months before, and the story it held that had set him on this latest and most dangerous of missions.

II: The Name

When Mackey had found the unmarked cassette tape resting in the centre of his desk during his spare period, an immediate sense of disquiet had come over him. He knew that this job was going to be different from all the others. It wasn't the clandestine nature of the communication, something Mackey was long accustomed to in this line of work. Sometimes a case simply stirred something in him that he could only liken to a primordial dread, something deep-rooted, like a species-memory stretching from the mind of a tree-dwelling ape-brother three hundred thousand years old and finding its way directly into his heart. This had been like that, only stronger than anything he'd felt before.

Mackey had eased shut the office door, muffling the sounds of the handful of fellow faculty members chatting in the hall. He didn't wonder too much about the deliverer of the item, or how they'd gotten past the seven locks on the door, four of which were of the invisible, totem-guard variety. Those who sought him out for services rendered outside of his more orthodox teaching duties at Kingston Military College often had access to means of bypassing obstacles like these.

To his fellow instructors, his additional job as a long-time military police investigator made strange visitors to his office and frequent hush-hush dealings simply part of his duties. Most never asked questions. Some colleagues, though, Mackey felt fairly certain, harboured suspicions about him, maybe even knew a thing or two about what went on behind his office door. It was in the way they looked at him, cautiously, uncertainly, as if they couldn't trust him completely. Which was okay with him, since he didn't trust them either; the only person he trusted wasn't a person at all, though she had more heart than anyone else he knew—Cerberus was as loyal as they came, and he'd entrusted his life to her too many times to count.

He set his briefcase down on the desk, and glanced at the index card lying beside the cassette. It held a concise listing of the particulars of the job, written in a tiny, meticulous hand that completely covered both sides of the paper:

Subject: *Lieutenant Ronald Emery Delson—last mission as member of US Army + post-military activities in Iraq.*

Known crimes: *Murder of 1 man during partnered CAP, Persian Gulf. Followed by desertion and disappearance into desert.*

Assessment: *Based on intel from agents and interviews w/ civilians in area, it has been determined that subject has assumed leadership role of cult group known locally as 'Bright Sons of the Morning'. Note: eyewitness accounts of subject's behaviour and actions strongly indicate he has been overtaken by otherling force. Delson has assumed alias/persona known as 'Kutt-Kutt II' (not found in Othertext, though otherling Kutt-Kutt "the Vast" sourced in OT, Volume II).*

Estimates suggest approx. 300–500 converts to BSOTM over 6-month period. Reports from villages at periphery of group's area of ops show approx. 50 people reported missing in months since Delson defection. Based on previous missions with similar otherling-led groups, it is assumed missing individuals are victims of inhabitation and/or homicide in service of Delson/KKII, who himself is in service to another, greater presence to whom BSOTM is devoted.

Given high number of group members and reported influence of D/KKII, group-wide possession suspected.

Identity of primary presence: *reports cite group members speaking of single deity—no record of its name exists in Othertext and related docs. Name* *withheld here for safety precautions. See accompanying audio recording for clarification. <u>Proceed with extreme caution + full battery of safeguards.</u>*

Mackey frowned at this last. Warnings like this were extremely rare. The Reclamation Society was afraid. Withholding a name in writing was less a safeguard for the person reading the message than it was for the person who wrote it. And though the office space was protected in every way Mackey knew to protect it, he felt more than a little uneasy at the thought of playing the recording. You never knew what might be summoned via an unintended audio trigger, and find its way through some breach in the protective web. Hooks were tricky and tenacious—once they wanted in, they tended to find their way; they got their "hooks" in deep and were nearly impossible to purge, which of course was where the epithet came from, coined by Dury fifty years before and still adopted by the few adepts working in the field today.

He scanned the remaining information written on the card.

Mission objectives: *Termination of subject, D/KKII. Reclamation of any group members.*

Last reported sighting of subject: *Dai-Rappur, Al-Dibdibah, Arabian Desert, Iraq. D/KKII believed to have founded colony east of D-R.*

- Further details to follow upon acceptance

Mackey knew how little hope there was of reclaiming any members of the Bright Sons of the Morning, but of course he would try. He would believe in the possibility of saving some of them because it was this same belief that allowed him to get out of bed every morning and face the new day. He had to believe, because belief, against all odds and all proofs saying otherwise, was the foundation of his greater overarching mission—his personal reclamation mission.

The satchel filled with unmarked bills sitting beside the cassette he hadn't bothered to count, though the staggering amount of money meant that in all likelihood this job was an important one to the

Reclamation Society. And though it was a great deal of money, as it usually was, it was as always nowhere near enough for what the mission asked of him. There could be no appropriate payment for work like this; only his one true objective compelled him to pocket the money and go ahead with the job, continuing to operate in the shadowside of normal life.

Mackey had long ago realized that he no longer felt so ill-fitting in this netherworld, but rather that the everyday world, the world as everyone else knew it, had ceased to feel the right place for him. When he was here—teaching, feigning genuine friendship with fellow instructors, offering remedial help to students toeing the academic line, pretending, in other words, that he was as normal as those around him—he found himself longing for the shadowside, to walk the secret depths of the world where his never-ending efforts might edge him a little closer to his objective; that light in the eternal abyss:

Her gentle green eyes, her easy smile, her soft, calming voice, the tiny vertical scar under her left eye where a stone skipped in childhood had ricocheted from a root jutting from the river and collided with her tender skin; a violent kiss that would mark her for her whole life, a small blemish adding to her uniqueness, never subtracting from her beauty but maybe emphasizing the fragility she shared with those she tended to; all these attributes that seemed to spring from the innate sensitivity that was her special magic, which served her so well in her work as a nurse caring for the battle-wounded at casualty clearing stations and proper hospitals alike.

A dread clung to him as he retrieved the recorder from his desk drawer and slipped the cassette into its mouth. He tried shrugging it aside but knew it meant something—his augmented senses telling him something was different about this contact. He'd never felt this strongly before, though he'd dealt with a catalogue of hooks on the job that had honed his senses in ways that all of his combined combat experience hadn't.

He steeled himself and pressed the 'play' button on the recorder.

Over the whirring of the tape came the subdued sound of conversation, a sizable number of people, it sounded like. There was a natural echo, hollow and rich, suggesting a fairly large space—a church, or a natural site; a cavern, or outdoors among cliff walls.

Momentarily, the crowd-voice fell silent.

"Blessed morning sun, deliver thine kisses upon my beautiful sons."

Mackey flinched at the loudness of that voice, booming from the little speaker and seeming to fill his office. He thumbed the volume down a notch, even as the emphatic response came from the group:

"*—Show us, teach us, lead us, Voice of Him—*"

Oh boy, Mackey thought, settling himself into his chair for what he could tell was going to be a lunatic's sermon for the ages.

"Firstly, I welcome our new initiates. Seven of you—a number touched with good fortune. Our ranks are stronger with your light. For you new recruits, you warriors seeking your wings to fly you into the Elysium we have forged here, I must start at the beginning. *My* beginning, my *real* beginning—my rebirth—because the me that came before all of this was meaningless, without purpose…the mere proto-human, like you all. What in the old savage world might be called a *military climber*, much-decorated and on my way to greater Earth-bound glories, but of course so very far from full realization.

"I am the door and the way, and through me you will come into His presence and find salvation in his kingdom of fire. I was a soldier but merely a toy soldier in the illusory world that exists on the other side of the great curtain—from lowly Pilot Officer to Flight Lieutenant, this was my paltry rise in rank in those days that seem a lifetime away. I saw my share of atrocity, watched my comrades-in-arms perpetrate sins like creatures born to it, which they were because all proto-men are born to sin. It is in their nature that, given free rein to do as they will, they shall. Like flies to feces, they are summoned to the act of atrocity. And yes, my brothers, I confess: I too sinned. I killed, I savaged, I tortured, I took what I wanted because I was able. I was stronger than *they* were, whoever they were, and I reaped what *I* wanted. I didn't know then what I know now. Oh, but my eyes were opened. Now I see how weak I really was, for now my power is beyond what I then could have comprehended.

"I had many missions, though only one mission could be called important. One mission with true purpose. This mission was classified as top secret, though its political and strategic military elements, I was to learn, were meaningless, for there was a mission within the mission, a secret mission, and it was a mission for me alone. I had been *chosen* for it, by something greater than all paltry military leaders. Some might say it was my fate. I know it was greater than that: I *was* chosen…by *Him*, our great orchestrator.

"Oh, yes…I was found. And given purpose. Awakened to the greater purpose for which all of you now give yourselves, too."

At this point in the recording, Mackey could discern scattered voices from the audience—the beginning mutterings of a demented revivalist gathering giving support to their preacher's sermon.

"I love you and I die for you, Voice of Him!"

"You are the door and the way!"

"Show us!"

"Like Lucifer I was cast down, like mighty Ool-Tuk-heemeer and Nel-o-Pek Kall before me, though lowly proto-man that I was, I was merely lured down in my CF-18 Hornet—another of the Army's failed attempts to attain the heavens. I had been deployed in Doha, Qatar, my mission to provide protection for Coalition ships in the northern Persian Gulf in the early days of the Gulf War. I had been flying a combat air patrol when, looking to the sun, I saw Him. He burned there, and has always and will always—the light in our darkness. And in my head and heart, I *heard* him. And he beckoned me to him, with a promise of ascension I had never before contemplated possible for me—He said to me, 'Come to me and your weak shell with be the house for the great Kutt-Kutt the Second, son of Kutt-Kutt the Vast. This destiny I have decided for you.'

"And knowing in that moment that I had been chosen like few others before me, I went to Him. I shot down my fellow proto-human in the plane flying combat air patrol with me, and turned my machine toward my new—my *true*—home. Behind enemy lines I flew, but where were lines in all that wasteland? Boundaries like these meant nothing anymore, as did the wars of proto-man. I ejected from my cockpit, letting my plane crash in the desert, and I parachuted into the holy land, too.

"There was nothing around me for days' hike in every compass direction but the burning land. Only occasional camel herds, beetles, deathstalkers, and ulleks inside of sand cats watching me with interest, for I was the first proto-man many of them had ever seen. There, too, I felt the presence of my first krulugs peering from within their coffin snake shells, hidden in their sandy burrows, watching this frail creature, me, walk where no proto-human belonged. I had left my fellow almost-men behind. Where I walked not even the migratory Bedouins dwelled. The armies of my old existence were long behind me, barely a memory."

Mackey hit the pause button on the recorder.

He'd heard something, a barely audible noise outside his office door, nearly drowned out by the recording. Mackey sat tensed, straining for some other disturbance, eyeing the narrow space at the bottom of the door, waiting for a sign of someone loitering outside, a shadow, a further sound, a signal that the door's totem-locks had been breached.

When nothing happened, only the distant murmur of echoing conversation from the matrix of the building, Mackey relaxed back into his chair. He contemplated what he'd heard so far. One deception in the recording was already clear. It might have been the Lieutenant's voice but it most definitely wasn't the Lieutenant captured on the tape—a Cro-Magnon by any other name, no way did the quasi-archaic lingo come from the much-decorated bully Mackey had met once before when Delson had toured the college the day he'd delivered his commencement speech to that year's graduating class. This Old-speak came from something on the shadowside—the thing inside the man.

The worry wormed its way into Mackey's mind: how had the person been able to record this, capturing what was undoubtedly considered a holy ritual among the cult? Had someone infiltrated the group? Or was it a defector? The latter seemed less likely, as most members of groups like these that Mackey had dealt with were lifers whether they wanted to be or not—escaping the clutches of otherling-habitation was next to impossible, after all, at least for non-adepts. Of course, there were exceptions to every rule, so maybe the defector was on the run, hiding from the Lieutenant's agents? Maybe this person had been the deliverer of the cassette tape in Mackey's possession—this might explain their ability to slip past his eclectic lock system.

Or maybe all of this was an elaborately constructed trap meant to lure Mackey to his death. He'd made few friends in this business over the decades, and more enemies than he was able to keep track of, though he did try—his meticulous paper filing system, a massive collection that documented every case he'd taken on since the days after Number One had ended, had come in handy on more than one occasion, whenever an old foe had resurfaced and he needed to refresh his memory on the particulars of the case in question. His filing cabinets, a half dozen in his office and the same number at home, would certainly prove a curious history to some future clerk or estate trustee clearing out his things if Mackey was ever gifted with the peace of death.

There was one especially curious aspect of the speech, a first among cases for Mackey, which was significant considering that his case file went all the way back to the mid-1940s: the speaker's repeated reference to himself as a *proto-human* before his invasion by the hook. A curious detail he'd never encountered before, maybe specific to this group. A mystery within the mystery.

Whatever the case, the monomaniacal psychopathic personality came through loud and clear—this old boy sounded one hundred-ten percent raving loonie. In this, at least, the otherling was like so many others Mackey had encountered.

Mackey glanced at the brief notes he'd made on the notepad at his elbow:

> *Ulleks*
> *Krulugs*
> *Ool-Tuk-heemeer*
> *Nel-o-Pek Kall?*
> *Kutt-Kutt II?*

So, Delson was real-deal otherling, then. Because no one who wasn't otherling knew of such things. Mackey had encountered each of these entities before, except for the last two. He'd never come across the names in the important grimoires or any other of the Othertexts or lesser Oldtexts. He grimaced, remembering the horror of those otherlings, wondering about the horror of these new mysterious beings, and whether their obscurity meant they were lesser entities, or more feared and therefore less spoken of.

Satisfied that he was alone, Mackey hit the "play" button and settled back into his desk chair.

> "I may not have belonged when I was floated down from my burning machine, but as soon as my boots touched the sand, I felt the kiss of Kutt-Kutt the Second. He had been waiting for me—waiting inside of me, for the true me to be born. I had lived my inconsequential life until I was called to awaken, and then I came home. I think the lower animals knew. They knew what it was that had fallen into their kingdom: the scorpion sacrificed itself to me, stinging itself with its own tail. The serpent ate its own tail to form a ring in the sand for me to wear like a necklace. The camel spider scuttled out from its hole to stand upon its rear legs, to throw its forelegs skyward and then collapse onto the earth, genuflecting before me; it, the worshipper, I, its living idol. The cheetah and the oryx returned from extinction to offer me their bodies in sacrifice—I ate their meat, and their energy hastened my progress to Him.
>
> "A single proto-man only did I meet—a nomadic holy man, who greeted me with friendship though before his end came he knew what I was. I saw it in his staring eyes as his life rivered from his broken shell, sustenance for my parched tongue. He knew then that I'd fallen down from above, and that I was remade, a new prince of the Earth. My superiors in the army would have commended me, could they understand my ascension. I'm fortunate to have learned how inferior they all are. They too will bow at my feet someday, and before you, and before the one we serve.
>
> "It took time for me to understand exactly what it was that had touched me, but I knew from the start that I was changed from who I'd been in the Before-Time. I was changed from *what* I'd been. Into something *more*. Soon enough, though, the power that had come into my heart would give me the power to see, like I'd never seen before. And I would come to understand that this power had always slept inside me, dormant, lying in wait, and that it had been woken by the word of the Bright Fire, by the Bright Fire's touch.

"I am here to guide you in His name, to act as His instrument in the one true mission. We will cleanse the world until only the un-evil animals remain. We will bring humankind to its pinnacle."

More voices from the audience erupted here, stirring Mackey, the shouts of the Bright Sons of the Morning more impassioned now. He listened, frowning deeply.

"Oh, I was graced then, like few men before me. I was honoured and *graced*. He came to me in the heart of the wilderness, many days into my pilgrimage. Kutt-Kutt the Second guided me but my proto-human shell suffered for the journey: starved and thirsting, blistered from the sun, I was near death.

"He gave me His hand, and I took it and it burned like the sun, and the fire, it filled me up—body, heart, soul. I was remade. I wept, like I cry before you now. These tears carry my love. My love for Him. The wisdoms he shared with me that fateful day, they…they were so *many*. I never knew. I never knew the beauty in the world. Nor had I any inkling of the power in me, to take from the world in any way I needed. He taught me—he showed me it so clearly—that I deserve to have anything I want. To satisfy all my wants and desires and needs, so that I want for nothing. But riches like these aren't simply handed to weak proto-humans like I was then. No, my sons. I had to prove I was deserving.

"I was tested.

"'Go, my son,' He bade me, that great king of the wasteland. 'Go and return only when you have captured the souls of others to bring into the tribe. Go!'

"I went. I walked into the dune seas, watched by vulture, stalked by wolves, though all these creatures of the land dared come no closer—they merely waited for my death, and knew in their savage hearts that while I lived and walked their country I was a danger to their peace. They felt a loyalty to me and, indeed, it wasn't long before they followed at my side, soared and trod ahead as my escort through the burning wastes. I searched, and I searched, and eventually I found what I sought.

"First, I met a child on my trek. A villager who asked me, 'Are you here to kill the men of my village, and take the women?' You see, the child tragically understood this as commonplace: only one aspect of the horrors of the proto-man, in a part of the world never far from the heart of war. The boy looked ashamed, as if he understood his belonging in this proto-human tribe. I said to him:

"'I am a servant to the Fire. I am therefore the annihilator of lesser worlds, and the desecrator of them. But the individual pieces of them—its animals, its almost-people, its nameless villages and its famed cities—these I am too great to see. I consume them, but in the same way a man may breathe in a mote of dust dancing in the air, keeping it to burn inside the fire of himself. But *my* fire is the oven to cook worlds. You, your village, your men and women and history and stories—these are nothing to me. They are nothing at all. I am blind to you. My words to you now are the rarest of gifts, *the* great blessing of your brief life. Rejoice, or die—it is all the same in the end.'

"I left the dust-mote-child, and in leaving him took his life: after witnessing me, his life meant nothing and he took his young life with the dagger he'd had hidden in his robe. I saw this inconsequential happening in the ever-seeing eye of my mind only moments after our encounter. The sacrifice was mine, another wood grain to stoke the growing fire of my eternity.

"The greatest test came at the end, as I prepared to walk home to Him with my sacrifices, and my converts. A group of proto-humans appeared from the desert. They had come from the world I had left behind. A special missions team of five soldiers, whose mission it was to find me, to *rescue* me—oh, the wicked humour of it. I think in the end they knew that the one they had been sent for was no more, as they lay dying in the sand, their weapons spent and useless, their blood the bathwater on my hands.

"I am grateful for my military upbringing, for it was a clue to my fate. You see, I was *good* at killing. The savage art of it. I was born to it. Like you all, too, were born to it. It is the one art we take with us in our evolution. But before I killed without purpose. Killing now is a cleansing, and our duty to the only cause in our existence, the source of our worship, our great star giving us light and love. Our father, the Bright Fire in the Heavens. Oh, the *wonder* of him. The *strength*. He is our sun. We are his sons. We are his servants and our reward is our servitude. We must rejoice in this, always. We must never ever, not *ever*, forget how fortune smiles on us.

"Now, the time is come for you all to want for nothing, like I want for nothing. To *ascend*. To *become*. Never again will this world deny you. Refuse you. Punish you. Take from you. No, the world is *yours*. The world is *ours*. And we will make it our paradise until the end of time, and when long from now that end is here, then we will enter the paradise beyond time, together."

The shouts from the congregation were loud now, frenzied. Mackey could feel the manic energy captured on the tape, conjured by the Lieutenant-thing's sermon.

"The world is ours, Voice of Him!"

"We follow you, Voice of Him!"

"Lead us! Show us the way!"

"Today, you join His army. His legions are endless, like the infinite scales that protect his dragon's heart. Rejoice! You are all soldiers now, and important, when yesterday you were nothing, less than dust, less than the shit you expel from the shells of your fragile bodies.

"Today, you are mighty.

"Pledge your bodies, minds, hearts and souls to Him. I, Kutt-Kutt the Second, am his vessel and through me you have heard His voice. Say the words with me, brothers:

"*All* for Kagll-uth.

"*All* for Kagll-uth.

"*All* for Kagll-uth."

It grew into an impassioned call-and-response, each turn growing more frenzied for both preacher and congregation.

"*All* for Kagll-uth!"

"All *for Kagll-uth!*"

"*All* for Kagll-uth!"

"All *for Kagll-uth!*"

And beneath it all, something else; less a voice than a sound, and yet it captured all of the fanatical devotion embodied in the group-voice pulsating from the recorder's inadequate speakers:

```
<>|<>|<>|<>|<>|<>|<>|<>|<>|<>|<>|<>|
<>|<>|<>|<>|<>|<>|<>|<>|<>|<>|<>|<>|
<>|<>|<>|<>|<>|<>|<>|<>|<>|<>|<>|<>|
<>|<>|<>|<>|<>|<>|<>|<>|<>|<>|<>|<>|
<>|<>|<>|<>|<>|<>|<>|<>|<>|<>|<>|<>|
<>|<>|<>|<>|<>|<>|<>|<>|<>|—
```

Mackey smashed his fist down on the player in a shock of recognition, cutting off the recording. The silence in the office was huge, though the call and response echoed in his skull. A chill had crept along his spine, stirred the nape hairs on his neck.

He sat tensely, waiting for…what?

Something, though nothing happened, at least nothing discernible to his natural or Change-augmented senses.

Mackey removed the battered cassette from the player and slipped it into a padded yellow envelope. He then filed it away in one of the voluminous filing cabinets beside his desk. He eased the filing cabinet drawer closed with a deep thud that reverberated in the room. He retrieved the bottle of vodka from his desk drawer and drank directly from it, undiluted and strong like he needed it to be. It did nothing to quiet his hammering heart.

There was no more noise from the hallway. A deep sense of solitude had settled over the building during his listening.

He crossed to the window, opened the blinds. Late morning light filled the office. He found the sun risen over the campus buildings in the east, and for the first time saw a darkness in its light. He turned away but caught his reflection in the small mirror over the sink in the bathroom, the door of which was ajar. He didn't like what he saw there either, and tried turning his thoughts back to his work, his drink, his home, his dog waiting there for their next move, loyal as ever—things he could trust.

But Mackey had his own trial to pass; he made no mistake about it—it was truly a trial unlike the lesser missions that came before. If he'd passed through metaphorical fire over the decades of this dark work he'd been subjugated to since his Change, then now he was preparing to enter a truer, palpable kind of inferno.

He took a final pull from the bottle before replacing it in the desk. He felt the old determination seep into him. He would use the remainder of the semester to prepare for the job, a task that would undoubtedly prove to be an obstacle to his academic duties—it was, after all, the obsession that would not let him go, the thing that had held him in thrall since the Somme. He'd get by without giving his full efforts to his teaching, though he naturally couldn't shirk his work entirely. The Military College demanded as much from its faculty as it did from its students, a fact that gave it its reputation as one of the top schools in the world. In a stroke of synchronicity, his long-awaited sabbatical began at the end of the term.

Two months was of course not time enough to prepare, though if he could he'd drop everything and start the mission right away.

But he'd do what he had to, researching all the particulars, so that he'd be as prepared as he could possibly be; and he would dig as deeply as possible into the man whose fate lay at the heart of the case: Lieutenant Robert Delson, otherwise known as Kutt-Kutt II. Of course, Mackey was driven by something that his contact couldn't have suspected: the greater otherling presence lurking behind the whole scenario, which held a very personal connection to him.

As if declaring a challenge, Mackey spoke the name:

"Kagll-uth."

Nothing happened, but of course something had already been set in motion.

It had been a long time since Mackey heard the name spoken—ninety years, in fact—though of course not one day had passed that he hadn't thought of it.

III: Origin

He was twenty-one when he'd been sent to France, a country famous for its beauty but that had been transformed like so many others by the hand of war. A sombreness hung over all: his fellow soldiers were plagued by it, of course, and the locals of Albert, the main town behind the lines, and the place itself, with its hushed streets and buildings. Even the wildlife wasn't exempt: emaciated mongrels loping apprehensively through the streets; cats peering from the tall grass with haunted eyes; the dirty crows cawing at passersby without gusto, like sculptures culled from the ashes of bomb-devastated streets and given a semblance of life. The ingredients of the country's beauty were all there, but no beauty was captured within them:

everywhere young Mackey looked was the ugliness of despair and death.

He'd been sent directly to the Western Front, a crash course in the realities of warfare. He dealt with it as well as could be hoped for, putting on a brave face even when fear ate at his heart. He learned during these months of fighting that the Germans were ordinary men, some frightened boys like himself, but boys it was his job to kill just as they in turn were duty-bound to try and kill him. Those first days at the Front were difficult and filled with much horror, but it was several months later when Mackey learned about the secret, darker thread sewn throughout the conflict.

It had been an hour before dawn on a frigid November morning, nothing but a huge stillness hanging in No Man's Land, where fog drifted, making shapes his tired mind had been moulding into hulking figures all throughout the endless stretch of his sentry duty. He drew comfort from the presence of the ambulance dog that sat obediently at his side, the emblem of the Red Cross emblazoned on the back of the jacket she wore. A few days before, the animal had begun following him around whenever she wasn't off on some life-saving mission or other. She was medium-sized, a mutt, and there was something about her that Mackey liked. She had kind eyes, and a fierceness of spirit—not knowing her name, he named her himself: Cerberus. They were in Hell, after all, and in Mackey's reinterpretation of the mythical beast, she stood guard at Hell's gates in an effort to keep him and his fellow soldiers on the outside, and alive. She had become his good luck charm.

"Not much longer, girl," he whispered to the dog, who continued staring out vigilantly across the churned earth of No Man's Land, sharing in Mackey's vigil.

As if one cue, Mackey was relieved from guard by a gaunt-faced kid even younger-looking than himself. They didn't exchange greetings, only nodded soberly to each other as the soldier took up the post along the top that Mackey had occupied for the past two hours.

Thankful to be able to relax his buzzing nerves a little and curl up in his dirty bedroll, he trudged through the trench, carefully stepping over the bundled-up forms of sleeping men, heading for his own place at the end of the line, Cerberus padding silently behind him. He realized then the persistent pressure in his bladder and cursed himself for not having relieved himself while alone on guard duty. How much easier it would have been to piss in an empty tin of bully beef and tossed it out of the trench, than to trudge to the latrines out past the trenches. He passed his bedroll and other belongings and, resigned to his fate, continued on down to the end of the trench a few feet away.

As he came to the end of the passage, something drew his attention—it was off to his right, where the trench made a sharp turn into a small area reserved for dumping shell casings before they were collected and brought to the dump at the rear of the lines. It was there that Mackey saw movement in the darkness. Frowning, and fearing an enemy infiltrator waiting for him, he silently unslung the Ross rifle from his shoulder. He crept forward as stealthily as he could. Details emerged from the darkness, made clear by the muted moonlight fighting its way through the clouds.

Mackey knew the moment he saw them that he'd stumbled across something he wasn't meant to have witnessed. His first thought, before he actually understood what it was he was seeing in the murk of the trench, was that two men were embracing. Their closeness, and their solitude away from the rest of the sleeping platoon, suggested an intimacy—emotional, maybe sexual. But even as that idea came to him, it was dispelled by another, a much different truth he understood in some deeply unshakable way: whatever it was he'd found, it was no such comforting or passionate encounter; it was a dark happening; perverse; *wrong*. Confirming this feeling, Cerberus, peering around Mackey's leg, growled threateningly at what she saw.

The moon peered through the parted clouds to cast light on the tableau, and Mackey gawked, immobilized by the madness of the vision.

A massive German Shepherd—an ambulance dog like Cerberus, designated by its own Red Cross jacket—stood hulking overtop a soldier, holding him pinned against the wall of the trench with its large paws planted firmly on his shoulders. The animal was hunched over the man, its jaws opened horrifyingly wide…and something—some appendage—protruded from the dog's mouth and was connected into the mouth of the soldier beneath. This appendage, whatever it was, was stretching the hapless soldier's jaws unnaturally wide, as well.

Mackey was startled when the grunt, somehow sensing his presence, turned his eyes in their sockets to watch him pleadingly, tears running trails down the man's filthy cheeks. Distantly, Mackey recognized that the stricken soldier was Perkins, a fellow Ontarian he'd gotten to know over the past few weeks; softspoken, brave, a lover of hockey and a romantic waiting for the right girl to cross his path; and there he was, lying in the mud of a trench, his body invaded in this unimaginable way.

The dog likewise sensed Mackey's presence and turned to him with a movement swift and violent. The appendage was torn from the mouth of Perkins with an audible cracking—the unmistakable sound of bone breaking.

Perkins slumped over, his seemingly lifeless body sliding down the chalk wall of the trench he'd been pinned against. The Shepherd stalked toward Mackey, its great head low to the ground. It was as he faced the animal head-on that Mackey realized its size was much bigger than he'd initially thought. The beast was gargantuan, somehow too big, not only for its breed but for any dog. It was as if its body was swollen, more muscular than was normal, bulging in places where regular canines didn't.

The dog growled deep in its throat, and then a second voice emerged from the animal—from within the growl, or superimposed on it, or so it seemed to Mackey. An angry hissing that was clear and distinct from the voice of the dog. And it was then that Mackey understood, instinctively picking out the weird appendage jutting from the dog's mouth. It was swaying from one side to the other as the dog advanced on him, the moonlight flashing across its red-scaled surface.

It was a snake bulging like some abominable tongue from the gaping mouth of the German Shepherd. Unimaginably, a voice that was comprised of many voices speaking in tandem came from the serpent:

"*All* for Kagll-uth. *All* for Kagll-uth."

The horror was magnified when a voice said from close to Mackey's ear:

"Go back, soldier. *This* war doesn't concern you—yet."

Jerking at the sound, Mackey saw the rat nestled along the uneven wall of the trench, its dark red eyes watching him, jaws parted unnaturally wide as the voice rose up from within its body.

Mackey stood shuddering a second or two longer, frozen. And then he acted without thinking.

He screamed. He screamed a scream of pure terror, of the unknown and the unknowable. And it went on and on and on, until the claustrophobic space of the trench around him was filled with men, shouting and bristling with arms, guns pointed everywhere at once.

"Mack, what is it, kid? Tell me."

Distantly, Mackey recognized the voice of his CO, concerned and frightened, for him, and them all.

Mackey couldn't find the words, for there were no words to express what he'd seen. But he was able to point to the dog, which had retreated to the back of the shadowy tunnel, its presence unnoticed by his fellow soldiers, its Red Cross jacket as ubiquitous in their everyday trench squalor as their own haggard, malnourished faces. But the dog, seeing that he'd drawn attention to it, did what it had to in order to escape.

Mackey and his comrades watched the animal scrabble up the wall of the trench with claws as long as bayonets, and for a fleeting second its profile stood etched against the night sky, broken-jawed, the snake protruding from its mouth lashing across the firmament; briefly turning its cold-eyed gaze on the men and hissing its defiance.

From the mouth of the snake, a voice grated, "Kagll-uth marks you, Jonathan Owen Mackey."

And with the delivery of this promise; spell; curse—and it was, Mackey understood, somehow all of those things—the horror disappeared soundlessly into the noxious mists of No Man's Land.

They all stared after it, aghast, speechless with terror.

And as the men all clambered to the trench rim in the hope of catching another glimpse of the retreating creature, perhaps to confirm the reality of it, a smaller but no less venomous refrain chittered in the claustrophobic embrace of the trench, heard by Mackey alone where he stood shuddering with cold and with the memory of the encounter:

"Oh *yes*, Kagll-uth marks you."

It was the rat, and Mackey turned in time to see it squeeze itself into a fissure in the trench floor near his boot, a hole within the greater hole that he and his fellow soldiers had dug; crawling that much closer to Hell.

Perkins survived, though his jaw was broken, the top and bottom front rows of his teeth had been knocked out, and his esophagus crushed, requiring emergency field surgery. Their medic had saved him, and Perkins had been stretchered to the nearest mobile hospital for proper surgical care. His mind, and his soul, though—Mackey wasn't sure what state they were in, in the aftermath of the experience. Nor would he ever learn what had become of the man— that encounter was to be the final memory he would have of him. He never had looked him up after the war.

Beyond the obvious horror of it all, was one other shocking fact that Mackey would wrestle with, endlessly: There were worlds outside of the world he existed in. He believed. He'd seen what few others had seen—how could he believe otherwise? In the span of that relatively brief interaction, Mackey had gone from agnostic to believer; a believer at least in some things he hadn't suspected to exist.

And he understood that he was afraid because what he'd witnessed went beyond the politics of the war he was serving in. That night in the trench he'd looked into a darkness of such depth that it could have been only one thing:

Evil.

IV: Bright Sons

His first thought when Cerberus's presence at his side awakened him from his meagre thirty minutes of sleep, was efficiently mission-focused—sitting up quickly and glancing at his wrist, he said, "The Scuttles haven't checked in."

Indeed, the screen's digital face was dark, and when he tried to tap it awake, his worst fears were confirmed. "That's not good," he murmured. "The whole web is down. Not even one active signal." Meaning that every single Scuttle had met with its doom out in the desert. Mackey turned to Cerberus. "Anything?" he said meaningfully, knowing of course that something was amiss for her to have awoken him before the end of her watch. She gave a low whine and looked pointedly from him to a point at the edge of the circle, then back to him and again to their boundary.

Mackey crept to the place and squinted at the strange flower that grew from the sand. It was huge, its serrated petals as large as his hand, their colour a black so deep the morning moonlight cast no lustre in them at all.

"That's wrong," Mackey said. And something about the flower really did feel un-right to him—his augmented senses were bristling, though he sensed no immediate danger.

He turned to Cerberus when she whined again. He followed where she was looking, out into the early morning darkness. He couldn't see anything, so grabbed the binocs and climbed the dune to squat beside her.

Still he saw nothing.

"Something out there, girl?"

The dog growled a low growl.

"I can't sleep for shit, girl—you go to sleep, Cerby."

Cerberus looked to him questioningly.

"Good girl," Mackey said, scratching her between her ears, ragged from fights of years past where the teeth of otherlings had got her. He motioned for her to lie down, and she slid down the dune to curl up in the centre of Mackey's sleeping bag.

Mackey ate a nutrient bar, settling in for his vigil.

He'd been an hour into his watch when the disturbance arrived. At first, he'd sensed rather than seen something out in the darkness. Then he picked out the dark line on the southern horizon that hadn't been there the last time he'd scanned that direction. Mackey used the binocs, which confirmed what appeared to be a ridge of rock emerging from the sands and extending in a straight line as far as he could see to east and west. As he watched the spot, with the pre-dawn creeping in more and more, he saw that it now stood out as paler against the desert vastness. How anything so large could have escaped his notice troubled him. Whether it had been there all along or arrived during his watch, he couldn't imagine what it might be—a colossal line of tents? Or merely a trick of the changing light, a sunrise mirage conjuring phantoms to his tired eyes?

He knew, of course, that it wasn't what it appeared to be. Not only had there been no strong winds that might have uncovered such a natural feature of the landscape, but like an ongoing rippling across his skin he sensed the wake of an enchantment.

Whatever it was, he determined after several minutes watching that it was stationary. He resolved to wait a while longer, allowing Cerberus to rest; besides which, their presence was known, so it made no difference whether they bided their time before they ventured southward at dawn to investigate. Or maybe they'd be paid a visit by another servant of the otherling they were hunting.

A sense of existing within a bubble-like calm fell over Mackey, similar to an enchantment he knew that achieved the same sensation. This, though, came from having been in similar scrapes as this before. His thoughts turned to the beginning of all of this, the true beginning in the trenches; and he realized that the memory had plagued his dreams before Cerberus had woken him. This wasn't surprising, as the same dream had been recurring so often for so long.

Kagll-uth—he'd found the otherling at last, or almost.

Kagll-uth, whose name existed in no Othertext or grimoire he'd come across, and that was unknown among the students and teachers of occultism Mackey had dealt with over the years. Kagll-uth, whose name it had taken Mackey ninety-plus years to hear again, spoken by a rogue Army Lieutenant of all people, captured on a cassette tape recording delivering a sermon to a cult devoted to their deity.

The universe, Mackey marvelled, was indeed connected in countless unknowable ways.

He thought of the ecstasy in the voice of the Lieutenant, exalting his master to the congregation—their *Bright Fire in the Heavens*—and worried at the fear gnawing at him. With fear came the likelihood of making mistakes, and a mistake in this work could be fatal—and if he wanted any chance of saving his wife then he needed to be at the very top of his game, physically, mentally, spiritually.

But of course his unease was inescapable: this job was unlike all those that came before. It was the single most important in his ninety years of missions.

He watched the horizon, wondering about the fate of the Scuttles and Invisibles, deciding that in all likelihood they'd been detected and destroyed, their debris destined to become buried beneath the sand drifts as if they'd never patrolled there at all.

When the dawn set the eastern horizon on fire, Mackey was startled to find what had somehow gone unnoticed by him during his watch, though he'd remained fully awake the whole time: the small dune was ringed with more of the ominous black flowers, with their huge, dangerous-looking, light-devouring petals. Cerberus, too, slept oblivious, very close to the protective circle Mackey had drawn in the sand, and the flowers stirring in the cold breeze only inches beyond.

Their presence, Mackey knew, and the inexplicable geological formation that had appeared out in the desert, were the darkest of omens.

Mackey's sense of otherling-presence was proven correct two hours later when he and Cerberus reached the demarcation in the sand. Indeed, the binocs had confirmed much sooner that this was no rocky escarpment rising from the sands.

It was a line of corpses—men and boys—laid head to feet and stretching to the horizons. Most within their immediate field of view looked as if they'd been dead some time, their skin parchment-like stretched over their emaciated frames, taut across their faces and revealing the skulls leering beneath. A couple of bodies were more recently deceased, their skin not yet waxy and pale, their frames not quite so gaunt as the others. All of the corpses bore identical, deep wounds encircling their throats—ritualistic murder by dagger, Mackey conjectured.

That neither wolf nor vulture had scavenged a single corpse from this buffet of the dead showed that they'd been tainted with the stench of otherness. Mackey and Cerberus had truly arrived at a more absolute border than any boundary found on a map: on one side, the Arabian Desert; on the other, a wilderness that led to the Bottom of the World; the country of Kagll-uth.

Cerberus sniffed the air, a subdued growling deep in her throat.

"You and me, girl," Mackey said, trying to soothe her and himself. "We got this."

But he wasn't so sure. He felt the momentousness of crossing into this region as he stepped over the corpses. Nothing changed physically, geographically—and yet everything felt different. It wasn't something that could be perceived with the regular senses, but his Changed awareness understood that he'd crossed a great divide. Cerberus leapt with effortlessness over the bodies, gliding down softly into the sand on the opposite side. He saw in the brief startle of her eyes that she felt it, too.

They stood still, scanning their surroundings, smelling the air, listening to the wind moaning across the sands. Mackey could tell that Cerberus sensed the changed atmosphere, too—something in the air that felt not only distinctly different to the desert behind them, but that he sensed deep in his bones, in his heart. The dog, fangs bared in a soundless snarl as she searched the landscape, surely felt the dark touch of crossing the boundary between lands, maybe more acutely than he did.

As if to emphasize their great translocation, Mackey felt himself caressed by a sudden wind that was so cold its touch burned. Infinitely colder than the desert's night-winds, and the sun had already risen high above the eastern horizon. It was as if Kagll-uth had bent nature itself to its will here within the bounds of its domain.

They walked on, waiting for something to happen.

It wasn't very long until Mackey's keen eye saw them, directly ahead.

"Company," Mackey said.

Hearing the word, one of many signifying the presence of danger that she'd long ago become familiar with, Cerberus followed where Mackey was looking. Mackey muttered under his breath, "We must be V.I.P. visitors out here, girl. That's some welcoming committee."

He didn't think he'd ever seen so many otherlings in one place at the same time. He guessed there were one hundred or more, spread before them in an impenetrable line from north to south. What Mackey had at first taken to be a trick of the heat causing the group to shimmer turned out to be something else entirely, and it sent a jolt of fear through Mackey, a fear that grew into terror the longer the spectacle went on.

The otherlings, all one hundred and more of them, weren't approaching Mackey and Cerberus at a walk—they were running across those burning miles. *Sprinting.* And they sprinted all the way, untiring beneath the molten touch of the sun, as if their bodies felt no pain, no fatigue. A certain sign, of course, that the bodies no longer belonged to their original owners, but were host to those who would wring them for every ounce of service they could until the physical shells crumbled. Adding to the lunatic vision was one other fact that became apparent the closer they got to Mackey and Cerberus: all the otherlings were completely naked. It made sense, Mackey reasoned—the human hosts *were* the clothing for the otherlings inside.

"Goddamned hooks," Mackey said.

It wasn't long before the hooks had arrived, the edges of the line curving to surround Mackey and Cerberus. Soon they were encircled. All of the otherlings were men, Mackey noted, though he saw a handful of children among the throng. Every one smiling ecstatically, with such fervour that they seemed to be wearing death rictuses.

Even if Mackey had been able to shoot his way out of the situation, he wouldn't sacrifice the people sharing their bodies with the otherling presences, doomed though they most likely were. Doing so, as with the wolf the previous day, wouldn't kill them anyways. Even destroying the bodies completely, with bombs, say, would only free the presences inside, potentially to launch an attack on him while in their non-corporeal forms, something more than likely given that they were deep inside their territory where their power was at its most potent. And despite the armour of cloakings Mackey and Cerberus wore, the fact remained that the otherlings outnumbered them one hundred to two.

There was nothing to do but surrender, and hope they would live long enough to infiltrate the Lieutenant's hidden base, and maybe, if luck was with them, find Kagll-uth itself.

"Stand down, Cerby," Mackey said. "It's okay, girl. We're going to get through this. Stand down, sweetheart."

As the manically smiling horde inched close, sending a chill rippling along Mackey's spine, he told himself to see the positive side to their plight: this, finally, was the opportunity he'd waited for for so long. And though he cautioned himself to be a realist, especially after the decades of fruitless searching, he couldn't help the excitement he felt. Surrendering to the otherlings would bring him that much closer to her.

Jenny.

Their voices spat the words in eerie unison, a single huge and exultant voice in the bright air:

"*All* for Kagll-uth. *All* for Kagll-uth."

Mackey had his arms raised high in the air in a clear show of surrender. He said, "I've heard this song before, guys."

Beside him, Cerberus whined nervously and moved closer to

Mackey, her body pressed up against his leg as the litany from the slaves of Kagll-uth rose louder than the icy wind, now an anguished howl raging across the wastes.

Mackey woke to find himself sprawled in the sand, a pain in his skull so all-encompassing he felt the threat of unconsciousness looming to claim him again. Gradually, he grew accustomed to it and was able to retrieve his last waking memory from the muddled fog of his thoughts: being hemmed in by the otherlings, and one of them stepping forward, leaning in close, the thing's disturbing smile breaking only when it unexpectedly darted its head forward like a cobra to spit into Mackey's face—a great spurt of liquid that stabbed painfully in his eyes. And with the impact of the liquid, an immediate and powerful vertigo had hit him.

He lay there for a while, willing the pain to ebb, slowly growing aware of pain in other parts of his body, too. The fanatical otherlings had done a number on him. Thankfully, as far as he could tell, it had been restricted to what was only a physical assault—he sensed no disturbance inside of himself, certainly no presence. The mystic fortress of his cloaks and warding spells had held against any would-be invaders; he knew with certainty that the otherlings had tried to take him over—their mystical fingerprints were all over him.

If only his long-dead dad could see him now, Mackey thought, beaten to a pulp the way his pops had done too many times to count; the world's oldest failure getting closer and closer to the end of a botched mission, and a botched life. But you could never say for sure what fate had in store for you, so Mackey contented himself in waiting and taking stock of his situation and conserving what strength he had left for what awaited him.

A vast leaden silence surrounded him, punctuated by the occasional soughing of the wind. He lifted his head up, allowing his blurry vision to focus. He was surprised, given the silence, to find that he was at the centre of a circle of otherlings. Beyond the bounds of the circle he saw other circles, rows upon rows of otherlings, dozens of them making up each ring, standing shoulder to shoulder in tight ranks, like some alien military formation. Even if he'd any doubts, Mackey wouldn't have felt the need to do a casting scan to determine that they were all shells housing otherlings: each of the faces he saw was devoid of emotion of any kind, despite the unsettling smile each wore; some of the bodies were ragged with old wounds, as if they'd been put through strenuous and reckless use.

These then, were the Bright Sons of the Morning.

Mackey was less alarmed at being hemmed in by the host of otherling fanatics, or the fact that, like them, he was naked, his body covered with dark bruises and congealed cuts, than by the absence of Cerberus. Not having the dog at his side felt wrong. They were nearly inseparable and relied on each other to such a degree that Mackey took it for granted until rare times like this when they were forced apart. And though she was an incredibly strong animal, with a canny mind, and even though she was cloaked in magics, still Mackey worried desperately. They were dealing with forces that swam in the most dangerous seas of arcane knowledge—if anyone or anything could cause him and Cerberus harm, it would be otherlings like these.

And their master.

Irritated at himself for having so easily succumbed to their trap and frightened for Cerberus and himself, Mackey slowly got to his feet. Once standing, and after he'd fought down his spinning vision, he looked at the people and called out, as indignantly as he could manage, "Hey slaves. Does a guy need an appointment to talk to your master?"

The silence from the ring of figures was unsettling, accentuating the unrelenting howling of the wind like some mournful Wendigo of the dune seas. More chilling still was the fanatics' seemingly unbreakable look of ecstasy—still, those smiling faces, eyes filled with such elation that it effectively erased all signs of their former humanity.

Then, a place in the circle parted to allow someone through.

V: The Battle

Mackey knew it was the rogue Lieutenant he faced, though he was barely recognizable as the man he'd met a few years before. His features were distorted, swollen. Indeed, his physique wasn't that of the man he remembered—though fit, Denning certainly didn't look like this. The muscles of his body were gigantic, giving him the appearance of an anatomy drawing come to life, where each muscle in his body was pushing outward to become grotesquely, impossibly defined. It didn't suggest a fit and athletically honed physique like that of a normal human being, or even the exaggerated proportions of a comic book hero, but rather as if such a state had been attained but then taken further, beyond the point where the human anatomy was capable of safely containing it; at which point, an evolution had begun to take shape, in which the musculature that had burst through its former confines was now being given new parameters to work within. Mackey got the impression that the otherling he faced wasn't yet fully formed, whole—that it was a horrific work in progress.

Once, when Mackey was ten years old, he'd been at the mall with his parents where a bodybuilders showcase was being held outside the local fitness centre. They'd stopped a moment to watch the spectacle, Mackey bewitched by the unsettling sight of the men and women, their oiled bodies rippling with muscles, sculpted to a degree that baffled him—he'd never believed that people could actually look like that, outside of superhero comics. He'd been overcome with revulsion, and the bodybuilders had followed him into his nightmares for months. Now, in the presence of this otherling, those same bodybuilders seemed like people in costume, play-acting a character that truly did exist, but so far outside of themselves that it was nearly unattainable.

Unlike his subordinates, Denning wasn't smiling. Utterly emotionless, he watched Mackey with inscrutable eyes as he strode forward, his hard chiselled body at home in the rugged landscape.

Mackey said, "A bright morning to you, Lieutenant Denning," trying to sound confident, though his voice only came out small, seemed snatched away by the night wind. In the distance, a wolf gave its voice to the desert.

Finally, Denning's face creased, lips pulled upwards into that hideous, emotionless semblance of a smile worn by all the Bright Sons.

"Denning is inside this frail house with us, buried deep."

If that was frail, Mackey didn't want to see the otherling at its physical peak. "Then who am I speaking with?"

"I am transformed. I am the vessel through which Kagll-uth speaks, for he will not deign to speak with dust such as you. I am his general like I was never a general in the small world of the proto-man military of which you are a cog. I am changed. I am re-named, for I am reborn. I am Kutt-Kutt the Second, the second General of the great host of Kagll-uth."

"You're a slave," Mackey told it. He wasn't going to be intimidated by big talk from another otherling slave, no matter how powerful this one might be.

"I am *blessed*," it spat back.

And *it* was indeed the appropriate signifier—Mackey could see that Denning was lost. This otherling radiated an aura of power that touched Mackey like a strong wind. But he'd driven it to anger, which was a shot landed on his part, so he'd goad it further and develop the chink in the armour it had allowed him to glimpse. Wannabe otherling deities were always full of themselves. Upping the theatrics, he barked a laugh that cut the silence like a knife.

"*Blessed?* In all of our shitty collective history, there's never been a single slave that could be called 'blessed'. Why don't you go fetch your master for me—and let the big boys talk this all out."

An expression of hatred contorted the muscles of the face, pushing them past their already supernormal limits, first into a hideous parody of fury, and then into something that was simply grotesque—though its smile remained. Mackey found it difficult to look at the face directly; not for fear, though it was one of the more unsettling things he'd seen—but because the extreme perversion of human physiognomy was revolting to behold. He couldn't help but flinch a little, feeling the face might rupture in places and spatter him with gore.

The Lieutenant-thing, seemingly giving in to its rage, took several steps toward Mackey. He tensed, assuming a fighter's pose while scrambling to clear his mind and prepare a barrage of wardings, though what his physical and arcane prowess could do against the presence that animated the man coming at him seemed negligible, especially while in his beat-up state. But the thing stopped, its smile growing, splitting its features into an even more hideous visage, less a human face than a mask made to resemble a human face and pulled over the head of some nameless beast.

"I must offer apology to you. I have been remiss. Because you still don't understand, do you, proto-man? No, I can see from your face that you don't. You see, all of this isn't the way you think it is at all. The Lord Kagll-uth is no abomination from some infernal domain of your invention—some colourful Hell inside the bowels of the world, or the blackness between stars. He is not some being from…" he drifted off, spread his arms to the stars, and finished, "No, soldier. He is in all of us."

Mackey frowned exaggeratedly. "Are you trying to bore me to death with children's fables? Sorry, Lieutenant Dungeon Master, but I left my twelve-sided dice back in the rec room, and anyways, I'm not in the mood to play your tabletop fantasy campaign. Pretend monsters don't do much for me anymore—I outgrew them back in the Forties, when I started killing your kind—the real monsters, every single one of which turned out to be real mortal."

He said it all with as much bravado as he could muster, but it was all show: something gnawed at him, a dark worry that threatened to blossom into a greater fear.

In the distance, came the howling of wolves again—a group of them this time. Mackey thought of Cerberus, and a vision of her being tracked by a pack of the beasts came to him, shuddering his heart.

Unsettlingly, Mackey saw that the Lieutenant-thing's demented smile had begun to cause damage to its physical shell. The skin at the corner of its lips, stretching beyond the natural bounds of the face, split, dark lines of blood trickling down. It took Mackey a second to realize that the raspy grunting spluttering from its mouth was mean laughter.

"Don't you *know*, proto-man? You don't *sense* it, even after all that I have hinted at? Kagll-uth is no *monster*. He is no spook from a pulp story. None of those blessed to be allowed entry into his kingdom is something so trivial, almost-man. Try to fathom with your infinitesimal mind the great truth: Kagll-uth is *human*. He is the gift inside *you*, and inside *me*, and inside all the rest of us. He is the great *potential* within us all, unlocked. He is greater than you only by virtue of having long ago accepted his natural transmogrification, abetting it and hastening it with the hard-won gift of Old magic. There is no ghostly presence that infiltrates the shells of proto-humans, taking them over like a puppeteer playing his theatre of marionettes—there is only the unlocking of the true human within. Though we do make use of the lower lifeforms—wolves, say, given transient sentience and sent out to deliver warnings to would-be heroes like yourself. Even the greatest of humans makes good use of lackeys. In the same way that the human recruits the proto-human slave, and wrings everything he can from him or her.

"The gift of our humanity unlocked—this is what Kagll-uth has given us. Don't you want to be *like* him? Can you *feel* this within you, dormant, waiting? This *beauty*? This *power*, without the debilitating weaknesses of the human-who-has-not-risen: morality—emotion—love." He barked a cruel laugh. "Kagll-uth has no use for failings like these. Kagll-uth has attained his humanity—what the almost-human calls *godhood*—and he is perfection and purity and power without limit. And anyone fool enough to oppose him, he merely returns to the dust without thought."

The Lieutenant-thing smiled wistfully, and added, "It saddens me to think of it: that so many of us will never—*can* never—become the true human—the god of fabulous invention—that lies sleeping inside the shell."

Mackey said, smiling wryly but with even less conviction in his voice than before, "I just can't quite see the hard scientific rigour in the claims you just made."

Kutt-Kutt the Second sneered, "You *see* nothing, because you seek to know the world through the wrong sciences."

"And what about wacko serial murderers like yourself? Do you make the upgrade to your version of *human*?"

"One step closer to my betterment."

"I think I'm fine with who and what I am, thanks."

A look of profound disappointment creased Kutt-Kutt II's face, and it said, "Jonathan Owen Mackey, you got a *lot* of growing up to do before you're man enough to stand up to your Pops like that."

It was, incredibly, Mackey's father's voice that came from the otherling's torn and bleeding mouth. Not only this, but it was the beginning of a lecture that Mackey knew well—*the* lecture, that had haunted him since his fifteenth year. Mackey was dragged back to that moment, saw his teenage self trying futilely to hide the tears stinging in his eyes where he lay sprawled on the oil-stained garage floor after his dad had knocked him down—one hard punch clipping him on the chin and taking all his adolescent dignity with it.

The Lieutenant, Kutt-Kutt the Second, in the voice of his father, went on.

"Johnny, she *deserved* what she got, like she deserves it every time she gets it. Do you hear me? Can you finally get that through that big thick dumb skull of yours? Your mom just needs reminding of her place in this house, just like you needed reminding just now. That's the *chain of command*. And any time you need reminding, I'll be here, bud. Your Pops—your superior—will *always* be here to teach you that lesson because, son, you ain't man enough yet to protect your mom from the teacher when she steps out of line and needs a lesson, so don't you even try. You got that, champ? Unless you want to go another round with your dad right now and make me prove it to you again? I can deliver TKOs all night long, champ."

There'd been tears in the lunatic's eyes even as he'd stood over his son, brandishing his fists in a way that wasn't supposed to happen between family. Eventually, he'd stomped off to get another beer and a handful of pills, leaving Mackey to try and pull himself together.

His dad had been right—all he'd been able to give his mom later that night, while his dad slept off an epic drunk on the couch, was his child's-tears and his dual professing of apology and love. And, like a stake driven into Mackey's heart, it was his mom—his oft-battered mom, black-eyed and strong—who told him that things were going to be alright, and that he was her brave boy, her guardian angel, her sunshine making every day a little brighter for her.

It took a lot but Mackey managed to come back from that unexpected and jarring place of memory, back to his confrontation with Kutt-Kutt II who, in a further show of travesty, was crying now, too. Mackey barked a laugh and made it sound full-on brazen, as if he were unmoved by what he'd just experienced. *"Pops*—been a while! Glad to know you ended up right where you belong…in Hell with all these other *slaves.*"

Kutt-Kutt the Second smiled its red smile, tears still flowing from its manic eyes. "Perhaps old *Pops* was enlightened all along, beating on your whore-mother while striving, if only blindly, toward his true humanity."

Though Mackey was able to keep up the self-assured front, an involuntary tremor crept over him. In all his many encounters with entities like this one, none had ever framed their existence—nor his own—in such terms. The oldest and most credible books written by occult science scholars never suggested the scenario. Always, the framework was essentially the same: evil coming up from a metaphysical underworld, or from some unfathomable other-dimensional beyond and nudging its way into our world, becoming the seed of some dim instinctual dread of the unknown in each of us. Though rarer, there were instances where humanity was depicted as the newcomer here, and the hooks as the original species that saw us as the interlopers, the disease spoiling a world that belonged to them. Still, in all the scenarios, the players had their roles: the hooks were the evil; and we were the innocent, at least in relation to the unspeakable malevolence that they represented.

It was the way Kutt-Kutt the Second made its revelation that showed Mackey the truth of it; eagerly, with a gleeful depravity, watching Mackey avidly for his reaction. Thinking of the countless otherlings he'd encountered over the years, Mackey found that he'd accepted the inconceivable truth of what he'd been told; the otherlings' outward monstrousness was nothing less than the physical fruition of their ultimate selves, once they'd attained their true humanity. He felt sick at the thought, that something so vile lurked inside himself, sleeping, waiting to be awoken.

No doubt Kutt-Kutt the Second had seen it in Mackey's stunned features when acceptance seeped into him. But he had to play the game as well as he could because so much depended on it. His reaction shocked the otherling in turn.

He burst into laughter, doubled over with it, felt himself slip into the character he was playing. Tears were in his eyes when he managed, "I don't believe your lies, Shakespeare," Mackey told the Lieutenant-that-was-no-longer-the-Lieutenant, but his voice betrayed him. He did believe. His heart knew it to be true, and his heart quavered at the knowledge.

The Lieutenant, again in the voice of Kutt-Kutt II speaking for the Lord Kagll-uth, smiled a feral smile that gleamed in the stifling air. "Oh, but you *do*." It watched him a moment, as if gauging his reaction, then, "But, in the end, what you believe matters nothing. You are a germ of disease in the face of the cure. The Lord is the great cure of humanity. Today, he snuffs you out through the arm of his power...me, Kutt-Kutt the Second. *Now* you die by my annihilating hand."

Kutt-Kutt II threw something at Mackey's feet: his commando dagger—unmistakable, he'd been using the same knife since he'd been issued it during his service in the Second World War. Where the otherling had been concealing the weapon, Mackey couldn't say— Kutt-Kutt II was naked, after all. It was as if the otherling had conjured it from the air. Just as magically, the hook was now holding his own knife—a dagger so long that it might have been a sword. Something in the weapon looked odd to Mackey, and even as he thought this he understood that Kutt-Kutt II held no weapon, but that his body itself was the weapon—the deadly-looking blade grew from his right wrist, appeared to be a keen-edged bone sharpened to a point.

Seeing his wide-eyed appraisal, Kutt-Kutt lifted his dagger-arm to his cheek. "I am the weapon of my Lord, living to strike in his name."

Mackey found his brave-voice. "It was awful nice of Lieutenant Delson to volunteer his body for your arts and crafts project,

Lieutenant Kutt. So, what? We duel like gladiators? Were you in the stands at the Coliseum, too?"

"I was in the sand, slaughtering your kind—the true slaves."

Before Mackey could retort, Kutt-Kutt the Second raised its face skyward and bellowed, "The glory of the battle between the warrior of the sun," with a pounding of a fist against its chest, and then stabbing the dagger of its arm toward Mackey, finished, "with the failed man, he who cannot ascend to his potential. I should just as easily have let my Sons tear you limb from limb. Consider this contest, blade against blade, a whim of my still not-quite-human self, Jonathan Mackey, a sickening part of me that a good solid butchering of you might just cure."

The Bright Sons surrounding them had begun a manic chanting. As it went on it sounded to Mackey less like the voices of men than the frenzied call of insects. He knew that sound well, remembering the eerie collective voice captured in the cassette recording. Now, sharing the same physical space with the disciples, Mackey felt the sound as a tangible pressure against his skin, hot and unwelcome, like a burning wind blowing in from the heart of the desert.

<>|<>|<>|<>|<>|<>|<>|<>|<>|<>|<>|<>|
<>|<>|<>|<>|<>|<>|<>|<>|<>|<>|<>|<>|
<>|<>|<>|<>|<>|<>|<>|<>|<>|<>|<>|<>|
<>|<>|<>|<>|<>|<>|<>|<>|<>|<>|<>|<>|
<>|<>|<>|<>|<>|<>|<>|<>|<>|<>|<>|<>|
<>|<>|<>|<>|<>|<>|<>|<>|<>|<>|<>|<>|
<>|<>|<>|<>|<>|<>|<>|<>|<>|<>|<>|<>|
<>|<>|<>—

Mackey was startled by Kutt-Kutt the Second's travesty of a smile, noting the extra-large protruding teeth crowding the mouth, like a pair of dentures meant for another man shoved into the leering maw before him; the eyes were yellow and cloudy, reminding him of the long-time heroin addict he knew from the veteran's club; the lumpen skin, as if the musculature beneath was expanding. The otherling was changing before his eyes, growing more and more—Mackey could no longer deny the truth of it—human.

"When you die by my hand, you will be spared the voracious hunger of the Lord. Your death will be my gift to you, so much less painful than what might have been your fate."

"Wait," said Mackey, holding up a hand. "Before we do this, I've been meaning to ask since I woke up into this lunacy ... Where is my dog?"

A look of confusion mixed with irritation crossed the otherling's features. "That even lower lifeform you were captured with? Being eaten by something, in all likelihood. What does it matter? You are about to die yourself."

Mackey narrowed his eyes. "Lieutenant Slave, you just don't make comments like that to unenlightened dog-lovers."

He sprinted at the otherling, knife held low.

Kutt-Kutt the Second was unprepared for the explosive swiftness of Mackey's charge, its seeming recklessness; and despite its own preternatural speed, barely dodged the dagger-strike that Mackey whipped upward. The strength of the blow, aimed for the otherling's throat, might have made a good start on an eventual decapitation, if the creature could be subdued long enough for Mackey to get the grisly work done with, and if its lunatic followers didn't kill him. But Kutt-Kutt the Second, despite being taken off its guard, was astonishingly fast. It lunged to one side so that the edge of Mackey's blade sliced a line down its cheek—far from a lethal strike.

Mackey knew his chances were bleak. There were only two ways to stop an otherling, after all. The first was to destroy its body to the degree that the thing inside of it would no longer have a physical shell to manipulate; dismembering, or the use of explosives were the ideal methods. Mackey didn't have the time for the former even if the otherling had given him a crude means by which to do so in the form of the knife it had granted him, and he didn't have any explosives to hand, so there was no chance of the latter, though under the present circumstances, explosives would mean his own death as well.

And though Mackey had had ample opportunity over the years

to practice the second means of vanquishing abominations like Kutt-Kutt the Second, he knew he was outclassed in the realm of magic. He'd fought formidable otherlings before but nothing nearly as strong as this. Being the General to the grandaddy of otherlings said as much.

But Mackey was still going to try. He was too stubborn to accept defeat, which was why he'd gotten his ass kicked so regularly by his father, the first real monster he'd known.

"What are you waiting for, dad?" he said, laughing. "Or Denning or Kutt-Kutt or whichever slave I'm dealing with—come on over here and let this almost-man cut you to pieces."

Kutt-Kutt the Second, seething at these barbs, ran at Mackey, its dagger-arm poised at its side for an upward strike intended to gut him. Maybe it hadn't been expecting Mackey to have the wherewithal to fight with any means besides the knife in his fist—whatever the case, the warding spell Mackey threw at it was simple but effective. The otherling, so intent on killing him, sensed nothing and crashed headlong into the invisible barrier; the impact sent it crashing heavily to the sand, its physical shell battered, the otherling within momentarily stunned.

Without pause, Mackey dropped the warding spell and dove onto Kutt-Kutt the Second, pinning its shoulders to the sand with his knees and driving the dagger into its face and neck over and over and over. He took out its eyes and crushed its throat; flesh was cut, blood spurted, tendons pulled loose, clinging to his blade.

The otherling regained its composure and swatted Mackey from itself with a backhanded blow that sent him reeling through the air. He smashed to the ground, winded, the world spinning. Through the blood pounding in his ears, he could hear the otherling getting to its feet and crunching across the sand toward him. He knew he hadn't inflicted enough damage—without its eyes it could still sense him, hunt him. He imagined its dagger-arm raised beside its face for a downward killing stroke. He turned to meet it, willing the strongest warding spell he knew, raising his own knife in an unlikely bid at parrying the impending blow.

Through his swimming vision, the destroyed face of Kutt-Kutt the Second glared down at him, red sockets seething with the otherling within. Its grotesquely muscled dagger-arm was raised high, pointed at his heart.

Mackey readied himself.

Something hit Mackey, hard. The blow struck him in the chest like a freight train, knocking him backward and nearly into unconsciousness. He lay there, vision swimming, thoughts reeling, pain engulfing his body, wondering whether he was going to die from the blow—all he knew for certain, as his befuddled senses strove to regain equilibrium, was that he'd been hit with a casting. A mindbogglingly violent casting, the likes of which he'd never experienced before. And he sensed somehow that it hadn't come from Kutt-Kutt the Second. The otherling had been far too engrossed in the impending violence of its physical assault on him, and any spells at its command would likely have been compromised by the punishment its shell had suffered, an attack designed to cripple the otherling in exactly this way.

What then, had smote Mackey down with such overwhelming force? The answer came to him, and he was in no condition to deal with it.

Through the pounding in his ears, he made out a voice: Kutt-Kutt the Second's, and he was pleading.

"No, Lord—*please*! Give me more time! Only a moment has passed. I would have killed the proto-m—"

Something crashed heavily to the ground directly in front of Mackey. He raised a hand instinctively and, peering through the sand thrown into the air at the impact, saw:

Kutt-Kutt the Second, the once-Lieutenant Delson. Its body was a broken wreck: limbs shattered, bones protruding from punctured skin, head askew at a horrific angle. A ragged hole encompassed the entirety of his chest, as if a sledgehammer the size of a truck had smote him down with a single pulverizing blow.

From the misshapen ruin of the face, the voice of Kutt-Kutt the Second spluttered, "Proto-man…I'll be waiting for you in the sun. A flock of us waits for you. The Lord has come for you now, and…"

The otherling died, a final choking death rattle signalling its demise. Mackey knew the moment it left the Lieutenant's shell—the body seemed to collapse in on itself, skin shrivelling like an animal in a time-lapse video. A soft exudation of stinking breath came from the slack-jawed mouth.

Mackey imagined he saw a shimmering in the air over the corpse, a brief glimmer as of some semi-corporeal shape heaving itself from the body and upwards, but when he followed its progress there was nothing, only the deep blue of the dusking sky and the first shuddering stars. The air was agitated, electric, though the wind was no more violent than it had been earlier.

And then the ground shook.

And the chanting of the otherlings ringing him in rose to a crescendo until even they became submerged beneath the booming percussion that seemed to fill his skull and rebound from the vault of stars above.

VI: Human

It crested the dune above him.

Mackey could only stare, astonished at the vision.

From the dune sea stalked a giant.

Mackey could actually feel a subtle reverberation of its footsteps transmitted through the ground. It was a man, and yet.

This mountain of a figure rose at least fifteen feet in height, and was, Mackey's reeling mind understood, the dark deity he'd sought for so long. Finally, he confronted the being that had set his life on its course.

Kagll-uth.

The human's shadow blanketed Mackey as it plodded down the dune. He shook with the thunder of the steps as it drew closer, and when the thunder ceased, Mackey looked up to behold him, the first true human he'd ever seen.

Kagll-uth.

Mackey found that he in turn was being studied by the giant.

He was at once horrific and beautiful—so beautiful that the

beauty veered into something abominable. Humans weren't supposed to be *this* beautiful, but then of course according to the doctrine of the Bright Sons, this is exactly what fully evolved humanity looked like. A beauty outside the experience and mindset of proto-humans like Mackey.

Kagll-uth bulged with power. Much like the otherlings and otherling-possessed wolf Mackey and Cerberus had encountered, the physical shell of Kagll-uth looked engorged to the point of fantastical improbability, as if his former frame, whatever it might have been, had been transmogrified, skeleton and musculature blossomed into something infinitely more colossal than what had been. He thought of Kutt-Kutt the Second, and its swollen, vein-strangled limbs, and understood that Kagll-uth was the ultimate expression of what the otherling servant had been evolving toward.

Beyond the terror that devoured his heart, Mackey felt the yearning to know who this human had been before he became Kagll-uth.

Kagll-uth, somehow hearing this yearning, told Mackey, in terms simple yet all-encompassing.

"I was no one. But now look upon me."

It was answer enough.

Like Kagll-uth's physical size, its voice—*his* voice, for truly he was a man—was too much; too loud, like the grinding of great bones, or thunder rumbling inside the confines of a vast cavern. Mackey recoiled several steps as he had when the giant first appeared over the dune.

And with this Kagll-uth forgot all about Mackey.

Mackey saw the human turn his beautiful monstrous head away, eyes scanning the miles over Mackey's head. He knew he was less than nothing to Kagll-uth, beneath notice but bestowed the gift of his attention for one fleeting moment, the gift of receiving an answer to a question Mackey had left unspoken but burning in his heart. Even as Mackey loathed the abomination, he felt a resentful gratitude seep into him, the exquisite giant granting him a privilege he didn't deserve.

As Kagll-uth contemplated the desert, Mackey admired the

human's beauty. It was more breathtaking, more awe-inspiring every moment that passed. And, suddenly, Mackey discerned something that Kagll-uth's horrible beauty had distracted him from noticing—across that supernormally muscular frame was an exterior covering—clothing, of a sort. It took Mackey a moment to extrapolate its elements from its overall pattern, and when he did he shuddered.

The human was clothed in the corpses of its proto-human victims—he could make out their frail limbs entwined with one another through some means he couldn't determine, like a hideous mesh armour. Peering closer, he saw that Kagll-uth wore a pair of almost-men strung by limb and entrail about his neck like a shawl; it brandished a petrified corpse in one fist like a staff. Pageantry perverse, Kagll-uth appeared dressed for some human saturnalia in the blistering heart of his realm. And in this realization, Mackey grew to understand that the corpses were no armour at all, but indeed a symbol of his sadism: it was mere costume.

The faces of the dead worn by Kagll-uth were etched in a uniform expression of final agony: mouths opened wide in hideous rictuses, eyes clenched tightly. Mackey wondered distantly who they'd been and what crimes they'd committed to deserve murder, and then this heinous display; or maybe they were Kagll-uth's Bright Sons of the Morning who had given their lives so that their liege might walk the desert in the clothing of their bodies.

The number of corpses was shocking—the physical strength required to bear their combined weight defied belief. The sense came to Mackey that Kagll-uth was engorged, with…what? The answer was simple, and became apparent even as he marvelled at the scale of the being:

Its unlocked humanity.

The titan couldn't be defeated, Mackey now knew.

It was invincible.

Mackey raised a hand. "Wait. Wait. Why am I here, if I mean nothing to you? I received a tape, with a recording of the Bright Sons…" He drifted off, too weary to go on, embarrassed at the hopeful note in his voice, feeling stupid conjuring such a mundane scene in the presence of Kagll-uth when in all likelihood it had been sheer luck that someone—a defector from the Bright Sons, a spy with the means to hide themselves from the vigilant eye of Kagll-uth?—had contacted the Reclamation Society, who'd sent this particular job his way like they'd sent him hundreds of others.

Kagll-uth frowned at him. "You presume that I, a human being, should know of you, an ant? I do not know who you are. I could never be bothered to know."

He'd been a fool, Mackey thought, full of hubris from past successes with lesser hooks, and with his longing to be reunited with his family had come the falsest of hopes. And now he would pay the price demanded by Kagll-uth; and even as he prepared himself for this toll, Kagll-uth said, voice full with casual mockery, "Worse still, now you must live your life knowing that you share the world with one such as myself."

At this, a sense of righteous fury filled Mackey. "You? *You?* I'm *better* than you. And I…I want to fight you. I'll *kill* you. And take her back from you. You evil, soulless man."

"So, you accept the truth of me."

Mackey and Kagll-uth watched one another. The wind gusted, blowing veils of sand from the dunes around them. The sun bore down with a heat that felt insidious.

"I have looked into the past and indeed found the inconsequential happening to which you refer, so important to your meaningless existence."

Kagll-uth, wreathed in corpses, lifted a hand eastward.

"Go into the desert. Your wife will be there waiting, or she will not be. It will be your choice." And, as if answering some question that might have been formulating in Mackey's mind, Kagll-uth added, "I too have a wife. She and her Bright Daughters of the Morning are wondrous, like the sun, the life-giver itself. Together, someday, our family will remake this world into the paradise it was always meant to be."

But Mackey had only heard what Kagll-uth said about Jenny. He struggled to his feet. His heart drove him on, one shaking step after another, in the direction the human had shown him. And without a backwards glance to the titan Kagll-uth, he plunged eastward. He felt neither the sun burning his skin, or the plagues of thirst and hunger and physical pain. He followed the vision of her that hung like a more nourishing sun in his mind's eye, though even that golden light grew sullied after a time when one other memory overtook it; the perennial night-memory to the daytime beauty of the woman herself.

And with this dark memory urging him on to fix his life's greatest mistake, Mackey trudged on into the heart of the desert.

VII: The Long Nightmare

Mackey strode back into the modest apartment bedroom from the adjoining kitchenette, brandishing the champagne bottle in one hand and a pair of glasses clinking in the other.

"Would my blushing bride fancy a nightcap before turning in for the—"

He took in the tableau, and in that moment began to understand what it was he'd wrought when, six months before, he'd acted on instinct and saved a fellow soldier's life on a night of terror in the trenches.

His wife, Mrs. Jennifer Mackey, nee Cartier, was gone. Where she'd stood waiting for him beside the garland-strung window was a smoking puddle of black liquid. Over it hovered a giant black hornet that Cerberus was glaring at, fangs bared, whining in fear. The dog and Mackey had been inseparable since their days in the trenches, their companionship and shared experiences inspiring his CO to recommend him as a handler—and Cerberus as his assistant canine— at the War Dog Training School established at the Shoeburyness Artillery School in Essex, England. She was as courageous as they came, and Mackey had seen her react in terror on only one occasion, when they'd witnessed something outside of normal experience in the theatre of war.

The din of the hornet's angry buzzing was the only sound in the room. The insect alighted on the wall and Mackey was able to take in the size of the thing—much larger than any hornet he'd seen, and fatter, its thorax and abdomen almost engorged-looking. The segmented antennae on its head were likewise incredibly long, twitching in the air. Its sleek pairs of wings were tucked neatly along the length of its body, the individual black hairs on their surface visible from across the room.

Mackey understood the meaning of his missing wife even as the voice left the hornet—a voice too-loud, a voice that seemed to threaten to destroy the insect's bloated body from within.

"Kagll-uth will delight in her. Consider this reparation for your righteousness. Kagll-uth will make her live forever. And *you* will live forever—your torment will likewise be eternal, though of a different sort. Perhaps you will see her again, some day long from this day."

Of course, Mackey knew the name the hornet spoke. That cold moon-washed trench in France was the landscape of his dreams, and the drama that had played out there was their dark theatre.

The hornet darted from the wall and buzzed an erratic flight around Mackey. He recoiled, tried batting it from the air with the wine bottle. He thought he'd succeeded when the insect seemed to have disappeared, only to find it clinging to the back of his hand. The moment he saw it he felt its sting—a touch that hurt worse than the shrapnel that had bit into his thigh and turned out to be his ticket home.

He managed to crush the thing, smacking his palm against his hand. The hornet dropped to the floor, crumpled and twitching. Mackey was lifting his foot to squash it under his heel when the insect erupted in flame. Fire licked from its body, sputtering along its wings even as it managed to crawl a few inches and take to the air. Eventually it fell to the floor again, still burning.

Mackey watched it turn to an ashen ruin with a hollowness growing inside of him. As the shock of the encounter wore off, and as the greater scenario came home to him, it birthed a desolation in him that would only grow as time wore on. The happiness that had been taken from him was the vengeance that had been wrought on

Mackey for his transgression. Because he'd interfered, stuck his meddlesome nose into business not his own, the business of those who trafficked in darker deeds than man-made wars on Earth. Adding to the weight on his conscience, he saw Cerberus stoop to lick her right forepaw, nursing her own wound—she'd been stung before he'd entered the room, he realized.

He wept, he screamed, because he didn't know what else he might possibly do, and his helplessness drove him on and on in this most primal response; and when the evil fire had finally sputtered out, still he sobbed, sitting useless vigil. Distantly, though, he understood a new duty, a new mission, a new life's work that was now his burden, though he couldn't imagine where or how he might begin his search for his wife.

The sensation that greeted Mackey as he swam from the clutches of the remembrance and into muddy consciousness was one of undiluted agony.

Slowly, as he lay there, he began testing his body, making small movements, gauging the sources of the greatest discomfort. In this way, he determined that his feet were certainly walked raw, and that he no doubt had a severe concussion from the incredible casting blow he'd been hit with (the dizziness wouldn't go away, and every attempt to sit up was met with sickening nausea). Realistically, the likelihood that he was suffering from internal bleeding was high. Most frightening of all, the awareness slowly came to him that his augmented senses had somehow been adversely effected; though he couldn't pinpoint how, he sensed that they had somehow been tampered with, sabotaged. He felt violated in a deeply personal way.

Mostly though, he was thirsty. His mouth tongue throat yearned for the cool kiss of water. But he had none. His canteen he'd left behind, unthinkingly, bent only on hurrying to find his wife out in these wastes, as Kagll-uth had promised.

Kagll-uth, the great deceiver.

Gingerly, he lifted his head up to scan around him. It took a moment for his eyes to become accustomed to the brilliant white glare of the sun. What greeted him was desolation that stretched as far as he could see. Endless panorama of sand, with occasional scrub brushes marking the miles. Nothing else. The only movement came from the ever-present heatwaves pulsating on the horizon like an army of restless spirits.

He eased his head back down, waves of nausea threatening to make him heave his guts out. Gradually they subsided, though the pain in his head throbbed and throbbed.

Laying there, his thoughts turned to the events of earlier that day, or had it been days and days ago?

He drifted, drifted, nightmarish snippets flitting through his thoughts: a headless wolf loping through the wastes; a boundary-line of dead in the dune sea; servants to a secret deity encircling him, eyes joyous with their madness; a bone-knife stabbing for his throat; the never-ending cataclysm of true humanity towering over him, erasing the sun with his shadow, that star for which the servants of Kagll-uth had been named.

He remembered the expression Kagll-uth had turned on him, echoed in the eyes of the corpses it wore—distantly mocking; inherently malicious; not rejoicing in what was certainly going to prove to be Mackey's doom but dismissing him entirely for what he was in comparison to it: nothing. As insignificant as a gnat, unworthy of the attention needed to single him out from the rest of the sand granules kicked up in the storm of Kagll-uth's footsteps, but to be forgotten even as those sand particles returned to their mother desert.

He drifted off again beneath the weight of these thoughts, the evil sun burning him.

When he came to sometime later, he sensed rather than heard something close to him, and craned his neck toward it. The movement sent lightning rods of pain shooting through him; his vision swam and it took him a moment to will away the vertigo.

Despite the pain pulsing in what felt like every inch of his body, Mackey couldn't help but smile as she materialized from the heatwaves shimmering up from the sand: Cerberus, limping severely, moving slowly, but whole. He was able to raise his hand in greeting, and promptly slid back groaning onto the sand from the effort.

When he felt the dog's shadow fall over him several minutes later, he managed, "Thank god you're okay, Cerby. You had me worried, sweetheart."

The relief he felt at their reunion was a salvation in that moment—on a pragmatic level, the two of them together would be much more likely to escape from their predicament alive. They'd beaten steep odds together many times before. And then there was the fact of how dear Cerberus was to him—very literally, she was, and had long been, his closest friend in the world.

"*All* for Kagll-uth."

The voice reached through Mackey's swirling fog of thoughts and dragged him back into full consciousness instantly. He sat bolt upright, barely aware of the piercing knives of pain the movement sent through his body. He winced in the sun-bright air, his surroundings swimming into focus.

Standing before him, inches from his face, was Cerberus—her blood-flecked jaws unhinged and gaping, the breath wafting from the maw powerfully foul, unfamiliar. Mackey searched the dog's dark eyes and saw it: a flickering dance somewhere between desperation and icy malevolence. Drool hung in long filaments from her lips. Her entire body was riven with tremors, the physical manifestation, it seemed, of the animal's mighty but futile struggle to escape its hook possessor. Instinctually, Mackey pulled the dagger from its sheath at his belt, brought the weapon up, bringing the blade between him and Cerberus.

Again, the voice came up out of the dog's mouth, from deep inside the animal; a deep and sonorous sound; the voice of a giant filtering through the narrow windpipe of an everyday mutt that was anything but unremarkable. The voice, and what it said, shook Mackey inside his bones.

"Your wife and the dog are here with us, proto-human—come join them, and make your family whole again. Kagll-uth opens to you this path, for which you've waited so long."

Mackey watched Cerberus, waiting, hoping for some sign of his dear friend to return into the malevolent eyes glaring hungrily at him. Tears blurred his vision, and a great loneliness seeped into his heart, a loneliness with a weight of years and years. How easy it would be to bare his throat to the otherling-possessed dog and, once the violence and pain was done with, find himself reunited with his wife in the hell she'd been in for nine decades, so that they could at least face the anguish together, if not live together again in the above-world. Or was there some hope left for him to escape this predicament, and rescue her so that they could be reunited here, in the world they belonged in? But what would his punishment and hers be if he tried and failed? Another ninety years of torture for each of them, kept apart and made to endure life alone, at the whim of a human like a god?

The sun flashed from the knife blade between the two old friends, a communication between the heavens and Earth.

Siege

The siege had entered its seventh week.

Three defenders remained of the nearly one hundred that had originally manned the tiny fort. They were exhausted, physically; mentally; spiritually. They had watched their brothers succumb to the relentless assaults of the invader, wave after wave after wave. And to starvation—there simply had not been enough food for so many. They were delirious with hunger, and the host outside their feeble, faltering walls was unwavering. They knew that the invader could sense their diminished, paltry numbers.

A final assault was imminent. Their end was nigh.

In the small warm-aired chamber, Pulchritudo growled in fury and frustration, "The enemy, he *toys* with us."

"The vile scum," spat Vi, tears welling in his eyes. "All of our brothers slain. Their screams echo in my skull. Our little sanctuary will collapse before long."

"One last stand then, brothers," smiled Nox. "Let us at last bring the battle to the enemy…and kill for as long as we are able."

His brothers smiled knowingly at Nox's mad gambit, their hearts rejoicing in his final command:

"Animate the fort!"

~

Inside the bedchamber, the saint continued his emphatic reading from the leatherbound Book opened across his left palm—*"May the dragon never be my guide!"*—wooden cross clutched resolutely in his right fist even when the sound of the ropes snapping sounded loudly in the room. He was still mouthing the formula when the lightning bolt of pain exploded in his throat, and his blood was splashing in a deluge across the flagstones.

The nurse fainted at the sight of the blood-spattered, snarling baby sprinting at her where she stood rinsing the soiled bedsheets in the washbasin. The young man stationed as guard at the door, Alfred, who dreamed of someday becoming a knight and defending the weak and the poor, rushed forward and stepped between them, dagger raised high.

Spiders in the Temple

Patrick Savinsky began his day as usual: rising from his bed of dilapidated cardboard and plastic bags, his makeshift fort against the elements; standing in the stinking murk of the pre-dawn alley slowly stretching his limbs sore from the night of restless, uncomfortable, cough syrup-dream-plagued sleep behind him. He was freezing. The temperature had plummeted in the night, and it took him longer than usual to massage warmth back into his shuddering, grimy hands.

Eyeing the crack of skyline he could glimpse through the alley—tall skyscrapers reflecting the blood-red light of the rising sun—he muttered, "Yeah, well, fuck you, too."

He hobbled down the alley in the direction of the nearby park and his bench—he thought of it as "his", as did the many regulars who daily passed by the bench en route to their day jobs and saw him stationed there, that ragged fixture of the park and a reminder of the bottommost social stratum of the city—his steps becoming steadier as he went, working out the kinks and numbness in his feet and legs, feeling circulation begin its gradual course again. He patted the pocket of his tatty coat, felt the familiar bulge of the squashed paper coffee cup nestled there, with which he would mark his place in the park as he panhandled the morning hours in an effort to acquire enough money for a noon-time coffee, or an evening bottle of cough syrup.

He made it to the alley mouth, where he spooked a fat rat from where it was rummaging in the trash to scurry into the open end of a rusted eaves trough. "Sorry, brother," he muttered, and made his way across the empty lot, with the park on its opposite side.

As he crossed the lawn his progress sent up a flock of pigeons to explode into the frostbitten air in a rain of feathers like dirty grey confetti heralding his arrival in the park.

He was dismayed to find his bench occupied.

Patrick eyed the man closely as he sidled toward the bench: immaculate designer suit; immaculate designer shoes; immaculate designer sunglasses sitting on his slender nose despite the overcast, more show of sleek style than utilitarian; hair slicked back efficiently with enough gel to fill a bathtub. He hated men like this one, who owned the world and, worse still, *believed* it was their entitlement to have it so. He saw them as predators, as voracious spiders preying on the oblivious, the more benevolent human moths fluttering along through their lives and chancing to get stuck in the webs of men like him. Back in his old life Patrick had seen many men like this man pounce on the unwary, viciously doing away with them for their own good.

He gave a theatrical scowl toward the dapper man, resenting his clean-shaven good looks and easy charisma. Let him smell my stink, Patrick thought. Let my piss-stained jeans and sweaty clothes hang like a gas cloud over his head. Let's see how long his royal highness sticks around on my bench *then*.

He sat down on the opposite end of the bench, closed his eyes, relishing his own bodily fumes, growing more pungent as the sun climbed into the sky and the first touch of humidity returned to bother the morning.

A curious thing happened then.

An elderly woman limped across the lawn toward the bench. She held a coffee cup in a shuddering hand, a trail of steam escaping its lip and drifting away behind her on the stiff breeze. A large and ancient brown leather purse hung from her shoulder and hugged her hip. She smiled a stain-teethed smile at him, and made a show of slowly—slowly, slowly—creaking herself into position on the bench directly between Patrick and the dapper man.

Something in Patrick always ached at the sight of elderly ladies like this woman. Maybe it was that they invariably reminded him of his mother, many years passed away. Perhaps it was the sort of innocence they imbued, as if life had left them so little that all they had left were the small pleasures: a meandering walk among the flowers of a city's downtown park; the warbling morning songs of pigeons; the warmth of a coffee on a cold A.M.; the easy pleasure of enjoying whatever breakfast they might bring with them to the park before heading home to a lonely apartment and lonely life but for the cat or dog that was their sole remaining companion in the mortal world.

Patrick smiled at her and then went to back to surveying the park stretching before them. He only turned back when the potent smell of tuna wafted to him. He saw the old woman holding a tuna sandwich in trembling liver spot-speckled hands. He watched her, a little horrified, as she took a bite from the sandwich and smiled at him, mouth full. He smiled and turned away again, quickly.

The old woman went about her noisy eating, smacking her lips while the suction-cup sound of her stained dentures dealing with the moist sticky mess of the tuna sandwich became a nauseating staccato rhythm. He grimaced. Disgusting. But then he chuckled, because the woman's grisly breakfast was of course nowhere near as disgusting as the suit-and-tie man beside her, who was no doubt being thoroughly repulsed by her theatrical performance as well.

Patrick nearly laughed out loud when, after a moment, she began a protracted gurgling, and he imagined her sucking back the hot coffee from her paper cup, washing down her loathsome sandwich, the mire of coffee and tuna congealing inside her stomach in the certain creation of violent diarrhea in her immediate future. Then she was apparently finished her grisly breakfast, continuing to sit quietly beside him, her silence broken only by a stuttering fart that made Patrick grimace even as he chuckled out loud: *Take that, suit-and-tie man! Ha! Take* that *bomb with you when you go back to your office cubicle!*

Right on cue, he felt the wood beneath him shift as the man at the opposite end of the bench rose abruptly from the seat. Patrick sat there, smiling with satisfaction. He listened to the sound of the man's shining shoes crunching through the autumn leaves in the direction of the downtown core. He cracked his eyelids and peered after him, his immaculate figure outlined starkly against the misty grey of the buildings rising from the business sector that fringed the park's western perimeter.

"What a fucking asshole," he said, unable to contain his resentment of the man—and men like him generally—who owned the world through their money and good looks and, worst offence of all, believed they deserved everything they got over everybody else. Patrick shook his head and spat in the direction of the receding figure. "Good riddance."

The old woman beside him said nothing. He turned to her, prepared to commend her for successfully having got rid of the man.

He stared at her blue face; her bulging yellow-speckled cataract eyes; her gaping mouth with drool dribbling from the corners onto her small round glistening chin with its cluster of virgin white hairs poking proudly in all directions; her scrawny throat, cut open to reveal the red tangle of her muscle and cartilage and exposed windpipe steaming on the cold air.

Between them on the bench, steam still curled from the open lip of her paper cup, the smell of coffee strong on the air.

It took several seconds for Patrick's mind to process these details and what they meant. Then he spun wildly on the bench, looking in the direction the man had went. He was still there, walking as casually as before, suit jacket neat, hair coifed and unmarred by the crisp breeze. He watched the man approach one of the several tall buildings rising alongside the sidewalk and spiking amid the dense fog hanging over the streets, and this is when he discerned movement where there should have been none. He stared, eyes bulging like the dead woman's frozen stare beside him.

The building rising up before the suited man, and those surrounding it, were crawling with men. He blinked to be certain his eyes weren't making mirages of ordinary city workers toiling away on their scaffolding, washing windows or patching ancient brickwork, but no, his eyes were true: the men were *crawling* across the sheer face of the towering structures like hideous humanoid insects clinging to the walls of their hives; each of them dressed much like the man who'd left the bench, debonair in tailor-cut suits, their ties trailing in the wind.

Patrick watched, horrified, nauseous, enthralled, as the killer of the elderly woman reached the base of the building and immediately began his own climb to meet the other crawling men far above. He went vertically, his feet carrying him as naturally as if he walked on a horizontal surface, a street, a sidewalk, a park lawn. He joined the others, and together they crawled higher and higher until the mist shrouded them.

Patrick blinked and blinked and rubbed at his tear-filled eyes. The city scene before him appeared as normal as it did every other day, but it was deeply changed in his mind's eye, where he would of course never see it the same way again.

"What's happening?" he said, directing his words to the lone pigeon pecking at the grass nearby. "What's *happened* to the world? Things were…Things were never this *bad* before. There was always some sanity left."

The pigeon warbled at him, deep in its throat, and then continued to peck in the dewy grass. Patrick watched it, envying it its simple vision and instinctual mission to seek sustenance this morning. His own stomach grumbled like a nervous Rottweiler. He hadn't eaten in a long time. But his appetite was gone. He wanted only a stiff hard pull from a bottle of cough syrup.

In the distance he saw a pair of police officers walking casually down the sidewalk, headed in his general direction. He could hear their voices, small with distance, their laughter as they shared some joke. They were oblivious to the buildings beneath which they walked, and the fog over their heads, and what lied hidden there and watching over them in their routine trek through the downtown core. A part of him wanted to run to them, and explain what he'd seen and what he'd learned about the world. But of course he knew how they would interpret this admission, and so he could only scurry away, leaving the grave of the bench to the old woman, who'd committed no crime worse than eating a disgusting breakfast in a revolting manner, and whose ancient beauty of gentleness hadn't been strong enough to repel the invader of her peace.

The sun crept forth from behind the clouds as he hurried across the park lawn, its cold wintry light touching the profusion of flowers spread in the peripheral gardens, making them appear brighter, healthier. But Patrick wasn't fooled by it: he saw the darkness hiding everywhere, and wanted very much to walk and walk and keep on walking, right on out of the city and into the rural county beyond, where no tall buildings scraped the bellies of the clouds gathered over the world, where farmland stretched into the horizon as far as the eye could see. But he was weak, and cold, and had no strength for journeys like these, which were journeys for younger men than he, and so all he was able to do was to hurry as fast as his weak, trembling legs would carry him back to the meagre sanctuary of his ramshackle cardboard castle in the little-frequented alley.

It was as good a place as any other to make his final stand.

Love-Goggles 1966

"You're welcome, friend!"

Stanley Dufferin jumped at the booming voice intruding into his muddled thoughts, letting one of the plastic shopping bags he'd been holding slip from his leather-gloved hands. It hit the tiled floor with a thud that didn't quite conceal the small but distinct cracking sound that accompanied it: the ceramic fishing boy that had topped Rebecca's Christmas list, the final piece she needed to complete her latest collection of tacky ceramic figurines; this one based on a Huck Finn-ish theme: a young scruffy boy, barefoot, bushy-haired and with fishing line dangling off his porcelain-pier base and into the imaginary waters beyond. And it had been the very last of the hideous fucking things on the shelf at Sears.

He levelled his gaze at the source of the disturbance, focusing all of his rising fury, skyrocketing stress levels, and thinking too of his wife's forthcoming disappointment in him.

A salesman was beaming at him with the brightest smile Stanley had ever seen. The man, round- and red-cheeked, seemed to be waiting expectantly for something. The knowledge that the man had actually been speaking to him increased Stanley's fury tenfold.

"What?" Stanley barked. Then gesturing to the bag at his feet, added, "Thanks—you yelling at me made me drop that and break the gift that's inside it."

The salesman's smile never faded. In fact, he heaved a hearty laugh, and said, "Big deal, friend! When you see what I'm selling, all the presents in this shopping mall—heck, in this *world*—will be forever paltry in comparison! Come have a look-see!" He was waving him over to the small fold-out table that was set up in the short annex that led to the food court, and the village of kiosks beyond. There were no actual businesses here, just a small photobooth tucked along the opposite wall close to the exit.

Curiosity moved Stanley's feet. He shuffled toward the salesman, skillfully manoeuvring through the people entering and leaving the mall. Arriving at the little display table Stanley saw a dozen black plastic-framed glasses on little velvet display stands. Several plain brown cardboard boxes were stacked behind the table, the top box's wings thrown wide to reveal rows of black plastic containers, presumably carrying cases each holding its own pair of glasses.

"I don't need glasses," Stanley said in a bored voice, his annoyance returning.

The salesman laughed. "These aren't ordinary specs, friend!"

Stanley cocked an eyebrow at the man. "Okay: what do these extraordinary glasses do?" He eyed the pair closest to him: their slightly tinted lenses reflected the loud overheads. Prescription sunglasses?

The salesman appeared completely impervious to Stanley's skepticism and sarcastic tone. "With these glasses on, everyone you look at will be transformed in your eyes. Every person you see will appear, in every exact detail, as…Mila Kunis!"

Stanley scowled at the salesman. "Who?" He was getting exasperated with the man. He only lingered out of curiosity. Mila Kunis? The name sounded vaguely familiar, though he couldn't place where he might have—

"The actress, friend," said the salesman. "Appearing in television and film, dark-haired and beautiful." He waited expectantly, smiling.

Stanley said, "Doesn't ring a bell. Look, I…" He drifted off, remembering the actress in that moment. He used to occasionally watch a sitcom in which she starred, about a group of high school friends in the '70s.

"Okay, yeah, I know who she is." He stared at the salesman, who continued to watch him expectantly. Then, "So, what do they do? The glasses."

The salesman assumed a patient expression. With great deliberation he said, "I told you, friend. With these glasses you'll see Miss Mila Kunis *everywhere you look*. Every woman you see—every man, even—will appear as Miss Kunis in every exacting detail. Are you married? Have a partner?"

"Why would…Why would anyone want this?" He heard how far-away his voice sounded, how small. He thought of Rebecca waiting at home for him: a couple of years his junior, she still had her figure, and after eleven-and-a-half years of marriage they still got along well enough, all things considered. Mila Kunis…she certainly *was* beautiful, from what he remembered, but…

A strained look came into the salesman's eyes. "Because none of us is happy, friend," he said. "Or didn't you know? What's this look? What, did you have yourself fooled a little, too? Deep down, though, you feel it, don't you? The huge unhappiness? The discontent? The pining for some thing that, when you think about it long and hard, you realize you've never had but have always yearned for and fear—and maybe even know in your heart—you'll never ever have? Look around here, friend, and tell me what you see."

The salesman's eyes roved among those passing by them in the bustling corridor. Stanley did the same, and saw:

Haggard faces; downcast eyes; expressions of sheer forced determination, as if the owners of those faces were doing everything they could to push themselves on their way through the crowds of their fellow shoppers and get to…where? And for what reason? The closest he saw to an expression of pure joy was a round-cheeked toddler gobbling his strawberry ice cream cone with a steady, focused mania while his mother hustled him along, guiding his progress with hands on his shoulders as if he were a brainless automaton.

"Here, friend: try a pair out."

The salesman was holding a small plastic case before Stanley, its blue velvet-lined door thrown open to reveal the pair of glasses folded neatly within. Stanley looked at them skeptically and, raising an eyebrow at the salesman, said, "You can't be serious."

The salesman's smile didn't waver as he said, "This is serious business, friend. I deal in happiness, after all. And it's at a crisis-level low these days."

Stanley wasn't sure whether to laugh or feel perturbed at the man's proposition and claims. He stared mutely at the proffered glasses. Then he chuckled and, setting his shopping bags and packages down at his feet, took the glasses from the case and slipped them on. Why not play along with the man? It was Christmas, after all, and—

A strangled cry escaped him.

Stanley looked among the throngs of Mila Kunis moving past them through the centre of the mall corridor. He stared and stared silently for several minutes, amazed at the warm smiles he was receiving from so many of the identical woman.

He plucked the glasses from his face.

The salesman's smile had grown larger, more ecstatic. With this Cheshire cat grin he said, "What's the verdict, friend?"

Stanley put the glasses back on. He murmured, voice far away, "How do you...How is it done?" Stanley was now alternately lifting the glasses from his nose so that he could peer beneath the rim of the lenses and replacing them over his eyes.

"Trade secret, friend," said the salesman. "I'm the inventor and if I shared my secret there'd be exploitation companies popping up everywhere overnight, taking my business with them. And business, even though it's the holidays, isn't exactly booming. So no thanks!"

Stanley looked to the table. The rows of plastic cases and glasses seemed a miraculous thing now.

"But why...her? What would I want with Mila Kunis?"

The salesman chuckled and gave him a wink. "Well, she's a pretty young woman for one thing. But then again, this season's line is an eclectic one, so if you don't fancy Mila, how about...Bruce Willis? No? What about Meg Ryan? Or the great Lance Henriksen? I know! Kurt Russell! Handsome and badass—who doesn't love Kurt, am I right?"

Stanley was staring into the crowd again with the glasses on, completely mesmerized. His voice came quietly, his words slowly. "Well, yeah, she is pretty, but...but beyond that, what would I want with her in my life? Mila Kunis, I mean."

The salesman smiled his larger-than-life smile. "Why *not* her to share your thoughts with? Your concerns, about your everyday, and the world at large? To have conversations with her that begin after dinner and end in the bottomless hours long after midnight when everyone else is fast asleep and you can both be free to rid your heart of the heavy burdens you carry day after day after day. To have someone—to have *something*—new in your life, and exciting, something that will give you the hope for tomorrow that new and exciting things bring with them. Because if you're like most of us, friend, you might have lost some of the old hope along the way, from wherever you started to where you are right now, today. And that hope is like a flower, friend—water it enough and it grows into the love you always wanted to have in your life but maybe never did, or if you did ever have it, it probably went away much too soon."

Stanley found it difficult to turn from the mob of Mila Kunis surging past them. A part of him wanted to laugh. Another part to weep with joy. Still another part wanted to shout about this discovery at the top of his voice. He turned to the salesman and said, "You're a good salesman."

Mila Kunis beamed back at him. Unsettled, Stanley pulled the glasses off, watched the smiling salesman appear in her place. She *was* attractive, this couldn't be denied. He thought of making love to his wife but experiencing her as some celebrity woman, young and beautiful. This would be like bonus points awarded after the more important experience of enjoying the totality of escape that having this weird miracle in his life would provide. He felt the first stirrings of arousal and, startled, embarrassed, shook his head and tried thinking of more practical aspects of the situation confronting him.

"What's your company name?" Stanley asked, voice distant with distraction and awe of the product in his trembling hand, uneasy standing at the edge of that surging sea of Mila Kunis rolling inexorably past them through the festively-decorated mall corridor. He felt it even then: his reluctance to replace the glasses in their case and return the case to the salesman.

The salesman beamed that Cheshire cat smile. "I'm my own

man, friend. Freelancing all the way through the holiday season."

"Who builds your glasses?"

The salesman held up his hands. "These are my partners, friend. Pinkies one through ten. Trustworthy to the bitter end."

"You make them all…by yourself?" There was awe in Stanley's voice. Hearing it, he understood in that moment that he'd accepted the miracle of the salesman's claims.

"All by my lonesome." There was undisguised pride in the salesman's voice.

"But…*how?* Where do you work from?"

The salesman shrugged. "I've got a workshop. I spend a lot of time in there." His smile never wavered. He was evidently relishing the mysterious air of his words and their effect on Stanley.

"What's your name?"

"*My* name? My name doesn't matter. Just think of me as the man with the vision. What's your name?"

"Stanley…" Stanley was back to wearing the glasses and staring around them at the passing people, his voice coming from miles away. "This all sounds…it doesn't seem real to me. It sounds made up."

The salesman guffawed. "Look around—you see much around here that's real, with or without my glasses?"

Almost against his will Stanley slipped the glasses from his nose to once again appraise those around him: the hurrying crowds of men and women, eyes hard and determined as they plowed through the unending waves of fellow shoppers, each loaded with shopping bags and gift-wrapped packages, each with the same emotionless eyes as they marched through that atmosphere so unique to malls during the holiday season—animosity just barely held in check, all wrapped up in colourful garland.

The Christmas music playing over the sound system sounded especially sorrowful to Stanley then.

He turned back to the salesman, found (of course) his expression of round-cheeked joviality waiting for him. The man watched him evenly, and Stanley couldn't decide whether he glimpsed any of the sadness there that he saw everywhere else, that was surely waiting for him in the mirror. The thought occurred to him, so he asked.

"And if I look in the mirror with these on?"

"There she'll be, as pretty as ever. Or there Kurt Russell will be, if you go that route."

"Do you make contacts, too? Or just the glasses?" Stanley felt guilty but the logistics of the potential scenario came to him: making love to his wife while wearing a pair of the bizarre glasses…

The salesman looked impressed and, pointing to his temple, said, "We think alike, you and I! They're in the works, friend, but there are only so many hours in the day, and only one pair of these to work through the night." He held up his hands as if surrendering to the inevitability of the situation.

Mostly to himself, Stanley murmured, "But it seems so…wrong."

The salesman was quick to answer, as though he'd argued this same point many times. "But who's to know? It's just fantasy, friend! No one gets hurt with my glasses!"

Speaking with studied caution, Stanley said, "Out of curiosity…How much?" His eyes turned toward the display table with the salesman's wares spread across its surface.

"Special sale price of five hundred even. I'll swallow the tax, my holiday gift to you."

Stanley's eyes grew big in his shiny face. His jaw dropped. A sardonic smile touched his lips. "That's highway robbery, *friend*."

The salesman affected a hurt expression (though his smile only grew a little smaller). "Even a saint has to eat, after production and labour costs are figured into the price," he said, chuckling. "Besides, five hundred bucks for happiness isn't much at all, all things considered."

Sudden and unexpected anger surged through Stanley. "Happiness? Oh, come on. You call something as superficial as this—if it even works, which I'm not one hundred percent convinced of yet, because maybe there's some trick here I'm not seeing yet—but you call that *happiness*?"

For the first time the salesman's face became serious. With as grave a voice as the expression he appraised Stanley with, he said, "It's more than most of them have got."

Stanley stared at the salesman in silence. He felt suddenly sick to his stomach. Nauseous and slick with a cold sweat. His elbow was jostled by a woman hurrying on her way. A moment later a surly-looking man nudged him, too. He jumped at the wailing child being toted off by a cursing mother somewhere behind him in the press of the crowd. He felt suddenly boxed in, claustrophobic in the people-clogged corridor. His heart leapt a little faster than it had been beating before, and it had been beating faster than usual since he'd donned those glasses.

With a barely discernable nod toward the display table, Stanley said, "I'll take a pair. And gimme a Kurt Russell, too."

The salesman beamed. With a flourish he pulled two pairs of glasses from behind his display table. He held them to his chest and held out his other hand expectantly. Stanley pulled the bills from his wallet and placed them into his hand, watched the salesman's fingers close over them and disappear into the folds of his jacket with a hand as deft as a magician's.

"You're welcome, Stanley," he said. Then, winking slyly, he added, "Enjoy your date night with your lady tonight, pal. Without love, after all, this world is l-o-s-t lost."

Stanley walked off, thinking of Rebecca, his steps burdened with a weird guilt the likes of which was very new to him. But of course it would be: he'd never indulged in the exploitative evils of technology like this before, if technology was even the right term. Maybe *magic* came closer to defining what he'd purchased—

"Stanley!"

Stanley spun around, startled.

The salesman was waving at him, half-jogging in his direction. Stanley stepped to the wall of the corridor, waiting, feeling uneasy. When the salesman arrived, huffing and smiling that most jovial of catalogue-perfect grins, he said, "Just thought I'd give you the inside scoop, Stan, being that you're a good customer of mine now. If you like the 2024 line, you'll love what we've got lined up." He leaned close to Stanley and, lowering his voice conspiratorially, said, "Next season we go summer-retro—how would you like to get cat scratch fever, friend, and go on a date with the Catwomen of the 1960s…Julie Newmar, Eartha Kitt, and Lee Meriwether?"

The names struck Stanley like a physical blow. He actually rocked back on his heels a little and blinked hard. Stanley was transported back in time: it was 1966 and he was 12 years old, hiding out in his childhood bedroom with his avid juvenile fixations on display in every comic book long-box, every shelf lined with pulp fiction paperbacks, every wall plastered with images of the heroes and heroines, the villains and villainesses he adored; this latter of which he was doomed to always pine for as if he'd actually had and lost the gift of their love. And he thought of the continuation of his childhood bedroom sanctuary, his adulthood man-cave where the child in him lived on, healthy but unhealthy while his wife turned a patient eye the other way. Oh, Stanley, will you ever grow up?

And he remembered his first secret crushes purring seductively inside the television screen, giving him his first erection and his first yearnings for the company of the fairer sex. Yes, Stanley had been hopelessly and embarrassingly head over heels for *all three* Catwomen between 1966 and '67. With glasses that could bring her into his life every day, everywhere he looked, well, life might be better than it had been during all those long-lost years since he'd been a boy growing flushed with excitement in his parents' basement where he worshipped at the foot of the television like a glowing idol. God, how he'd loved them all. It had been a love so pure, so innocent and simple and good-feeling. Sigh…

"Put me down for all three pairs," Stanley told the salesman, the smile spreading helplessly across his face.

The salesman laughed, clawing at the air. "*Mrow!* You're welcome!" he said. "Here's my card. Add yourself to my mailing list—you're the early bird, first in line and first to meet the Catwomen of his dreams!"

And he turned and was trotting back to his makeshift display table in the centre of the mall hubbub, in time to greet a new group of men and women who had gathered over his demonic or miraculous wares.

Stanley turned and wove his way through the throngs of people, the plastic cases with their very special gift to himself a warm presence nestled inside his coat pocket. Behind him the salesman's voice came to him, full of good humour and jubilant madness like a balm to the noisy commercial unpleasantness of the holidays.

"Merry Christmas, and you're all welcome!"

Laundromatricide and the Wrath

"Welcome, filthy one, to the humble temple of the Final Fraternity, a fitting site for what will happen here tonight."

The Great Cleanser spread his arms wide to take in the entirety of the basement storage space, and the building above them. The smile he gave the woman clutching her blanket-wrapped baby to her chest was ecstatic.

His followers, rapt eyes on their leader, felt the rumble of the machines in their bones as clearly as they could hear them shuddering the ceiling of wooden timbers and plastic tubing and insulation.

And the Great Cleanser finished the encomium: "This sacred place of great and ongoing cleansing, this site from which the purification of our world will be accomplished."

His followers echoed the words, their single voice adding to the thunder of the machines above to send echoing reverberations through the large subterranean room.

"This sacred place of great and ongoing cleansing, this site from which the purification of our world will be accomplished."

"Cleaners," intoned the Great Cleanser. "Hold her."

The men surrounding the woman drew closer, clamped hands on her arms and shoulders. Someone pried the child from her arms, ignoring her screams of protest. When she scratched at the man cradling her baby another bonked her over the head with a shorn broom handle, sending her to the tiles in a heap. A moment later she was hauled to her feet and held firmly in place to witness the leader of the cabal accepting the gift of the infant.

He unwound the blanket from the small form and let it drift to the floor. He smiled his rapturous smile, a distant dislocated look in his eyes as he appraised the baby. One of the Cleaners opened the door of the single hulking industrial-sized washing machine that occupied the centre of the floor, its stout power cable trailing behind it to plug into the wall. The machine's place in the middle of the room gave it a sense of importance, like an idol at whose door these men were gathered to worship.

With extreme gentleness, the Great Cleanser placed the wailing child deep inside the mouth of the machine. He stood back, looking down at the baby as its cries rebounded from the inside of the washer's cavernous stainless steel innards. One of the Cleaners added the symbolic capful of detergent into the machine's cleaning liquid drawer, then closed it reverently.

The child's mother, gleaning the madness of what was intended, lunged forward but was held back by the Great Cleanser's bodyguards.

"The child first, and then its mother," intoned the Great Cleanser.

"The child first, and then its mother," repeated the Cleaners.

"One more step toward peace in the world."

"One more step toward peace in the world."

The woman understood then that she would also be fed to the machine.

The Great Cleanser closed the lid of the machine and turned it on.

Its roaring motor drowned out all other sound: the chanting of the men repeating the final line of the soliloquy like a prayer; the strident screaming of the mother; the clattering and thudding from inside the machine's steel tub.

The men's eyes were full of ecstasy.

Their smiles were radiant.

They were all that much closer to becoming stardust in the Heavens.

~

The following evening.

"Background?"

"Prostitute. We found her trolling for johns in an alley off Wyandotte West. We were quick. Nobody saw. Even if someone had they wouldn't have cared."

The Great Cleanser smiled coldly from where he stood before the massive industrial washing machine in the centre of the basement. A pair of Cleaners was busy with washcloths and a bucketful of water, one wiping the red-spattered interior of the machine, the other working on the red window.

"Efficiency. This keeps us hidden, and strong."

His words echoed in the vast room, and he turned to the bag-headed woman struggling hopelessly against her rope bonds. She was kneeling on the floor between another pair of his men. He squatted and pulled the sack from her shoulders. A mess of blonde hair hid her features, though her pale brown eyes burned frantically upward at him.

The Great Cleanser examined her arms. "I don't see track marks." His tone was questioning, curious.

The Cleaner who'd provided the report was quick to reply. "She's definitely a streetwalker. We've seen her a few times on our rounds."

"It makes no difference, of course," the Great Cleanser said. "It has a certain satisfaction to it, though, when the vanquished is both trash like this one…and with child."

Part of their sanctifying membership dues required that prospective group members bring in one sacrifice. More often than not these tended to be someone related to or with some connection to the member: a sister, mother, girlfriend or wife; or a friend or acquaintance. But as one's standing in the group rose and his time as a member grew, he was required to bring in unknowns on a regular basis. Although they had on occasion been visited by those who volunteered themselves freely—sacrifices who understood the greater good toward which the group worked so hard—the vast majority of their sacrifices were of course abductees. These were frequently taken from the street: the homeless provided an ideal and endless population to steal from; as well as the local prostitutes and drug addicts. The group had to fulfill its duties, as other brothers' groups in other cities did their duties, too.

The Great Cleanser spread his fingers and placed his hand on the woman's stomach. She shrank from his touch, but he held her firmly.

"Ah, there you are. He's a strong one in there. Good. We've caught one in time."

The woman found her voice. "*What?*! What do you *mean?* What do you want? Leave me alone. I'm not *pregnant* or anything."

The Great Cleanser said, "But you are."

"No, no, I'm *not*," she said, the words tumbling from her. "Even if I was, I'm not a bad person. I—I'd never hurt my baby, if I was going to have one. I'd be a good mom. But I'm not pregnant, and—"

"Even if you weren't with child now—and you are, because I felt the child kicking as my hand graced your filthy body—even then you would always have the *potential* to be a mother."

"But I'm a good person." She was crying freely now, trying to fathom what was happening to her.

"Why, darling, you don't understand us at all." The Great Cleanser's tone had changed: he spoke with a great gentleness, as if he were explaining an easy concept to a dull child.

The woman watched him, any shred of hope she'd had wilting beneath his moon-eyed maniacal gaze.

"We don't presume to repopulate the Earth with some new kind of humanity and wisdom. We're not *that* kind of group. We understand this would be a fruitless project. Our mission is completely different to that sort of thing. We want simply to ensure through our humble efforts that life *ceases.* We don't deserve to go on at all. We want *every* human being to die. Ourselves included. Once our mission is done, of course. Then and only then will we follow all those who we've sent as dust to rejoin the stars and become stardust ourselves."

He leaned close to her to emphasize his final point on the matter. "We believe that the best way to expedite our goal is to focus our attention first and foremost on those who bring us forth into this regretful world of misery and damnation."

The woman stared at him until understanding slowly dawned on her through the diminishing strength of the heroin electrifying her system. *Women.* The lunatic and his lunatic followers were women-killers.

The Great Cleanser's smile glowed down at her. The murmured agreements of the man's compatriots rumbled around her. The irony of it all didn't escape her as she told them the truth about herself like she hadn't yet shared it with anyone in the world, not even her pimp boyfriend.

"I'm barren. I couldn't conceive if I wanted to. I've wrecked my body..." She drifted off, less ashamed than unable to encapsulate all of the poor decisions she'd made in her life in a brief plea to the man in front of her.

The Great Cleanser frowned. "What you say does make sense. But then I *felt* the child move..." He drifted off, lost in thought. Snippets of whispered conversation between his followers came to him, deepening his frown:

"If the whore's ruined her body, how could she be..."

"Impossible..."

"Or a miracle?"

"Immaculate conception—"

The telephone on the wall erupted into a jangling cacophony that sent echoes bouncing from the bare walls.

"Shit," seethed the Great Cleanser, incensed at the interruption to his musings and to the ritual at hand. Snatching the phone from its cradle with a darting hand like a snake, he said with smooth fury, "Yes. Stanley here." He listened a moment, a muscle in his jaw twitching angrily. "Yes? *Now?* Which machine? Why don't they just use another machine? We have many. What? But why? That makes no sense. Well, why don't you make her see the *logic* in it? What? Really? Oh, come *on. Seriously?* Now? *Now?* We're in the middle of business. The *real* business. She said what? That we have to pay her for the out of order machine? What? That we're going to pay for *what we do here?* Oh, we *steal money from people*, do we? Is she still there? Yes. Oh, it's one of *those.* The holier-than-thou Bible-thumping whores. Of *course* it is. Okay, okay. Fine. Give me a minute and I'll refund her the measly two dollars. And next time do your job better or you won't have a job."

The Great Cleanser hung the phone up with a calculatedly gentle hand, and turned back to his waiting men and the captive woman. "I apologize, but I must excuse myself to deal with the incompetence of others. We do have a front to maintain in the world above."

His men nodded solemnly. They of course understood the need for maintaining a position in the real world so that their important venture in directing the future according to the Great Cleanser's prophecies could continue unhindered. The laundromat above their heads, with its mundane public function, provided the perfect front and poetic beauty for their covert mission and gatherings. That its nature as a brick-and-mortar business required their leader's attention from time to time was understandable.

The Great Cleanser let his hand drift gently down to his side. His fingers caressed the hilt of the ceremonial dagger sheathed in the scabbard he wore. It had been a pawn shop find, the weapon's history unknown to the seller—but that was irrelevant, because its function in dispatching the group's victims endowed it with its new ceremonial power. In any case, it was quieter than the handguns they'd used in the early days, and of course had a grace lacking with firearms.

His manic smile was returning. "But this interruption doesn't change the outcome of our meeting here, only hastens it. Your fate is the same. Your life is meant to end now, along with that of your unborn."

"But there *is* no unborn. There can't be." The words spilled from her in a desperate flood, even as her eyes filled with tears of resignation to her circumstances.

"For the greater good," he intoned.

"All for the greater good," his disciples echoed.

He plunged the dagger into her belly. She shrieked and crumpled onto the blade, nearly tearing it from his fingers as she slid to writhe on the floor. His men turned her onto her back and the Great Cleanser straddled her, pulled the blade free, and stabbed her in her belly again and again and again and again and again. He stabbed with a great ferocity, seeking not only to end the woman's life but to claim the life she denied having been able to conceive.

As she lay there in the fast-gathering pool of her blood, the prostitute was fated to hear the first rumbles that trembled the walls of the temple in which she was about to lose her life.

A great and ponderous thunder, louder than the machines above, louder than the ecstatic voices of the men watching the ritual of her murder.

Then she was gone.

But the thunder grew.

A couple was making their way slowly down the sidewalk. Between them they carried three black garbage bags filled to brimming with dirty laundry. The plan was their usual Sunday itinerary: first to dump the contents into a washing machine at the neighbourhood laundromat and then to beeline it for the liquor store across the street, there to spend a good chunk of the social services cheque burning a hole in the pocket of the man's jogging pants. They'd wait out the forty-minute laundry cycle across the street in the park, drinking a beer each while keeping vigilant for the bike cops who casually patrolled the grounds. They'd go back to transfer their laundered clothes into a dryer and spend the next forty minutes across the street for round two, a beer or two each while looking ahead to a night of fast food and pro wrestling on the T.V.

All in all, it was going to be a damn fine Sunday.

"Holy fuck," said the man under his breath, stopping fully in his tracks as a pervasive sense of something very, very amiss came over him.

"What?" demanded the girl at his side, squinting in the sun glaring from the pavement.

"When in the fuck did this all happen?"

They found themselves at the edge of a wasteland.

Stretching as far as the eye could see, the usual landscape of street, sidewalk, and parking lots was submerged beneath what appeared to be a very viscous, dark liquid. Some parts appeared waterier, but mostly a thick, mud-like texture characterized the substance that covered the streets.

The stink was nearly gag-inducing.

"Jesus *fuck*," swore the man, pulling off his doo-rag and covering his nose and mouth with it, to little effect.

"What the fuck is this shit?" The woman had pulled her t-shirt collar up over her mouth and nose. Her eyes watered at the pungency of the smell.

"*Shit's* right, babe. It's sewage, smells like," said the man, voice muffled. A sewer overflowing? A subterranean water main burst? In the heat-hazed distance, on the opposite side of the immense sewage-pool, they could just make out an excited flashing of lights: cops, maybe fire trucks and ambulances, too.

"What the Hell's *that?*" There was an angry, accusatory tone in the girl's voice, as if she were daring the scene to become even darker and more fucked-up than it was already. He followed where she was looking, at a distant point approximately where the parking lot of the laundromat they'd been headed to was located. There, a series of white-robed shapes lay scattered in the sewage water, amid the floating debris of cardboard and garbage and branches. The longer they looked at them the more certain they became of what they were.

Bodies. People drowned in the great flood of septic and sludge.

"Holy shit, when the Hell did this happen?" said the woman. Then, more pragmatically, she added, "Now where are we supposed to do our fuckin' laundry? We got nothin' clean to wear." Indeed, even the oversized t-shirt and shorts she was wearing were grease-stained in several places. They could clearly see the remains of the Stardust Laundromat building, its ceiling collapsed and its brick façade shattered and poured down into the sewage-filled street. Fire roared from the rubble, and black smoke added to the overpowering stench.

The young man shook his head in wonder at the epic spectacle of mud and sludge and death and property damage. He jingled the coins in his pocket, saved up throughout the week so that they'd have the required change to complete their usual two loads of laundry. "The world is fucked, babe. Just *fucked*."

Just then an elderly man shuffled past them down the sidewalk. He'd been standing at the edge of the devastation, staring out across the desolation of brown-black water and sludge before turning away. His clothes were sodden, and his hands and face were filthy too, as if he'd trudged through the sewage wasteland.

The young man stopped him. "Hey man, what the Hell *happened*?"

The man's rheumy eyes turned to him. There was terror there. He said, "The sewers just…exploded. Flooded. They're still flooding. No one knows why or how—we've been smack in the middle of this heatwave for almost two weeks now. There hasn't been a drop of rain in ages. It's a mystery but ask me and I'll say this was no accident."

The young man and his girl exchanged uncertain looks.

"What do you mean?"

The old man leaned in close, his whisper full of conspiracy and fear. "There's a divine hand in this. We are at war, after all."

He turned and limped on his way.

The young man and woman looked down the intersecting side street and the promise of its meagre shop fronts stretching into the smog-hazed distance. He wiped a hand across his sweaty face, said, "Let's go, babe. We'll find something down there. But let's get some beer first. Thank God the LCBO's on this side of the fuckin' neighbourhood."

"Yeah, baby," said the woman through a cloud of exhaled cigarette smoke. "I need a drink or three after seein' fuckin' crazy shit like this today."

They continued on their way.

"Ow! Fuck!"

The young man looked back to find his girl had stopped on the sidewalk, hand on her belly. "Hurry up, babe."

"Wait a sec," she said. "It's just junior. He's kicking like fuckin' crazy today." Slowly she resumed walking, though she continued rubbing her stomach.

"Future UFC champ in there," piped the young man, all paternal pride, smiling appreciatively at the vision of violence and blood. "One hundred percent killing machine."

A voice stopped them.

"In the name of the great purity, I channel the cleansing powers bestowed on me through membership in the Final Fraternity. All for the greater good. The battle continues."

They turned to look the way they'd come.

It was the filth-drenched old man they'd spoken with a moment earlier, standing on the sidewalk. His avid eyes shone like jewels in his dirty face, and the sun flashed from the pistol he aimed toward their family.

Gods Great and Gods Small

"Why.
Why.
Why.
Why.
Why?"

The word haunted the road, as the speaker himself haunted it: the farm boy shambling onward on shaking legs, feet dragging, eyes lost and seeing nothing but the pictures playing in his memory.

Around him the countryside was placid in the sunshine, the fields stretching into the distance, fringed by the crooked arms of woodland. Birdsong called from the stone pines, the only other voice besides his own.

"Why," the farm boy droned on. "Why. Why. Wh–"

He stopped, startled to have collided with another traveller on the little-frequented road. He recoiled, looked at the man before him, saw, rubbed at his eyes and looked again. But the man—the apparition?—remained.

"I'm sorry to have frightened you, young man," said the traveller to the farm boy, now speechless. "Though perhaps we were meant to meet like this."

The boy goggled a moment longer and then, accepting the miracle of what he saw, found his voice.

"Forgive me. I'd heard stories of…others like you. Those put to death in the same manner, who rose up and walked with their fellow men to speak the good word like they spoke it before they were killed. The martyred. Saints. Here in Rome but elsewhere too, in far lands. France, and Egypt, and…and other places. I confess I didn't quite believe the tales…"

He drifted off, his stunned expression quickly becoming one of joy. His smile shone like the sun. He was witness to God's hand making miracles, on a day that otherwise had threatened to destroy his belief in any goodness remaining in the world.

"Why do you ask 'why', friend?" said the head of the Saint, from where it lay tucked protectively within the crook of the decapitated body's arm. The ragged edge of the severed neck was pale in the bright light, as if long ago healed of the grave wound that had separated it from its head.

The farm boy frowned, the memory of his recent sorrow returned. Knowing in his heart that he could be open with this miraculous traveller, he said, "I saw things today… Wicked things, that put a sadness in me. I…I saw soldiers burn my village to the ground. They put men to death, and the young and the old, though not all of these were Christian. Some were, but not all. The women they rounded up, tied together in chains. I ran away. I lost my courage at the sight of all the horror. You ask why I ask 'why'—these visions haunt me, and they don't go away, and I see them and I ask 'why' because I wonder why do things like this happen today? Why are these things *allowed* to happen? My father, he was a good man, who worshipped in secret…"

The farm boy was crying now. His eyes were pleading as he stared at the head held in the hands of the Saint, for if anyone in the wide world might be able to answer the question, it was this holy man before him.

The Saint, eyes shining with a kindness rare to find, said, "Some say we are at war."

"Yes, of course. I know that Nero has executed many, but–"

"No, friend," said the Saint in his gentle voice. "There is a greater struggle than the paltry affairs of men, though it is true that some men believe divinity rushes through their veins like blood. I too have seen such scenes as you describe, many times over. And I fear tomorrow will see many more. Perhaps such scenes are guided by a greater hand."

This made sense to the farm boy. The things he'd witnessed that morning had been enough to make him question the death of all goodness and righteousness, and to believe that the Devil had planted his seeds everywhere, to bloom evil flowers in the world at large. A great war indeed, if the good Lord must meet and crush such a merciless foe.

They watched one another for a moment and then the Saint said, "You ask 'why' and I give you your answer: *but we will do what we can.*"

The farm boy thought about what the Saint had told him, and the more he pondered these things the more he felt a change come over him. The great weight he'd carried with him since the morning was still upon him—it would remain on him always, he felt—but it was perhaps a little lighter than it had been.

"Thank you for the blessing of your wisdom. It fills me up, truly it does. I feel…I am a new man, different from who I was before our meeting. I was lost, and was found."

It was the first time he'd thought of himself as a man rather than a boy. His initial embarrassment at his boldness melted away after a moment, when he understood the truth in it: he *was* a man today, after witnessing what he had and coming through it with new wisdom and a new hardness in his heart. His father would have been proud of him.

The expression on the face of the Saint had become one of sorrow. He said, "I must be on my way, friend. I have much work to do. Be well, and may He guide your travels."

The farmer watched the head-carrying Saint continue on his way, until he disappeared around the bend in the road to the east. It was only then he realized that he'd forgotten to ask the Saint's name, though he reasoned it didn't matter, because the man embodied goodness and in the end that was what mattered most: there was goodness left in the world.

~

The day was idyllic, warm and sun-washed and serene. The fields outside of Aquileia were busy with birds, chorusing in the leafy embrace of the trees, skimming over the gentle waters of the lagoon to the west.

The farmer spoke to the four men gathered before him on the grass to one side of the road. His dusty travelling pack and bag lay at their feet, and they were engrossed in his oration, a fact that pleased him as much as it had initially made him uneasy. He'd never before been so eloquent as to hold the attention of others. But since his encounter with the head-carrier months before, he'd found a new voice awakened inside himself. He'd never before been so fluent with those words his father would read to him from the Bible at bedtime each night, and though it felt strange to hear the words fall with such assurance from his lips, he'd learned to not question this gift too much; instead he gave himself up to the power of the words, and relished the light he saw dawn in his listeners' eyes as he recited them.

"…and I saw the souls of those who had been beheaded because of their testimony about Jesus and because of the word of God. They had not worshipped the beast or its image and had not received its mark on their foreheads or their hands. They came to life and reigned with Christ a thousand years."

The farmer stopped his sermon and followed where his listeners looked, to the west. A noise could be heard in the distance. Together they listened, and worry spread among them. The land had become unsafe for travellers.

"Is it thunder?" said one man, cocking his ear westward, though the sky there was blue and clear.

"It *sounds* like thunder," said the farmer, "though it is thunder of a different sort, I reckon. Listen closely: it is the thunder of many footsteps upon the road."

Indeed, when the truth of it was pointed out the men could all hear it plainly. They grew more nervous, and cast wary eyes down the road.

"Be brave, friends," said the farmer, who saw their discomfiture. "We commit no crime. Someday His worship will be permitted, celebrated. Though I am only a humble farmer, my heart says it is so, and I know the truth in this."

But the men knew what other men might believe of it, and so they fled, with apologies and promises to return and find the farmer again, so they might hear his wisdoms once more. The farmer remained standing at the side of the road, waiting. Soon enough, around the bend in the road he saw the host come into view, their crimson pennants waving on the air, their golden armour gleaming in the sunlight.

"Hello, travellers," called the man to this grim-eyed troupe when it drew close. "Will you join me, and rest yourselves from your journey? My brothers have left me, and I yearn for conversation. I bring the good word of Jesus Christ."

The men exchanged hard looks. The centurion of the group frowned at him. He spoke to one of the men behind him, though his eyes remained fixed on the farmer.

"Vitus—deliver this criminal to his god." He sounded bored, his command lacking conviction, as if he were much accustomed to saying the words.

Vitus stepped forward. He was young-looking, and fierce-eyed. He strode to the farmer and, grabbing him by the neck, thrust him to the ground. He positioned the farmer's head upon a large stone conveniently embedded in the dirt, and tore the gladius from its scabbard at his hip and raised it over his head. The farmer hadn't struggled through any of it, and remained calmly awaiting his fate. He was filled with a great peace. What was going to happen, would happen. That was all.

It wasn't a clean cut, because of course the shortsword was not made for killing in such a way. After several attempts which left the farmer screaming and thrashing and spurting blood in the dust, another soldier shouldered his companion aside, and resumed the grisly work. Soon enough, though they'd made a messy job of it, the thing was done.

The soldiers continued their march down the road. Some sneered at the body and its head as they went, which together had only moments ago comprised a foolish beggarly man preaching sacrilegious words he should never have uttered.

Vitus spat on the corpse. "Go be with your god. Nero delivers you to your angels."

The soldier in the column behind him nudged the bloody head with his pilum, sending it rolling off the road into the grass.

The host continued down the road. The birds remained silent in the trees.

A moment passed. The sounds of the Legionaries quieted with distance, faded away completely. The body of the farmer, once a boy and then a man and now something else, sat up. Struggling to its feet, it followed the trail of blood to the edge of the road and began parting the long grass there, searching. A moment later it withdrew its head, shaking off the black flies and fat wasps and blood-red serpent that crawled over it.

Tucking it beneath an arm, the Saint began walking westward along the road, to seek an answer his heart already ached in knowing. Behind him, from the direction in which the Legionaries had gone, a great clamour arose—the sounding of a trumpet; the clash of steel on steel; the screams of the dying—giving the sun-painted day its darkness, its balance.

Wild Animals at Play

Mark Shadley, eccentric locally famous homeless beggar of the downtown core easily recognized for the tie-died t-shirt he always wore and the perpetual stink of piss that hung like a mist around him, squinted into the sun-bright haze. He'd started at the strident shriek that had pierced the hung-over quiet on that Sunday morning as he made his regular circuit rummaging in the garbage bins marking the periphery of the lot at irregular intervals. In the distance, at the edge of the weed-choked empty lot—once, in more affluent decades past, a Canadian Tire had stood there, surrounded by a string of coffee shops and delis—he saw a group of children.

They stood in a loose circle, as if examining something between them. A moment later their collective voice rose, loud and feral, as whatever game they played took its next course. Mark Shadley watched them a moment longer, feeling a small unease he couldn't quite fathom. Then he shook his head and turned away, saddened by that scene of youth and potential now so utterly long-lost to him. He limped toward the main drag, and the scant promise of a few coins tossed into his empty coffee cup by early morning pedestrians en route to a coffee shop to cure their hangovers.

As he left the children behind in their play, he continued to feel the ache in his heart for the things that had remained behind in the distant days of his youth.

~

But up close, in the smashing heart of the children's gathering on the vacant lot, it was a different story unfolding.

The six boys, between ten and fourteen years of age, encircled a girl of twelve. They moved inward, kicking viciously, hitting with their hard little fists. They beat the girl in the head, on the face, all over her body. The apocalyptic cracking of her ankle snapping where one burly boy leapt down on her foot hushed their roaring voices a moment; then, as the girl fell onto the cement and her high-pitched scream tore across the weed-choked lot, their fury was reignited; as if the sound of her voice was a grease for the fire of the anger that smouldered in each of them.

The beating resumed.

The sun crawled westward across the blue.

When at last the pack was finished, and stepped away to examine what they'd done, little was left of the girl that had wandered into their midst and insulted them with her observations about their home-lives. Call them fatherless trash? Their mothers welfare-cases and whores? Their siblings junkies or the dealers who made junkies, shooting rock behind dumpsters? Time to go to school, little girl. Some personal six-on-one tutoring for you, to teach you things you'll never need to remember.

Her fragile limbs were blood-streaked; blood poured from her head and pooled around her body where several boys' boots had stomped her hard. Her face was swollen and purple with bruises. Her jaw was unhinged and dangled at an angle that gave her the look of a deranged person, one of the meth-heads shambling zombie-like down the streets, smilingly mockingly, maniacally. Teeth were scattered around her body too, brilliantly white in the burning sunlight but for one filling-lined tooth glinting a dull silver, looking somehow older than the rest of her. Her broken ankle was turned all the way around, disgusting and astonishing and not quite believable, like a bad special effect in a B-budget horror movie they might watch and laugh at and be unafraid of.

One of the boys, the youngest of the six, watched his older brother prod the body with a toe. The child began to cry. Turning at his sniffling, his brother gave him a hard smack on the back of the head. The slapping sound shot across the lot. It silenced the boy. He began nodding his head, as if suddenly understanding a lesson imparted in the blow.

"Let's go to the store."

This was the oldest boy, who already boasted the faint flowering of upper lip hair and occasional pimples on his forehead that marked passage into the teenage kingdom sprawling before them all. He made a show of hawking and spitting a huge yellow-green snot-ball at the motionless girl before turning to walk toward the downtown core.

They followed him across the lot, and through the streets toward the neighbourhood convenience store and whatever penny candies they could steal while one of their number distracted the Vietnamese teller. The body they left behind glistened wetly in the bright air, looking right at home among the wild grass and flowers struggling through the ancient, broken cement.

As the pack moved through the streets they came upon old Mark Shadley at his morning station, seated cross-legged on the stoop of a derelict hair salon begging for change. An empty paper coffee cup stood on the sidewalk at his feet, waiting for coins to fall from the hands of sympathetic pedestrians, or from the sky.

The leader of the child-pack, seeing the old man hunched over the sidewalk, smirked, and casually kicked his paper cup away down the sidewalk as he passed him. Several of his minions laughed loudly, as if it were the wittiest of jokes.

Mark Shadley was startled and raised himself up with an unsteady hand on the brick wall beside him.

"Sit down, old man," said the pack leader, stopping in his tracks to raise a fist on the air while his lackeys scooped up the spilled coins from the sidewalk. "You don't want me to *make* you sit down." His pack members chortled, bristling at the expectant violence, giddy at the unexpected comedy of confrontation between their strong leader and this frail old rummy daring to occupy a place in their territory of the city.

But Mark Shadley wasn't having any of it. He wouldn't have

taken disrespect served up like a hot breakfast from anyone, let alone a litter of shit-stained puppies like these. His voice was gruff, and full of all the threat wielded by one who's been beaten down by the world time and again only to rise time and again just the same.

"You're gonna pick up my cup and put it right back where it was, you little ugly cocksucker. And you're gonna put every hard-fought coin back inside it. Or else I'm gonna spank you and then go have a talk with the dirty whore of a trash woman that squirted you out of her shamefully filthy pussy."

Then, suddenly, recognition came: these were the children he'd seen earlier that morning, in the vacant lot. He recognized several of the boys' colourful t-shirts, and the shortest boy's Detroit Tigers baseball cap. He saw the leader's fancy hover-board tucked beneath his arm, noting its decidedly un-macho decals: bright-coloured unicorns and butterflies and cartoon stars; and the juvenile foolishness of the teddy-copter, its rubber cord attached to the boy's belt, its other end affixed to a paw of the powder blue plush bear whose whirring chopper blades sprouting from its head held it aloft a foot above the gang of grimy teenagers. These items, attached to this ragged, sallow-faced, cruel-eyed rat of a boy, were, Mark Hadley knew, nothing other than trophies, and he wondered absently what a child so evidently savage as this one had done to acquire them: who had he stolen them from, and how badly had he hurt them to lay claim to the things?

Suddenly, with a pang, he remembered the little girl he'd seen with them, and recalled his unease while he'd stood watching the children, trying to guess the game they played. And understanding came over him like the swell of a great wave, drowning any hope he might have had for the boys gathered in front of him, for their future, for their humanity. Into the stunned silence he added, his new melancholy creasing his wrinkled face with even deeper lines as if he were perhaps reliving a memory years and years and years old, but no less bitter for all the passage of time:

"That girl back there didn't deserve what you little monsters did to her. She was better than you all, and I think you know that."

The outrage the words bloomed in the alpha male pack leader

evaporated the instant he saw Mark Shadley's eyes fixed on him. The boy's puffed-out chest deflated instantly, and he took one faltering step back, bumping elbows among his lackeys and lieutenants. There was something in his eyes that the children had only felt sputtering inside themselves—here, in this shabby old man towering over them like some living scarecrow that had climbed down from its wooden post in a corn field and strode in from the outlying county, that thing was alive and vital and smouldering like a wildfire.

The old man didn't want to do what he did then—his was an act of survival, in order to endure in the world like he'd survived for over sixty years so far. And Mark Shadley made fists of his large, vein-strangled hands and stepped among them; and he taught those lost, world-fucked children the pure and the true way of the wild.

People-Eater & the Wolf Inside

On the ragged edge of the world I'll roam, and the home of the
wolf shall be my home.

- Robert Service, *The Nostomaniac* (1912)

The pines were limned in lunar light. Starlight quivered the sky.
Polaris trembled like a precious jewel overhead. In the glade, the fire
crackled and spat sparks in tireless fury. Its flickering light cast
dancing shadows all the way across the tree-line fringing the upper
slopes of the basin to the north.

The man and woman huddled over the flames, rubbing their
hands together for warmth. Occasionally the sharp cracking of a
branch sounded like a breaking bone in the huge quiet of the woods
around them. Somewhere near at hand, just beyond the perimeter of
fire glow, something rustled through the brush—a raccoon or fox or
night bird foraging by the night's light. Possibly a coyote or wolf
drawn by the fire—both species had been growing bolder in recent
years, forced by development in the area to enter the small outlying
towns for food. Sightings of wolf packs rummaging in the dump had
become more frequent; sightings in the woods fringing the town
were commonplace. One had to be careful. Only a few days earlier a
pack had attacked a woman walking her dog on one of the trails that
wound through the Ojibway conservation forest, not far from there.
The woman had managed to escape—her terrier had been taken by
the wolves.

The man's voice was loud in the great hush, though he spoke quietly.

"I knew that The Wolf Inside would prefer to meet out here rather than a more everyday place. A coffee shop, say, or a bar."

She smiled at his use of her correspondence name. "The Wolf Inside thought it was appropriate that People-Eater chose this place. It has a great romance to it." The thought of those places he'd mentioned—bars, coffee houses, or any place that was a part of the nearby small-town civilization—felt more unsavoury to her than usual. In that moment in the naked moonlight, it seemed utterly alien.

In an age of ubiquitous social media and online dating platforms, they'd found each other through a suitably arcane method; the traditional paper, snail-mail service called Other Halves would seem downright obsolete to most modern bachelors looking to meet their next partner. But then the two of them were anything but modern in their ways. Part of their bond had been forged when they'd realized that the term *old soul* truly applied to themselves. Their souls were older than most. This made them a rare species, one near to extinction maybe. It didn't matter—they would repopulate the Earth. Their discovery that Other Halves was quietly known for the fringe religious and philosophical beliefs of its members had seemed nothing short of miraculous. That they'd found one another within the group was a downright spiritual occurrence, given their unique appetites.

"What *is* your name?" she said. "I guess we should know each other's names at this point, right?" The smile she gave him was uncertain, her nervousness betrayed by a flickering in her eyes as she watched him closely in the firelight.

"My name is People-Eater," he said. "That *is* my name, now and forever."

She watched him a moment and then something new came into her eyes: a revelatory boldness, a courage. She nodded vigorously, as if affirming something to herself that was very important.

"Okay," said The Wolf Inside, and she turned to stare into the fire.

He decided to bring the conversation to its destined place.

"I found Him during my years further north, up in White Horse. When did you find Him?" He was admiring her face in the flickering light, its dark-eyed beauty. He longed to explore the rest of her. He longed to know her in all her power.

"*He* found *me*. He finds us all."

It was her turn to take charge of the conversation, he saw, to declare who and what they were in relation to the rest of the world. There was an accusatory sharpness in her voice that startled him. She was watching him closely.

Closing his eyes, he said, "My *deepest* apologies, Master. I'm humbled for my thoughtlessness. *You* find all. You *are* all."

She watched him a moment longer, then smiled. She looked satisfied.

Tendrils of fire seemed to lick toward them from the blaze. Somewhere in the night, a rumble sounded, like thunder, but also a faint tremor in the ground, like seismic quaking. Like a great voice awakening in the world.

"Since we're asking the big questions," she said, "How many for you? We never said, during our correspondence."

They'd only ever hinted at their actual respective numbers, a tantalizing possibility, an ongoing thrilling potentiality they'd both yearned to know and which she finally dared bring up during the momentousness of this, their first physical meeting. The moment the words were spoken a new energy seemed born between them: electric, sexual, and more than this. A spell cast, a ritual begun.

"Seventeen and counting," he said simply.

He saw them as he often did, like a fast-running movie-reel montage of blood and dismemberment, the internal being brought into the outside world—the freeing of souls from their hideous prisons. A perpetual collective screaming accompanied the images, and it felt like the very stretching of the fabric of reality—and it was, he knew. It was the sound of this world being pushed to its near breaking point by the reality that he, People-Eater, embodied. With her, The Wolf Inside, at his side, his reality would come to pass. The better reality would invade and usurp the lesser. The ghost-taste of the dead was like liquid fire on his tongue. It felt good being able to be so open with a person, this wondrous woman like a wolf. The relief was like the shift of the world's weight from his shoulders. Someone now shared that burden with him. He breathed deeply, cherishing the chill clean air, this moment on the cusp of nirvana.

Heart smashing with excitement, he said, "How many for you?"

He saw how she steeled herself, a look of barely bridled excitement filling her eyes. "I made my one-hundredth last night," she said, watching the moon frosting overhead. "A milestone. It was like a celebration, looking ahead to tonight." She held a hand up, close to the licking flames. It visibly trembled. "I'm still shaking from it. It was…It was so good. But of course, words can't do it justice."

He turned to look at her. The cold beauty of her. So small compared to his hulking body, and yet just as strong—stronger, maybe. The pulse in her throat, the fire reflected in her face. (Or flickering from inside her?) His smile was one of awe and admiration. Truly, a beast lived in her exquisite shell. He could learn from her. He would learn from her. She had so much to teach him. He gave her the gift of his openness.

"My first was a woman. She was my girlfriend at the time. It happened when I was twenty years old. She was a year older. It seems so long ago. I didn't know why I did it. I was young. I was scared at first."

Her voice was hushed with excitement: "Did she provoke you, or…"

He was quick to answer. "No. No. We just weren't good for each other. She was a good person, though. But we weren't right to be together. We never should have went out. And for as long as we did. Six years. It didn't make sense. We wanted different things. But no, she was good, as far as people go."

She waited. She admired his pensive eyes. They reflected firelight and lunar light or maybe the same light from within him that she felt burning inside herself.

He went on. He could do this now.

"We were talking. Sitting in the car. We were parked not too far from here, actually, just off the farmer's track we took tonight. These woods are a good place for talking. It was nice. We started kissing. It was good. Then I hit her. That's how it started. I didn't know why. I guess I *wanted* to do it. It made sense. It felt right to do, so I did it. We were kissing and I stopped kissing her and it started. I'd never wanted to do anything like that before. Not really. Not *really*. That was the beginning for me. The hunger the thirst the need woke up that night. It's been growing ever since. It followed me everywhere, my whole life. It followed me into the army. To Iraq, in the Gulf War. The more I…quenched it, the stronger it got. It gets stronger all the time. I was fighting a secret war that my fellow soldiers didn't have a clue about. They had no idea. I'm still fighting it. The hunger's stronger than ever. Sometimes I feel like I'm starving."

She watched him closely. His profile seemed to waver uncertainly in the firelight. The flames danced in his eyes.

"How did you do it?" she said. "What did you use to do it?"

"My hands. Just my hands. And then my teeth."

"I like your hands. They're strong." She reached a hand to his. She stroked his knuckles with her fingers. He shivered. He was cold. She warmed him with her touch, though her skin was cold, too. His smile gleamed in the firelight. She smiled, too.

People-Eater thought of his desk back home, its drawers filled with her letters, lovingly read and re-read so many times he'd lost count. One year of correspondence and now, finally, here they were. Finally, he could be free with another person. He could do this now. He was excited. He was alive. He was burning. He went on.

"I squeezed her throat, and she died soon after. In my hands. She fought a bit but there was no way. I watched her for a long time. She turned blue. Her face was blue and her eyes were huge and full of what I thought at first was fear, until I understood that it was something else…Realization. As if she finally understood something greater than herself, and me. Soon I gave in to my need, and I bit into her. I spent most of the night with her. It was…a feast. After I was finished, I carried what was left of her into the woods and left her there. They're deep. Nobody comes out here. I never heard about her again." Looking into the trees he murmured, "She's still there."

Silence fell. Only the wind in the trees and the nearly inaudible and indefinable but ever-present murmur of the night. An owl warbled somewhere far away.

The Wolf Inside said, "Only bones. She's only bones now. Whatever she was before is gone. She'll never hurt you again."

He looked to her, a look of startled wonder in his eyes.

She said, "I could feel your pain from your very first letter to me. I know it well."

"But it wasn't her…*She* didn't do anything."

"But someone did."

He turned back to the fire. "The world hurts us all."

"Yeah."

"It's hard to be alone."

"*Yes.*"

"Nobody can do it. Nobody."

"No even the wolves."

"Not even."

He fed a branch to the fire. His voice was eager:

"Who was your first?"

She could feel it: he yearned to know her in all her mystery. She leaned to him. Her heart hammered. Her lips brushed his ear. His skin was cold. Her lips burned. She trembled. He did, too. She told him.

"A child. A teenager. A stranger. I'd never seen him before. He'd been smoking a cigarette in a playground, alone. I was a few years older. I could tell when he saw me that he wanted me. But I wanted something else. It was so easy. When you promise a person something that they want, and they think it's within their reach—sometimes it's like a spell. You make the promise and that's the spell you cast and their yours. I left him there, bleeding in the sand, the bottle glass sticking in his throat. My family was packed and ready to move, waiting for me in our empty house, reminiscing, being nostalgic, while I said goodbye to the neighbourhood. We were gone for good after that night. I'd been so excited to get away. Doing what I did to that boy was so…freeing. I felt free to do what I'd done, and it freed me to do it after, again and again. Suddenly there was a long road in front of me where before there was just a dead-end. I started following it that night, with that broken bottle and that boy. And here we are tonight. It gets harder, it seems, there's so many cameras everywhere, and city-eyes in the sky, but...but it almost makes it better, too. More fulfilling. It's like a challenge. Like trials that I have to pass."

"Like a war."

"A calling."

His voice nearly caught in his throat. "Did you ever question why? What it was that made you do what you did, that first time?"

"Never. I did it because I had to. If I hadn't then something in me would have starved. There wasn't a choice. There is no choice."

He watched her a moment, worship in his eyes. They'd talked about such things during their correspondence, but to hear them from each other in person, here, now—it was creating an energy between them that was palpable. She could feel that he cherished the gift of her; his goddess his companion his other half that made him whole when he'd always only ever been incomplete. It was how she felt, too.

People-Eater said, "No one will ever hurt you again either."

The Wolf Inside smiled. "We have each other."

"And Him. We have Him."

"We're His."

"Yeah."

"Together, we can wipe away everything that came before. Make it all clean."

"A new beginning."

"Yes."

They sat looking out across the woods. The pines were made over by the moon into an otherworldly landscape. It was as if the world had been replaced by another, or that they'd left the world they'd known for this world of silver peace and whispering trees like fellow conspirators in their private trading of secrets. The breeze moaned among the trees like a flock of lost children in the night. Sparks from the fire wheeled on the air, more abundantly than before. The fire crackled noisily. Its voice soothed. Its touch staved off the chill while glorious scenes of carnage replayed in their memories.

The Wolf Inside said, "I brought you something."

People-Eater looked up. "I…brought you something, too."

"A present?"

"A gift, yeah."

They stood and crunched through the snow to where they'd parked their vehicles a stone's throw away, his truck in the shadow of the camper trailer she drove. He opened the trunk and there, in the truck bed, lay her gift: an elderly man and woman, each tied securely with thick loops of rope lashed around wrists and ankles. Trussed like this, they huddled close, seeking the comfort of each other in their hopeless situation. The rectangles of grey electrical tape across their mouths stifled their protests; giving them the appearance of bearing the ironic mouths of automatons, steely and emotionless.

"Thank you." Her whisper shook with excitement. "Thank you so much. I've never…No one ever gave me a gift like this. Not ever."

He followed her as she hurried around to her camper trailer's passenger side. He heard her muffled footsteps inside the vehicle, the quiet groaning of its large frame as she moved around inside. She came back with a blanketed bundle, holding it out to him.

People-Eater felt his heart race. Gingerly he reached his hands to the blanket, parted its thick folds, though he heard the quiet burbling before he saw her. The plump-cheeked infant, sleepy-eyed, twitching in her arms, reaching a tiny hand blindly toward him, her shock of red hair like fire curling across her forehead.

He couldn't find his voice, his emotion was so great. Seeing him struggle, The Wolf Inside waited patiently, the child held out for him.

At last, he accepted the gift, and managed, "Where did you get it?"

"It doesn't matter. It's yours now."

They cried together.

A minute passed, then they went back to the warmth of the fire. Once there, People-Eater felt a pull. Without thinking he placed his hand into the fire, held it there a moment; then he closed his fingers and withdrew the hand. He held his fist out for her.

The Wolf Inside cupped her hands beneath and accepted his gift. The flame danced frantically on her palm.

His eyes drew hers.

They kissed. It was another burning in the night.

A crunching behind them. They turned.

Wolves.

A group of the animals was loitering beyond the reach of the firelight. Their silhouettes were a shaggy hulking mass. He imagined he could smell the freshness of a recent kill on their collective body. Their amber eyes glowed in the light thrown from the flames, watching them with what looked like a fanatical devotion.

She said, "Hunters. Appropriate. They're beautiful."

"So pure. They hunt because they must."

People-Eater raised a hand in welcome, beckoning them to come closer.

The wolves watched them warily a moment longer, then crept cautiously into the circle of the firelight, their avid eyes staring into the flames. Their smell of wild death grew more potent.

Something compelled People-Eater and The Wolf Inside to turn back to the fire.

It had grown. It was a ten-foot pillar shuddering toward the stars. Wreathed in the flames stood a great figure. Its face was obscured, its trinity of arched horns silhouetted clearly in the furious blaze. Its long arms reached heavenward like a challenge to the stars; its saurian tail lashed slowly from side to side; its phallus spiked starwards like an obelisk.

It radiated strength, and the wildest beauty. Its voice was the thunder they'd felt shuddering the world and its fragile but savage people for so long. From the thunder words formed, which seemed to reverberate inside their thoughts like an echo from a far place.

"You've found your way."

"I'm your servant," People-Eater said, and bowed low.

"And I am, too," intoned The Wolf Inside, prostrating herself, tears on her cheeks.

Behind them they could hear the muffled cries of the old man and woman, watching from the opened truck bed, trying feebly, hopelessly to free themselves from their fate.

People-Eater and The Wolf Inside got up, clasped hands. They were two lost travellers trapped on a dark world spinning through the eternity of space. But they'd found each other. They had each other. They *had* each other, forever.

The moment marked the first time in their lives that People-Eater and The Wolf Inside felt the warmth of belonging, of truly, *truly* belonging. They were now part of a tribe. They felt exultant, invincible. The long hard years were finished. New roads lied ahead. The world was theirs for the remaking.

All around them, the wolves gave the night their howling song, frenzied; ecstatic; a voice of celebration.

People-Eater gave the infant to The Wolf Inside to hold, while he reached into the truck bed. He hoisted out the elderly couple with ease—ragged and thin, it was like lifting sheafs of paper for someone with so much power running through his veins.

Overhead, the sky was awash with the ancient starlight, pushing back the darkness.

Together, man and woman—with their sacrificial gifts—joined the figure in the fire.

This great hunt was begun.

Sister-Biter

The sun had been bigger when she was younger.

This is how she remembered it being: more expansive, blanketing the world and shining into its darkest nooks. It had felt *better* somehow, too. It was so good she could *taste* it.

What did it taste like? Her mother had asked her this once, after Julie had remarked that she liked the taste of the sun even more than her favourite food, which at the time was rocky road ice cream.

Like Heaven, ten-year-old Julie had answered without hesitation, arms thrown sunward where she stood in the centre of the backyard lawn, cherub-cheeked and content, while her brother Stanley dug determinedly in the nearby sandbox with the plastic shovel in his chubby fist.

Those days seemed far, far away as Julie sat staring out through the windshield past the dew-beaded lawn lining the perimeter of the parking lot, the tinted windows of the brick building beyond staring at her stoically. Her hand was shoved inside the sleeve of her denim jacket, fingering the scars crisscrossing her forearm. Under her light shawl she imagined the long raised purple weal at the base of her throat, the mark left by something feral having once gone for her jugular, and very nearly taken her away from witnessing sunny days forever.

~

Teeth were to become his preferred weapon against his sister, though exactly why was to remain a mystery.

The various doctors and psychiatrists in Stanley's future would have their theories: maybe the primal quality of the violence represented the manifestation of an instinctually animalistic form of aggression; or perhaps it had its origins in an early childhood oral fixation that had never been fully assimilated into a healthy and mature temperament. Whatever the case, everyone agreed that the onset of the behaviour had certainly coincided with the beginning of Stanley's departure from normal reality.

The first time Stanley bit Julie was on a pleasant summer day, smack in the heart of the season, July fifteenth and so humid that the mayflies stippling the sidewalks and house fronts didn't even put up a fight if you plucked them from the cement but seemed instead to wait with patience and relief for their fate in your hands. But like all children, Stanley and Julie were impervious to extreme weather and were absorbed in their respective play on that fateful humid afternoon.

He'd been eleven years old, she fourteen. He'd been methodically dismembering his umpteenth mayfly, slowly pulling the long filaments from its tail and watching its body stretch into an erect posture of all-consuming agony, when he turned to his sister seated on the driveway a few feet away. Her sticker book was opened in her lap, nubs of chalk abandoned beside her where she sat cross-legged in the middle of the thick-lined yellow circle she'd outlined on the cement. Stanley had halted his torture of the insect and stared at her. He parted his fingers and the mayfly continued to cling to him, its sticky bodily juices trapping it against his sweaty thumb until he absently wiped it to dust on the leg of his shorts.

Julie felt her brother watching her.

"What?" she'd demanded, annoyed by whatever game her younger brother was playing at and that she didn't want to be a part of. When he only continued to stare mutely at her with vapid eyes, completely engrossed in her and disengaged from the world around them, she shook her head and turned back to the stickers on the page before her. "Weirdo."

Stanley had always been a little peculiar but, as far as little brothers went when compared to the younger brothers of her friends, Stan was quickly reaching the very top of the weirdo list: the extended periods of quietness into which he'd fall, staring at nothing while seated at the kitchen table with his lunch forgotten in front of him, deaf to their mother telling him to finish his meal; his newfound habit of talking to himself in unsettling whispers that she and their mom could hear coming from behind closed doors, and often in distinctly different voices; and, creepiest of all in her opinion, his tendency to constantly spy on her, peering through the ajar bedroom door at Julie reading on her bed, or watching her skipping rope with her friends on the driveway from the upstairs bathroom window, his shadowy presence given away by the subtle stirring of the gauze-like curtains.

And so Julie didn't bat an eyelash when she sensed him marching up to her and standing just outside the chalk circle on the driveway that afternoon, continuing his steadfast, silent vigil over her. Just Stan the Weird, doing his weird thing. She ignored him, her annoyance quickly turning to satisfaction the longer she successfully dismissed his efforts at luring her into his silly game. It was only as his shadow fell fully across her and darkened the bright stickers that a sudden trepidation was triggered in her. By then it was too late to do anything.

Stanley, surprisingly strong for an eleven-year-old—even though at one hundred pounds he *was* a very big eleven-year-old— had reached into the circle, clamped his hand around her wrist, and yanked her beyond its chalk boundary and toward himself. In the same motion he brought his sister's arm to his mouth and sank his teeth into her wrist.

It marked the beginning of what Julie would eventually come to think of as the weird and ongoing war between them. There always had to be a first bullet fired.

~

The first time Janice Buckler asked her son about it his answer left her stunned, speechless where they shared the kitchen table, the gurgle of percolating coffee filling the room.

"Stan honey, why did you bite your sister?"

Janice had tried using her casual-voice, as though the subject weren't of any particular consequence, sounding as non-accusatory as she could make herself sound so as to not ignite the anger in him that mention of his sister seemed to evoke more and more those days.

"With my teeth I will vanquish the evil from the face of the Earth."

It sounded Biblical and sweeping, and very dark. It threatened to wipe away the placid sunshine and mellow morning atmosphere. This, from her eleven-year-old boy.

"Is that from the Bible?" she asked evenly, keeping her eyes on the slice of burnt toast she was buttering with a hand that had only just begun to quiver. If it was from the Bible she had no idea where he'd come across it: she hadn't taken the kids to church once since Henry had left them when Stan was five, and they were enrolled in a public school so had very little exposure to religious studies.

Stan said, "It's from me." His pudgy right hand had risen to clutch emphatically at his left breast, the gesture startling her to look up from the toast in her hand. His love-handle shuddered between his clutching sausage fingers, his eyes watching her avidly.

"Where did you hear it?" she reiterated, fighting to hold his intense stare.

"It's. From. Me," Stan repeated with such precise fury that she never asked the question of him again, even though the biting would continue.

~

Janice found him early one morning in the garden, staring down intently at something obscured to her by the daffodils shuddering in the stiff breeze.

This was toward summer's end, a chilly Saturday morning in September, a couple of weeks into the school year. She'd been standing on the patio, garden hose in hand and about to water the backyard lawn when she'd spotted him. She was going to call out to him, but something stopped her and, instead, she crept up behind him and peered over his shoulder.

A cat was lying stiffly among the flowers, its head twisted all the way round its scrawny neck; its eyes were gauged out, and bluebell flies were clustered in each of its black orbital cavities like shimmering jewels. A great hole gaped in its belly, likewise busy with flies. Dirt and bits of leaf clung to its matted black fur.

"Stan, honey," she said, quietly so as not to startle him, quietly because her voice just came out that way, small and quavering. Quietly because in that moment she was afraid of her son. Truly and deeply afraid. And when he turned around and found her standing there, it was the look in his eyes—completely impassive, utterly tranquil—that somehow made it all the more horrific.

She saw the dirt on his hands, and what looked like dried blood under his fingernails. She never did ask him whether he'd killed the animal, or why he would have done something so senseless and cruel. She only told him it was time for breakfast, and urged him toward the patio door and the sharing of another terribly silent meal.

Eight months later Stanley bit his sister again.

They'd been enjoying a lazy Sunday together in the family room—Janice leafing through the day's newspaper with Julie sprawled beside her, reading a book on the First World War spread across her knees (a subject that, precocious girl that she was, she'd become strangely absorbed with). Stanley was seated on the carpet in front of them, watching a matinee science fiction movie on the T.V., entranced by the black-and-white images of space men battling earthmen except for when he would occasionally scramble from his place to fiddle with the rabbit-ears antennae on top of the set. Then, satisfied that the white noise and distracting moving horizon-lines had been vanquished, he'd return to his place on the carpet, leaning back against the sofa on which his mom and sister sat engrossed in their respective reading.

So placid was the scene—and Stanley so engaged in the movie—that Janice figured it would be safe to leave brother and sister alone together for a while. She hoped that whatever had triggered the bizarre biting incident of the previous summer had passed into family lore, never to be repeated again. Besides, her brother Gary was over again, as he'd been over a lot of late, helping out with around-the-house stuff that she had neither the time nor the skill to deal with herself: cleaning the eaves troughs, patching loose boards in the backyard fence, and, currently, putting windshield wiper fluid in her car and replacing her burnt-out left headlight. She could hear the muted sound of his mucking about in the garage filter through the family room wall, along with the tinny voice of the ghetto blaster spitting out music, and smiled to herself: thank goodness for big-hearted big brothers.

She folded the newspaper neatly, depositing it on the end-table beside the couch, and slipped wordlessly out of the room. She paused at the door that led into the garage and poked her head in.

"Rock on, Gary."

Her brother stopped in mid-strum, right hand raised high in the air over the wrench that served as his imaginary guitar. He smiled sheepishly, his cheeks ruddier than usual from his work (and play) in the garage. "The crowd wanted an encore. A man has to oblige."

He'd just finished installing the new headlight. His mind had been wandering all day, in part because he was worried about his sister, who'd been more despondent of late than usual, which was saying something; in part because his was simply a wandering mind. On this particular afternoon he'd allowed his imagination to skip back in time, and he'd been imagining how different his life might have turned out had he kept his high school rock band together and gone out on the cross-country summer tour the way they'd planned before the big falling-out (over a girl who'd made the rounds of three of their five members, himself not included) that had broken their band up for good. He'd been listening to the Who while pacing languidly back and forth across the grease-stained concrete floor of the congested space, strumming the wrench in his hands like a Rickenbacker.

Janice laughed. "Thanks, Gary. The kids are in the family room. I'm going to check on my garden. Help yourself to a beer from the fridge."

Gary let his arm windmill down and around, doing his best Pete Townsend impersonation in time to the song crackling from the radio.

She smiled and ducked back inside, continuing down the hall to the kitchen where she let herself out through the sliding door onto the backyard patio. Though there was a nip in the air, the sun was bright and she could taste spring on the breeze. She crossed the lawn to where she'd left her weeding unfinished before breaking for lunch, retrieved the small held-held shovel and knelt in the soil. She didn't mind that the ground was still hard as rock and that she wasn't going to achieve much until maybe a month from then: she was content to just keep her hands busy, her mind focused on a tangible task like attacking the earth with the steel spade-tip.

Inside the house, it was midway through the movie when, possessed of no visible reason, Stan turned from the television and promptly champed his jaws down on Julie's forearm. He simultaneously clambered on top of her, pinning her against the couch cushions. His jaws clenched tightly, and he began to whip his head side to side in the same way a dog will do in order to kill a rabbit by breaking its neck. His sister's screams echoed through the house and out the windows flung open to the early spring air, summoning their mother from where she'd been weeding and their uncle Gary from the garage.

They arrived in the family room at the same time, breathless and staring aghast from the doorway at the sight of Stanley straddling Julie, tearing at her arm while she battered his head with her free fist, screaming hoarsely. There was blood on the couch, and on the kids. They ran to them, and it took all their strength to pull Stan from his sister. When they finally separated them they were shocked to see the expression of ecstasy infusing the eleven-year-old boy's face: eyes wide and transported to some other place far removed from the family room; his teeth bared in a bloody grin that looked about as feral as a human being could be before it stopped looking like a human being at all.

This second bite left his teeth-marks in Julie's flesh. It was a bonafide *wound*, that if left untreated their family doctor confirmed would have become infected, possibly severely. She would have needed extensive treatment, possibly surgical. As it stood, she had to take antibiotics for a week, and this after the doctor had disinfected the wound and cleaned it thoroughly. She'd required stitches. Fifteen of them.

It was later that same night, while peeking beneath the thick bandage to admire the injury with awe, that Julie told Boris the plush cat—the only stuffed toy she'd kept from her younger years, for the sentimental reason that it had been given to her by her dad the year before he'd went away—that it was like a signature, and evidence that Stanley the Weird, crazy kid brother, had been here.

Boris the cat stared mutely at her with his blank button eyes and, suddenly reminding Julie of her brother's creepy dead-eye expression, she deposited him without ceremony into the clutter of her bedroom closet and slammed its door. Then she stared at her reflection in her full-length mirror, wondering what her brother saw when he looked at her; wondering about the things living behind the eyes watching her in the mirror.

The Brother-Sister War saw many skirmishes over the years, some of less consequence than others. It became a sort of fixture in their family's peculiar life, so that nothing serious was ever done to deal with it: Stanley's aberrant behaviour was essentially swept under the rug while their mother dealt with individual incidents on an as-needed basis. Bitings, scratchings, howling fights that saw the siblings rolling around on the carpet until their mother tore them apart: this became commonplace.

And the animals Janice and Gary found dead and mutilated in semi-secluded places around their property—the cats, dogs, squirrels, raccoons, garter snakes, even one white rabbit, all left in the garden to rot and be bleached by the sun—these they stopped discussing too. There were coyotes in the county, after all—maybe the new housing developments were forcing them to expand their hunting territory into the surrounding neighbourhoods. This is what they told themselves, before burying the subject for good.

The conflict between the siblings couldn't be ignored forever, though, and culminated in tragedy, as all prolonged conflict does. The tragedy took the form of another premeditated ambush laid by Stanley for Julie. The cunning involved in planning and executing this particular strategy for a child so young—he was fourteen years old by this time—was astonishing, and confirmed that nothing but the most extreme measures had to be taken to deal with his illness.

It was a Thursday and Julie had come home early from the yearbook committee meeting. Her mom was at work and, not having expected Julie to be finished so early, had left Stan at home alone. Julie had felt some trepidation, but it had been months since Stan's last violent episode, and he even occasionally talked to her at the dinner table, so Julie figured she'd be okay for the few hours until their mom got home, especially if she kept to herself.

She'd eaten a light supper in her room while finishing her math homework. Then, she'd decided to wind down in front of the T.V. before turning in for the night, and had just made herself a mug of hot chocolate and brought it to the family room when the doorbell rang. She waited, hoping Stanley would answer. When the doorbell kept ringing, she cautiously padded over to the door and peered through the peephole—nobody was there. Now thoroughly weirded out, she checked that the locks were in place and hurried back to the T.V. and her hot chocolate. She'd channel-surfed until she found a nature documentary about the African savannah. Curiously lulled by the narrator's soothing voice, she'd seemingly fallen asleep at some point during the program.

When she came to, she immediately felt something was amiss. Her skull ached fiercely, and turning her eyes in her sockets to look around the room caused explosions of white-hot pain to in her temples. Her whole face felt puffy and numb, and the sound of the T.V. came muddied, like she was hearing it through a wall.

She lay still a while longer, thinking she must be very sick, maybe with the flu, because she was much too young for anything more serious, like a stroke or brain aneurysm. She tried again and, with great effort, succeeded in turning her head to her side, and found herself looking at the clutter of dishes and magazines on the coffee table. She saw her empty hot chocolate mug on its stained coaster and, placed directly beside it, an opened plastic medicine bottle lying on its side, that hadn't been there when she'd last looked.

She read its label: *Melatonin.* Her mom had been taking the stuff for years to help her sleep when her insomnia got the better of her, as it often did.

She felt his presence a moment before his shadow fell over her. She revolved her eyes in their sockets and there, of course, was Stan the Weird, round-shouldered and big-bellied, his eyes fixed on her with the same expression a shark might watch a swimmer dog-paddling where the water level plunges into the open ocean.

She opened her mouth to say something, then decided to not push him. Her tongue felt too large and sluggish in her mouth anyways, like the time she'd had a tooth pulled and the dentist had injected her with Novocaine. And the ache in her head was *tremendous.* Instead, she turned and examined her body, not quite surprised to see—it was almost as if she'd expected it—the complex web of her bonds: thick loops of rope were wound about her, pinning her arms to her side. These were reinforced with a series of bungee cords affixed in different places, as well as a length of chain she recognized as the leash of their deceased Doberman pinscher, and that their mom didn't have the heart to get rid of. Stan the Weird had evidently made a thorough raid of the garage, cleaning out their uncle's meticulously ordered shelves.

In the days following, they would learn that the amount of Melatonin Stanley had drugged her drink with could easily have been fatal had Julie not been taken to hospital as soon as she had.

Stanley leaned close to her and whispered, quiet as a mouse:

"I know what you are, sister."

His shark-eyes watched her hungrily. She feigned ignoring him, though the words startled her. Maybe he sensed this, because his voice grew louder, the triumph in it clearer.

"Forbidden woman, immoral sorceress—I. Know. What. You. *Are*."

He was taunting her. She flexed her numb arm muscles as much as she could, felt the bungee cords stretch a little, though the rope didn't yield at all.

Maybe her brother didn't appreciate being ignored as his victory over her was imminent. He shouted: "I know what you are! I know what you are! I *know* what you *are*!"

"*What* am I?" she exploded, shouting at her brother for the first time in her life; shouting possibly for the first time in her life ever, docile child that she was. The words came out with difficulty, sounding thick-tongued and sludgy. His response struck a chord in her; a chord that rang in her heart, and sent reverberations outward into every part of her: physical, mental, emotional. His words *hurt*.

"You're...*wrong*!"

He hadn't meant she was wrong *about* something. No: there was something wrong *with* her. Something was wrong *inside* of her.

It was a condemnation—a judgment—that confirmed something she'd felt for as long as she could remember. It left her stunned, and feeling more exposed than all of her brother's previous claims about her.

He finished his judgement: "But I shall cure this now, and make everything in this house right again. As for murderers, the sexually immoral, sorcerers, idolaters, and all liars, their portion will be in the lake that burns with fire and sulfur, which is the second death."

Stanley came toward her in a hideously predatory manner, padding on his toes, shoulders hunched, fingers poised to clutch and hold her in place. His teeth were bared, revealing gums swollen and red with gingivitis. The mania in his eyes was as soulless as she'd ever seen it.

It might have been fate that intervened then.

Their uncle Gary, concerned that nobody had answered his repeated calls that evening, had decided to drop by on his way home from the construction site to make sure everything was alright. As was customary he let himself inside with the key Janice had given him and hurried in search of the children. He burst into the family room and took in the scene at a glance. Clamping a beefy hand on Stan's shoulder, he spun him around. "Stan!" he said in a voice full of threat. "Hold it right there, mister. This has gone *way* too far this time."

He cast a glance to Julie entangled in the bungee cords to add emphasis to the statement. It was a moment's distraction, but a fateful fraction of a second that Stan used to his advantage. Quicker than one might have thought possible for a lumbering fourteen-year-old and without any hesitation whatsoever, Stan snatched the box-cutter slung through the array of tools on his uncle's tool belt and thrust it upward with all his strength. The blade sank fully to its plastic nose in the softness of Gary's throat.

Stan stepped back to give his uncle room. Gary's mouth snapped open in surprise and his eyes grew comically wide. A second later he toppled to one knee, and from there fell to his hands, all the while blood ran from his throat and spattered the carpet. He was trying to speak but only a grotesque gurgling sputtered from his mouth. His eyes continued to bug out and he was sweating profusely. He raised a hand toward the plastic handle of the box-cutter but, either from pain or fear of causing more damage, didn't try to remove the blade. A moment later he'd collapsed onto his side, his body heaving.

Julie, head smashing and body numb, could only watch through tear-filled eyes as their uncle died on the family room floor in front of her. When at last his spasms stilled she threw all her energy into a renewed attempt to free herself. She succeeded in swaying side to side, all while willing sensation into her unresponsive limbs.

"Finally, sister, I will cast you out."

She looked up to see Stanley grinning at her malevolently. He came onward champing his teeth together again and again and again in anticipation of sating his inexplicable hunger. And just as Julie summoned all of her strength and tore loose from her bonds her brother lunged forward and fastened his teeth onto her throat.

The vision came to her:

A fox hunting among chickens; a lion choosing its prey from among a herd of gazelle.

It had been a long and difficult winter.

The decision to consult a psychiatrist about Stan's behaviour was, of course, unavoidable. Committing him to the rigorous rehabilitation program for mentally ill and violent children at Higher Hopes was even more trying. But, according to his doctors, he'd been making progress in leaps and bounds and, as of a few weeks earlier, had even been allowed to meet with his sister for the first time since the incident that had sent him there. Their meetings were supervised by both Janice and a clinician, of course, and outside of Stan's reticence around Julie, the meetings had gone peacefully enough.

Her brother Gary's death lived with Janice every day. She thanked God that he'd been there, and gave his life so that Julie had the time to extricate herself from her bonds and escape her mentally ill brother. The ensuing months had been made more difficult by the distance that had slowly grown between her and Julie. She thought it was just her daughter's way of coping with the trauma of what had happened. But the more time passed, Janice saw less and less of Julie, who'd taken to locking herself away in her room as soon as she was home from school. And it wasn't just that she was isolating herself from her mother—weekend nights, which before had been spent at the mall or at the movies with friends, Julie likewise spent reading in her room, or listlessly channel-surfing, or just sitting staring into space. Mimicking, in this way, her brother's emotionally detached behaviour over the years.

With all this behind her, the traditional spring cleaning of the house was symbolically important for Janice. The catharsis she'd felt when she finished scrubbing the floors in the kitchen and both upstairs and downstairs bathrooms had been invigorating, and she'd just started dusting in the family room when fate seemed to conspire to send her a sign.

She'd removed the DVDs and handful of old VHS tapes from

the top shelf of the entertainment cabinet, and was vigorously dusting the bare shelf. She'd reached the feather duster to the very back of the shelf to get at where the dust was thickest when, pulling it out, the duster's plastic hilt snagged on something and pulled it out as well. She jumped a little as the object thumped down heavily beside her foot. She'd stared at it a moment, startled, as if it had fallen from the sky. She hadn't noticed it because its black leather colour camouflaged it inside the shadowed cubicle of the similarly black furniture.

It was Julie's most recent yearbook, which her graduating class had received a week before. She must have been leafing through it recently and forgotten to bring it into her bedroom, to be filed neatly alongside her others, something she did both because she was a tidy person and because she'd served on the yearbook committee for each of her five years in high school and so the books meant a lot to her.

Janice picked it up and flipped through it randomly, actively respecting her daughter's privacy and ignoring the many handwritten messages from her classmates that filled its pages. She stopped page-turning and found herself staring at Julie's class picture.

"Hey, I know you," she said. She was struck by the quiet, sure beauty of her daughter. She looked at ease, and confident, though not in a haughty way. In a word, she looked like an adult. Janice felt a pang in her chest at the thought, but resigned herself to facts: Julie was eighteen, and an emotionally mature eighteen at that. She wouldn't resent her growing up.

An idea came to her then, and she crossed the room to pull open the door to the crawlspace. She clicked on its hanging bare lightbulb and went in search of her own collection of yearbooks (mother like daughter, she also kept them neatly together, in a carefully-labelled cardboard box). She had to stoop to avoid banging her head from the latticework of wooden ceiling beams in the claustrophobically narrow space, carefully navigating the clutter of Tupperware containers stacked everywhere, and the assortment of cardboard boxes, each labelled in her meticulous hand: *Christmas ornaments 1*, *Christmas ornaments 2*, *Christmas lights*, *board games*, etc.

"There you are," she said in quiet triumph, and proceeded to drag the box designated *Yesterdays* (it struck her as an incredibly corny label to have written on the box, but whatever) from its place sandwiched between two other cardboard boxes of roughly the same size. The underside of the box scraped a trail through the thin carpet of dust in the little-frequented space and though she bumped knees on plastic containers and grazed her head on the sharp edge of a ventilation grill protruding lower than the wooden crossbeams, she succeeded in getting the heavy box out of the musty storage space and dragging it into the adjacent family room.

She sat cross-legged on the carpet flipping through the yearbooks one by one. She went in chronological order, chuckling at her first year class photograph: her deer-in-headlights expression of fear captured in that long-ago gymnasium cum photo studio, wondering what was in store for her between those walls for the next five years of her life. My God, she was a *child* in the picture. She put the yearbook to one side and opened the next with a creaking of long-untouched pages.

Minutes passed. The house was silent around her, Julie reading in her bedroom and no T.V. or radio on anywhere. She found herself flipping to the graduates section of her final-year yearbook and found her picture: it was certainly an upgrade from four years earlier. The discovery in those intervening years of things such as a hair straightener and the effective application of makeup had ushered in a new era for her. The era of the attractive young woman.

"Damn, I was cute," she said. And when she came across her prom picture several pages later, she amended, "Goddamn it, I was fucking *hot*." And holy shit wasn't Julie just the spitting image of this little hottie from another day, a long, long time ago.

It got her thinking about a subject that had been troubling her in recent years: her daughter's sexuality. It was a little mystifying, really—a girl as drop-dead gorgeous as Julie no doubt had her share of admirers at school, and yet as far as Janice was aware, Julie had never shown any interest in anyone. She'd given Julie the Talk at the start of her freshmen year, of course, making sure she knew that she could be open with her when it came to who she was seeing, boy or girl; but though Julie had seemed receptive to everything Janice said, there never had been any boys or girls.

Looking back with a shudder to her own high school years, Janice thought of the phase of her social life when she'd experimented, meaning she'd slept around…a lot. Too much, maybe, but part of that she thought might have come from not being given the same Talk from her own mother, prompting her to do what she did in secret. It wasn't until her graduating year that she'd started going steady with someone, a young man she'd finally felt okay with bringing home to her parents. Janice supposed she'd just been waiting for Julie to bring her own person home one day, but that day simply hadn't materialized. Was her daughter still a virgin? Or had she taken after Janice, and been sleeping around while, for reasons unknown, keeping it a secret from her mom?

Janice sighed, shook her head in resignation. Whatever the case, she knew Julie was a good kid, and that she'd always done her best to keep open lines of communication with her. Someday she'd meet her person, and introduce them to her mom. After all, Janice reasoned, Julie always had been a bit of a loner, enjoying her moments of solitude rather than constantly socializing with her friends.

She stood, having bookmarked two of the yearbooks—those with her and Julie's respective senior year pictures—and headed upstairs to offer proof to her daughter that beauty and brains were in the blood, that the two of them were alike and that if the past was an apt predictor of the future then things were destined to turn out alright for Julie, too, despite the recent difficult months. Janice quelled the inevitable negative thoughts that came to her because she wasn't going to have her good spirits ruined by hard facts like her husband having never witnessed the sight of their daughter in full bloom. His loss. She was going to bask in Julie's successes as any proud mom should.

And so with these trophies that captured their mutual young adulthoods tucked beneath her arm, and with renewed confidence in her role in Julie's life not just as her mother but as the friend and confidante she'd once been, Mrs. Janice Buckler walked smilingly into her daughter's bedroom, and found her clinging upside down in the ceiling corner over the bed via no means discernible to her eye; naked from head to toe, with legs spread wide. Protruding from between her buttocks was, incredibly—*inconceivably*—an earth-coloured garter snake, its lifeless length draped between her thighs and dangling down through her breasts, its bullet-shaped head nearly grazing the mattress. The stiff-looking corpse of a plump raccoon was gripped by the tail in her other hand, blood from the gaping wound in the animal's belly smeared around Julie's mouth and splashed down her chin and lacquered over her neck. Her usually placid blue eyes were rolled back in her skull to show not the whites—no, oh dear God no—but a hideous mottled white-and-black like speckled bird's eggs.

But then Janice saw the huge, grotesque grey appendage invading Julie's vagina, like a thorn-crusted vine but on a scale too vast to do anything other than kill the human being it was inside of; and it was when, against her will, Janice followed the path of that appendage that she began to fathom the truly otherworldly scope of the scene before her: the loathsome member rose up and up, past the place where the room's ceiling should have been, tethering her daughter to a star-stippled sky that brewed beyond. She understood innately that it wasn't the same sky that was outside of their house— she knew the house was still there, its roof intact, the neighbourhood as quiet and unremarkable as on any other week night; what she saw from the vantage of the bedroom doorway was a glimpse into a different place entirely, a plane beyond, an existence on the other side of this room's reality.

Defying gravity, mocking sanity, a sprawling cityscape hung upside down in the western quadrant of this sky, the tops of its buildings spiking into space, its ground hidden behind layers of cosmic gases; the city's architecture was alien to any she'd known, its shapes and dimensions hypnotically deceptive—more organic than anything, they resembled colossal stone edifices sculpted by the winds of eons into their amorphous shapes. From this monstrous megalopolis came a procession of weird many-legged machines, like silver insects followed by a train of animals pulling a dais on which reclined a giant being made from what appeared to be burning trees. The large floating stones dotting the skyscape she realized were disembodied heads drifting past outside of the house in which she stood, disbelieving her senses; these heads moaned, giving the scene its clamour of wind—with their mouths wide, she saw into their star-filled maws, while their scattering of eyes goggled at the pulsing sky in pained-looking ecstasy.

The *wrongness* of the scene struck her as potently as its horror, its marriage of Escher and Dali as a perverted montage spliced into a Brakhage cosmological film epic. Lesser details in this incomprehensible tableau came to her, slowly: the cloud of large black flies buzzing furiously around her; amid them several giant black moths flapped their petal-like wings anxiously; a legion of them furred the walls around Julie. The bed beneath her daughter was spattered with blood: the raccoon's; the trickle of red-tinged spittle from the serpent's mouth; her own cunt-blood streaked downward from where the grey protuberance stretched her open.

And then Julie sensed her mother's invasive presence.

She swung her head around and found her mother petrified in the bedroom doorway. A look of fury contorted the young woman's features from their ecstasy into a hateful mask; and a low guttural growl rumbled in her throat like that of a rabid dog. The girl floated gently down through the air, her body performing a slow and soundless and graceful somersault. She came to rest straddling the monstrous appendage that pierced her until, a moment later, the thing pulled itself from her body with an intolerably loud and prolonged flatulence that filled the bedroom like stuttering thunder.

Her mother wet herself in her terror, crying.

Julie dropped the dead raccoon at her feet and, gripping the stout snake with both hands, pulled it from her anus. She draped it across her shoulders like a horrific shawl and took a step toward her mother, who shrank beneath her daughter's Stygian stare. Breath wafted from their mouths in streams of fog in the cosmic chill of the bedroom. A putrescent stink hung over everything.

This was the child that Janice knew so well, whom she'd bathed as a baby, and coddled, and watched grow over her eighteen years into a beautiful, intelligent young woman, who'd made the honour roll five years straight and was destined to begin a post-secondary academic career in any university she chose to apply to; the same young woman who played lead clarinet in the senior band, and who'd served as a chairman on the yearbook committee five years running, and who excelled not only academically but was a precocious reader and thinker outside of the classroom. This young woman had come *from her.*

The growling, bloody thing before her, with the hateful black eyes, and the stench coming off her in waves—a pong of death—was like a great negation of the world Janice Buckler had always known.

She found herself once more thinking of—and yearning for— her husband, Peter, who'd slipped away like a mystery she knew she would never solve. Without him there with her, and without her dear brother Gary, and beneath the black gaze of her daughter, Janice felt completely and unequivocally alone in the world.

The yearbooks in her hand made her feel suddenly embarrassed, and she let them slip through her shaking fingers to fall on the carpet.

And, just like that, the moment poised on the precipice of darkness and disaster passed.

Janice and Julie stood watching one another in the placid sunshine streaming through the bedroom window. Julie, blue-eyed, gentle-eyed again, her mother unable to speak. All was quiet around them, disturbed only by the distant clicking of the grandfather clock's hands from in the depths of the house.

The comforter, pulled from the bed by Julie a moment earlier, lay draped over the animal carcasses: the smooth mounds and curvatures of the blanket might have hidden nothing more outlandish than a plush toy or a pile of clothing. Where the black flies and moths had disappeared to her mother couldn't say, but they were gone as if they hadn't buzzed and flapped there at all. Julie looked small in the baggy blue hoody she'd snatched from the hamper and pulled over herself. Her bare legs poking out beneath, her mother noticed distantly, were goose-pimpled with cold. Janice was shivering, too, though of course it wasn't the icy air that caused it.

"Mom," Julie said, drawing her mother's attention—her wide eyes had been darting fearfully around the bedroom, as if everything in the world was a threat to her. "Mom: it's okay. Let's pretend everything's normal."

The plaintive note in her words hung in the air between them.

It took a moment of working her mouth silently before Julie's mom found her voice again, though when she spoke it quavered uncertainly.

"Pretend everything's *normal?* Oh dear God, what *was* that, Julie? What's a mom supposed to do, or think, when she sees a thing like that? What's…what does it *mean?* What does it all *mean?*" She was crying, and clutching her arms around her shaking body.

Julie chose her words carefully. It felt like a great deal depended on what she said then. When she spoke, she spoke deliberately, slowly, and while looking right into her mother's eyes of despair.

"It means everybody's different, mom. All of us. In our own ways. This, to me—what you saw—to me, that *is* normal." She laughed a laugh of anxiety, and her mother laughed too, involuntarily, unable to thwart the mad comedy of their conversation, of the world, of life.

"But…but *why* are you like this?"

"Why are you not?" Julie winced a little at the hard accusation in the words, reminding herself of her mom's innocence in all of this.

Janice was desperate for a concrete, definable answer to the incomprehensible thing she'd seen. She clutched at him as desperately as her terror had conjured him a moment earlier: "Is it your father? Is this his fault? Did he—"

"I'm sure dad was as good as you are, mom," Julie said quickly. "I'm not…*his fault.*"

Janice was shaking her head. "I didn't mean it like that, honey. I'm just trying to understand."

"I know, mom."

"But…But…But for how *long?* How long have you been…"

Tears threatened to come into Julie's eyes now too. "Always, I think. I've never *not* been this way. But the past few years, the way I am has been getting…stronger." It was the only way she knew how to put it that sounded even halfway right, though really it was all beyond words.

Her mother shook her head frantically, trying to deny or expel the vision. She continued to weep, openly and without any effort to staunch her tears. The only words she managed were, "I'm so scared, honey."

"Mom," Julie said imploringly, her eyes begging her mom's belief in her like she'd never begged her for anything before in all her eighteen years. She gathered herself a moment, deciding to say what had to be said. "You're my family. I'd never hurt you. Not ever. I…I *could* hurt you, easily, and very much, in ways you can't even begin to imagine. But I'd never. What you have to understand is that, my whole life…I've *protected* you. Watched over you. The world, it's…it's a hungry place. That's something I learned a long time ago. But with me, you've always been safe. With me, you'll always *be* safe."

From this world, and the worlds of other Masters.

The thought hung in Julie's head like a black cloud, but she successfully fought down the urge to inundate her mother with too much honesty. She was only beginning to make sense of things herself, and couldn't expect her mom to understand.

And, as if to stave off the darkness of the moment, another thought came to her, quickly on the heels of the first:

There was love in this world.

Julie pulled her mother to her. Janice let herself be held the way moms never allowed themselves to be held by their children. But this was okay, she felt the acceptable nature of it in her daughter's arms; it was an embrace whose strength, physical and beyond-physical, she felt acutely. It awed her, and she showed her awe in the same way that she showed her grief, and her great fear, and her anger at the unfairness of a world that allowed husbands to abandon their families so easily: she cried and clutched her daughter's iron arms tightly, tightly.

"Thank you for telling me, Julie," she said. And, "I think…I think I maybe always knew, somehow. I could never put it into words—I still can't—but I knew. I knew *something*."

Of course she'd known, thought Julie, relief flooding her. She was her mom. No matter what Julie might be, a part of her also came from this kind woman she'd known her whole life.

Janice said, "Your brother knows, too, doesn't he?"

At this Julie's emotions overcame her. She cried, too, nodding as the memory came back to her as powerfully as a physical blow: herself one year earlier, gathering her strength and snapping the bonds her brother had entangled her in during his final attack on her; breaking the rope and bungee cords and chain like so much paper confetti and for the first time using her secret strength to fling him away from herself like a ragdoll; fleeing the family room, her throat sputtering blood like a spigot where his teeth had found her, while he watched her run away from where he lay bloody-mouthed on the carpet, shaken at her show of uncanny power.

Her mother's arms around her were the greatest comfort she could imagine in that moment, warm as sunshine. She'd never felt anything so good before in all her million years of life.

Late-June sunshine painted the dewy grass of the grounds in a gentle light as Julie stepped from the car. She crossed the nearly deserted parking lot, the many-windowed façade of the building looming over her, depressing for what it represented for her brother: a prison, whose staff didn't, nor could ever, totally understand him and the things that would always haunt him. She tried to brighten her mood, telling herself the school year had ended, a new summer was waiting and, beyond it, university. A new world, a new life.

First things first, she thought, pulling open the heavy glass door and entering the cool, quiet lobby.

"Hello, Julie," came the greeting from Margaret, the stocky nurse stationed at the desk. "Have a seat and we'll have Stan come to the meeting area in a moment."

Julie visited her brother on a regular basis. She used to come with their mother but a few months ago had been given the okay to visit alone. She took a seat now with her back to the window overlooking the lot. She scanned the magazines strewn across the low table in front of her but felt too anxious to peruse any of them. She always felt a little nervous before seeing her brother, though once they were seated across from one another, with the protective Plexiglas window between them, all of her apprehensions evaporated and they were big sister and little brother again. And, despite their usual lack of meaningful communication during these visits—usually Stan would just sit there in his typical catatonic state and stare through her like she wasn't even there at all—Julie always felt pleased afterward, both because she felt like she'd fulfilled some familial duty, and also because she liked seeing him. He was her brother. She loved him, despite of everything.

This visit, though, she met an unexpectedly animated version of her brother. This was the Stan of old. This was Stan the Weird, veteran of the Brother-Sister War.

He smiled a sardonic smile as he took his seat. "Hello, sister. How nice of you to come see me again."

"Hi Stan."

He hissed at her and ran his tongue across the observation glass. His voice had sounded muted through the barrier but she heard him clearly when he said, voice strangled, "I'll kill you, evil whore! Just *give me* the chance!"

Julie watched Stan with pained eyes. Then, smiling the sad smile that had won her several classmates' hearts, she said, "I love you, Stanley."

"Don't you call me *Stanley*! Evil-whore, don't call me *Stanley*! I am *Perseus* and I will vanquish, you, Gorgon bitch! I am the guardian standing strong against your infiltration of the goodness in the world!"

His eyes, manic and glaring with fury and terror, told her that he believed he was fighting for his very soul while in her presence. So did the cross he made of his fingers, thrust toward her in as much a gesture of loathing as attack.

Julie chuckled, shaking her head at the sight of him. She had to admire him his conviction: Stan believed he knew her, on one very deep level, and played his part the way his heart told him he needed to. He'd always known about her, without her having ever given him so much as a sign or hint. His fury and hatred was founded on something like faith.

But there was a time for everything, she decided. Glancing around to ensure none of the monitors were looking their way and waving a hand to blind the sole camera watching their cubicle with its cold Cyclopean eye, she turned back to her brother watching her hatefully through the glass. She willed herself to drift up from the plastic chair and to float suspended across from him watching her in awe; she opened her mouth wide, wider, inhumanly wider, until the dry-bone clattering of her jaws unhinging sounded nauseatingly in the cubicle; a moment later the pulped semi-digested remains of a possum was regurgitated and filling her mouth, fur glistening in its blanket of digestive fluids.

Stanley erupted in a fit of incoherent, lunatic screaming, all of his heart's suspicions and certainties validated utterly in that moment. He thrashed his fists across the window glass, heedless of the damage and pain the assault was inflicting on himself. He tore the small silver crucifix from the chain around his neck and stabbed it knife-like against the glass.

Julie swallowed back the possum remains as his assault on the barrier grew, reconfiguring her jaws as she dropped softly back into the chair. A blink from her eyes and the camera-eye was un-blinded. She watched him as a pair of male nurses approached, blowing a kiss off the palm of her hand to him screaming and pounding on the plastic barrier. She watched as long as it took for the nurses to haul him from the cubicle, kicking and teeth-gnashing and howling in holy outrage, his words echoing back to where she sat in her chair.

"I have seen it with my eyes! I have seen, *Lord! Bless your soldier with the strength to fight the Adversary, o Lord!"*

Julie said, "Thanks for always watching out for mom. But you don't ever have to worry about me."

Stanley, of course, heard nothing that she said to him then, as he fought the nurses and gnashed his teeth at the memory of his sister's flesh in his righteous grasp.

She loved him, it was true. But she found that she also loved driving him just a little more bat-shit crazy than he was already bat-shit crazy. She was the older sister, after all, and this was one of her sibling privileges to enjoy now and then. She was okay with this, and didn't feel in the least guilty for it. All told, she was as good a person as she could be considering the worlds in which she lived, and the ways they often influenced their denizens to do bad things to their weaker neighbours. She had, after all, all the power in the universe to wield if she wanted.

"Until next time, Perseus," she said, and left him praying for goodness on the opposite side of the window that separated their worlds.

~

She checked herself out at the reception desk, making the requisite small-talk with Margaret: yes, it had been nice seeing her brother; no, nothing much else was new with her; yes, she was excited about school next year; no she hadn't decided on her major yet but she'd see; etc. etc.

Five minutes later she was exiting the building, imagining she heard the ghost-echo of her brother's vehement curses following her. She involuntarily touched her arm, there and there and there, and then removed her shawl to run a finger along her throat, where the scars of his bites marked her forever. She was okay with these scars: first off, it was Stanley's story more than it was hers, he was the bright centre of the story like he'd always been the centre of their family's strange little universe, and so it made sense that he should have left his stamp on her, as if he were keeping her in check, as if he were acting the hero to the darkness inside her. As if, opposites that they were, they kept a sort of balance in the world, even though she knew she had all the power in the world to do with as she pleased, and she chose to keep safe those few people she called her earthly family, including the brother that had always sought to expose her. Plus, she was a veteran of a war, and any veteran worth their salt had scars to prove they were there, fighting for what their hearts told them was right.

She stopped when she reached the car and looked skyward. A smile spread across her face. It was spring, and summer was around the corner, soon to be in full glorious bloom: the sun would be reaching its golden fingers into every nook of the world, its light burning away all the darkness the world outside one's home could throw your way. And she decided right then that she was going to go home and ask her mom to accompany her to the movies that night; a girls' night out, because ancient and wise and all-powerful she was, but her mom's friend and confidante she was always happy to be.

And besides, nights like this they *should* savour while they still could: the end of the world, her heart told her, was rushing toward them faster than all the light in the universe.

Rat-Eaters
in Lucifer's Land

He dreamed the same dream that had plagued his sleep for what seemed like forever: the dream of the Eating Things. The things always occupied a melancholy, mist-shrouded field strewn with dead, where the pickings were plentiful for their obscene, ravenous appetite. He never saw them clearly—always they remained shrouded in the perpetual fog that hung in thick curtains over the crater-pocked ground. But always he could *hear* them: the hideous crunching and chewing as they cannibalized the dead in that most dangerous-feeling of places.

As always, he was held helpless in the preternatural terror of the vision, listening appalled while the things continued their feast. Often he would see the silhouettes of them dragging corpses over the broken earth to some unknown place, like demented farmers picking grisly fruit from their garden. What were these dream-creatures? Harpies of dark European folklore? Demons spawned from some collective, trauma-born nightmare? Biblical angels of apocalypse? He didn't know, though some remote, lucid part of himself sensed even within the tenuous fabric of the dream that they'd grown to haunt his waking world as well; that they'd be waiting for him when he awoke.

Wind gusted, and a charnel stench wafted through the dream, that familiar gut-wrenching miasma of decomposing bodies and poison gas. And the mists swirled, became tattered, and were erased and replaced by a vision more horrific still, as he opened his eyes to find himself materialized into shuddering wakefulness in the trench that had been his prison for two endless weeks. And he remembered who he was, Captain Patrick Denning, acting commander of the men known in some parts of the continent as the Death Angels.

And with waking, the desperate realization came to him again: the war had invaded and perverted even his meagre once-sanctuary of sleep.

He glanced around. There they were scattered in the trench: the ragtag remnants of his company, a mere dozen men including himself, some with wounds serious enough to keep them out of action indefinitely. All of them wearing the same expression of resignation to their dire circumstances. And dire they were.

The supply lines had been severed nearly two weeks before, leaving the company in a desperate place: ammunitions nearly spent while the German lines received replenishment daily. Jacoby, their radio man, had suffered a direct hit one week ago, the shell leaving little but mechanical garbage beyond salvaging, and ragged pieces of meat nearly unrecognizable as having once constituted a human being; their CO had been picked off by sniper fire three days before, dropping like a stone from where he'd been crouching on the trench's lip to survey the enemy lines through his binoculars— clutching his destroyed throat, he'd writhed in the mud and died even while the medic, Coulter, tried to stanch the blood gushing between his fingers. He could only do so much with the limited supplies of plasma and bandages, and the men he patched together daily saw the strain in his haggard face as he went stoically about his endless, bloody work.

Stranded, pinned down, flanked on all sides by an ever-encroaching enemy, the men awaited what in all likelihood would be an imminent and final German assault on their position, both from beyond the threadbare copse of trees to the east and from the western fields. It was the first week of winter, and the temperatures were plummeting steadily with each day passing. Their hunger now bordered on starvation and had forced the company to turn to catching the vermin infesting the trenches in order to stay alive.

"The last stand of the dreaded Death Angels," Denning murmured to himself, looking to the gaunt-cheeked soldier seated in the mud midway down the trench, turning rats impaled on a makeshift skewer. Their bodies had been blackened by the small, sputtering fire, their calcified tails jutting stiffly in death. Fires were dangerous out here but it didn't matter now—their position and predicament were only too clear to the enemy.

Private Casey Findley was one of the replacements, a newbie who'd proved himself time and again in those endless fourteen days they'd lain pinned in their trench. The blood-soaked bandages around his skinny bicep and thigh signified his true rank in the eyes of the men. He'd suffered those wounds while saving a man hit by fire and trapped in No Man's Land during their first futile attempt to break out and take the German line to the west. Never mind that the man—a corporal by the name of Bruce Chalmers—had since died: the replacement had brought him back, still breathing. Miraculously, the paratrooper company's arrival in the French countryside a little over two weeks before had not only been Findley's first jump with the Death Angels—it had been his first jump ever. No one remarked on it anymore. They were all seasoned soldiers now.

Denning turned to examine the rest.

Sadler was peering cautiously over the top of the trench into the devastated fields, idly fingering the hockey card clipped to his helmet, the good luck totem he'd brought with him from the old world; Hicks, Spencer, Johnson and Mackinaw leaned against the muddy trench wall and stared forlornly into the desolate sky they'd dropped from two endless weeks ago. One soldier, Private Charles Bennett, hacked with a rasping cough, huddled inside a dirty wool blanket: he had pneumonia and was suffering. Another, Private Michael Garrety, frantically scratched an itch on his cheek and neck that had been bothering him for days—a sign of nerves. His fingers had left raw red wheals on his skin, but still he kept at it. All of the men continually rechecked their guns, as if willing more ammunition into the chambers.

Only one of their company, Corporal McCall, stood apart from the others, smiling his weird, incongruous smile while running a dirty finger along the helmet in his hands, tracing the faded lines of the black, winged human silhouette etched against the olive green as he watched the rats cooking over the fire. A trueborn angel of death if he'd ever seen one, mused Denning, unsure whether this fact pleased or saddened or frightened him.

"They're ready," said Findley, startling the captain from his reverie. Denning looked at him, seeing that he'd spoken to no one in particular and was now simply staring into the fire. *My God, he's a child, a boy.* This fact, though not new to Denning, still had the power to hit him like a bullet in the stomach. Findley could be a boy scout tending a bonfire at an overnight camp. But of course he was not that, and this place was not that, either.

The stink of the cooked rats hung in the air, making the men grimace and fidget nervously in their places and avoid each other's eyes. Captain Denning made a point of being the first to crawl to the fire and pull one of the rodents from the skewer. He used his knife to slice into its soft belly—it came with an exhalation of gas that whispered like a voice into the tense silence. He willed his thoughts elsewhere as he'd become so proficient at doing, and sank his teeth into the warm flesh.

"It's not steak, but it'll have to do."

In the wake of those words, spoken through a full mouth, he felt the bravest he'd ever felt while serving his country.

Seeing their Captain do what had to be done, their great hunger overpowered their nausea and his men followed, huddling closer around their loathsome supper.

The revolting taste of rat meat still clung in their mouths when the great wailing of descending shells began again.

"Get down!"

Denning's voice was swallowed in the cacophony. He needn't have bothered, of course—his men were already trying their best to squeeze themselves as deeply as possible into the meagre shelter of the trench, cradling their heads in their hands as the concussive impact shook the earth, sending clods of dirt and stones raining down everywhere.

Screaming erupted along the line, from men wounded by

shrapnel or untouched by anything but their mortal terror, punctuated always by the great thunder continuing to crash down from a sky dirty with artillery.

It seemed that the shelling lasted for days. It pummelled the earth like a punishment of insane gods and melted the marrow in the bones of the Canadian line clutching the ground; it froze the blood in their veins and loosened their bowels so some of them shit themselves where they clung.

And it went on and on and on and on and on.

This latest barrage left the ground all around the trench punctured with immense craters. Sometime during the tumult, the clouds had opened as well, and heavy snowfall was coming down.

There was no respite for the men though, even after this, for out in the heavy smoke of No Man's Land, they could make out the sounds of furtive movement; the advance of the German line, a final assault in the immediate aftermath of the heaviest shelling the Canadians had suffered in days. Word spread along their line and those men who were able steeled themselves for the fighting to come. Coulter made his bloody rounds, maintaining his emotionless efficiency, though some of the men noticed that his hands had started to shake so badly that he was barely able to see to their wounds.

Slowly, the smoke cleared, and through the snow, they could make out shapes beyond the debris of bodies and limbs and churned earth clogging No Man's Land. They clutched their weapons, preparing themselves for the enemy charge, and the inevitable close-quarters combat that would follow their failure to hold them back. They exchanged hard, knowing glances: this, they knew, would likely be the end for them.

"Be ready!" Denning sighted along his rifle's scope, willing his hands to hold the weapon steady.

Minutes crawled past.

In the aftermath of the prolonged shelling, the tension was electric. In the quiet, a new sound came to Denning's ears, and it took him a moment to understand that it had followed him from his dreams: the gnashing of hideous teeth; the ripping of uniform and flesh; the sharp snapping of bones like pistol-cracks. A chill snaked down his spine, tickling his balls with an icy finger. Cold sweat broke out on his forehead.

He listened raptly, heart smashing; but no, thank God no: it wasn't the sounds of some grisly feast drifting across the field, but the crunch and clank of something mechanical; something heavy and cumbersome and made of screeching steel components advancing across the uneven ground, crushing to pulp the bodies covering the graveyard that was No Man's Land.

More unnervingly, another sound became audible: the anguished cries of people. Prolonged moanings, shrill screams were drifting from the field, sounding inseparable from the mechanical noises.

Denning put binoculars to his eyes and probed the snow-shrouded distance, expecting Tigers to materialize.

Dark shapes coalesced there, but no tanks, these.

"Aww, what the fuck is this?" This was Hicks. He'd spotted them, too, whatever they were.

The men stared entranced into the snow, and saw.

A line of men marched there, though the nebulous conditions made them appear strange, their shapes burly and elongated.

"Maybe they're surrendering," chortled Hicks, voice wavering with nerves. "Maybe this war's done with us, eh, boys?"

"This war ain't never going to be done with us, soldier." McCall, of course, always the best at speaking the ugliest truths the men never wanted to hear.

"Wait a minute," murmured Denning. "What *is* this?"

"Captain?" Spencer looked to him. He was shuddering with cold, and fear.

The men exchanged uneasy glances, clutching their rifles tighter.

"Is that…It looks like…Is that *armour*? I can't tell—it looks like those men are wearing armour of some type."

"Armour?" echoed Harding. "*What?*"

"I can't tell for sure. I haven't seen this before though. This is new."

"*You* ain't seen this before?" said Harding with raised eyebrows. Their captain had seen a lot of action, far more than most of them. If this was new to him, it didn't bode well for a situation that had begun appearing doomed days before. "Why do we always hear about *something new* when it's suddenly being shoved down our fuckin' throats?"

"Welcome to the paratroopers, Death Angel," someone down the line quipped grimly, though nobody laughed.

The line of weird armoured men continued to march toward them.

The sound of their progress grew louder, chilling the Canadians: the heavy metallic clanking, the loud clomp of their footsteps smashing down onto the frozen earth with tremendous force; the grating of great machine limbs. And, now much more clearly, the strangled cries of men coming with each of those crashing steps.

The men sighted along their weapons with a focus borne of terror and desperation.

"What the fuck are they?" Hicks' whisper cut the tense silence.

"They're the new knights of a new Round Table, fit for deeds in Lucifer's garden, looks like," said McCall. No one noticed the maniacal gleam in his eyes as he stared at the approaching horde, though he sounded as straitjacket-ready as he usually did.

"What the hell are they, sir?" said Private Hicks again, ignoring McCall.

"Targets for your bullets, Private," said Denning with practiced bravado. Then, movement caught his eye, beyond the marching things trampling the dead. "Some of the Krauts are still in their trench. You can see them moving around."

They looked and, indeed, saw them: the line of helmets visible over the rim of the trench behind the armoured host, taking turns peeking up at the advancing line.

Their footsteps made a growing thunder that the Canadians felt trembling the earth beneath their boots.

~

The Death Angels got their first clear look at the armoured host, and it shattered the semblance of calm they clung to.

Huge and box-like, the machine-men lumbered slowly but were no less dangerous for it. The right arm of each tapered into what appeared to be some variation of the MG 42 machine gun—operated one-handed, the weapon wasn't meant for accuracy, which became clear when the point-man spattered fire over the heads of the Death Angels, though as suppression fire it was getting the job done.

The machine-men's left arms were also weaponized, though in a different way that became apparent when the same point-man sent a long tongue of fire licking out to scald the frostbitten air only metres from the Canadians' trench.

Flamethrowers.

Horror of horrors. A flashback to wartime crimes of years before, incomprehensibly confronting the men now in this modern age of 1944.

But even worse were the naked men strapped across the chests of each armoured figure with tangles of barbed wire. They were emaciated, their pale complexions making the lacerations and bruises on their skin stand out starkly. Their limbs were stretched to their limits and each step of the armoured men must have sent bolts of pain through them. Denning and his men didn't discuss it, but they knew these were Allied soldiers. Psychological warfare of the most powerful and perverse kind.

As if this weren't horrifying enough, the men looked for the source of the chugging motor and spotted a handful of rectangular machines bouncing over the uneven ground toward them. As they drew closer, their details emerged: their gaping front ends, the mouths filled with six-inch steel teeth, with long concave shovels on all four sides of the machines' faces designed to scoop soldiers into the churning maws.

Eaters.

Insane horror of insane horrors. These converted

woodchippers were equally effective as psychological weapons than as actual killing machines. The sight of the remote-controlled monstrosities with their gnashing teeth, rolling inexorably closer was the stuff of nightmares. It sent chills through every soldier who'd heard the dark stories about their use.

For the briefest of moments, the Death Angels stared bewitched by the oncoming Eaters, and the brilliant fire spitting from the flamethrowers, the only brightness amid the dismal grey landscape of trench and muddy fields and winter sky. The heat from the flame was a shock to their cold-numbed faces and hands. With this heat panic swept through the trench.

"Sir!" said Bennett where he lay against the trench wall. "What the hell do we do?"

Though the men could hardly believe what their eyes told them, they knew to trust in and follow the example of their captain, the steadiest man they knew, who'd reliably gotten them out of so many hopeless situations they'd lost count.

"We do the only thing we can do if we want to get through this," said Denning. "We hit them with everything we've got. Don't think. Just do. Grenades first, on my command."

His command came a few seconds later.

The soldiers pulled the pins from their grenades and hurled them at the armoured horde. One of their number went over the top of the trench even as the symphony of explosions shook the world: McCall, eyes reflecting the great fire, Browning machine gun blazing.

Denning watched him run into the wall of flame before them. And then, mouthing a habitual prayer to a divinity that had failed him repeatedly over the past two weeks, he rose from the mud and signalled for his men to follow him into the fire.

Denning would later look back on what happened and consider it something of a miracle.

Their initial grenade attack destroyed a pair of the armoured men, and their lunatic charge among the cumbersome enemy was both unexpected and confusing. They picked them off with close-range fire, finding vulnerable places in their heads and joints. It was over within minutes, though they wouldn't get away unscathed: two of their men were hit simultaneously—Spencer and Johnson. Burned to death at close range with the incendiary force of those monstrous flamethrowers, Denning and his men could only hope their friends' deaths had been quick.

One of the Eaters swallowed the grenade Denning threw into its mouth, erupting in flame and grinding to a halt in the mud. It had inadvertently snatched a corpse from the many littering No Man's Land—Denning saw its masticated remains exiting through the machine's rear chute like a massive explosion of spaghetti.

Beside him, Hicks gawped, swore, "Oh Jesus fucking Christ."

Denning took him by the arm and pulled him to cover alongside the dead Eater, out of sight of the pulped body. "Snap out of it, Hicks," he shouted at him before turning to shoot a volley at the second Eater, which was turning around to chase down Sadler. Denning stopped when he saw Sadler's plan, cursing himself for having wasted valuable ammo on the thing. Still, he watched with satisfaction when the thing followed Sadler as he leapt into the trench—the machine's operators, slow to realize what had happened, weren't able to turn the Eater from its course in time. It toppled into the trench, and lay pinned between its opposing walls, wheels spinning helplessly.

The final pair of armoured soldiers were gunned down. They toppled to the ground with a colossal crashing and groaning.

"Everyone down!"

Denning dropped to a knee, scanning the snowy distance, all too aware of their exposed position. It was as he was frantically trying to decide whether to order a retreat or a final adrenalin-fuelled assault on the German line before them that it happened: a barrage of fire concentrated on the enemy trench from its rear side. They watched in disbelief as waves of men moved in, pumping the trench with bullets.

Allied ambush! Reinforcements! Rescue!

"He shoots, he scores," said Sadler, his tone one of utter disbelief, oblivious to the long gash across his cheek where a sliver of shrapnel had cut him.

"Sir?"

Denning turned from the fighting, saw Bennett standing off to one side, staring absorbed into the wreckage. The men approached him, navigating amid the series of small fires smouldering all around. The naked human that had been tied to its chest had been shot to ribbons—little remained now but a bloody husk. Amid the smoke and blood and warped steel and sparking, fried circuitry of the fallen armoured figure, they saw:

A bullet or shrapnel had loosed the face-plate to reveal a human face. Its distinctly Slavic features were drawn and deathly, grey-white as if long ago drained of all vitality, like a hideous sculpture set within the greater steel sarcophagus of the armour. The bullets that had destroyed its face-plate also revealed complex tangles of wires and tubing that ran from the steel head-piece directly into the back of the man's skull; other filaments disappeared into his temples and cheeks, snaked up his nostrils.

This wasn't a man wearing armour, they realized: this was a man sewn with wires and cables and tubing into a mechanical body like some hideous gestalt creature born in a pulp story.

"Jesus Goddamned Christ." This was Harding, goggling at the sight.

"Knights," said McCall, eyes brimming with more mania than usual. "Truly, knights." Incredibly—inconceivably—he raised a hand rigidly to his brow, saluting them. After his suicide run into their midst, machine gun spitting and cutting down several of the towering machine-men at point-blank range, fire licking all around him and devouring two of his comrades alive, McCall had it in him to salute this latest horror produced by the mind of the enemy.

The men stared at him, speechless. Then, without a word, McCall hunkered low, and moved out across the smoky ground, eyes avid and seeking…something. He went in a northerly direction, skirting the German line to the west, and running loosely parallel with it. Denning opened his mouth to call, and then something stopped him. Instead, they only watched him disappear amid the smoke and snow.

Then, "Oh, fuck!"

The men started at Bennett's cry, following his wide-eyed stare and instinctively bringing their guns to bear on the wreckage: the steel-framed face they'd been examining had at some point opened its eyes, and was watching them with an expression that could only be described as lost.

Warily, Denning leaned close. "Can you talk? What—*who* are you?" He kept his Number 4 aimed guardedly toward the chest of the thing. Its limbs seemed lifeless, incapable of any sudden movement, but as he'd learned all too often, no precaution was too much.

The voice that answered him spoke a muddled hybrid of languages: he recognized English, Czech, Italian, German, though the garbled dialogue lacked all humanity; it sputtered out its erratic message in a mechanical monotone completely empty of emotion before lapsing into silence and its tragic-looking appraisal of them.

"Bennett," Denning said, and the multi-lingual Private stepped to the front of the men to provide as accurate a translation of the garbled words as he could.

"We are…Axis and we…are slaves…"

A seizure wracked the thing's face, its bloodless features contorting horribly. Its blood-filled eyes snapped open wide, and the glare looking out at the men now was distinctly different from its previous pitiful gaze.

"What's it mean, *slaves?*" Bennett sounded as scared as he looked, wide-eyed and shaking.

"What are you a slave to?" Denning asked it.

"The Lord…of Light…Light to your Darkness. The baby Jesus, the sheep for…the wolf…Now…angels fall every day. His host is…greater force…"

Its tone was different now, too:

"Surrender is…your only…choice. You number…few…We are… millions strong…all…around you…All…hope gone…"

A fire flashed into sputtering life amid the circuitry at the back of its head, followed by another spasming of the face. The expression in its eyes fluctuated rapidly between a maniacal glare and its former sorrow. A line of blood seeped from its nostrils, bloody froth bubbled in the corners of its mouth.

Bennett muttered under his breath. "What is this, Kraut propaganda or…"

The machine-man interrupted him, its pleading-voice returned.

"Please…we were…men once…too…Mercy, friend…Kill…me…We…the…experiment…We…deserve…peace …" And then, changed again, it spat: "The lesser…will die… You…death…is…all…awaits…But for…German…superi…ority…and…its brothers…and the…Lord…"

Its wrecked limbs struggled to right themselves, to sight along its flamethrower-tipped hand and kill the men gathered around it; but its broken body failed it, and the machine-man only shuddered in its place on the ground, smoking, wheezing, burning, dying.

"It sounds…broken," said Sadler.

Garrety's voice was hushed. "What it said, about the Krauts controlling them. Is that…What did it mean? Is this some new Kraut weapon? Like, remote control? Like with the Eaters?"

"But so much worse," said Denning.

The men could only exchange uneasy looks.

"Oh God, look."

They looked, found Hicks pointing at a place where the machine-man's steel casing had been stripped by bullets, and part of its naked arm—its human arm—lay exposed: on the bare pale skin a dark tattoo stood out starkly. A series of numbers. A serial code.

The men had heard rumours of the extermination camps, where Germans took captured Jews, Poles, cataloguing them with numbers like sheep. They'd heard of unimaginable atrocities, mass murders committed, though seeing actual evidence of the horror manifested like this—another escalation in the demented mania of the war—it was too much. The men stared, speechless, sick at the sight and the implications it conjured.

They jumped at a sudden movement and mechanical groaning, bringing their guns up again. Amid the debris close to them, another machine-man had risen to its hands, its human eyes watching them from behind its helmet's cracked plastic visor. One of its legs was missing, shorn at the knee, and it left a trail of blood and sparks as it crawled toward them. The steel tip of the flamethrower-hand it held toward them was twisted and wrecked, but still the soldiers held their weapons at the ready.

It came to rest beside its dying companion, the man it wore barbed-wired to itself long-dead, too, his face missing completely. Pieces of the machine-man's tattered steel hide had come apart as it made its way to them, clanging along the ground. A skeletal man lay revealed inside the shell. The men saw the steel Waffen SS medallion nailed prominently into the grey flesh of its emaciated chest, as well as an array of other medals—they saw Italian military insignias and strange ornate, archaic-looking symbols they'd never seen before—stabbed across its body like a proclamation of Axis military institutions; the vision like a mockery of humankind. They knew, of course, that another serial number would be found tattooed somewhere on its skin.

It spoke, this one's voice like the wheels of a railcar grinding along its track, and like its companion, its words tumbled in a staccato hybrid of languages that Bennett translated as best he could. "The weak na...nation you... serve, it will serve...us, as...all nations...serve. This is...the hi...hi...hierarchy...now, as it...has been...the...hier-er...archy al...waysssss...." A hideous smile creased its face, revealing a mouthful of black teeth. Incongruously, tears ran from its eyes. "You serve...the Father...land, too...of...course. To...day...you've served...us a feast...fit for...the kings...of old..."

It raised its twisted flamethrower-hand to the men. They stiffened, fingers tightening on the triggers of their guns, though the machine-man's weapon only smoked and sputtered harmlessly.

"I heard they use magic in the war," murmured Harding, sounding young and unhinged. "Magic and machines, together. They make...weapons. I thought it was just rumours, more propaganda..."

"That's bullshit," said Garrety, his quavering voice sounding anything but convinced.

"Yeah," said Hicks. "This poor son-of-a-bitch's just a remote control car for those Kraut loonies."

No one else said anything. They only stood staring at the dying machine-men while the sounds of fighting continued from the

German line. The second creature before them tried to say something more but only a violent cough erupted from it, sounding somewhere between the barking of a dog and a man vomiting. Bloody, oily effluvium dripped and hung like webbing from its lips to the earth. Its face, they saw, was changed now: terror-filled, pain-filled, it pleaded silently for an end to its misery.

Denning squatted before the first creature. "What is all this? *Why* all this? Tell us." He swept his arm out across the charred ground, the machine-men dead and fire-blackened Canadian dead.

The machine-man focused its mournful eyes on him. Its bloody smile stretched its papery skin grotesquely. "We make…good sport   and…experi…ment..ation…even if…failed…experiment…ation." And it cackled, as if at the bitter irony of things, and then its laughter erupted into another fit of blood-foamed coughing.

Without orders, without warning, Sadler raised his gun and fired several rounds at each of the things in turn, point-blank. In the aftermath of the shots, he looked to the captain, eyes filled with alarm, as if he were as startled by his actions as the rest of the men.

"Mercy-kill, sir. I…I couldn't help it. I'm sorry, sir." His voice was hushed, barely audible at all amid the wind and distant gunfire.

Denning only nodded, wondering whether Sadler had meant mercy for the machine-men or themselves.

"Everybody says this war is Hell," said Harding. "But it's the people. *People* are Hell."

"Not all," said Denning, without any conviction. He could hear it clearly in his voice, didn't bother trying to disguise it at all: disingenuousness, going through the motions the way he'd never done before in his life, with anything. He was changed on this day, from the man he'd been. His eyes saw the world differently than they had before all of this.

"He was right, sir," said Sadler. "McCall. This *is* Lucifer's land."

He was eyeing the devastation with a grim eye, absently running a finger along the curled edge of his lucky hockey card; the face of the player photographed there, Syl Apps, stared outwards from a sepia-tinted ice rink an ocean away. Noxious smoke swirled in wind-swept eddies, veiling and unveiling the dead and the pieces of the dead moment to moment.

In the snow-veiled distance, a series of shouts took the place of the gunfire. They made out the shapes of soldiers climbing from the German trench and coming toward them with shouted greetings: men of the cavalry that had rode in at zero hour, saving the Death Angels who more often than not were the saviours of others.

Denning said nothing to Sadler. He only lifted an arm in weary greeting to the approaching soldiers. They'd figure this out, he reasoned. He'd speak with the brass and sort out this ugly mess. Soon the world would make a little more sense. He turned to his men. "Alright boys, we pack up fast. Harding, you help Coulter—"

The sudden explosion at the edge of the circle of soldiers was catastrophic: Bennett was killed instantly, taking the brunt of the blast from behind; several others were wounded by shrapnel; all of them were sent flying through the air like ragdolls.

Other explosions followed immediately after: grenades? Mortar shells? They couldn't tell—all was chaos, thunder, fire.

Fate saw to it that two of the men were hurled directly into an old foxhole that had become uncovered during the earlier artillery shelling. Denning and Sadler lay crumpled and tangled in each other's limbs in the shallow hole and, even as their vision cleared, they saw the rushing darkness as the great oak tree became uprooted in the blasts and came crashing down across their hole, bringing night fully and firmly.

They came to in the foxhole, suffocating in the stale air with the massive tree shrouding their view of the sky. Peering out between the small gaps in the tangle of branches they saw, though they wondered at the reality of the vision:

It was the men who had taken out the German fortification, and seemingly saved them, engaged in a flurry of activity amid the ruins. They were a small team, special missions, their markings American. Swarming the site, they were methodically putting bullets into the Canadians, dead and wounded alike.

"Good work, men. Your valour will be remembered."

This was a general striding through the carnage, unperturbed, his emotionless voice carrying on the wind. Denning and Sadler realized he was addressing the Canadians being gunned down at close range. In the immense silence following the mass execution, the general's orders came briskly and clearly:

"Quickly. Burn them like the Germans would have, except for this one." He gestured to where one of his men was kneeling beside a fallen Canadian. "His wounds are superficial. He'll be fine for what we need."

Squinting, Denning saw, and his heart sank: it was Private Casey Findley, bravest boy scout Canada had given the war, being carted off to what horror he didn't want to contemplate. He opened his mouth, considered his options and what giving away his and Sadler's existence would achieve. And he shut his mouth, and silently hated everything in the world.

The American general clapped his hands together like he might applaud a symphony's impeccable performance. "Looking good, men, but chop-chop. Pack up and move out. Team two, take out the Krauts behind the tree-line, then meet us at camp two."

He turned and marched toward the smashed German line, beyond which Denning and Sadler could make out the vague shapes of vehicles. Half of the force that remained behind began a disciplined gathering of the fallen machine-men and disparate pieces of them that lay scattered in the vicinity. The remaining soldiers made a pile of the corpses of the Death Angels, which a pair of them razed with flamethrowers. The stench of burning meat carried quickly on the brisk wind. Two dozen soldiers trotted past their foxhole toward the German line behind the tree-wall to the east, weapons clanking.

The seek-and-destroy-and-gather operation was a model of efficiency and ruthlessness that left Denning and Sadler stunned. Within minutes the two soldiers were watching the American convoy roar off across the broken, snowy landscape, their secret atrocity unknown but to the two of them.

It took a great deal of effort but eventually the two men succeeded in digging themselves out of the earth. Finding that the weight of the tree was too great for their combined strength to shift, they opted to use a shovel they found in the foxhole to dig a new tunnel into the side of the hole, and upward to freedom.

Working in cramped quarters and with ebbing strength made it a formidable task, and when they crawled tentatively into the light nearly two hours later, they were trembling with weakness. They took in the sight of their dead friends piled in the snow, a scorched mound with stinking smoke still rising from them: Harding, Coulter, Bennett, Johnson, Mackinaw, all burned into black, tortured statues. It was as inhumane a death as could be given a man.

"Sir?"

"Yeah."

"What the Hell was all that? And…*why?*"

But Denning had no answers for his sole remaining soldier. He only stared at the bodies, feeling something in him that had been growing increasingly unhinged come apart completely. Time seemed stretched, stilled. The moment felt like a dream, but of course he knew it was not. His dreams had never been this dark with death and depravity. After a moment he heard his voice coming to him as if from a very great distance:

"I'm so hungry."

Sadler turned to Denning, saw that he was staring at the hill of burned men. It took a moment for meaning to seep its way through Sadler's instinctual denial.

"But…sir?" Sadler was watching his captain, aghast. "We can walk. The western line is open now. The Krauts to the east are probably going to pull back, too. They're engaged with the team that was here. There might be a base nearby. If we head—"

"There's no base," said Denning, still staring at the black human hill before them. "There'll never be a base again." Then, turning to look at Sadler, "Aren't you tired? Aren't you *hungry?* We haven't eaten in so long." Somewhere, he thought, a boy scout named Casey Findley was becoming a new kind of man. "I'm hungrier than I ever remember being. It's like I could eat all the food in the world if someone could give it to me."

Sadler stared at his captain, and then looked back to the burnt corpses. He forced himself to soak up the details of the bodies: their wizened black flesh; the spoiled pudding of their eyes seeping from gaping sockets; their features preserved into rictuses of agony. These had been his comrades, friends. Now they were lifeless husks, a part of the bleak landscape like the destroyed forest, the shattered earth with its rocks hurled into the air by shelling, like confetti in some mad celebration of the evil times they found themselves living in, in this incomprehensible place.

Sadler grunted in the affirmative, aware suddenly of a great ache, in his bones, in his muscles, in some other, deeper place. And then he heard his voice say, "I'll start a fire." And then his voice added, sounding practical and efficient and soldierly, "Because it's so cold, sir." Because the meat didn't require it, he meant—it was already cooked; the fire was to keep them warm while they ate and the winter dusk came on; they needed to conserve what strength they had before beginning their march to find…what?

He wasn't sure, so he busied himself with things he understood. And he was squatting to gather together the branches from trees that had been obliterated during the day's shelling. Fires were dangerous out here, but the captain said nothing: they were Death Angels—they were beyond the weakness of fear just like they were beyond paltry pride—they ate danger for breakfast. They ate rats like it was the Last Supper.

As Denning watched Sadler piling the branches, his thoughts turned to what day it might be, what date. He had no idea, but had a suspicion that maybe somewhere an old world had continued marching onward. He said, as if testing the truth of the idea, "Your Leafs are playing back home, I bet."

"What are the Leafs, sir, and what's home?"

Sadler was the most avid hockey fan of their company. He lived and breathed the sport, had collected hockey cards until the companies had ceased making them at the beginning of the war, and kept up with all the scores from overseas as best he could, especially when it concerned his beloved Toronto Maple Leafs; he'd even spent a couple of seasons playing on his college team, in Kingston. His tenure as a right-winger was cut short, of course, and a different fate had awaited him, on far distant shores.

Denning nodded at his man's words. This made sense. It confirmed something he felt but couldn't quite put into words. Appropriately, he noticed that Sadler's talismanic hockey card was no longer clipped to his dirty helmet; dislodged during the recent fighting, it was lost somewhere amid the mud and snow.

Their fire was ready. Its warmth felt good on their cold-numbed hands. They took turns cutting themselves slabs of meat from the body closest to them. The dog-tags clinging in the charred skin told them it had been Mackinaw, once; but it was now only meat; a meal; energy for them to take into their own bodies and use to walk onward from this site of battle to another.

After some time of chewing the gamey meat in silence, the thought escaped Denning, dropping from his mouth like a little shell between them.

"They're not just in my dreams. They're there. It's us. We're out there." He was staring out across the desolate fields. This couldn't be France, could it? Where was the postcard-beauty? Where were the pretty girls? Had they erased it all? Had he dreamed it all?

Sadler raised an eyebrow. "Sir?"

Denning turned to the man, a look of surprise on his face, as if startled to find him there at all. "It's *us*. *We're* out there. And here we are now, living the dream. The Death Angels are dead. Long live the Rat-Eaters."

Sadler's eyes widened. He watched his captain a moment. He said, "Yes, sir."

Denning shook his head, as if clearing his thoughts, then turned away to continue eating.

Sadler turned back to his own meat. After a moment he said, through a full mouth, "Where do we go now, sir?"

Denning eyed the horizon, ugly with smoke.

"That *is* the question, isn't it?"

As if to punctuate their exchange, a distant thunder erupted in the west, sending a rumble through the earth that they felt shuddering deep in their bones. Artillery: a new night, a new struggle.

Then: "Sir."

Denning looked where Sadler looked, to a point in the fields stretching away in the dreary west. He squinted in the uncertain light, picked the figure out, marching through the ravaged land.

"Sir, is that..."

"McCall."

"He survived."

"Of course he did. The meek shall not inherit *this* Earth. He's one of the strong."

"What's he doing?"

The last the men had seen of the corporal had been his courageous and mad gambit during the battle with the machine-men; rushing into the fray, laughing maniacally with gun blazing, before creeping into the smoke of No Man's Land in search of Germans or Americans or Tiger tanks or machine-men, or whatever it was he was looking for.

"He's going to get his answer."

"Should...Should we go after him, sir?" Then Sadler added, hopefully, "Make sure he gets his Purple Heart? He deserves one for what he did back there, right? He took out two or three of those machine-soldiers all on his own."

"No need, Private. He doesn't want a medal. We'll probably see him again sometime."

Sadler said nothing to this, turned back to the charred meat in his hands. In the east, gunfire erupted, like a counterpoint to the concussive drumming in the west—the covert missions team laying siege to the German line. This, of course, was nothing new. They were accustomed to being hemmed in by fighting. They were paratroopers.

"Sir?"

But Denning had already heard it and was watching the snow-besieged distance directly ahead of where they sat, and from where the new sound came: a heavy, repetitive thudding. Of course they were familiar with this sound, and a moment later they saw its hulking shape materialize amid the precipitation: a machine-man. A moment later, though, they saw how this creature differed from its companions: it had been decapitated during the combat (wounded by shrapnel from a grenade? Or a direct hit from a machine gun?) and lumbered on its way with its head tucked neatly within the crook of its steel arm. Sparks sputtered from the bushel of wires stretching tautly from the head's temples and to its neck, these hideous electric ganglia reminding the two soldiers that they fought in a war whose scale they'd only just begun to understand.

They watched the machine-man trudge determinedly on, like a cephalophore in holy pursuit of a Devil, until it was swallowed by the sheeting snowfall.

Denning said, "We'll let him go, too. We'll let them both go. They'll find each other if they're meant to."

They said nothing more. There was nothing else to say. This was just another vision conjured in the world they lived in, outside of their control.

They continued eating. The sky darkened, and though the snowfall dwindled, a ferocious wind swept out of the north. Full night settled over the already gloomy land, transforming the landscape of severed tree stumps into the jagged profile of a primitive fortress: one could imagine the array of ghostly shadows being Visigoths and Huns stealing through the darkness, a barbarian horde waiting for their chance to tear down what other men had built.

They finished their supper.

Captain Denning stood, gathered together his meagre pack and slung his weapon across a shoulder. Sadler did the same. The two men turned westward and began their wordless trek across the wasteland toward the new thunder.

A Savage Path

By the muted milky light filtering through the dirty glass of the window set over her desk in the cramped musty garage, Abigail Delores stared at the sheaf of papers stacked as thick as a phone book before her.

She lifted the title page, and read:

Chapter 1

The purple clouds churned against a black sky, heralding its arrival from among the stars. It appeared: a gargantuan egg-shaped object. It descended to hang over the city of Windsor Ontario, where it remained for years. Once an unremarkable place, the city became a new mecca of pilgrimage.

People journeyed from afar to see it.

Some called it the God-Egg, others more simply but profoundly: God.

She looked to the wall of the garage opposite the steel door, to the shelves stacked neatly beside one another. She read her name emblazoned on the spines of the many books lined up there in a variety of fonts and colours, amazed as always that she'd written so much, feeling as ever that she hadn't truly written any of it, that she was merely the vessel through which the words, omniscient and of their own volition, poured, from some unknown place of origin. She scanned the titles; as always they summed up in her mind the overall emotion of the books but never more than this, never any details relating to their plots or characters or themes, much of which she'd forgotten over time:

A Lonely Child

A Starless Map

A Godless Girl

A Moonless Life

She admired the colourful cover of a paperback displayed facing outward: a green-skinned woman with a classically beautiful face, her head encased within a large glass bubble, her silver space suit standing out starkly against the backdrop of a dark purpling sky stitched with stars. Over the woman's shoulder a rocket was lifting from the rocky landscape into the sky. The title of the book held a melancholy quality at odds with the vibrant yellow cartoon font in which it appeared:

A Weeping World

She cocked an ear at the sound of steps within the house. It was a muffled sound through the thick door that led from the garage, where she'd been banished, from the kitchen beyond. There her husband prowled: she could hear the sounds of him making coffee, the familiar pattern he went through so many times a day; the running of water from the faucet, the plastic noises of the coffee maker being opened and its filter being replaced and, a minute later, the chugging, gurgling sounds of percolation. He would bring her her supper in the next few hours, like always. Had she banished herself here this time, or had it been him punishing her? In the end it didn't matter: either way she was in this world and he in another. They punished themselves more than each other. This was how it had always been, even in the early days of their marriage before either of them had begun to fully appreciate the individual paths on which they were heading.

She saw his shadow blot out the tiny slice of light between the door and the rotting jamb, felt his presence there on the opposite side of the door, on the threshold of speaking to her. But he didn't, and after a minute the shadow departed, giving her back the sliver of light into the house in which she no longer belonged.

She turned to stare at the shelves again, their colourful spines and colourful covers offering her a small comfort. She looked from the shelves to the sheaf of papers on the small desk. All of the books, everything she'd ever written or dreamed of writing, had coalesced into her new manuscript. It would be her final book, she'd known that even as she'd begun the fevered writing sessions that, two months of hard work and sleepless nights later, she'd only just completed that very morning. This would be her final testament and message to the world, if the world ever deigned to notice her epic efforts. The title page stared up at her, its words awakening a deep depression in her:

A Savage Path

It was all the more melancholic to her ear for it designating the first non-fiction manuscript she'd written, and certainly the last.

She lifted the stack of papers, leaving only the final page resting naked and revealed on the desk. She read the words on this page.

Chapter 777

And so the great Egg hung in the sky for eleven long years of mystery and debate and prophesying.

And then, on the eleven-year anniversary of its arrival, the Egg leapt away into the sky; without warning, without sign, it was gone instantaneously.

It was never to return.

In the years following its great exodus, major changes swept the world: many new religions were founded; and rates of suicide climbed staggeringly. Some cried out that the world's judgement had been passed, and that humankind had, collectively, failed some divine test of its moral good, and was now destined to plunge into its darkest epoch yet. Some waited for the great Egg's return. Others claimed their hearts told them it would never return.

Either way, happiness seemed to have been snuffed from the world.

She stood from the manuscript, dissatisfied with it, with the day, with the world outside the tiny claustrophobic and melancholy world inside her skull. She wondered vaguely, beyond the great weariness pulling her toward the couch tucked into one corner of the musty garage, about her desire to go out into the streets and kill whoever crossed her path. She wondered about it, but no longer as fearfully or with as much anxiety as when the inclination had first begun to seize her months and months before. Now its presence in her heart was a peculiar comfort, and a quiet certainty. With it like a heavy stone inside her she pulled the garage door open to the city waiting for her outside, thinking as she did that, though her husband's territory may have included the house they'd shared uncomfortably for fifteen years, hers was the bigger country.

The first thing she saw was a pair of teenagers idling past on the sidewalk running close to the house; two boys, one walking alongside his companion, who puttered along on a bright red air-scooter a half-foot over the ground, its sleek sides spattered with colourful sports stickers and decals. The boys became aware of the woman watching them from the shade of the garage, and cast a casually suspicious eye on her.

She looked up. The stars were out, and the moon, but they were remote as ever, wintry and unattainable. She felt that winter inside her heart. It had frozen her inside, crystallized long ago any tears she may have shed for the way things always turned out.

The woman, seeing the street and the houses and the teenagers with an exacting clarity she didn't recall having ever before possessed, did what she had to. She pulled the pistol from the waistband of her gym shorts where she'd tucked it after finishing her novel hours earlier, aimed at the boys, and pulled the trigger twice in succession. The shots were apocalyptically loud in the mellow gloaming, like thunder. The blood from the shattered skull of one of the boys shot so violently through the air that it spattered across her face and shoulders, staining the cement around her, even making it so far as to stipple the cover page of her manuscript; a splash of red across the title like a stamp or seal.

The book was done.

Unbeknownst to her, the sliver of light between garage door and jamb was again briefly blotted out by her husband's shadow as he stood there listening in the huge aftermath of gunfire, before slipping away back into the depths of the house.

Finally, she could rest too, and taking one step back into the warm, comforting shadows of the garage, she placed the barrel of the gun inside her mouth, pulled the trigger, and joined the way of the world around her.

Cry for Mother

A tree house, a free house,
A secret you and me house,
A high up in the leafy branches
Cozy as can be house.

- Shel Silverstein, *Tree House*

Audrey Deloise navigated her way in the kitchen by the moonlight spilling through the patio doors at the far end of the room. The digital clock on the microwave said 2:17 A.M. She took a glass from the cupboard and filled it from the tap. She stood there in the moon darkness, drinking thirstily. Something had awoken her again. What had it been? What was it always? Her sleep had gotten so bad during the past few months. She'd been parched. Maybe her thirst had woken her? Of course she knew that it hadn't, but tried to believe it had.

She finished her water and remained standing in the darkness, listening to the huge silence of the sleeping house around her. Then she noticed the note paper pinned to the freezer door, standing out pale and stark in the darkness. She whispered across the tiles, and plucked the paper from beneath the colourful plastic magnet. She cracked the refrigerator door and by the spear of escaping light read:

Mom,

I can't anymore.

Love,
D

Audrey Deloise became instantaneously numb. All feeling, physical and emotional, was absent. It was as if a great void had opened up inside of her while her thoughts continued to circle its periphery in a jumble. She thought distantly of the space documentary she'd watched a couple of nights before—her thoughts were asteroids or other space debris drifting along the edge of a hungry black hole, the black hole yawning dangerously inside of her.

Of course, she knew even as it was happening that it was a direct result of reading the brief note from her daughter; the acceptance of the note's meaning had evoked this, whatever *this* was.

Slowly, slowly, she could feel the old pain growing up inside her again. A return of the familiar brew of guilt and despair her mind seemed to always push away, just beyond awareness, but that had plagued her on and off for years. Now it rose up in her again, only so much more strongly than she'd ever experienced it. It hurt so much—both emotionally and physically—that she doubled over from the pain, dropping her glass to smash on the floor. She fell to her knees; collapsed onto her side and spasmed in its throes, cracking an ankle against a wooden leg of the kitchen table and sending a coffee cup left there after dinner crashing on the tiles. She wept and wailed; she clutched her chest as she flailed about on the linoleum, because it was there that the unbearable agony pulsed strongest, in tandem with every beat of her heart, though of course this was no heart attack, at least not in the conventional medical definition of the term.

It grew and grew like it never had before, pushing outward, filling her up, filling the world.

~

A stifling heatwave tyrannized the August night.

The pizza joint sweltered. The small window unit air conditioner had died the week before and the restaurant owner, too cheap to buy a replacement machine this late into the summer, let his employees suffer the record temperatures. The single door was propped open in a desperate attempt to allow fresh air into the stuffy space, but to no avail. Mosquitoes hovered lethargically overtop the tomato sauces simmering in their stainless steel vats. Dozens of the insects lay mired in the dried, sticky sauce spotting the countertop like adventurers baked into effigies by ancient lava flows. The bleary-eyed night manager and two employees working at that wee hour of cemetery stillness, as well as the pair of teenage patrons splitting a medium pepperoni and cheese at the corner table, each felt bludgeoned by the formidable heat.

The patrons, Jerry and Della, were in love. They were runaways, and this was their first night on the lam. The pizza joint—Outskirts Pizza, located as the name suggested in the city limits along the dark stretch of Highway 3 between Windsor and Belle River—had long been their favourite fast food place, one they'd ordered from constantly throughout the years. Tonight had been their first trip there without parental supervision, an expedition that had taken them an hour on foot because no buses went out that far from Windsor. Shortcutting it through the countless farmers' fields and scraggly woods had been an arduous trek, but worth every step.

It was all very exciting, and they were going to savour their pizza slices and colas and they were going to make love again before dawn, in the tent they'd pitched in the woods behind the pizza joint, and come sunrise they were going to be thumbing their way far away from there. It was all so thrilling. Who knew where they'd end up tomorrow, and the things they'd see? One town, two towns, a big city over to the west. Who could even guess what lay ahead? Tomorrow, next week, and then the fall like a cool refreshing dream coming after the vicious and endless summer heatwave.

The future was theirs. They had no ties to their hometown. They had no real friends besides one another, steadfastly shunning people like a ritual of wolves. Yup, the world was theirs for the taking.

"How do you like your pizza?" Jerry said through a mouthful of cheesy bread. He seemed oblivious to the glob of tomato sauce on his old, faded Deathray Bradburys t-shirt.

"Mmm," answered Della, mid-bite, nodding her head for emphasis.

They knew they were the perfect couple, and jokingly combined their names to call themselves "Jelly" as if they were Hollywood celebrities (not that they'd ever be that, because they hated rich shallow people like those they imagined existed in the Hollyverse). But still it went to show what kind of couple they were: the kind that was meant to be. Like stars—celestial bodies, not famous people—destined to burn together in all the darkness of the universe.

And the things they were running away from were meant to stay away forever. These were the Secret Things, known only to each other, and that was the way it was supposed to be. Together they could survive anything. Together the world was going to get better, and turn into a good place, somewhere sometime somehow. That's the kind of power Jerry and Della a.k.a. Jelly wielded when they were together. That was the magic they made between them.

"Do you think they know yet?" Jerry tried to make his voice casual, maybe a little tough. She loved him for it.

Della said, "Mom knows, I'm sure. She gets up a lot in the night to use the bathroom or get water and would have found the note I left on the fridge. Dad's working the graveyard shift at the plant so she wouldn't be able to tell him until a few hours from now."

Sensing the unease in her voice Jerry was quick to say, "We'll be long gone by then. No worries."

She smiled at him. He was so thoughtful. He was so strong for her. With him she was stronger. She said, "I'm not worried."

They finished their pizza slices. They sipped their pops and enjoyed the sleepy, secret atmosphere of the wee-hour eatery.

The night manager gasped.

Jerry and Della looked up, saw him and the two employees staring toward the door with expressions of terror. They looked there in time to see the abomination shamble its way into the pizzeria.

As one, without thought but acting instinctually in a shared bid for self-preservation, the five occupants of the pizza joint bolted toward the questionable safety of the kitchen area, and then the storeroom beyond.

They stood gathered there now, speechless, trembling, and stomachs rebelling at the memory of what they'd witnessed, the thing that had invaded the pizzeria. The thick steel storeroom door with its massive deadbolt slammed into place didn't seem nearly secure enough considering what was on the opposite side.

"What the Hell is that Godforsaken thing?"

The night manager's voice was hushed and quivering. He was pale with fear. His sickly colour made his thin brown moustache stand out, quivering on his lip like a living thing. One of the cashiers, a pimply sandy-haired sixteen-year-old boy, was trying hopelessly to cover the wet spot darkening his khaki uniform trousers with his hands. The girl employee stood with her hands clamped across her mouth, as if stifling a scream waiting inside her mouth.

Della and Jerry clung to each other, unspeaking.

The thing outside, though the five of them had only glimpsed it briefly before fleeing to the storeroom, would remain etched into the matrices of their minds: a true monstrosity, summoned straight from direct-to-video B-grade pulp horror movies: a humanoid thing of raw nerve endings gleaming wetly in its raw-meat flesh, with what had appeared—God's honest truth—as its internal organs pulsing and pumping on its *exterior shell* like some demented medical dummy come to hideous life; its glistening brain bulging from its skull like a tumour exploded outward; its spongy lungs like twin alien organisms engaged in deep, rhythmic communication; and its heart, oh it had worn it plainly for them to see, too, and to hear, the organ clinging like a hideous parasite to the left of its rotting, pungent chest cavity and beating an audible percussion they could still hear despite the storeroom door separating themselves from it. The thing bled everywhere from its vein-wreathed body, from a million places that gaped and dripped and spluttered and splashed onto the tiles of the eatery.

Even now, a thin line of its blood seeped beneath the door, threatening their running shoed feet.

But more hideous even than its appearance—and so much more chilling—was the thing's *voice*: it howled and it caterwauled and it keened an ongoing din that sounded like the very epitome of pain. That, more than anything else, was the true horror of the thing: they could detect no aggressiveness in its voice that might suggest that it was a danger to them. Only a nerve-wracking *agony* as it wailed and wailed and wailed and wailed and wailed.

"Oh my God, have we lost our minds?" the piss-stained cashier cried, hands clutched over his ears in a futile attempt to drown out the thing's lamenting cries. A sheen of sweat made his pale face oily and sickly. "Is that thing for *real?*" he said, the very real noise of the thing's cries nearly swallowing his words.

"What is it?" cried his co-worker, the pudgy seventeen-year-old girl with her blonde hair pulled into a severe little bun at the back of her head. She was shaking violently, her pouty lips quivering. "And why won't it stop that noise?"

"We're safe here," said the night manager, his frantic darting eyes betraying his true feelings, though he continued trying to reassure them and himself. "It's okay. We're safe in here. Nothing can get in here." He placed a wildly shaking hand on the door.

"But the way out's blocked!" cried the boy, pointing to the rear exit.

They all turned to it with sinking hearts: indeed, the exit was blocked with a formidable mountain of wooden pallets and heavy cardboard boxes stacked to the ceiling.

Raising his voice over the noise of the thing, which at that moment began pounding on the storeroom door with its bloody hands, the night manager said, "Get to work!"

He set the example himself like he never did during more mundane work shifts, unfolding the stepladder that leaned against the wall and, clambering to its top step, pulled down the topmost pallet. "Watch out," he warned, and dropped it to smash into splinters on the floor. He methodically worked his way downward, until the employees could reach the pallets themselves. Soon a mountain of wooden splinters and upended cardboard boxes lay all around them, and the way to the door was open.

The night manager slammed his palms onto the crash bar and the door swung open onto the sweaty night.

It took a moment for him and his employees to realize that the patrons weren't with them in the small back lot. They saw them, still inside the storeroom, huddled close against the interior door. The night manager leaned back inside, whispering urgently, "Come *on*. What are you *doing?*"

They ignored him. The boy had a hand pressed reassuringly against the girl's back, and she was leaning close against the steel, tears streaming from her eyes.

"It's okay, Della," the boy said over the screaming of the thing. "Go on."

What she said baffled and horrified the night manager.

"Mom. *Mom*. I know…I *know* it's you. I can *feel* that it's you. And…I know why you're here and…"

She drifted off, and the abomination's screaming stopped. A huge hush descended, in which the people could hear their own frantic breathing, and the girl's trembling voice, and the beating of the thing's heart from the opposite side of the door. The unreality of the moment became even more incomprehensible.

"Mom," the girl went on. "I don't know what's happened to you exactly, but…I know it has to do with things at home…Mom…I *know* you know, mom. I know you knew for a long time."

At this the thing on the other side of the door resumed, a low, agonized moaning now.

Della went on, making her voice louder to be heard. "I used to hate you for it, mom," she said. "But I don't anymore. I understand how scared you must have been, just like I was. Dad can be really scary. He can be the worst thing in the world. Nobody knows that he's a secret monster, but we do. But it's over now, mom. For me it's all done, and me and Jerry are going away from all of it. We made a pact, and we're going away. I love you, mom."

It was these last words that shattered the relative stasis of the moment and drove the thing on the other side of the door into a new kind of hysteria.

It roared. It keened. Its grief shook not only the door in its frame but trembled some thing deep inside each of them.

Jerry and Della stood outside the pizzeria, watching the night manager and two employees run off into the darkness. The early morning air, though muggy, felt much less oppressive than the storeroom.

Inside the pizzeria the thing that was Audrey Deloise continued its awful cacophony a while longer, before abruptly stopping.

They waited tensely, but no more screaming ruined the quiet. They stood holding each other for a few more minutes, taking comfort in each other.

"What happened to her?" Jerry's voice was hushed, awed. His eyes were tender, and his hands held Della's. "What made her change into..." He drifted off, not knowing what to say. It was unexplainable, and yet nothing made more sense than that the horror in the pizzeria was the same woman they'd known their whole lives.

Della said, "She knew about it all along. But I think the letter I left her must have really made her realize, and somehow...I don't know. I never talked to her about it. Maybe finally hearing about it from me did something to her."

It was unexplainable and yet, to Della, who'd lived through those sixteen years in their un-right home, it all made a demented and fantastical and perfect sense. Everyone reacted to terrible and hard things in their own way. She and Jerry were running away from those things. Their mother...had been changed when the things had been brought into the light.

"It's like evil science," Jerry said.

"Or science reacting to evil."

"It's not her fault we're so messed up, Del. Not really."

Della said, "No, not really. It's hard to be strong."

And with that, they freed themselves from the world they'd known, and Della held on tight to her brother Jerry's hand as they fled into the moon-washed summer night, onward to days of adventure and freedom, and they never looked back that night or for the rest of their lives after.

Not ever.

Not *ever.*

Through the deep still August morning the woeful, lamenting thing shambled onward. It clutched a long knife in its bloody fist, snatched from the countertop of the pizzeria, moonlight glimmering in the silver blade. As it moved through the darkness words escaped it, guttural-sounding and harsh gritted through its new raw vocal cords, a repeated phrase like a mantra:

I am strong now. I am strong now. I am strong now.

And it was, like it had never been before.

I am strong now. I am strong now. I am strong now.

Over star-bright hill and across moon-silvered field and down sleeping streets the thing went, until it reached the hushed house in the quiet suburban street where it had lived in secret agony for sixteen endless years. It crept inside, vengeance in its naked heart.

Not long after, a car pulled into the driveway and nestled inside the garage. A man got out, his steel-toed work boots clunking on the cement as he entered the home through the door inside the garage.

A few minutes later his shrill screams stabbed through the open windows and into the sleepy neighbourhood before being cut abruptly short, letting the night's great silence return like a blessing of peace.

We Are Alone

I

The TV wall filled the cottage's basement with light. Bradley Wilson fidgeted within the luxurious folds of the leather massaging couch, his finger hesitating over the 'play' button on the remote in his hand. The scene paused in the TV's screen showed a small stage empty but for the lone lectern in its centre. The symbol adorning its front was the same as that sewn into the fabric of the tapestry hanging on the wall at the rear of the stage: the stylized molecule, riven in two by a spear of lightning, the emblem of the Experimental Sciences Division. This was their headquarters at Cape Canaveral, the site of this emergency meeting.

Bradley had known beforehand why his dad, Dr. Robert Wilson, had called the meeting, and what he'd done in the days immediately leading up to it. Besides himself, his dad had told a few colleagues only, mostly those who'd worked closely with him on the project. The greater scientific community, and the world, had been entirely caught off-guard with the revelation. If what his dad had done felt like a betrayal to these colleagues, then what was felt by the majority in the wake of his father's address could only be described as a sense that a sacrilege had been committed. The project had come to represent an almost sacred quest to so many people, after all.

Robert had looked his eighty-five years when he'd taken his place at the podium at the Science Institute, a noticeable tremor marking his progress, his steps slow and deliberate, though many would remark on the youthfulness in his ruddy features. His paused image now stood before the audience of five hundred in attendance, and a televised and live-streamed global audience of millions.

Bradley pressed 'play' and tossed the remote onto the coffee table, out of easy reach, as if defying the reluctance he felt in rewatching the Speech. Part of him though—the dutiful son—felt that he should, as if through his constant devotion to the Speech, he might show his support of his father's courage and ideals, maybe even begin to understand what it all meant.

Too late to switch the thing off again now, he thought, as the basement filled with the sounds of the murmuring crowd, blotting out the chatter of Jean and the kids upstairs—he was committed.

"Greetings, fellow scientists and friends, seekers and questioners. Thank you for joining me here today on such short notice. Many of you were active in the field during those exciting days of the early puncture technology that saw humankind ascend like angels into the heavens."

Hidden away in the electric basement darkness, it was easy for Bradley to remember those days. He'd been young, coddled by his parents in a way that being in this basement conjured. His dad's baritone voice, his measured and erudite delivery, it was soothing to Bradley, a touch of familiarity during a time of chaos.

"Because I am a scientist, and therefore a realist, and because I am an explorer, and therefore a romantic, I will not mislead you today. I will be truthful and I will show you the romance in that truth. Let me be both as brief and clear as I'm able, because we all have other places to be, and others with whom to be. First, I owe you an apology.

"The romantic in me couldn't wait, and made the leap. *The* leap. Without permission, without sharing my intention with any of my colleagues, I went ahead and used the lightweb system I designed and made the first jump."

An immediate murmur arose, stunned and angry.

Wilson raised his hands in the air.

"Please, let me finish, and then we can have a conversation. And then you may judge me and my actions."

The crowd-voice subsided, though the atmosphere was charged now, electric and anxious.

"I did what I did for two reasons. Firstly, I admit it was because I wanted to be the first, and an eighty-five-year-old man certainly wouldn't have been considered for the journey, even if he'd invented the technology. But more importantly, something compelled me to do it. Some worry, that wormed its way into me and wouldn't let me be. I felt a sense of…danger, that I hadn't felt in relation to the project before, and because the mission was as important as it was, I went ahead and faced the danger so that no one else would have to. This sounds braver than it was. I was terribly scared and, as I said, I also simply wanted to be the first."

People were talking among themselves again, but Wilson went on.

"The first thing I need to tell you is that the technology…did not work as intended. Wait, no, that isn't exactly accurate…the technology itself worked, though in an entirely… *different* way than we'd intended, and in an utterly *unexpected* way. But what it *revealed…that* lay in diametric opposition to what we had all predicted, and hoped for. This has nothing to do with the premature nature of my trip, mind you—as I said, the technology worked. The goal of the lightweb is, as you all know, to encode its traveller—in this case, myself—into pure light, and to send that light on an interstellar journey, focusing on the nodes of the lightweb as jump-points, all the while, crucially, retaining my consciousness. Our lofty goal was to reach the limits of our solar system, and then to send that light-ray back, to reel it home, here into the light-chamber at Cape Canaveral, where all the building blocks of the human traveller—myself—would be reconstituted, my mind to be mined for all the new knowledge gleaned from the journey.

"Alas, what did happen on my journey—what I learned— broke my heart. And though it further breaks my heart to tell you, I must because I owe you all this truth."

Absolute silence in the auditorium now as Wilson paused a moment to gather his thoughts.

In the cottage basement darkness, Bradley shivered with goosebumps, immersed all over again in the wonder of his father's dream, wishing helplessly that, this time, the Speech would go differently.

"It was…It was a science that I don't understand. Maybe we never will. Whatever it was that happened, it felt miraculous, as a discovery of this magnitude always must. Or maybe…maybe it *was* miraculous. This admission comes from a dyed-in-the-wool man of science, yes, but I'm being honest with you. No science I know of can explain to my satisfaction what happened, what I experienced and witnessed, though I welcome any and all thoughts on the subject. Forgive me, I'm digressing. I will *try* to explain.

"Everything started out as planned: my encoding went through, and I was transmitted through the lightweb. It was astounding. In a sense, in a very special sense, I was conscious through it all, still alive in the moment in my new light-coded form. This part of the journey deserves its own speech, of course—its own book, in fact—but there are more pressing details to address. So, as I say, my journey through the lightweb began as intended. But then…"

Robert Wilson paused once more. He stared off into space, over the heads of the audience members. He seemed to be choosing his next words with great deliberation.

In the basement, Bradley fidgeted with nervousness, though he'd watched the video countless times. Dimly, he was aware of the kids' voices shouting in play upstairs, Jean's laughter underneath.

After an uncomfortable moment, Robert Wilson went on.

"My goal for this maiden voyage was to reach the edge of our solar system and return home, a feat of a lifetime, of our generation, but…something else happened. A happy accident, you might say, though the ending to my story is bittersweet. It seemed impossible that what happened had indeed come to pass. But I knew. I wasn't able to understand, at first. But some part of me knew. I *felt* it. This is what happened:

"I felt the lightyears unravelling like thread beneath a movement that was so relentless, so fast that all felt still. I was…My being, my consciousness, within the light—some might call this my *soul*—was…stretched. But rather than following the plotted trajectory along the lightweb, I found myself…everywhere. An infinity inside and outside of space-time. A whisper of consciousness that covered all the corners of our galaxy, of all galaxies, on and on and on to the final rim that represents the distance light may travel before…the end of time. In what felt simultaneously like an instant and an eternity, I had experienced light years too vast for my intellect to fathom. Where even light years were so small as to be beyond perception.

"And everywhere I went, it—"

Bradley, hearing Jean calling to him over the TV, struggled forward from the folds of the massaging couch to snag the remote from the table. Pausing the video, he yelled back, more testily than he should have. They were on vacation, after all, and here he was holed up in the basement like a mole, rewatching the Speech for the umpteenth time. "Yes? What is it?"

Jean's voice came down from the top of the stairs, apologetic, "I said, 'how about ten minutes or so and you come up'—the rugrats are restless. We promised them the beach this afternoon."

Jean was so much better than him, always as busy as he was with her own work at the lab and yet always shouldering the bulk of the load at home, too. He acquiesced, feeling guilty and grateful. "Of course, hon'. Ten minutes."

"Okay, basement-dweller."

The door eased closed and he heard the delighted giggles from the kids. Reggie said, "Dad's a *basement-dweller.*"

Julie laughed gleefully, said eagerly, "What's a basement-dweller?"

Reggie: "A troll!"

Jean: "That is *not* what that means."

Reggie wasn't exactly wrong, Bradley thought, unpausing the TV. The image of his father unfroze.

"—was the same. Stars, planets, galaxies, superclusters on their ancient journeys…I saw *everything*. And it was the same everywhere. In my light-shard, my awareness was limitless, along a lightweb that stretched, inconceivably, everywhere at once and everywhen that those photons would ever experience. It was somehow *faster* than light because time had slowed. It was more than I have the scientific vocabulary to describe. If I were so inclined, I might liken it to a spiritual experience, simply because it lay entirely outside of any scientific system I could explain it with. A new definition of godspeed. This isn't hyperbole or fantasy, though I know how it must sound. The lightweb was an *instantaneous* awareness, an infinite consciousness. Immediately—or so it felt, truly it felt this way—I was pulled *everywhere*, whether through some unforeseen glitch in the lightweb itself, or whether I was pulled by some force I can't explain. And somehow I knew that this journey was absolute in its comprehensiveness—I was very literally pulled everywhere, and everytime within the lifespan of this light itself. And everywhere I visited, every light year travelled, it was the same.

"There was nothing."

Robert Wilson paused here, looking as if he were gathering himself. He waited until the latest rumble of voices in the audience had quieted before going on.

"This is the thing you need to know, and to understand. And to accept.

"There *is* nothing out there. And more to the point…There is no *one*. There is no habitable planet conducive to human life. There are no sentient beings like ourselves, or unlike us. There is nothing like *this*, what we have *here*. There is no world like ours. There are no worlds at all like this. Each class-M planet we thought was out there, is not. That I promise you.

"I travelled, and I searched, in this miraculous way, for distances in space whose temporal translation is billions and billions and billions of years. *Deep time*. I'm the oldest human being who has ever lived, from a certain perspective. Certainly, I'm the man with the most pain in my heart for the truth it is my duty as a scientist to deliver to you, though my science will no doubt sound scant to you and my story one of fantastical invention.

"I repeat, though, for it's the truth and it must be stressed: There is nothing. And what you all must come to terms with is a very difficult thing, as it was for me, at least at first. But you must come to terms with it nonetheless.

"We are alone.

"In the entire, infinite, ever-expanding universe: We. Are. Alone."

A renewed murmur had begun to emanate from the crowd, much louder than previously. Several voices rose higher, beginning the portion of the recording that most upset Bradley—the beginning of the conflict between the science community and one of its pillars, his father.

"What about the microbial life found already in ice from space?"

Wilson answered quickly: "Flukes, random occurrences from which nothing remotely significant could ever grow. I hoped, too. I looked. I saw. There is nothing."

"Come on. Where's the science, Bob? Where's the rigour in that type of statement? And what you're saying about class-M planets—we know these exist. What you're saying is preposterous."

Robert Wilson's amplified voice rose over these voices: "You have the right to investigate and try to disprove what I've told you. I promise you will be disappointed, like I was disappointed."

But the crowd-voices continued.

"Wait now, Carl's right. My thoughts exactly—you're a scientist, Mr. Wilson—you know better than to expect us to go by your word on a statement this…radical."

"I agree, Bob. This project is of such importance, and this…fantasy you've described is…it's not science at all. This isn't like you."

Bradley watched his father's face, noting that he never once shed the dignity he wore so plainly. Here, during this harangue from the audience, he was even nodding along to the accusations, sagely, accepting it all, understanding it. Even when, most demeaning of all, laughter could be heard, mocking and ugly, filling Bradley with anger at the insult. And still Robert Wilson looked dignified. And, once this latest hubbub had quieted, he went on as before.

"As I've said, if you investigate my claims, hoping to disprove them, you'll be disappointed. You have every right to do so. My technology is waiting for you to use."

It was clear that Robert Wilson's revelation was not what the audience had anticipated, or wanted to hear. The people had come that day to hear news of some development in the project they believed and trusted in, moving it one step closer to fruition, so that they would have proof that their lifelong dreams did, in fact, have a basis in scientific fact, that the careers and pursuits they'd been engaged in for all their adult lives were noble, important; that there was hope for future generations, for the children of their children's children to have a new home elsewhere, away from the mess they'd made of things here, and the mess that had already begun to take shape in the Mars colony, echoes of the same old all-too-human troubles.

But like a mantra, the man they'd entrusted their hopes to—one of history's most celebrated scientific intellects—only continued to repeat the words of this seeming fantasy, or delusion:

"We. Are. Alone."

He stayed at the lectern, bearing a swell in the audience-voice, angry and restless, before continuing.

"I'm sorry. You'll go ahead and follow where I led, no doubt, using my lightweb technology—do it. It is in our nature to do this. So you'll see for yourselves. Or don't do it. Believe what I've told you, and don't do it, and save yourselves the heartache, and instead go spend time with your families." And, like coffin nails being driven home: "We. Are. Alone."

More cries from the audience, this time outright spiteful, full of rage. How dare he make such claims? How dare he crush dreams they'd all nurtured since childhood?

"I don't believe it!"

"You call yourself a scientist—you should be ashamed of yourself!"

"We don't believe you!"

"Are you feeling okay, Bob?" (This was, from the sound of it, the concerned voice of a colleague.)

"My friends, my colleagues. It does not matter what you *believe*. The truth remains unchanged. I have no reason to lie. I have nothing to gain from it. I have devoted my life to science. I want the truth you want. I've wanted it since I was a boy looking through my first telescope, bewitched by the Milky Way. I *want* the truth you want. You know this. But that truth is a lie, a fantasy.

"We.

"Are.

"Alone.

"This is the very difficult truth you all must accept.

"And so my message—my *plea*—with you is this:

"After you look, and once you've found for yourselves what I've already told you here today, then let us make the most of this world we call our own. Because it is the *only* Paradise, though we wreck it year after year, generation after generation. And if we are to discover who we are—and why we are here—the answer does not lie out there, among the stars, where there is nothing, and, perhaps, where we don't belong. It is here, somewhere in our world and within ourselves. Because we *are* alone, but for each other.

"Thank you for listening. It has been my privilege to work with you and for you, toward our mutual goals all these years. Goodnight."

Robert Wilson stepped from the lectern and walked toward the side of the stage from which he'd emerged fifteen minutes earlier, when the world had been a different place than it was now. He was followed by the violent din from the audience. Some were shouting unintelligibly. Many people were now standing—these were the shouters, Bradley guessed, though it was difficult to tell from the footage.

Bradley paused the video close to its conclusion, the frozen scene showing his father being met at the edge of the stage by Susan Barlow, one of his father's oldest friends and staunchest supporters; her face looked stricken, and she was leaning toward him conspiratorially to say something close to his ear (Bradley wondered about those words, what she thought of his dad's claims). Other figures milled at the side of the stage: scientists all, astrophysicists, mostly; a retired astronaut by the name of Brett Collings, and Jack Gedravski, author of a half dozen wildly successful popular science books, and the emcee for the evening, looking stunned.

His father had been a pioneer—his puncture system had revolutionized interstellar travel and paved the way for the founding of the first Mars colony. Not satisfied with this, he'd gone one giant step further when a mere decade later, he announced the ambitious project of the much more advanced light-code travel system. It was leading the way toward making exploration on a potentially limitless scale a reality. A brave explorer—and ever the boy adventurer at heart—he'd been the first to volunteer for the inaugural mission, which had been scheduled to take place ten or more years down the road, knowing of course that his advanced age wouldn't allow him to go.

Nobody had known back then, not even Wilson himself, that he would be the first to make the jump, and that the journey would simultaneously be such a brief one and an infinite one; and certainly no one would have guessed that its findings could be as darkly conclusive as he'd claimed them to be.

The consensus among the scientific community was that his father was mentally ill, and had imagined or invented the outrageous details of his journey. Even Bradley had to admit that it sounded more than a little fanciful, and without any hard science to back up the claims his dad had made...

The tantalizingly inexplicable fact remained, though, that a voyage of some type *had* taken place, the evidence of which was corroborated when the lightweb chamber was examined. And so one couldn't help but entertain the notion—*had* his dad been telling the truth? *Had* he somehow inadvertently stumbled on the creation of a technology that led to travel at a speed the human mind simply wasn't able to process? Could the fantasy be *real?* Was something at work here that went beyond science?

Sighing, feeling the weight of the recent days pushing down on him, Bradley stood, the massaging couch also sighing as it returned to its unoccupied form. He trudged up the stairs, squinting when he pushed open the door at the top and the harshness of daylight hit him, and the heavy atmosphere of humid air that seeped in through the opened cottage windows. The kids began yelling excitedly, ready for the beach. He gave them a smile, but it came with difficulty.

Despite having left the Speech behind, he couldn't unhear it; those three words that had caused such disruption and unrest amid the usually sedate audience of intellectuals, and throughout the world:

We are alone.

The most frightening words for every member of the human race to hear.

II

The kids were playing in the sand close to where Bradley and Jean had spread their beach blankets among the shale and tufts of scraggly grass. Gulls wheeled against the milky sky, dappling the sand with frenzied shadows. The ruined lake, black and listless, was given some life by the weak sun glimmering in its swells. In the distance, the little research station towered from the water, a pair of water walkers just visible where they hugged the station's west side, their long legs folded alongside their bodies, giving the machines the appearance of huge tree trunks lashed to the building. A pair of motorboats was docked on the other side, within sight of the limnocorrals, where simulated contamination environments existed in their respective enclosures, a half dozen in total.

The Wilsons had walked down to the beach through the woods, exiting the deep quiet and forest gloom for this brighter, wide-open vista. Julie had remarked in typically grand fashion that it looked like the edge of the world. Looking at the horizon now, hazy with distance and pollutants, Bradley could understand it. In some dark and metaphorical ways, he felt that they might in fact be exactly there.

In harmony with his thoughts, Jean called to the children, "You're too close to the water, guys—back it up, or we're heading back to the cottage." To Bradley, she murmured, "Jesus—this is what a sunny vacation is, in the summer of '58. It's worse than when we were here last year."

"It was two summers ago," Bradley corrected her. "And yeah, it is worse. I think we should forego nostalgia from now on, and keep our vacations on dry land. Maybe indoors, too. Even if the sun-suits make it safe."

Lake Chakotay held sentimental value for them—it was where

they'd first met when they were still undergrads and, eight years after that, where they were married. A small wedding, but as scenic as they could have wanted, the entire ceremony taking place on the deck of a friend's yacht. Even then, though, fifteen years ago, the amount of garbage everywhere had been shocking. Now, floating islands of trash were scattered across the lake, cans, plastic bottles and bags, fishing nets, and other non-biodegradable junk held together by tangles of watergrasses. Worse still was last year's oil spill from a nearby pipeline failure, resulting in over one thousand litres of crude oil flowing downslope and reaching the lake and its surrounding marshland. All of this had earned it the nickname among cottagers as Garbage Island Lake.

Instead of the cleanup needed to help restore the lake, it had been designated as a research site, where the ailing ecosystem was being studied in the hope of devising ways of dealing with similar situations but on a much larger scale, like the Great Pacific Garbage Patch. While it was nice that the lake's predicament was being used to help a global situation, it was still sad.

"Without a body of water *in sight*," she agreed. "And this isn't anywhere near as bad as the oceans."

They left it unspoken, the blatant proof that they'd been too engrossed in their work to take even this most rudimentary of vacations as a family for two entire years. They were constantly bringing the kids to the lab during their summer vacation from school, while taking turns treating them to matinee movies or visits to the mall on weekends—that was usually the extent of the time they spent with their children in the summers. Bradley hoped that exposing them to the lab might help foster an interest in science, though so far neither Reggie or Julie showed signs of it.

When the kids didn't budge from where they stood looking at the water, Jean made her voice stern: "*Now.*"

Julie dutifully scampered further back from the scummy tideline, followed a moment later by Reggie, sulky, shoulders drooping less with annoyance at being reprimanded than with the cumbersome grip of his transparent air-suit.

"Thank you," Jean called, the good-natured humour in her

voice infectious—Reggie raised his eyes to her, trying to suppress a smile but not quite managing it. In his defeat, he changed tack and shouted at his mother, "I'm gonna dunk you in the dead sea!"

Julie froze where she was furling the hot sand with her sun-suit-shod feet, making an exaggerated 'o' of her mouth, eyes comically wide.

"It's a lake, not a sea, bud," said Bradley.

"Okay, Doctor basement-dweller."

Julie giggled, and her brother laughed, backing up in mock nervousness when Bradley peered at him over the top of his sunglasses, giving him his angry-look. That got the siblings playing together quietly, diligently digging in the sand with plastic shovels.

Bradley and Jean settled into the hot laze of the moment, savouring the quiet. It was inevitable that the subject, tactfully ignored in front of the kids, would surface, especially since they'd had so little time together for private conversation in the past few weeks. Jean had been out of state at a conference on the day of the Speech, though of course she and Bradley had talked briefly over the telephone in the aftermath of it. She'd only heard the latest developments once she'd gotten back. By then, there were so many other things to try and process, not to mention the endless bureaucratic red tape to wade through, and dealing with the efforts of the voracious news correspondents to reach them—

They needed this time, to talk, and to not talk but to be together in the not talking.

It was Jean who broached it.

"So."

"So?"

"What are your thoughts?

"On the Speech?"

"Of course, the speech. And all the rest."

Bradley said, "Of course the Speech."

This is what it had become known as, and would remain known as, between them and for everyone else in the world: the Speech, with a capital 'S'.

"Well…" he began, but found he was at a loss for words. He

settled on, "It's a lot to think about. To process. I suppose I haven't had enough time yet, though God knows I've thought about it non-stop. You?"

"The same." Her eyes were squinting beneath the floppy brim of her beach hat, staring at the uncertain zone of haze where sky met horizon. "The same."

For a lot of people, Robert Wilson's suicide the day following his historic address was a decisive punctuation mark on everything he'd said. The method of his suicide likewise seemed like a statement of sorts: he'd entered the lightweb chamber, and deliberately operated the system incorrectly, with the result that an incomplete encoding process was set in motion. This resulted in his physical body being destroyed, but not encoded into light. Wilson simply ceased to be. This led some of the more romantic to speculate that perhaps some essence of Wilson had survived and had been sent to wander the universe once more, eternally. Nobody seemed to know how to disprove this idea, though plans were already underway to expedite the second light-code mission. Experimental Sciences was hopeful that they could move the launch date from ten years to eight, maybe less given the number of resources now being thrown at the project.

The machine itself Wilson left unharmed, though he'd had the opportunity to destroy it if he'd wanted to; if was as if he were reiterating his position that his technology remained for others to use, despite his advisement against it when there were more important matters to attend to here.

The news of Wilson's passing, much like his Speech itself, was the most talked-about subject everywhere they turned. And among all the discussions, from science panels and forums, entertainment talk shows and news programs, to scholarly articles and books, friends sharing personal conversations; the conversation inevitably turned to the next, perhaps only, logical question: if Wilson was right, and we *are* truly alone in an infinite universe…*why* are we here at all?

Bradley certainly had been thinking about little else. It devoured his waking thoughts. He'd taken a leave of absence from the Institute, but found himself unable to do anything resembling mentally or emotionally restorative activities. He simply wasn't able to do much of anything at all besides sleep, and waking briefly and spending a few despondent hours each afternoon puttering around the house, eating the bare minimum to sustain himself before retreating back to the sanctuary of sleep.

When Jean had told him they were taking a family vacation to the cottage, he acquiesced without any argument. When he continued watching the Speech in the cool shadows of the cottage's basement, Jean let him be. She made a point of telling him, though, that she'd scored a victory when she convinced him to join her and the kids at the beach that afternoon. He hadn't quite managed a smile for her, but dutifully donned his sun-suit and followed her and the children out onto the rear deck and from there, down the path through the woods to the beach spread out below.

It was late afternoon, Saturday. Early enough in the weekend that Jean could still ignore the horizon of the work week ahead. She'd taken a few days off but, a couple of days after the funeral, had returned, mostly in an effort to keep herself busy while giving Brad the time to himself that he seemed to need.

But of course, they both had bigger things on their mind. Who didn't?

"If logic can't," she began, then found herself distracted by a gull fluttering down to land among the cattails on the sludgy shoreline, pecking at something in the water, and began again, "I mean, if your dad was right, and the logic of science can't explain us—this planet, alone in the universe, so abundant with life, and *sentient* life at that—then what can?"

"There's…" Bradley drifted off, also struggling to find words, which was unlike him, he who spoke loudest among all his peers and doctoral students. He watched another gull wheeling against the cerulean sky, as much a miracle as every other element making up this moment he was sharing with his wife, she herself a work of boundless genius contained in every molecule that comprised her attractive physical body, her keen intellect, her soft laughter, delicate as the tinkling of glass under the hopping dance of a bird's feet. And slowly, as if stirring from a long-lasting dream, he said, "There is a design."

"Yes," Jean said immediately, her voice quietly emphatic. "There is a design, in all of this."

She meant the world; the world spinning under them, revolving in all the infinite blackness of the universe. She said, "But is it a miracle of science, or just a miracle?"

Bradley took a moment, ordering his thoughts. "The last time we spoke, dad and I, the day after the Speech, when he came over for dinner. You'd gone to bed early, you were so jetlagged and wiped from your conference, and the two of us sat up talking on the patio outside. And the last thing he told me that night before he went home was how, on his light-code trip he'd finally seen the Great Annihilator."

Jean cocked an eye at him. "Really?" She'd assumed the two of them had spoken about the Speech, and planned on asking Bradley about it in the morning. But by then an assistant at the labs had already called the house with the news of Robert's suicide. When Bradley hadn't volunteered any details about that night, his last with his father, she'd assumed it was too difficult a memory, and didn't bring it up. The subject had never materialized, until now.

"Yeah. Believe it or not, it was the only thing he told me about his journey. We didn't even talk about the Speech. I didn't know how to bring it up, it was all so…crazy. And if he was sick, then I didn't want to…It just felt like this one moment, the two of us sitting outside on the patio, in the quiet and the dark, was this moment of peace that we'd never get back again. Like the moment he went home, the world would barge back into our lives and it would be all about the Speech and questioning his cognitive functioning and his betrayal of the project by jumping the gun and flying solo. All of it. So I didn't say anything. I just let him lead the conversation, and we talked about this, that, just small-talk, inconsequential things. Until, from out of the blue, he told me he'd seen it. The GA."

"That's fitting," Jean said. "If he was going to talk about anything, in the context of this…this impossible cosmic journey, then it's fitting it would be the GA."

Robert Wilson had long had a fascination with this microquasar in the Milky Way. He'd written his graduate thesis on the subject, specifically setting out to prove that this black hole and its sun weren't alone out there near the sky's Galactic Centre. He'd believed he'd detected spectral evidence of a second sun, though his adviser hadn't been so sure. 'The eyes and mouth of the Galactic Centre', he'd called it. He'd also published several papers on the subject in later years, each adding more evidence, though these appeared in pseudoscience journals, unlike the rest of his extensive bibliography, which included several scholarly, highly influential books. Jean, and the rest of the family and scientific community, were well aware of Robert's obsession. It was the only detail of his long career that had ever been met with criticism from his peers. 'Lack of sufficient evidence' was the general consensus on the subject, though Wilson never recanted, always standing by his convictions, vowing to prove his idea someday. Now people asked whether this fixation was simply a quirk of an eccentric genius's personality, or the first sign that, genius though he undoubtedly had been, underneath the scientific intellect lurked a propensity toward delusion, the beginning of mental illness?

"Fitting indeed," said Bradley. "And he said that he'd been right all along."

"Really? He said that?" Jean was mesmerized by this return to familiar territory. Legendary territory in family lore.

"Dad said it was just as he'd predicted: the eyes and the mouth. But…he said it was also not at all like he'd always pictured. He said that…the suns—the eyes—he said they gave off what he could only describe as loneliness. These two blazing stars, staring into the void, emanating the greatest loneliness he'd ever seen. He said it broke his heart. He said he knew it then, that there was no point in continuing his journey, though it was outside his control and he did continue. But he said he knew the truth then. That there was nothing out there at all.

"He wasn't looking at me—we were sitting side by side on the deck, looking at the stars, irony of ironies—but I saw that he had tears in his eyes when he told me."

"My God," said Jean, because it was the only thing possible to say.

"And so I ask you: Robert Wilson—genius or madman? His light-code trip: truth or fantasy? And if truth, was it a miracle of science we can't explain yet, or just a miracle we'll never explain? And if it's the latter—what now? What do we do? Do we wait? For what? Do we pray? For what? Do we keep on working to figure it all out? Or do we shelve our research and focus on keeping up our gardens at home?"

"Can it be both types of miracles?" Jean said. "I'm in awe of it whatever it is." And she added, "I'm not sure if focusing on our home gardens would be all that bad." And then after a brief pause, she added, "If there was one thing your dad was not, it was crazy."

Bradley turned to her. "Do you mean that?"

Jean nodded.

They looked out to the lake. A two-person crew was clambering into one of the motorboats, loading in gear. A minute later they were puttering over to the limnocorrals.

"So what do we do?" Bradley said, snagging a blade of grass from beside him and absently twirling it between his fingers. "Do we throw ourselves into our work? Our purpose is to disprove the old man? 'Sorry, pops—you may have been the greatest genius of modern times but, you know, we have to see for ourselves.'"

She smiled. "He did say that, in the Speech. That we'd follow in his steps."

Bradley went on as if she hadn't spoken. "Or do we try and fix what we've damaged here? Ideally, we pursue both, of course, preserve what we can here while continuing with the work. There's so much to work for."

He waved a hand skyward. It was a weak gesture, lacking the sweep and conviction it had once held. He felt the twinge of belief in his father's cosmic verdict, as he'd been feeling it more and more in the days since the Speech, and resented the old man. He felt ashamed that his belief on this most important of subjects had begun to undergo a change so quickly. He'd followed in his father's footsteps, after all, dedicated his life to science, specifically to exploratory space research, and here he was questioning his life's work in the wake of the goddamned Speech. He felt betrayed, even if he knew it was wrong of him to feel it.

"Brad," Jean said.

He followed where she looked—the scientists in the motorboat were at the first of the limnocorrals. One of them was leaning from the boat and dipping a long steel-handled net into the water inside the man-made ecosystem-within-the-greater-ecosystem, fishing about. A moment later and he pulled the instrument out with its catch inside the netting: a duck, it looked like, though it could have been a different species of bird. At that distance, they saw only flapping wings as the animal struggled in the net.

"Those assholes put a duck in one of their cages?" She was outraged, glaring at the scene with her fists balled at her sides.

Bradley said, "Maybe it flew in on its own? Maybe we're seeing a rescue op in progress?"

"They better be rescuing him," Jean said, sounding helpless.

A minute later the boat was on its way back to the station.

In the minutes since he'd told Jean about his father's revelation concerning the Great Annihilator, Bradley had felt something resilient slowly come awake in him. He said, "It was a rescue mission."

Jean cocked an eye at him. "Yeah?"

Bradley was nodding, watching the men debark from the boat and ascend into the belly of the station with their cargo. "Yeah. They're going to clean that bird up so he can fly again."

The kids were still digging in the sand, talking quietly. Bradley and Jean sat watching the lake, saw a gargantuan water walker disengage itself from the research station like a mechanical spider from its steel web and walk with long and precise steps toward the horizon, to learn what it might from the deeps of the poisoned lake.

An hour later, they were trudging along a little footpath toward the cottage, the leafy canopy over their heads bringing a deep and satisfying gloom and quiet following the relative brightness of the beach and the constant susurration of the chemical waves. Bradley and Jean carried their hastily folded sun-suits, along with the kids' suits, in the packs on their backs. Bradley also had a smaller bag slung across a shoulder, stuffed with blankets and various things. Jean carried the cooler pressed with both arms to her body as if it were a precious cargo.

Reggie led, with his clumsy stomping steps, then Julie quiet as a moth, with Bradley and Jean bringing up the rear. Midway back, Julie spotted a colony of giant white puffball mushrooms sprouting from the earth a little way off the path. Pointing excitedly, she posed the same sort of questions she did whenever she found herself in the presence of some great natural mystery: "Are those fairy balloons? Is it a pixie city? Do fairies live here?"

She accompanied this last with a spreading of her arms to encompass the woods stretching all around them before turning questioningly to her mother. Reggie followed where she was pointing, then turned back to kicking stones from the path and into the foliage.

Jean imagined the puffballs uprooting themselves from the moist soil, lifting skywards, the tiny hidden pilots of this incredible flying city bidding goodbye to the family of giants invading the serenity of their forest. But as she looked among the mushrooms, she saw a great amorphous light pulsing among them, casting its glow across the ivy-laced oaks. She squinted, trying to determine what it might be, whether it was some trick of the sunlight filtering down through the canopy. The notion came to her that it could be a sign of the miraculous that they'd been debating on the beach. Was it some phenomenon of the woods, and part of the greater design; or was it God truly, and the designer Himself, the one behind all the fish and ducks and seashells and trees and wonder and misery in the world, all of the beauty and balancing darkness that made up everything, the architect of this single astonishing jewel embedded in the desolate fabric of eternity.

But then the light dimmed and dimmed, and from it coalesced Robert Wilson, no less miraculous than any other vision would have been; and Jean could tell by Bradley's soft exhalation on the path beside her that he saw his father, too, or whatever this was—a psychic emanation of him, or some lingering trace of the man returning after the annihilation of his physical body in the lightweb machine's energies. Indeed, the body wavered, and from time to time flickered, like a projected image, as if it were being beamed into the forest from elsewhere, or produced naturally like some magical phosphorescent effulgence of the mushrooms.

The apparition watched them with the familiar gaze, part mischievous, part adoring, and somehow conveying the easy fearlessness all who'd known Robert Wilson spoke of so fondly when reminiscing about him. It looked tangible now, its shadow etched clearly against the oak beside it by the spears of sunlight filtering through the leafy canopy.

Bradley cried silently, bewitched by the spectre, heart full with rapture. Through his tears, voice barely audible, he whispered to it, "I'm going to destroy the lightweb lab, and all of your research. Consequences be damned."

Jean knew he meant consequences to his career, his reputation among his peers, all those things that were less important to him today, in that moment, than they had been yesterday.

Jean, blinking away tears, clutched her husband's hand, giving him her support in this as they'd always supported each other in all endeavours.

A smile of radiance appeared on the apparition's wavering features, the exact smile the man himself had worn on those occasions when the burden of constant work had been cleared for some brief moment of respite—like when he took on the joyous role of grandfatherhood and took the kids on adventures to the science museum where the universe could be explained, and to the park, where it could be explained just as well, maybe better. It watched them a moment longer before turning and drifting off between the wildflowers to disappear among the paradise of shadows and sunbeams and oaks as old as time.

Reggie, oblivious to the visitation, had tramped down the path ahead of everyone, humming to himself, lost in thought.

Julie was tugging on her mother's shirt. "*Mom*—do they? Do fairies live here?" She'd missed the visitation completely, too, so committed was she to wringing the answer she wanted from her mother.

Jean turned to her daughter, taking in her rosy cheeks, her wind-tossed hair coming loose from the high ponytail she wore, her eager green eyes like jewels lighting the way through the dim forest paths. All beauty, all promise. And, catching up with Julie's question, she said, "There's only us, sweetheart. Only us."

Together, the Wilsons continued on their way, deeper into the hushed woods.

The Punished World

I

His Africa lay etched in crystal
Jewelled fauna and flora bewitched
in a remade Cameroon
If this dark-dream of beauty lived today
would lepers walk into the shining jungle heart?
Should we follow?

II

A 1962 world-drowning
and New Paleozoic,
return to primordial Eden
where the scattered found a gift inside:
species memory; falling back, and back
to the start of a savage story

III

And the oracle cried for the water gone away,
industrial waste-crust the cancer of the waves
as crops to dust and rivers to streams
splintered the tribe again

IV

Read him well, our timeless lastronaut
before we bed down in our caves,
prophet as much as mirror-bearer
The satellite dead speak to us from above

Commander Ballard sends commiserations
from his orbit overhead
Cape Canaveral the site of starts and vigils
without end

Roads of Peace

<<At long, *long* last,>> he said, looking out across the blackened landscape. <<It's…It's…>>

Emotion seized him at the sight of the desolation, and he was lost for the right way to express himself.

Beside him his billionth-and-first brother appeared, and said: <<They're *quiet.*>>

And then their five hundred thousandth-three hundred-fifty-third aunt scuttled forth and amended, <<They're *gone.*>>

They absorbed the fact of this. The weight of it.

Then from behind them their two millionth-seven thousandth-one hundredth-and-fourth sister said, <<Let's go!>> and she scuttled between them and onto the flaking earth. She was young, one of the hatchlings who flaunted a new mutation: a light pulsed from within her shell, red and bright and strong in the dusty air.

They followed.

The others came, too.

Brothers and sisters, fathers and mothers and newborn hatchlings and grandparents, they exited through the cracks and holes in the earth. In long lines, and in haphazard waves the great tribe spread outward, outward, rejoicing as the sun—the sun! Muddied and muted through the poisonous black clouds but still, *the sun!*—flashed from their resilient carapaces; their antennae reaching and reaching heavenwards for the sheer freedom in the gesture after their long self-interment in the deep-dark miles below; their legs cutting trails through the brittle ashes, forging new roads of peace that would lead to Paradise.

About the Author

Alexander Zelenyj is the author of the books ***Blacker Against the Deep Dark, Songs for the Lost, Experiments at 3 Billion A.M., Black Sunshine***, and others. A compendium of his work, ***These Long Teeth of the Night: The Best Short Stories 1999-2019***, was recently released by Fourth Horseman Press.

Zelenyj lives in Windsor, Ontario, Canada with his wife and their animals.

Discover more about the author and his other works at

www.alexanderzelenyj.com